the
stranger

the stranger

SARAH SINGLETON

SIMON AND SCHUSTER

Thanks to Marc Huynh and Ian Watson for their various contributions, and to Simon Smart for being a brilliant India travelling companion.

First published in Great Britain in 2011 by Simon and Schuster UK Ltd,
A CBS COMPANY.

Copyright © 2011 Sarah Singleton

Simon & Schuster UK Ltd
1st Floor, 222 Gray's Inn Road, London WC1X 8HB

A CIP catalogue record for this book is available from the British Library.

978-0-85707-073-9

1 3 5 7 9 10 8 6 4 2

Printed in the UK by CPI Cox & Wyman, Reading RG1 8SX

www.simonandschuster.co.uk

www.crowmaiden.plus.com

For my beloved sister Ruth

Charlotte

The train slowed, brakes screeching, as it drew into the station. The perfume of diesel drifted into the carriage through windows open in the heat. Then other smells too – spicy food cooking on stalls, musky pink blossoms heaped on a wooden handcart, decaying refuse and underneath, the faint odour of old urine. It was still early. Beyond the village, rice fields spread away. As the train halted, the quiet platform stirred, coming to life, as a dozen vendors emerged from the shadows, descending on the train with rice-cakes, hard-boiled eggs, cups of tea, newspapers. Voices clamoured, announcing what was offered. The men – for they were mostly men – brandished their wares beyond the train windows, fighting for attention.

Charlotte rubbed her eyes. She was still half asleep. The carriage was tatty and old-fashioned, divided into compartments. She rose from the hard wooden seat, clambered over her fellow passengers and their baggage, out of her compartment to the carriage door, to overlook the throng on the platform. Ahead, a slender woman in a saffron-yellow sari walked across the tracks, a basket resting elegantly on her head. Charlotte took a deep breath, drawing it all inside, feasting on it, the colour, the babble, the complex scent, the clarity of the morning air, the curl of steam and cinnamon rising from the teacup a man thrust under her nose – and felt emotion swelling inside her chest, thrill and contentment together, to be in India, this strange, beautiful, intriguing place.

Passengers embarked and disembarked. Some bought a breakfast through the window. Charlotte stepped down onto the platform and bought curry and rice in a foil dish, along with a large chapatti folded like a piece of cloth, and a copy of *The Times of India*. A large reddish monkey, a baby clinging to her front, scampered over the platform roof. A whistle blew and the doors to the carriages began to slam shut. Charlotte, clutching her breakfast, hopped back onto the train just in time. She scrambled back into her seat as the train started to move, juggling newspaper, breakfast, the leather bag hanging over her shoulder.

A fat Indian man in a tight suit, nursing a briefcase on his lap, sniffed with an air of disapproval, but said in English, friendly enough:

'Where are you going?'

'The Golden Tiger Reserve. I'm working there.' She dropped her bag at her feet, stuffed the newspaper down the side of the seat and opened the foil dish. The curry, which had cost only a few rupees, was rich and delicious. The smell of it filled the compartment so the woman sitting next to Charlotte twitched her nose and briefly woke up. Charlotte dunked the end of her chapatti into the curry and took a big, satisfying bite.

The man in the suit – a businessman he seemed – nodded with interest and eyed her breakfast.

'Ah. I wondered what you were doing on this little branch line. I've visited the reserve,' he said. Then, waxing philosophical: 'It is very beautiful. You know, sometimes we need to step away from modern life, all its demands, and connect with the natural world.'

Charlotte nodded. 'Would you like some?' She held out the foil dish but the man politely waved it away.

'Thank you, no. I have eaten already, and,' he tapped the briefcase with affectionate fingers, 'I have my lunch in here.' He leaned

2

forward, as though honouring her with a secret. 'My wi[...]
it for me.' He beamed – a big, satisfied smile, then leaned b[...]
his seat, eyes closed, perhaps enjoying the prospect of this lu[...]
or else congratulating himself on having such a thoughtful wif[...]
Charlotte smiled too, glancing at the other passengers in the
compartment: the sleeping woman next to her; the young couple
sitting opposite each other, all loved up judging by the affectionate
little smiles and glances they shared; an old woman with a long,
grey plait holding a basket of oranges, and a mother with a daughter of about twelve, sitting side by side. The mother was brushing
the girl's curtain of long, long, glossy black hair, talking to her in
a low, kind voice.

Charlotte settled back into her seat, eating happily. In another
hour she'd get off the train and drive back to the reserve head-
quarters. She'd spent the previous night at Yercaud, after delivering
plant samples to the Horticultural Research Station – part of her
job as a volunteer at the Golden Tiger Reserve. She was eight
weeks into her three-month placement, and the reserve, India itself,
had started to feel like home.

The mother plaited the girl's lavish hair, creating a gleaming
black rope down her back. The young couple exchanged looks,
and smiled. Beyond the window, the lush, sumptuous landscape
of Tamil Nadu flowed past, little villages amid undulating stretches
of verdant meadow and emerald-green rice fields.

The compartment door opened. A white man, probably in his
early twenties, lugging a battered blue backpack, stared in. He
glanced around. His eyes settled on Charlotte.

'Any seats free?' He was English, had longish red-brown hair,
a sunburned face and thin, bare limbs.

'Sorry, no,' Charlotte said. The answer was evident. Still the
young man waited, as though hoping one of the passengers might
sacrifice their seat for him. Why on earth should they? Charlotte
thought, with a ripple of annoyance.

heading for?' he asked. Ah, that was it. She was
... her young adventurer in India, and he had
... araderie that existed between such travellers.

... Golden Tiger Reserve. I'm working there –
... nteer placement. What about you?'

... don't know. I'm just travelling, you know?'

'Great.' Charlotte didn't feel inclined to talk. She wanted to
read her newspaper and anyway, something about the young man
irritated her. The way he'd ignored everyone else in the compartment, as though they were invisible, speaking only to her, a
complete stranger, just because she was another young European.
She picked up the *Times* and glanced at the front page. The Englishman waited another few moments on the threshold, moving his
weight from one foot to the other, shifting the heavy backpack.

'You're English, right? How long've you been in India?'

Really, couldn't he take the hint? Charlotte sighed, looking up
from the paper.

'Yes, I'm English. I've been here a couple of months. You?'

'Oh, it's nearly ten months now,' he said with some pride. 'I'm
here for the long haul. Love the place.' He looked around the
compartment again, as though an empty seat might magically
appear and he could sit down and harangue Charlotte with his
trove of traveller's tales. Fortunately, Charlotte thought, that wasn't
going to happen. She turned her attention back to the newspaper
and, finally, with an audible sigh, the man drew back, closed the
compartment door and wandered off along the corridor outside.
When she glanced up from the newspaper the businessman caught
her eye and gave a quick, warm smile. She sensed he hadn't been
impressed by the Englishman either.

The sun rose higher, throwing heat through the train window.
Charlotte's thighs began to burn, even through her cotton trousers.
Beyond the window, a water buffalo with its crescent of horns

wallowed in the shallows of a wide brown river. Half a dozen children scampered along a dirt path, on their way to school judging by the uniform and satchels, the girls' hair bound up in neat pigtails.

The train was approaching the reserve now. The cultivated land gave way to wilder places, to the forest, with its teak and rosewood trees, the pillars of the natural cathedral where deer wandered.

Charlotte's attention drifted between the window view and the newspaper spread on her lap. A story about relations with China, soldiers missing in Kashmir, some scandal involving a famous cricket player, lifestyle features about keeping a marriage alive . . . not so different from the news at home, except that the names were Indian instead of English. She turned the page and an article jumped out – a picture of a tiger by a pool of mahogany-coloured water, the fierce, striped face repeated in its reflection. The headline: *Rescue Effort for Golden Tiger Reserve*, then a subtitle: *Sanctuary in line for international support*. Charlotte narrowed her eyes as sunlight flashed into her face. She glanced at her fellow travellers. How sweet the young couple were. They hadn't touched each other once during the length of the journey but the connection between them was palpable, in looks and quiet smiles, the way their bodies seemed to mirror each other, yearning across the space between the facing seats. The sleeping woman woke and rummaged in the large bag at her feet. The young girl read from an English storybook to her mother, while the old woman with the oranges glanced over her shoulder and nodded encouragement.

The train plunged into darker shade, galloping through a dense clump of trees. The whistle shrieked, once, twice – then brilliant sunlight washed over them again, the sticky golden heat of it filling the carriage. Charlotte stretched out her legs and wriggled on the hard seat.

A crash, the scream of metal.

The carriage bucked, leaping from the rail. Charlotte flew from her seat into the air, slammed against the businessman and the compartment wall, then against the window as the entire world turned upside down.

How long did it take? A few moments. Yet it seemed to last an eternity, every instant stretched out, every detail etching itself on her mind as though in a slow, vivid, terrifying dream.

The carriage jumped into the air, flung itself against the preceding carriage, and was struck in turn at the rear by the one behind. A moment of cataclysmic collisions, carriages barging and crashing one against another. Terrible sounds – metal warping, wood smashed and ripped apart. Inside, helpless passengers were thrown against each other, smashed into compartment walls, windows, luggage racks. Bags, baskets and cases tumbled and bounced, fell open, discharging cargos of clothes and fruit. For one insane, lucid moment Charlotte's stunned brain caught a snapshot – the eight of them seemingly afloat in the compartment like Alice falling down the rabbit hole to Wonderland. The girl was upside down, plait aloft, mouth open, the storybook still in her hand. The old woman had her hands in the air, amid an impossible cloud of oranges. The young lovers were tossed over each other; the businessman and his briefcase loomed over Charlotte, horribly large, threatening to crush her to smithereens. Her body instinctively recoiled but the momentum of the train, the impact, held her in place, the compartment a drum in which they bounced like helpless peas.

The noise was deafening, overwhelming, the crash and slam and scream as wood, glass and metal broke, smashed and exploded. The businessman was sucked back against the wall and Charlotte thrown against him, the briefcase thumping into her stomach. People, luggage, possessions, oranges, dropped to the floor as though released from a spell. The carriage lurched to one side. For a long, horrible moment it teetered, giant and ungainly. Then it leaned and toppled, and they were thrown again, the eight of them, against each other and the window, helpless to protect themselves. The track ran along the top of an embankment, and the carriage crashed onto its steep side and slid down.

Crushed, obliterated by shock and the weight of the other passengers, Charlotte waited for the final impact. Was she going to die? The thought flashed through her mind and, on its tail, dismay in a brilliant blaze. How could that be it? But calm followed, like a cool, white mist in her mind. Scenes from her life flashed before her – playing in a summer garden as a child, walking along a winter beach hand in hand with her mother under striped thunder clouds – each tableau curiously brilliant, charged with intensity. Well, perhaps she would die. She let it go, the thought, the fear. Far away, the screeching carriage ground to a halt. Something, or someone, fell against her with enormous force. Charlotte shut her eyes, and the world blacked out.

Cries, moans, and the thin, wavering screams that went on and on, as though Charlotte had woken in hell, among thousands of tormented souls. She didn't move, in the darkness, for an indefinable length of time, unable to think clearly who or where she might be. Only the terrible sounds existed, the cries that filled her ears, grated on her nerves, kept her from sinking back into unconsciousness.

At first her body was remote. She couldn't feel it or make it move, but gradually she became aware of a generalised pain, a weight pressing down on her legs, needles of pain in her knees and hips. Her mouth tasted strange and she couldn't swallow.

The wailing went on, unbearably.

Charlotte's mind came into focus, second by second. She opened her eyes. Why couldn't she see? Where was she? She concentrated on moving, lifted her hands to touch her face, and discovered something had covered it. In a panic she pushed it aside, whatever it was. Charlotte tried to sit up but her knees and hips refused to move. The joints hurt more than ever. Looking around, nothing made sense – the proportions and orientation of the carriage, the position of the window. She reached for her legs and realised she couldn't move because someone was lying on top of them. A heavy, unconscious someone. She tried to wriggle her legs free, to push the someone off. Pain screamed in her legs, agonising stabs in her knees which were bent at a strange angle, crushed beneath her fellow passenger. She pushed again with all her strength, dragged out her legs, the pain almost overcoming her as bones seemed to crack in her feet, and her knees finally straightened. The ligaments in her legs burned as though red hot. A sob escaped her, a long hiss of pain. But at last, she was free.

Charlotte looked around her, trying to make sense of the scene. The carriage lay on its side on the embankment, sloping, the ceiling downwards. The carriage window, seen through the compartment door, showed an oblong of brilliant blue sky, fringed with foliage. Inside – a catastrophe of people and luggage. The businessman lay at her feet, unconscious but muttering. He was the one who had crushed her legs. A random jacket lay beside her; this had been covering her face. The other passengers were beginning to stir. She scanned them, the other seven, heaped against each other like broken dolls. Dust floated in the air, agitated, spinning in the sunlight.

The infernal screaming went on, the backdrop to everything. The sound came from outside the carriage – some other passenger.

Inside Charlotte's compartment, the mother sat up and cried out for her daughter. The girl raised her head, and said in English:

'Mother? Here I am. Here!'

Something about the woman's arm didn't look right. Charlotte suspected it was broken. The other passengers struggled away from each other, tried to sit up. The old woman had a vivid red gash on her forehead, the skin sagging open. The young couple were trying to stand up and neither appeared to be seriously injured. Everyone was shocked, bruised and bewildered.

The worst case, the most worrying, was the businessman lying at Charlotte's feet, still unconscious though his lips were moving. It was hard to say how he was hurt, except that he looked wrong. The big body lay heavily, wedged between the carriage wall and the roof. Internal injuries perhaps?

'Are you hurt?' Someone was speaking. Charlotte turned round. The young man was studying her.

'Yes, I'm okay,' she said.

'You have blood all over your face.'

'Do I?' she said, wondering. Charlotte put her hand to her cheek. Blood made the skin slick; her fingers came away a dark red. She ran her tongue over her teeth, noticing for the first time how much they ached, feeling loose in her gums, and the strange taste in her mouth, that was blood too.

'I think I bit my lip. And my nose is bleeding,' she said. 'How about you? Are you okay?' Still the screaming went on outside. Charlotte couldn't filter it out. Like a needle it pushed into her brain.

'Yes I'm fine, and so is my wife, thank god.'

'He's the one I'm worried about.' She gestured to the businessman. 'I think he's badly hurt.'

The young man nodded. 'We have to get everyone out of here,' he said.

'How are we going to do that?'

He looked around. 'We climb out of the compartment door and either smash the window or crawl along the corridor, to the main carriage door.'

Charlotte looked up. The carriage lay on its side, roof downwards, so they would have to climb up through the compartment door and then sideways along the corridor. That might be easier and safer than trying to break the window. The young man briefed the others.

'I'll go first, to check we can get through, and then I'll come

9

back and help everyone out,' he said. The compartment door was already open, hanging down, so he wriggled through and crawled away along the sideways corridor. The rest of them looked at one another, shocked and bloodied. Charlotte felt a sudden, whelming urge to cry but swallowed it back – this was no time to lose control – turning to the businessman instead. She folded up the jacket and placed it under his head. Shouldn't she try to place him in the recovery position? But what if he'd hurt his back, or had internal injuries? Wouldn't that make it worse?

'I don't know what to do,' she said, helpless. 'What should I do?' The other passengers stared at her, also at a loss. Charlotte longed for help to come, for someone to take over, professionals – police, paramedics, air ambulance. But they were out in the middle of nowhere. How long till the emergency services reached them?

The young man returned, out of breath and sweating. They looked at him expectantly. He said something in Hindi. Then, in English:

'It's okay, we can get through. The carriage door was jammed but I managed to kick it open.' He gestured to the young girl and her mother. 'Come on, you first,' he said.

The mother winced, cradling her broken arm, but spoke encouraging words to her daughter. The mother struggled to climb out with her injury but the young man helped. The old woman followed, then the young man's wife, and finally the woman who had slept in the seat beside Charlotte. When only she and the businessman remained, Charlotte said to the young man:

'What shall we do with him?'

'I don't know. He looks serious to me, but we have no way of moving him. He looks very heavy. Besides, we might make his injuries worse.'

'But we can't just leave him!'

The young man shook his head. Charlotte noticed tiny freckles of blood on his smooth, handsome face. He had blood on the back of his hands, too. Where had that come from? He wrinkled his brow.

'I'll stay with him for now,' he said. 'You must get out, see what needs to be done.'

'I'll tell them you're in here, and I'll come back,' she nodded, wondering who 'they' were, the rescuers, how long it would take for them to come. Inwardly she breathed a prayer of relief, that she didn't have to stay in the compartment with the injured man. The young man had taken the burden from her. But she'd come back and take her turn, once she'd got outside, escaped this carriage tomb, breathed fresh air.

Her legs quivered with pain as she climbed up through the compartment door and into the slanted corridor. Her knees – worse now – hurt with a constant, distracting throb. Shouts and cries filled the corridor. Further along she could see other people trying to get out of the carriage through the door at the other end. Charlotte crawled along, slowly, slowly. The closest door was open, and she emerged through it into the sunshine.

What a scene awaited her. The train, derailed, rested on its side like a fallen animal. Broken carriages lay concertinaed, tumbled down the embankment. The black, iron wheels poked towards the sky, the filthy undersides of the carriages indecently exposed in the sunlight. Passengers in ones and twos, and small, huddled groups, sat on the embankment nursing themselves.

And the screaming went on. It hadn't stopped. Who was it? Why didn't they shut up? The banshee sound of extreme, intolerable pain, horrible to hear. Someone in another carriage, closer to the engine she thought. The smell of diesel and burning hung in the air. For the first time, Charlotte had room in her mind to wonder, what had caused the crash? Why had the train derailed?

'Do you need a hand?' The voice, English, male, came from beneath her. Charlotte was standing on top of the fallen carriage, gazing along the length of the devastated train. The wild landscape spread around it, open grassland, stands of tropical hardwoods.

Charlotte looked down. It took her a moment to work out why she recognised the speaker. He was the backpacker who'd spoken to her earlier (how long ago that seemed now).

'No it's okay, thanks. I can manage.' She clambered to the edge of the train and jumped over the wheels to the embankment. The impact was agony for her knees; she cried out and her legs buckled so she sprawled on the ground amid the dry, yellow grass. The man ran over.

'You're hurt? Here let me help you.' He put his arm around her, lifted her into a sitting position on the sloping bank.

'What about you? Are you hurt?' she said.

'No. Bruises, that's all.'

'Has anyone called the emergency services, do you know? Is anyone in charge?'

The man shook his head. 'I don't know. I've only just got out of the train myself.' He looked at her intently. 'I'm Jack, by the way.'

'Charlotte. Charlie,' she said.

'Are you sure you're okay? Your teeth are chattering.' He was staring at her, with small, brown eyes.

'Shock, that's all. Look, we've got to do something – find out what's going on. People have been badly hurt. There's a man in my compartment – he's in a bad way I think. We have to get moving.'

'Look, why don't you just sit for a few minutes – get your breath back.'

Charlotte shook her head. 'No time,' she said. 'Do you have some water? I'm very thirsty.'

'In my bag. Hold on.' Jack stood up and ran over to his backpack, discarded on the grass. He fished in a side pocket and returned seconds later with a plastic bottle. Charlotte took it gratefully, unscrewed the top and gulped down three large mouthfuls of water. She left a smear of blood on the bottle mouth. At first the water made her mouth sting, and the cut on her lip began to bleed anew, but it was such a relief to drink and wash away the bad taste. She took another mouthful, wiped the bottle neck and handed it back.

'Thanks, Jack. Now, we have work to do.' She clambered to her feet, climbed the embankment, and began to walk along, looking for someone from the railway company – someone who should know an emergency procedure and take charge. Did such a person exist? Jack came hurrying after her.

Towards the front of the train the concertina effect of the carriages grew more dramatic, the damage more extreme. Then she saw the locomotive itself and the reason for the crash became evident. To the east, the land had been cleared of trees and a large gash in the vegetation revealed the existence of a makeshift quarry, one of several illegal and unregulated small-scale quarrying operations that had sprung up on the reserve.

The embankment had subsided. A quantity of soil, stone and its binding layer of scrub grass, had slid away from under the rails, downhill, towards the wound created by the quarry. A stretch of rail, several metres long, was exposed and unsupported, and the train had tumbled off.

'This bloody country. What are they like?' Jack said. 'We could have been killed.'

Charlotte flashed him a look of dislike. 'There are train crashes in England too. We have to find out what we can do to help.'

Jack looked distinctly restless, as though what he'd like to do most of all was walk away and leave the horrible mess behind.

'Surely the emergency services will be here soon. What can we do?'

'We don't know how long it will take for help to come. We're in the middle of nowhere. You go off, if you like. I'm going to see what I can do.' Her teeth were still chattering despite the heat, but she continued to walk the length of the train.

People were clambering out, others were sitting or lying on the embankment. A man carried a little girl with blood all over her white dress. Was she still alive? Charlotte looked away, afraid to see. An old man sitting on the grass cradled his wife in his arms, while she cried with her hands over her face. The smell of burning diesel grew stronger as she drew closer. Fuel had spilled out onto the grass.

'Stay where you are!' A man in a uniform stepped forward, holding out his arm.

'What? Who are you?' She was rude, abrupt even. The accident had taken away her instinctive politeness.

'You don't want to see,' the man said. 'The driver's dead. He was thrown out of the cab and the locomotive crushed him when it fell.'

Charlotte saw the man properly. He had a deep cut along his cheek and blood on his scalp, visible at the roots of his hair and on his forehead. He was wild-eyed, in a state of shock, as she was.

'Who are you? Do you work for the railway?' she said more gently.

'He's the co-driver.' Another, older, man in a uniform had appeared beside Charlotte. He said something in Tamil and put his hand out to the co-driver, a gesture of comfort.

'Does anyone know what has happened yet? Has anyone called the emergency services?'

'Yes. Rescue and medical teams are on their way from Coimbatore.'

'How far is that? How long will it take?'

'They'll be here soon – it's about fifty miles.' He drew out a packet of cigarettes from his jacket pocket, lit one, and then passed the packet to the co-driver, Charlotte and Jack, who was hovering behind her. They all declined.

14

'Is that a good idea? What about the spilled fuel?' she said. The man continued to smoke but he did at least move further from the train.

Charlotte shook her head. 'Fifty miles? That's a long way! People are dying!'

A throng of other passengers, many of them cut and bruised, was moving towards them, seeking help and reassurance, wanting to know what was going on. Variously angry, worried, agitated they began to harangue the co-driver and the smoking employee. Charlotte couldn't understand what they were saying but the gist was obvious enough. Someone started shouting and the smoking man tried to calm them down. He raised his voice above the clamour, no doubt appealing for order.

'Look, there are people coming,' Jack said, tapping Charlotte on the shoulder. She turned round. Several men were running towards the train. Others were following.

'Who are they?'

'I don't know. People from a nearby village perhaps? I 'spect they heard the accident.' Jack frowned, sizing them up, these would-be rescuers. Seeing the group near the locomotive, they ran up talking excitedly, and soon everyone was looking to the train official for instructions and information. An image flashed into Charlotte's mind, the businessman still in her compartment with the young man, awaiting rescue, and she wondered if she should go back to see how they were getting on.

The train official lifted his arms in a bid to silence the crowd.

'The rescue and medical teams will be here soon,' he shouted in English. 'Please, be calm. Listen! We want to evacuate any remaining passengers from the train, except for the seriously wounded, who must be identified and tended till the emergency services arrive. If you are able to help, then do so. If you are injured, please sit on the bank away from the train.'

More people were arriving all the time. The able passengers

15

and the locals spread out along the length of the train, helping any remaining travellers from the carriages and carrying out the most basic first aid. No-one held back, all throwing their efforts and energies into helping one another. The sound of voices, encouraging shouts and cries for assistance filled the air.

Charlotte approached one of the carriages at the front of the train, bent almost in two from the impact of the derailment. The windows had exploded, releasing a hail of glass which now lay on the grass. She stepped forward gingerly, afraid of what she might find.

'Hello? Is anybody in there?'

Something stirred. Charlotte clambered onto the side of the carriage and peered into the gloom.

'Can you see anything?' Jack had followed her. He stood on the embankment, looking up, shading his eyes. Sweat coated his face. The heat was growing more intense, minute by minute.

'There're people still inside, but I'm not sure who, how many.' No point even trying to open the door, it had buckled and jammed into the distorted, broken carriage wall. 'I'll try getting in through the window.'

'Be careful of the broken glass. Here – take my jacket and throw it over the window frame before you climb over.' Jack rummaged in his backpack and drew out a thick fleece. Charlotte dropped the fleece on the glass, swung her legs over and dropped inside.

Charlotte

The carriage was twisted out of shape, like a crazy house in a fairground. The thin wall separating the compartment from the corridor had split open, exposing shards of spiky, splintered wood. Dust again, spinning in spears of sunshine, then dark shadows, in which, as her eyes adjusted, Charlotte made out a heap of people and luggage at the bottom. How many people? Four or five, she thought. Somebody moaned.

'Hello? Can anybody hear me?' Her voice sounded very small and strange. Somebody muttered something she couldn't understand, and she heard another moan. At least they weren't all dead . . . did she think that thought? But what if someone were horribly hurt and mangled? She felt the first premonition of a terrible headache to come, a certain cloudiness in her thinking. She pushed it to one side.

'My name's Charlotte,' she said, trying to sound competent. 'Can I help anyone get out of here?'

Someone coughed and muttered again, though Charlotte couldn't understand what they were saying. She edged closer, struggling to keep her footing on the slope.

'Do you need any help?' Jack had jumped in beside her. He had a torch. 'This any use?'

'You're very well prepared,' Charlotte said.

'A useful man to have around in emergencies, yes.'

Charlotte squatted and edged closer to the people still lying together in a heap. An old man raised his head. He said something, then tried to stand up, but his left leg gave way and he staggered back again.

'Here, help him!' Charlotte said to Jack. 'Put your arm around him, help him out of the carriage.'

Jack did as he was told. The old man was thin as a bird, with long, white hair and a beard. Pain darkened his face, but he made no complaint as Jack half carried him out into the sunshine. Three left, Charlotte thought. A plump woman in a white nylon suit and two boys – her sons maybe? One looked about fifteen, the other a couple of years younger. They were also dressed in smart clothes – perhaps the three of them had been off to some happy family occasion?

Charlotte stared. She was certain the woman was dead. Her head lay at a peculiar angle and her body was utterly still. Charlotte stretched out a hand and touched the woman's throat, checking for any indication of a pulse or breath, but she felt nothing.

Charlotte waited for a moment, too shocked to know how to proceed. How many times had she seen simulated deaths on films and televisions? Yet here she was, eighteen years old, confronting death for real. The woman – probably a mother – snatched away, broken, just like that, and all her plans, worries, hopes, dreams and fears snuffed out too. Charlotte swallowed. Nothing she could do to help. What about the boys?

Jack reappeared, crouching beside her.

'This woman's dead,' Charlotte whispered.

'Are you sure? How do you know?'

'Look at her. I think her neck's broken. And I couldn't feel a pulse.'

Jack touched the woman's face with careful, lingering fingers. A beam of sunlight illuminated his face. He had an expression of strange wonderment, his eyes very round.

'Yes, you're right,' he said. They looked at one another, Charlotte and Jack – in the oven heat of the carriage, amid the train's broken architecture, the stray stabs of sunshine, the glittering dust, in the presence of the unknown dead woman.

Jack stared at Charlotte, his expression intense. 'I'll never forget this moment,' he said. 'Not as long as I live.'

One of the boys shifted and cried out, breaking the spell.

'Do you think they're badly hurt?' Jack said.

'I don't know. I haven't looked at them yet. I think we need to move the woman first, she's pressed against them.' They were both a little uneasy at the prospect of handling the dead woman, but the boy murmured and then made what Charlotte guessed was a cry for help. They had no time to lose.

'Come on,' she said, as much to herself as to Jack. 'Don't think about it, just do it.'

She took the woman's arm and heaved the inert body. Jack didn't help, still mesmerised by the body, by the idea of the woman's death. Charlotte struggled. The woman's head lolled horribly, rolling on the broken neck. Charlotte gave one final heave, and shoved the body aside, trying not to look into the dead face, striving to keep her mind focused on the task of helping the two boys still in the compartment.

'Please! Jack, please help me here. Have a look at the boys – see if they're hurt.' The sharpness in her voice stirred him into action. Jack slid forward and checked out the boys.

'One's unconscious, the older boy. Hey, do you speak English? Can you sit up?' Freed from the constriction of the woman's body (their mother? – surely she was) the younger boy sat up, his face shocked and confused.

'My hand hurts,' he said, holding it aloft. 'I can't move my fingers.'

'I think you've broken them,' Jack said. 'Can you stand up? I'd like to help you out of here.' The little boy nodded.

19

'Where's my mother?' he said. Jack glanced at Charlotte, looking for help. What should he say?

'Your mother's here,' Charlotte said. 'You go outside. It'll be safer there.' She nodded at Jack. 'Go on, help him get out.'

Jack manoeuvred the boy from the carriage and out of the broken window, and Charlotte turned her attention to the older boy. How badly was he hurt? A bruise was already rising on his forehead and a little blood had seeped from his nose. No other wound was immediately visible. A head injury then? That could be serious. She touched the boy's face.

'Can you hear me? Can you wake up?'

The boy's eyes moved under closed lids and he made a convulsive gulp.

'Wake up – please,' Charlotte said, as much to herself as the boy. His head twitched from side to side and his eyes flicked open. He gulped again and swallowed, then stared up, beyond Charlotte. What was he looking at? Something beyond the confines of the carriage, she thought. He didn't seem to be quite present in the ordinary world – though nothing about the accident, this day, could be considered ordinary. The boy's mother was lying dead behind them – nothing would be the same for him again.

'I'm back.' Jack clambered into the compartment.

'We need to get you out of here,' Charlotte said to the boy. 'Can you sit up?' She was so hot, sweat trickling down her face, making her eyes sting. She wanted to get outside, away from the dead woman, the dust and confined space, into the fresh air. Still the boy stared into nowhere.

'Help me, Jack,' she said.

'Is he hurt?'

'I don't know. I'm no expert but I think he banged his head.'

'Is it safe to move him?' Jack edged closer, wrinkling his brow again, looking at the boy and then intently at Charlotte, peering into her face.

20

The boy shifted and blinked.

'Can you sit up?' she repeated.

The boy didn't answer but the question must have registered because he struggled, flailing his arms. Jack and Charlotte hurried to help him. He seemed unable to manage his limbs, but nothing, apparently, was broken.

'He's like Bambi,' Jack tittered nervously. 'You know, when Bambi tries to ice-skate.'

'Hold him!' Charlotte said. 'Please – I want to get out of here.' Sweat dripped over her lips, making the cut smart. Together they half carried the boy out of the compartment and through the carriage door. Outside, a group of people had gathered; they reached out to help the boy down.

'Is there anyone else inside?' a man demanded.

'One,' Charlotte answered. Then, when the boy was out of earshot: 'It's the boys' mother. She's dead.'

She took a deep breath and jumped off the carriage onto the embankment. The place was swarming with people now – local rescuers helping people out of the carriages, tending to the wounded. The air buzzed with the sound of urgent voices, people shouting instructions and encouragement, the screams and cries of the wounded and bereaved. Charlotte thought about the businessman in her own compartment, ran back along the train to see how he was and if someone had relieved the young man.

Yes! The injured man was lying on the embankment. The young man was sitting close beside him, his arm around his wife.

'You're okay?' She squatted beside them.

'Yes, thank god. People came, helped me get him out. It was so hot in there! I thought he would die.' The husband studied Charlotte. 'But you – you're very pale.' He looked concerned.

Charlotte felt all remaining strength drain away. The shock and hurt she'd ignored and overridden washed over her, properly noticed for the first time. It had taken somebody else's attention to alert her to her own condition. Her legs weakened, her body sagged and she half collapsed onto the ground. Her vision swam. As her mind clouded, Charlotte thought, surely the rescue services would be here soon? How long since the crash? She had no idea. Time had lost meaning, since that moment after the impact, when she'd wondered if she would die.

She blinked in the bright sunshine, the view becoming hazy. She was lying on her back now, the ground seeming to rise and hold her up. The spiky grass tickled. Faces peered at her – the young husband, an Indian woman she didn't recognise, and Jack – Jack too. Something about this scene was deeply familiar, though long forgotten. Was it a memory from infancy, lying in a cot and seeing giant faces looking down? What a curious thought. She closed her eyes, wanting a rest from the sun. The world faded away.

An indeterminate time later, she opened her eyes again. Her entire body ached but particular pain beat like a drum in her knees and her jaw, as though every tooth on the left side of her face had been drilled without anaesthetic. And her skin burned, probably from lying in the ferocious sunshine. She blinked, raised her hands to rub her eyes, which alerted her to the ache in her shoulders.

A tremendous noise filled the air. What was it, making such a deafening racket? Charlotte lifted her head, propped herself on her elbows. A helicopter, standing on a patch of open ground at the bottom of the embankment, beyond the felled train, was starting up its rotor blades. The entire scene had transformed in the time Charlotte had been unconscious, with the arrival of the rescue services. Men and women in uniforms moved among the local rescuers. Two people on stretchers were being loaded into the helicopter. Paramedics tended the walking wounded. The entire atmosphere of the scene had altered, from frantic panic to ordered industry.

'Excuse me, may I speak with you? Do you need any treatment?' A young woman in a paramedic's uniform squatted beside

Charlotte. She carried a clipboard. 'You were travelling on the train? Could you tell me your name?' She had an attractive heart-shaped face, caramel-coloured skin and a long, glossy ponytail.

Charlotte supplied her with the details – about herself and her journey. Yes she was travelling alone, British, staying at the Golden Tiger Reserve on a volunteer placement.

'No serious injuries,' Charlotte said. But the paramedic scrutinised her, stretched out a hand and touched the side of Charlotte's face, wearing a cool, professional expression.

'You took a blow to the head? There's some dried blood on your face.'

'I'm not exactly sure.'

'Any pain?'

'My jaw hurts. And my knees. I think someone fell on them. My knees are the worst.'

'Let me see.'

Charlotte rolled up her cotton trousers. Purple bruises blossomed. Her knees were puffy, their familiar, slender shape obliterated by swelling. The shock of the spectacle made them hurt all the more.

'Can you bend them? Can you walk?'

'Yes. Well, I was walking, till I sat down.' She moved too abruptly and had to sit down again.

'She was fabulous! You should have seen her – unstoppable. She went into the train to rescue people.' Jack. Jack of course, squatting beside the paramedic. Charlotte smiled weakly.

'Can you tell me something? There were two young boys . . . their mother – I think she was dead. Do you know if they were okay?'

The paramedic shook her head. 'I don't know. We haven't collated all the information yet. We're doing the best we can. Don't worry, it sounds as though you've done more than your fair share. You take it easy, look after yourself. We'll manage things now.'

23

The paramedic examined Charlotte's knees, felt them, asked her to bend and straighten them.

'Only bruising,' she said. 'You were lucky. They'll be very sore for a few days though. Take it easy.' When she'd satisfied herself Charlotte had no serious injuries and made a note of her contact details, the paramedic rose to her feet and strode off to the next crash victim.

Jack sat down beside Charlotte.

'How are you?' she asked.

'I'm fine. Just fine. Very lucky. They took all my details too.'

'What happens now?' Charlotte sank back onto the grass, the effort of sitting upright too much for her.

'They're organising transport to get us away from here, to the next station,' Jack said. 'Here, have some more water. They're handing out bottles.'

Charlotte took the bottle gratefully, unscrewed the top and took several large mouthfuls. The afternoon was nearly over, the sun low in the sky. The colours of the forest deepened, rich emeralds, a sheen of chestnut brown on the trunks of the giant trees. Not far away, on a single low shrub, like a visitation from a fairy tale, a peacock perched, oblivious to the grand drama and individual tragedies unfolding in front of it. The peacock was beautiful, a splash of deep, petrol blue, its folded tail pouring down from the little tree.

Charlotte sighed. After the storm of the day, all emotion had drained away. She felt empty and scoured out. Jack was sitting beside her, silent. She wondered about all the people involved in the accident, each of them dealing with their own personal hurts, losses, disrupted plans or lives. None of them would ever forget this day. None of them would be untouched by what had happened.

'Are you okay?' she said to Jack.

He nodded. 'Yes. Just very, very tired. I feel as though I could sleep for a week. But when I see what some of the other people here are suffering – well, we were both lucky, weren't we?'

'Yes. Yes you're right.'

Jack reached out and took Charlotte's hand. 'It's changed me. Do you know what I mean? Nothing can ever be the same again, after this. I've seen death. I've looked it in the face. We could have died – both of us. Just being here – now, it's a gift. Do you know what I mean? Do you understand what I'm saying?' He was gripping her hand.

'Yes. Yes I do know,' she said. But something about this fervour made Charlotte uneasy. She tried to extricate her hand politely, but Jack held it tight.

'Let me have your mobile number,' he said. 'We need to keep in contact after this. We need to talk about it, what we've shared.'

Again, the warning tremor. But politeness won over. He was only asking for her mobile number. Why should she refuse? He was waiting with his phone in his hand, to type the number in. She gave it to him. Then Jack started to talk.

'It's not like anything else, is it? This travelling. When you cut your ties and just leave everything behind. Family, friends, home, all the familiar things. And you're adrift, nothing to rely on but yourself. Everything seems to mean more, doesn't it? To be more significant – like a story. An adventure story. You don't have anything solid, no structure or routine. So what you do have – words, conversations, encounters, dreams – they shine. They gleam. Do you know what I mean? It's like I've never been so much alive as these last months, travelling. I've been so awake. And today, the most alive of all. Because I nearly died.'

He looked at her, eyes fever-bright, wanting her to agree – wanting affirmation. Charlotte nodded. She did know what he meant. She had thought these things herself, how vivid and crowded with incident every day was in this foreign place. Still something about Jack's rapture was perturbing and she pulled her hand away, more definitely this time, wanting to free herself.

The noise from the helicopter intensified and it lifted from the

25

ground. The rotor blades spread a simoom, laden with dust and grit. Charlotte shielded her eyes, watched it rise into the air above the fallen train, slowly turn and then head off into the darkening sky.

An official-looking person in a railway uniform called out. A bus was bouncing its way over the dry ground, to take the stranded passengers away from the accident site. Several ambulances were already parked up, taking on board a cargo of wounded. She noticed a photographer, and a small camera crew, filming an interview with one of the railway officials, and thought of Otto, her best friend. He wanted to be a photojournalist.

'It's time to go,' Jack said. 'Come on, Charlotte.'

She tried to stand up but the pain in her knees screamed out and she half collapsed back to the ground.

'Here, let me help you,' he said, reaching out his hand. She struggled to her feet, reluctantly allowing Jack to help. She certainly couldn't walk without him.

'Put your arm round my waist,' he said. Slowly he propped her up as she hobbled painfully down the embankment.

One of the men attached to the camera crew spotted them and hurried over.

'You're tourists? Can we speak to you on camera about the crash? Only a minute, we'd be most grateful.'

Jack shook his head and backed away, taking Charlotte with him, but the man, dressed in jeans and a leather jacket despite the heat, followed them, persisting with the request.

'We'd appreciate a tourist's point of view, just a few words?'

'Okay,' Charlotte said weakly. 'Hang on, Jack. I'll help them out.'

The man called out to his colleagues and a moment later the camera was pointing at Charlotte. A woman in a smart suit and perfect lipstick asked her where she was from and what she was doing in India. 'Now I'd like you to tell us what you remember of the accident – what it was like for you,' the woman said. She was cucumber cool, despite the carnage all around. 'Look at me, not into the camera.' She nodded to the cameraman.

Charlotte blinked, suddenly lost for words. She swallowed hard. 'It's hard to describe. A terrible crash, and we were thrown about in the compartment. People were screaming.' She dried up.

The woman prompted her: 'How would you rate the emergency response?'

'Oh, well. Considering the accident happened in the middle of nowhere, I think they've done a good job.' Words failed her again. She sounded like an idiot but her brain refused to engage.

Jack edged closer.

'Come on, we have to get on the bus,' he said. The interviewing woman nodded, already looking for another victim.

Charlotte and Jack joined the other unharmed or only lightly injured passengers queuing for the bus. Behind her, Charlotte glimpsed a large black body-bag, hoisted by two paramedics, and felt a shudder of horror. Was it the woman, the mother of the two boys? She remembered seeing the dead woman's face and how it had felt to move the body.

'Come along, please.'

Charlotte quickly looked away, allowed herself to be ushered onto the bus. She climbed the steep steps with some difficulty, wincing at the pain in her knees, Jack close behind her, helping her up. She found an empty seat and sat down, keeping her eyes away from the window, not wanting to look out. Everyone was subdued, worn out by the day and eager to be away from the site of the crash. Still they had to wait as names were checked, and some kind of argument broke out between the bus driver and an official from the train company. At last, the door closed, the engine started up and the bus started to move. Charlotte sensed the collective relief of the passengers as they drew away from the embankment and she caught one last glimpse of the wrecked train as the bus turned and bumped over the rough ground.

27

'It was the quarrying,' she said.

'What?' Jack was sitting close beside her.

'It was the quarrying – caused the subsidence and the derailment. It's a big problem on the reserve. Illegal work. That and logging and poaching.' Her voice was flat. She was too tired to muster any real emotion. The jerking of the bus made her knees throb.

'Where are you staying?'

'I'm lodging with the reserve manager – with his family. They've got a nice place. And they'll be wondering where I am. I should have been back hours ago.'

'I expect they'll have heard about the crash by now,' Jack said. And then, impulsively: 'Do you think I could stay there too? Just for tonight? I've got nowhere to go.'

'Where were you planning to stay, before the crash?' Charlotte was reluctant to agree.

'I don't know. I didn't have any particular plans. You know how it is. Maybe they'll have some work I can do at the reserve? It would be great to stay with you for a while.'

Again Charlotte felt a peculiar shrinking. Jack was gazing at her with a needy intensity she found discomfiting.

'That's unlikely. I sorted out my placement months ago. I don't think you can just turn up and take a job. It doesn't work like that.'

Jack shrugged, picking at his nails. 'Well I could try. Nothing ventured, nothing gained. Wouldn't it be great to spend a little more time together?'

How could she answer that? She wanted to say no – but politeness restrained her. So she said nothing, instead turning her attention to the window now the train wreck was out of sight. The sun was sinking fast, throwing golden light through the bus.

The journey took about half an hour. The bus reached a track, and then a road and the drive became smoother. They drove into a town and drew up at the railway station, where a train was already

28

waiting for those who wished to continue their journey. Just now Charlotte felt she never wanted to get on a train again.

She climbed carefully from the bus and looked around, wondering how she would get back to her lodgings.

'Charlie! Charlie! There you are!' A female voice shouted out above the hubbub at the front of the station. A young Indian woman was running over, hair bouncing on her shoulders, sunglasses pushed back on her head, dressed in smart jeans and a white blouse.

'Amrita!' Charlotte waved.

'Oh thank goodness you're safe! I was so worried. I heard about the crash, I was going crazy! Why didn't you ring to tell me you were okay?' Amrita seized Charlotte in her arms and gave her an enormous hug, sending Charlotte into a painful totter.

'I'm sorry, I should have called. So much was going on.'

Amrita examined her. 'Are you hurt? Was it terrible? We heard people had been killed!' Amrita was eighteen, the same age as Charlotte. She was the reserve manager's daughter, and soon off to university to study engineering. The two young women had become great friends over the weeks Charlotte had been working at the reserve.

'I'm okay,' Charlotte said. 'Bruised knees, that's the worst of it.'

'I've got the pick-up,' Amrita said. 'Come on, I'll drive you home. You look terrible.'

Jack hovered, keeping close to Charlotte. Amrita glanced up at him and he said: 'Hi, I'm Jack. I met Charlotte on the train. We were working together, in the rescue.'

Amrita shook his hand.

'Do you have any spare beds? I'm so sorry to ask, it's just that I haven't anywhere to stay tonight,' Jack said.

Amrita blinked. 'Well, I expect we could sort something out. I think the train company is sorting out accommodation for people who don't want to travel tonight – they want to look after everyone, because of the crash. But – well, any friend of Charlotte is a friend of ours, so come with us if you'd like.'

Charlotte felt a sinking inside as Jack climbed into the pick-up. Wasn't that mean of her? Jack had helped courageously after the rail crash, and he'd taken care of her too, with great generosity. She should be grateful – and she was. Still, something about him made her uneasy. She didn't like the way he looked at her so intently.

Amrita drove them back to the reserve. She was clearly bursting with questions about the train crash but she kept quiet, out of consideration for her weary passengers.

Their house was new, built on the edge of the village with a garden and flowering creepers growing over a veranda, shuttered windows and white-plastered walls. Amrita's father and mother hurried out to greet them when the car drew up. Charlotte received another ferocious hug from Amrita's mother, and they were all talking at once, the family, relieved and worried and trying to find out about the accident.

Daylight finally faded as Charlotte and Jack were ushered into the house. Amrita's mother, Prina, as slender and elegant as her daughter, took her guests into the large living room, and then hurried into the kitchen to make cups of tea.

Amrita sat next to Charlotte and put her hand on her shoulder. 'What would you like to do? Are you hungry? Do you need to lie down?'

'I'd like to take a shower, if that's okay.' Charlotte felt weak and tearful all over again but she reined in her emotions and headed for the bathroom. Slowly and carefully, because of her bruised knees, she took off her clothes and stepped under the shower. She turned the tap and closed her eyes as the deluge of delicious cool water fell over her, rinsing away the dirt, blood and sweat of the long, appalling day. She lathered herself with soap and washed her hair, wanting a ritual of cleansing, to rid herself of the residues of the crash and its aftermath. She dried attentively, noting the various cuts and bruises, the tenderness of her jaw, the pain and swelling in her knees. All these things would heal soon enough. The cuts would close and disappear, the bruising would subside. But the images haunting her mind – how long would she carry them?

Prina served a generous meal that evening. They all sat around the low table in the living room, laden with plates of coconut rice, lentil puree, fried fish, chutneys and poppadams. At first Charlotte wondered how she could possibly eat, but once started she found she was ravenous.

Jaideep, Amrita's father, was sitting at the head of the table. In his late forties, lean and grey-haired, he didn't say much to begin with. Jack tried to engage him in conversation, asking questions about the management of the Golden Tiger Reserve, but Jaideep, while polite, remained at the periphery of the conversation. Then, when the meal was finished, Jaideep sat forward and asked Charlotte to tell him everything that had happened.

Charlotte sighed and Prina shook her head, scolding her husband for asking this of her now, when she was tired out and hurting. But Charlotte reassured Prina it was fine, and perhaps now was the best time to tell them, while the entire incident was so keenly in her mind.

They were an attentive, sympathetic audience. From time to time Jaideep gently interrupted with a question or a request for clarification. Now and then Jack interjected some detail of his own, or praised Charlotte's capability and courage after the accident, when she'd helped the other passengers. When Charlotte had finished, Amrita gave her a big hug and Prina cleared away the dishes. Jaideep turned on the television for the news and an item on the train accident.

Eight killed, a hundred injured. Footage filmed from a helicopter, then a view along the side of the fallen train and interviews with train company officials. The accident was blamed on subsidence created by illegal quarrying in the Golden Tiger Reserve.

Charlotte glanced at Jaideep, who was staring intently at the screen. Apart from the catastrophe of the crash itself, this was an ill-timed disaster for the sanctuary. Undermanned, underfunded, the wardens and volunteers waged a constant battle against poachers, loggers and quarrying. And with the new grant application, this was the last thing they needed. It made the reserve management seem dangerously incompetent.

The news switched to another item and Charlotte's eyes grew heavy. She excused herself and went to the neat little bedroom she shared with Amrita. The night was warm, the air fragrant with the perfume of the blossoms on the creepers which drifted into the house. Charlotte stood at the window, seeing the dark outlines of trees in the distance, a fat white moon overhead. She could hear the insect chorus.

She left the windows open but drew the shutters closed, changed into her cotton pyjamas and slipped into bed. As soon as she turned out the light and put her head down on the pillow, the bedroom door opened. She assumed it was Amrita, but as soon as the silhouette appeared in the doorway Charlotte realised her mistake. It was Jack.

'Charlotte?' he said softly.

'Yes? What is it?' She moved awkwardly in bed.

Jack, stepped into the room and pushed the door closed behind him.

'Jack, I need to sleep. What do you want?' She was brisk and irritated.

Jack didn't take the hint. Instead he crept forward and without asking, sat himself on the edge of her bed. Charlotte wriggled away.

'I'm sorry, I don't want to trouble you,' he said. 'I just wanted to talk for a minute.' His voice had a peculiar oily quality, as though he wanted to wheedle something from her.

'What is it, Jack? Can't it wait till morning? I don't want our hosts catching you here. They are very strict about that kind of thing and since you've foisted yourself on them tonight, I think you should abide by the rules.'

Jack ignored her chilly tone. She could see him smiling at her in the darkness.

'I just wanted to say goodnight,' he said. 'This has been such a day, hasn't it? And we shared it, you and I. There's a bond between us. You can sense it too. Whatever else happens, we're bound by that time together. It means something.'

Charlotte shook her head. 'It was just an accident. Something random and terrible. Now please go away. You shouldn't be in here and I really need to sleep.'

Jack, still smiling, rose to his feet and walked to the door. Just before he left he turned and said: 'Goodnight, Charlotte.' Then he whispered something she couldn't hear, before stepping outside and closing the door behind him.

Otto

Otto bought another drink. Except for the cheapness of the beer and the fact that most of the revellers were well-dressed Indians, the Mumbai bar was much the same as those back home. The air conditioning alleviated the Indian heat. A city bar like all city bars – bright lights, loud music, talking and drinking.

He was alone. Another Brit staying at his backpackers' hostel had recommended the place, suggesting he would like it. But why come all the way to India to hang out in a bar like this? To meet the locals? They all looked much smarter than he did. He felt like a scruff in his cut-off jeans. He'd tied back his hair into a ponytail because it needed washing.

A large television screen showed a quiz show of some kind, though he couldn't hear the dialogue because the music was too loud.

Otto felt miserable. He'd planned this trip to India with his friends Charlotte and Jen. But Jen had decided to stay on in Goa, and Charlotte was undertaking her volunteer placement at the Golden Tiger Reserve in the south. He'd travelled alone for several weeks, taking long, solitary train journeys, seeing vistas of India through the window. Now he was back in Mumbai, the huge, crowded, colourful metropolis: high-rise offices, miles of slums; swish new housing developments and decaying Victorian mansions;

flashy modern shopping malls and women selling heaped vegetables on the pavement. He'd wanted to roam alone for a time – it was challenging and exciting. The solitary traveller always has more adventures, meets more people. But things hadn't turned out quite as he'd planned. However far he went, he couldn't escape his memories of Maria, the beautiful girl he'd met in Goa, the infatuation he'd fallen into, and the recollection of her violent death on the paradise beach.

Maria. Whenever his mind wasn't occupied, he thought of her. The murder hung like a cold, dark shadow over his Indian odyssey.

'Another beer please.'

The barman nodded. Three slick young Indian men in colourful shirts and tight denim jeans pushed their way to the bar, beside him. One glanced over, eying Otto's dishevelled appearance.

'Hello, you're British?' he said.

'How did you guess?'

'Ah you look British,' the young man said. 'Welcome to Mumbai. Can I buy you a drink?'

Otto hadn't touched his last one, but he nodded. 'Please,' he said. 'Another beer.'

The young man smiled, revealing a set of astonishingly white, perfect teeth. Otto looked at him more carefully, noting the healthy gleam of his skin, the designer clothes.

'So how do you like Mumbai? I'm Faarooq, by the way.' He held out his hand. 'My father runs a chain of restaurants in the city. I'm studying for an MBA.' His tone wasn't boastful. The newly wealthy in Mumbai seemed much less embarrassed by success than their British counterparts.

'Otto,' he said, shaking the hand. Faarooq smelled of some expensive aftershave and wore a thick gold necklace that appeared a little vulgar to Otto. Then again, how vulgar must he seem, with three days' stubble and hair a week unwashed? Faarooq started talking about restaurants and business, and Otto's attention

35

wandered to the television screen above Faarooq's head. The news came on, with English subtitles, useful against the loud music.

A train crash in Tamil Nadu, out in the country. Eight dead, a hundred injured. He thought of Charlotte – hoped she wasn't involved. That's unlikely, he admonished himself – don't worry.

'So what do you do, Otto?'

'Sorry?' He looked away from the screen.

'You're a student?'

'Oh, yes. Media. I want to be a photojournalist.'

They talked some more and Faarooq invited Otto to a private party but Otto's heart wasn't in it. He was tired. Tonight the drink had made him heavy and dull. He made a polite farewell and headed out of the bar, into the heat of the late, un-air-conditioned Mumbai night.

The city was always busy, even so late. Cars, scooters and bicycles filled the streets. Neon lights blazed above the crowded pavements. Waiting at the traffic lights, two glamorous young women in an open-topped car laughed together, tossing glossy hair over their shoulders, while perched on the kerb, an emaciated, elderly beggar held out his hand for a few rupees.

The night city smelled ripe; rot, rubbish, spice, smoke, diesel fumes and, distantly, the perfume of the Arabian Sea. Otto pushed his way through the thick, heated Mumbai air. It was a forty-five-minute walk to the hostel. He could have taken an auto-rickshaw – several drove past, yellow and black, buzzing like giant bees – but he wanted to be moving, and in any case, walking was always the best way to see a city, particularly a city like Mumbai.

Lots of people about, mostly men, walking, or standing in little clusters drinking tea, smoking and talking. Garish posters on hoardings advertised new Bollywood films. At first Otto had found it alien and intimidating, but as the days went by, he started to relax and feel at home. He'd bought a large map of the city and spent many hours exploring Mumbai on foot, learning the shape of it – the old and the new, high places and low, claiming it, making it his own.

Otto had done all the tourist things. He visited the Prince of Wales Museum and admired elegant statues and exquisite, hypnotising miniature paintings. He spent two days working as an extra in a Bollywood film, a favour organised by a man he met in a restaurant who worked at Film City. Otto played a British soldier – the enemy in a musical drama set in nineteenth-century India during the Raj, the time of British rule. He spent most of those two days hanging about, enjoying an opportunity to watch the process of film-making.

The evenings he hung out with other backpackers at the hostel – enjoyed the diversity of the young travellers: Europeans like himself, Americans, several young Israelis just out of the army. They ate, drank, talked and talked. About travel, India, politics, books, films. And women; he met several interesting young women but never felt the urge to make a move, to take things any further. The memory of Maria, his longing for her, the brutality of her murder, hung over all his adventures, taking the shine from them. She haunted him. Even as he admired a statue of the Buddha or strolled through the Hanging Gardens, he found he was talking to her in his mind, sharing what he could see.

It was stupid of course. He'd only met Maria a few days before her death and he hadn't really known her. She'd been a fantasy figure, beautiful and exotic, a seductive beach babe. Foolish to pine for a fantasy, but nonetheless, he did. From time to time he'd glimpse a European girl who looked a little like her and his heart would leap.

Otto had walked into a poorer part of the city. The hoardings and illuminated advertisements gave way to small shops and street stalls, many open even so late. From time to time he passed people sleeping on mats or pieces of cardboard, under makeshift shelters, tucked against walls. Close to the hostel he ordered three hot, oily samosas from a vendor with a barrow stall. The effects of the beer had worn off. His mind was clear but he felt tired.

The hostel was a curious, higgledy-piggledy building, an old Victorian house with several random extensions. The front door led to a tatty black-and-white tiled hallway with a door at the far end, leading to a small, walled garden. Posters, postcards and maps adorned the walls, pasted and pinned one on top of another, presumably going back years, or decades. According to the hostel brochure, all sorts of famous people had stayed since it opened in the sixties, though Otto was sceptical about a claim the Beatles had visited.

He ambled through the hallway, eating a samosa, and stepped into the garden. Three men were sitting at a table, smoking and drinking beer. A television in the communal lounge was visible to the drinkers through an open window.

'Hey, Otto! How's it going?' one of the men called out. 'You wanna drink?'

'No thanks. I'm worn out. Off to bed.' He sat down though. Even going to bed seemed like too much effort.

A string of coloured light bulbs illuminated the garden, a dry, dusty place with neglected plants in pots and discarded cigarette butts on the ground. Still Otto liked it. When the noise and cease-less crowds of the city grew too much, this was his place of retreat, where no-one would beg from him or try to sell him something.

Music, a female voice, spilled from one of the upstairs windows. The men at the table laughed at a joke Otto didn't hear. He put his last samosa on the table, too weary to eat.

The news came on the television again, repeating the article about the train crash in Tamil Nadu. The death toll had risen to nine. Aerial footage of the wrecked train, an interview with a shocked passenger and a railway official – then a profoundly famil-iar face appeared on the screen.

Charlotte. The shock knocked Otto for six. So unexpected – to see that long-known, lovely face on the screen. Thoughts tumbled in his mind. She had been caught up in the crash? She was hurt? She was okay? She might have been killed – one of the nine casualties, about whom he'd been so unmoved, until now, realising one of those nine might have been his best friend.

Charlotte didn't look well. She had a strange expression on her face and he could see dried blood at the roots of her hair. She said something about the rescue effort and then the scene cut to a journalist. Charlotte had been on the screen for, what – ten seconds? But in that time the hostel, the drinkers and the city had faded away. Charlotte had been involved in the train crash. She could have died. He might have lost her too. Charlotte – the friend he could talk with for hours and who knew so much about him. What if he'd lost her?

Shock and dread blossomed inside him, one after the other. Was she okay? Alive, at least. Yes alive – but hurt? She'd looked terrible. Were they taking care of her?

Charlotte

Charlotte's phone was ringing. The shrill tone invaded her sleeping mind, breaking into her dreams. How long had it been ringing? Would someone else answer it? Surely the noise would stop soon, and the call would switch to the answering service? Charlotte didn't want to wake up. Sleep held her tight.

The phone continued to ring. She slipped her hand out of bed and groped over the bedside table to find it.

'Hello?' she croaked: her jaw hurt, her lower lip was puffy and sore. Moving gingerly in the bed, she set off a chorus of aches and pains. It was nine o'clock, according to Amrita's alarm clock. Amrita's bed was empty.

'Charlotte? Is that you?' A friendly male voice.

'Yes, who's this?'

'Mark. It's Mark! You've forgotten me already?' This with an affectionately teasing tone.

'Mark! No of course not. But this number – your name didn't come up on my phone.'

She'd met Mark in Goa. He was a freelance journalist living and working in India. He'd covered the story of Maria's murder and, after initially distrusting and disliking him, Charlotte and he had enjoyed a surprising flirtation. The sound of his voice gave her a pleasurable frisson. She gathered her wits.

'Though I might well have forgotten you,' she said. 'You haven't exactly been keeping in touch.'

'No, sorry about that. Busy. You know how it is. I'm calling from my office, not my mobile, that's why you didn't recognise the number.'

'So – to what do I owe this pleasure?' Charlotte sat up in bed, wincing at the pain in her knees. Of course she knew instantly why Mark had phoned her – but she let him ask.

Amrita, presumably, had opened the shutters. Morning sunshine poured into the room. The window offered a view of the burning blue sky, an undulating landscape of grassland and trees. Closer to the house, a narrow road, an auburn-coloured cow grazing on the verge while its exquisite, pale-golden calf frolicked.

'I saw you on the news late last night. Are you okay? God, what a surprise that was, seeing your face all pale and shocked. Were you hurt? Was Otto with you? Is he okay?'

'Cuts and bruises. Nothing serious. I was lucky. Otto wasn't there. He's in Mumbai,' she said. 'Thanks for your concern though. It's kind of you to call.'

'Well of course I'd call. It's not every day one of your friends is involved in a railway accident. Nine killed, did you know that? I don't suppose you took any photos?'

Despite everything, Charlotte laughed. 'Ah, now we get to the nub of it. You're writing a story? And there was I, thinking you were worried about me.'

Mark laughed too. 'I was worried about you, Charlie, believe me. You looked bloody awful in the interview, but at least I knew you weren't dead. You know how it is. I have to make a living, and there you are, a man on the ground. How could I miss such a stroke of luck?'

'Yeah, it's okay. I didn't take any photos; strangely that was far from my mind. I'll tell you what I know but if you're going to quote me, let me contact my parents first so I can reassure them I'm whole and unharmed. They'll get a horrible shock otherwise.'

'Sure, sure. Whatever you say. So tell me about it. Where were you travelling to and from?'

It took her some time to recount the story to Mark's satisfaction. He was exacting, asking her numerous questions about the crash and her experience, about the emergency response, her thoughts on the causes of the derailment. From time to time he would ask her to clarify something she'd said. He wanted to know about the other passengers, how they'd reacted and what was said. She told him only a little about her role in the rescue effort and didn't mention anything about the boys and their dead mother. She could hardly bear to think about this, and certainly didn't want Mark writing about it. Even so, the interview took over an hour and by the end, Charlotte felt worn out, as though she'd lived through the accident all over again.

'I need a picture of you,' he said. 'Can you email me one?'

'I don't want my picture with the story.'

'Please? A head and shoulders shot will do. It'll make the story come alive. I've got some agency pictures of the accident itself, but a picture of you will make it more personal.' He was friendly but pushy, trying to cajole her into agreeing.

'Sorry, Mark, no. I don't want my picture in the paper, okay?'

He let it go and changed track. 'You're working on the reserve where the accident happened, yes? How much do you know about this big grant application to World Wildlife?'

'I know some. The reserve manager's talked about it – I'm staying at his house, with his family. And there was a story in the *Times of India* yesterday.' The memory of the newspaper article flashed into her mind. She'd seen it just moments before the crash. Moments before the noise, the hurt and the horror.

'Well, because of the accident I've been doing some research myself, about the tiger sanctuary and this World Wildlife grant,'

Mark said. 'Do you know how important it is? If the reserve doesn't get this funding, their tiger protection project could be finished. They need a lot of money to keep it running and don't have a very successful track record when it comes to keeping tigers safe.'

'I know. It's a very difficult job,' Charlotte cut in defensively. 'Have you any idea of the size of this place? They can't afford many professional staff, jeeps or surveillance equipment and they're threatened by well-equipped and determined poachers, as well as encroachments by loggers and illegal quarrying. It's a constant struggle.'

'Okay, okay, keep your hair on,' he said. 'How about an interview with this guy, the reserve manager? You think you could sort that out? Ask him for me? Tell him we're friends?'

Friends? Charlotte gave a wry smile into the phone.

'Why don't I come out there and see you? I could get a load of background info, interview your reserve manager guy – and we'd get to spend some more time together? What d'you reckon?'

Charlotte laughed. She had to admit it was a tempting proposition, even if Mark's main motivation was the prospect of a story. He was good company, entertaining and easy to talk to.

'Well I don't know,' she said. 'I can hardly stop you, can I?'

'No you can't stop me, but would you like to see me? And would you talk to your boss guy?'

She heard the faint wheedling tone beneath the flirty bonhomie. Had Mark already tried and failed to speak with Jaideep?

'Look, I'll think about it,' she said.

'I'll call you later, okay?'

'Sure. I've got to go now. Bye, Mark.' He was still talking, trying to extract some kind of promise, as she cut the call. A faint smile played across her face until another male voice interrupted her thoughts, accompanied by a brisk rap on the door.

'Charlotte? You awake?'

'Oh, Jack.' Her smile disappeared. Had he been listening to her phone conversation?

'You sleep okay?' He hovered in the doorway.

'Yes fine. Look, will you let me get dressed? I told you about the house rules. I think you should have some respect for them.'

Jack looked at her with the hungry expression she'd seen before. No doubt about it, he was starting to seem very creepy.

'Yeah, right,' he said. 'Just wanted to check, you know, that you were awake. I didn't sleep that well, to be honest. Kept thinking about the accident, over and over—'

'Please, Jack.' She cut him off. 'We'll talk in a bit. Go away now, let me sort myself out.'

He stopped talking, blinked at her once, twice, as though he could hardly stand to tear himself away. Then he nodded and retreated from the room. Charlotte jumped out of bed and closed the door. She took a deep breath, in and out, and leaned her back against the door, as though to prevent Jack from pushing his way in. She ran her hands through her hair. He'd be leaving today, she reminded herself. He'd be moving on and she'd never have to see him again. Thank goodness. She had too much else to worry about and he was starting to freak her out.

Charlotte dressed and wandered out of her bedroom. Her knees were stiff and she walked awkwardly. Everyone else was out and it was after ten. Prina had left a note in the kitchen, telling Charlotte they'd left her to sleep in and she didn't have to work, because of the accident. Charlotte helped herself to tea, fruit and yoghurt for breakfast. She was sitting at the table, picking at pieces of lush golden pineapple, when Jack came in and sat down at the other side.

He didn't look great. His skin possessed a peculiar greyness, even under his tan. Charlotte narrowed her eyes and examined him.

'How old are you, Jack?'

'Twenty. You?'

'Eighteen. You look older.'

'Do I?' He seemed to take this as a compliment but she hadn't meant it as such. He had an air of dereliction – like a man who'd spent a lifetime drinking too much. Hard to say exactly why she thought this; most likely it was simply because she was disliking him more and more. He was wearing a bleached pair of jeans and a T-shirt decorated with a large smiley. His fingers tapped out an irritating tattoo on the table.

'So, when are you off? And to where?' She tried to keep her voice light and friendly.

Jack twitched his mouth to one side, shrugged, reached out a hand and took a piece of fruit from her plate. He placed it in his mouth, very slowly, looking at her all the while. Charlotte shivered. She pushed the plate away.

'Oh, I have to check the train times,' he said, with a shrug. 'It's very nice here, isn't it?'

Charlotte ignored the comment. 'The trains are pretty regular. I can drive you down to the station if you like. I'm allowed to use the pick-up.' Would she be able to drive with her bruised knees? She'd give it a go, if it meant getting rid of Jack.

Jack nodded his head from side to side, non-committal. 'Thanks, that would be kind of you,' he said. 'I've noticed that, Charlie, what a kind person you are. Maybe I'll do that, later. How about you show me around the reserve first, before I go?'

'I don't think so. I've got a lot to do.'

'Like what? You've been given a day off work.'

Charlotte sighed. So Jack had read Prina's note? She was cornered. Couldn't she simply say no?

'Look I don't know if I can drive very far, my knees are very painful. I'll give it a go. I'll drive you round a bit of the reserve and then I can drop you at the station afterwards.'

Anyone else would have picked up the edge of hostility in her voice, but Jack seemed oblivious. She didn't look at him or speak

45

at all as she tidied up her breakfast things. She picked up the keys and led the way to the battered old pick-up Jaideep had said she could use. Jack hopped into the passenger seat.

She'd grown used to driving in India these past few weeks. Fortunately the roads in the area were quiet, but you never knew when you might encounter livestock in the road, or a bullock cart, children walking to school, or simply an unexpected pothole. The old pick-up was quirky too; certainly it wouldn't pass an MoT test in Britain. The driver's door didn't open, requiring Charlotte to climb inside through the passenger door or the window, the engine had a tendency to stall whenever you stopped at a junction, and the handbrake didn't work at all so you had to park on the level and leave it in gear to make sure it didn't roll away.

It hurt her legs to clamber inside, but driving didn't prove as painful as walking. The sun was high, a cauldron pouring heat on the gently rolling hills, the voluptuously green forest and the intervals of golden grassland. Charlotte slid on her sunglasses and a peaked cap against the sudden stabs of sunlight falling between the trees. She didn't speak to Jack, trying instead to focus on her surroundings. At the back of her mind though, like a shadow, thoughts and memories of the train crash bubbled up and played themselves out in the theatre of her mind, as though the shock and fear she'd pushed aside during the aftermath of the accident were waiting for her now.

'Look! Oh my god, look!' She slammed on the brakes, sending a lance of pain through her right knee. The troublesome engine stalled and the wheels kicked up a plume of reddish dust. She pointed through a break in the trees to her right. It hadn't been Jack in particular she was talking to – probably she had exclaimed aloud for herself, expressing her own irrepressible excitement.

Elephants.

A little family group: five she thought, visible about a hundred metres away.

'Oh my god,' Jack breathed, echoing what Charlotte had said. Neither of them spoke for a few moments, mesmerised by the spectacle of the elephants, gently striding across the clearing into a clump of trees. They made no sound from this distance. The last was evidently a juvenile, trotting to keep up with the others, swinging its trunk aloft. Then they were gone – and the forest was still.

An insect whined in the pick-up cab. The dust thrown up by the wheels settled again on the rough road and the bonnet. Charlotte smiled. For a moment – just a moment – she'd forgotten about the train crash, the dead, even annoying Jack sitting by her side.

'Amazing,' Jack said, pushing his way into her consciousness again. 'Absolutely amazing. I've never seen wild elephants before. What is it about being with you, Charlie? Astonishing things happen.'

Something seemed to catch in her throat. She wanted to trample all over his peculiar reverent tone.

'I wouldn't call a train accident astonishing,' she said. 'How can you say that? It was horrific. Isn't it inside your head, what we saw? What we heard?'

'Yes of course it is!' He was gazing at her. 'When I say astonishing I mean – extraordinary. Life-changing. Don't you see that? Don't you understand?' He stared into her face, looking for something. Then he nodded. 'You do understand. Of course you do. You have to. It isn't possible it could be otherwise.'

'What isn't possible? What're you talking about, Jack?' She thrust the gear stick forward into first, pressed her foot carefully onto the clutch and started up the engine again, to break the conversation. She stared out through the windscreen, wanting not to see his peculiar face.

'The moment in the train, with the dead woman,' Jack said. His voice was patient: the priest who can afford to wait, knowing salvation comes in the end.

'For crying out loud,' she said. 'I want to forget about it, Jack. It wasn't special, it was horrible! The woman died. She's left

47

two sons behind. Certainly their lives are never going to be the same again.'

But she was rattled. It had been an extraordinary moment, no doubt. But she didn't want weird Jack hanging on to it, creating some kind of mystic significance, a cosmic connection binding them together forever. And that was what he was trying to do, wasn't it? Was something wrong with him? Was he mentally or emotionally unstable?

She planted her foot on the accelerator, hurting her knee again and causing the pick-up to jump forward with such force they were both thrown back against their seats. Why had she agreed to drive him? Because the prospect of leaving him at the station was so appealing. Yes, that was worth the pain.

Jack didn't speak again, but when Charlotte glanced over, he was still looking at her, only now his expression was smug – as though he were the fount of all knowledge and had only to wait for foolish, resistant Charlotte to see for herself the Truth. With a capital T.

'Here. Drop me here,' Jack said.

'What?'

'Please, stop. Let me get out here.'

'We're in the middle of nowhere. It's two miles to the reserve office,' Charlotte said. 'This isn't England – there are wild animals here. Elephants, leopards, tigers.'

'I'll be fine,' Jack shrugged. 'Honestly – how often do people get attacked by tigers? Just pull over.'

Charlotte sighed and shook her head. 'Okay, a tiger attack on a man is pretty rare, but elephants can sometimes be dangerous.'

'I'll take my chances, okay?'

The engine cut out when she stopped. Jack leaned over and put his hand on her upper arm. She could smell him, the acrid heat and sweat of his body, something unpleasant and unhealthy. She tried to wriggle away.

'You're an extraordinary woman,' he said. 'I can see who you

48

are, Charlotte. I know what you did yesterday – how you behaved. You were remarkable – so brave. So capable. I admire that. We were stripped bare. No pretence, no barriers, no false manners. I truly saw you. I shall never forget it.'

Charlotte swallowed. She didn't know what to say. He both repelled and perversely fascinated her. It was flattering, yes, but far outweighing the flattery was a distrust. Something wasn't right about him, she could see it in his face, smell it, hear it in the words he spoke.

'Get out then,' she said. 'You wanted to walk? Then walk. Don't say I didn't warn you. You'll have to get a lift from the reserve office to the train station. I'm going home.'

Jack drew back. He smiled. 'Sure.' He climbed out of the pick-up and lifted his backpack from behind the cab. 'See you,' he said, closing the passenger door.

'Goodbye, Jack.' She started the engine and drove away, watching his diminishing figure in the rear-view mirror. She shouldn't have left him to walk alone but she was utterly relieved to be rid of him.

Charlotte headed back to the house. Her mood was dark. Images of the accident kept rising in her mind, making her anxious, all tight and constricted inside. She felt very tired and lay down on her bed hoping to sleep, but couldn't calm her thoughts. A gentle breeze moved through the house, tempering the mid-day heat. She closed her eyes.

Charlotte woke up. For one delicious moment, her mind was still and empty. She didn't move, wanting to remain in this place, to savour the peace. The sun had passed from the window and a warm, golden light filled the room. She could hear someone moving in the house, Prina probably, tidying and preparing for the return of her husband. Charlotte could smell something cooking, the tang of fried garlic.

This instant of mind-quiet didn't last long. Memories of the accident came crowding back, carrying with them an irrational burden of guilt. Because she should have done more? She pushed it aside, swung her legs over the side of the bed and rubbed her face. Her mouth tasted dry and sour; she needed something to drink. She wished she were at home, safe and sound, with people she knew and loved, where she could be entirely relaxed. Amrita and her family were lovely, of course, but she'd only known them a few weeks and she was a guest in their home. Just now she yearned for stability and familiarity, for her mother, for Otto and Jen, the friends who knew her best. And for Otto in particular.

She had to phone them, her parents. They might have heard about the train crash on the news. Although it would hardly hit the headlines in Britain, her mother and father would be looking in particular for news about India, and she didn't want them to be worried. And there was Mark's story: he said he'd give her time to contact her family first, but she wasn't confident she could trust him to hold out long. Just now, the thought of their response, of having to explain the story all over again, put her off calling. She'd do it later.

Charlotte stood up. Jaideep's jeep, with the name Golden Tiger Reserve painted on its side, drew up outside the house. Through the window she watched him park. She glimpsed someone in the passenger seat. Jaideep said something to this someone, who opened the door and jumped out.

It was Jack. Why hadn't he gone? He was walking towards the front door, side by side with Jaideep, and they were talking like old friends, man to man, Jaideep laughing out loud at something Jack had said.

Had Jack forgotten something, is that why he'd returned?

Charlotte shivered. She'd thought she was rid of him, that she wouldn't have to see him again, and here he was. The front door opened and closed. Jaideep called out a greeting to his wife.

Charlotte stood frozen. She should go out and say hello, but she didn't want to leave the relative safety of her room. She didn't want to encounter Jack. No such luck. Someone knocked on the door – it was Prina. Was Charlotte awake? Did she want a cup of tea?

Charlotte sighed. Pull yourself together, she told herself. What was her problem? Was it simply that Jack was so closely connected with the accident that she'd developed this antipathy towards him? He was a bit odd, certainly, but he hadn't actually done anything wrong. Except, of course, the intensity of the attachment he'd formed with her. Was she paranoid to think he'd come back to the house because of that? She would just have to be straightforward and give him the brush-off.

She pushed the hair from her face, stood up straight. Her knees had stiffened again after her sleep, so she found herself half hobbling into the living room.

'Hi, Jaideep – you're home early today. Everything okay?'

He had a lot to deal with, following the train crash on the reserve, the funding application. He had a difficult job at the best of times, though he seemed to love it.

'Oh Charlie,' he said, the laughter fading quickly from his face. 'There is so much to do. So much.' Jaideep turned to his wife and they conversed in Tamil for a few moments, obviously sharing some worry about the reserve. Charlotte glanced at Jack who was standing with his hands tucked into his jeans pockets. He grinned.

'I didn't think I'd see you again,' she said. 'When's your train?'

'Actually, I don't think I'll be taking the train today.'

'What?'

Jaideep turned to her. 'Some good news, eh? Jack and I have been talking this afternoon, and he says he'd like to help out for a while. He has some skills we could use, and we've so much work to do, I said he'd be welcome to join us. Isn't that great? He told me you'd be pleased.' Jaideep beamed, as though he'd done Charlotte an enormous favour.

Charlotte tried to smile in return, conscious they were all looking at her, and that Jack's eyes in particular were boring into her.

'Yes, well, that's great,' she said. 'Are you sure you can spare the time, Jack? Where are you going to stay?'

'Oh don't worry about that,' Jaideep said. 'One of the other reserve wardens can put him up for a while. I invited him to come and eat with us here this evening. I thought you'd like to welcome our new British guest!'

Jaideep looked rather pleased with himself, Jack was smiling and smiling, Prina put her hands together at the prospect of a gathering, and right on cue, Amrita came home from the local school, where she was working temporarily as an assistant.

They all sat down together. Prina brought in a pot of sweet, spiced tea and Jaideep updated them on the aftermath of the crash. The train had finally been removed from the line, and the train company had drafted in equipment and ground workers to restore and shore up the collapsed embankment. All kinds of wrangling had already begun – about who was to blame for the derailment, who'd carried out the quarrying, why it hadn't been stopped. Whichever way this argument went, it didn't look good for the reserve. Why weren't they on top of things?

'It is complicated,' Jaideep said. 'We report any incidences of illegal quarrying to the state authorities, then the company involved applies retrospectively for a licence. That application – the preparation, presentation, appeals and so on – can take such a long time that the damage is done before the licence is refused. This isn't just our responsibility. We need more support from the authorities.'

Charlotte found it hard to concentrate on the conversation. When she'd finished her tea she went back to her room and sat on her bed. She took her journal from her bag, intending to write something about the accident, but still hadn't managed a single word when Amrita came into the room a few minutes later. Amrita sat beside her. 'What's wrong, Charlie?' She put her arm around Charlotte's shoulders. 'Is it the accident? You don't like to hear us talking about it? You look so pale and tired.'

Charlotte shook her head. 'Maybe. Partly at least.' Then, the words coming out in a rush: 'Actually, it's Jack. I don't like him. He gives me the creeps. He's been saying some very weird stuff to me and I'd really like him to back off.'

Amrita's eyes widened.

'What sort of weird stuff?'

'He seems to think we have some big connection because of the accident. He gets all intense and heavy and tells me how special I am, it is totally freaking me out. I can't believe he's wheedled his way into your dad's good books. I was hoping he'd be on a train out of here by now.'

Amrita's eyes widened further.

'Shall I speak to my father? Ask him to make Jack leave?'

Charlotte considered. A voice inside her head screamed yes, yes, yes! Make him go away! Out loud, she said: 'Maybe I'm overreacting. He won't be staying at the house so perhaps I can avoid him and Jaideep seems to think he might be of use. But I feel very uncomfortable about it. I'll have to keep out of his way and somehow get the message across loud and clear that I'm not interested – that I don't like him.' She put her journal down. 'And I need to call my parents, tell them what happened. I'm not looking forward to that either. They'll be all worried.'

Charlotte took her mobile phone from her bag. She hadn't checked it all day and noticed a text had arrived very late the previous night, when she'd been asleep. A message from Otto:

Saw you on the news last night – the train crash – couldn't believe it. Hope you're not hurt. Must have been terrible. Call / txt asap and tell me how you are. Lots of love, Otto xxx

Otto. She felt such a flood of affection, seeing the message, hearing Otto's voice in her mind.

'What is it?' Amrita asked, seeing Charlotte smile.

'It's from my friend, Otto.' She kept her eyes fixed on the text, reading it again and again.

'Ah yes, Otto,' Amrita said wisely. She'd heard a lot about Otto and Jen over the weeks.

'I'd better call him,' Charlotte said.

Amrita stood up. 'I'll leave you to it,' she said.

The phone rang once, twice. Charlotte was assailed by an enormous longing to hear his voice and absurdly afraid he wouldn't answer.

'Hello? Charlie?' He had to raise his voice, so much noise in the background, traffic and the hubbub of a crowd.

'Otto! I just got your text! Where are you?'

'In the middle of a busy street – can you hear it? Sorry, it's very loud here. Just a minute.' The noise subsided a little. 'Okay, that's better. I'm in a bar. So – tell me, what about this accident? Were you hurt?'

'No, nothing serious. My knees hurt. It was grim, Otto. I can't tell you.' Tears welled. A lump caught in her throat, making it impossible to speak.

'Charlie? You still there?'

'Yes. Yes, sorry. It's all been a bit much.' She choked back the sobs.

'Look, do you want me to come down? I could take a train. Tomorrow – I'll come tomorrow.'

'You don't have to do that,' Charlotte said.

'I know I don't. But bloody hell, Charlie, what you've been through. I want to be with you.'

Inside her mind, Charlotte was crying out – I want to be with you too, please come; leave tomorrow. She took a tight little breath.

'I don't want you to break your plans for me. I'll be fine. Haven't

54

you things to do in Mumbai? It's a long way to come.' She yearned for him to gainsay her, to tell her nothing in Mumbai mattered that much, that he'd travel hundreds of miles across India to be with her now, in the hour of her need.

'It's no problem. I'm getting a bit bored of the place, to be honest. I'd be happy to come.'

Charlotte felt a flutter inside her chest – a wary gladness.

'I'd love to see you,' she said. 'Thanks, Otto. I appreciate it.'

They spoke for a few more minutes. When the call ended, Charlotte sent a text to her parents, and they called her back. Another long conversation ensued, in which she played down and reassured. It was a pleasure to hear the voices of her parents, to know that safe place still existed, waiting for her return.

At last she returned to the living room, to Jack and the family, with a lightness in her step. She would soon see Otto.

'Everything okay?' Amrita said.

'Yes, fine thanks. Otto's travelling down to see me.'

'Otto?' Jack said, a querulous note in his voice.

Amrita, cool as a cucumber, turned to him and said: 'Yes, Charlie's boyfriend. I'm dying to meet him, she's talked about him so much.'

Jack's mouth opened and shut. A curious congested colour filled his face. Amrita turned to Charlotte and winked.

Charlotte smiled. Amrita was a clever girl.

Otto

Otto went early to the Chhatrapati Shivaji Terminus. He'd signed out of the hostel and at the station bought a ticket for the Trivandrum Express. It left just after noon and would take him to Salem, Tamil Nadu, in – so the timetable said – an intimidating twenty-seven hours and forty-five minutes. With twenty-two stops.

A pale lemon light filled Mumbai in the morning. People flooded through the station in a great tide. The terminus was a palace of Victorian gothic, with columns and domes, stained glass and gargoyles, where farmers brought vegetables and milk from their villages to sell, where office clerks and call centre workers poured off commuter trains for a long day's work. On the steps outside the station, five little boys lined up with boot polish and brushes, offering to shine shoes.

Otto had an eight-hundred-mile journey ahead. A day and a night on the train. He bought a coffee and sat down on the steps outside the station, his backpack close beside him, watching the endless stream of people. With every passing minute the heat intensified. He thought of Charlotte at the end of the journey, out in the wilds, all that way from the unceasing, noisy crowds. Odd how much he wanted to see her, the quiet ache of it. He was worried about her, of course. A train crash – people killed. She could so easily have been one of them. He might have lost her.

How would he have felt then? Of course she represented home for him, familiarity, in this sea of strangeness. He loved the strangeness, the challenge it offered him, the abrasion of the new culture and way of life, but it was tiring too, a constant effort. It would be a great pleasure to relax with his old friend.

At the end of the morning, the Trivandrum Express drew in. People thronged the platform along the length of the train, talking amongst themselves, sometimes shouting and gesticulating: families lugging bags and boxes, women in brilliantly coloured saris, groups of young men, a party of glamorous girls in Western clothes, several old women with crates and sacks, perhaps heading back to their villages, a few soldiers dressed in khaki. How many would stay the distance to Salem, or beyond?

Otto, hefting his backpack, pushed his way through the crowd and climbed onto the train. All sorts of negotiations seemed to be going on, about who was sitting where and with whom, seat reservations, journey plans. The interior of the train was heating up although the windows were open, as though the feverish discussions, disputes and anxieties of the travellers were further increasing the temperature. The air smelled of hot bodies, hair oil, perfume and spicy food, and beneath it all, the city's perpetual base-notes of diesel and decaying refuse. Otto found his seat, fortunately by the window, and stowed his backpack. Eventually the passengers began to settle and, bang on time, the train drew out of the station.

It was a long journey, but Otto enjoyed it. Nothing for it, except to surrender to the experience, the view, the passengers who variously read the paper, dozed, chatted to him or each other. They succeeded each other in waves, some getting off and others getting on. It was like a reality show, all these insights into everyday Indian life, played out before him hour after hour. Sometimes he read his book (something by Irvine Welsh he'd picked up at a second-hand bookshop in Mumbai) but more often, he stared out of the window and watched the endlessly fascinating vista of India pass by.

57

From time to time he thought about Charlotte and the train accident, feeling a moment of anxiety about his own journey and the risk of something similar happening to him. The crash had happened on a different and minor branch line, at the edge of the reserve – so was an accident on a main line like this one more or less likely? Hard to say. Better not to think about it.

He dined on the cheap, excellent food provided by the train's catering service and once or twice disembarked at a station to stretch his legs for a minute or two before the express resumed its journey. Late in the evening, bunks were folded down to sleep six, and he enjoyed a surprisingly good night's rest. It was strangely pleasing to know how many hundreds of miles were passing as he slept, oblivious, lulled by the gentle motion of the train.

Very early in the morning a new contingent of passengers joined the train, another batch of commuters, more women with baskets of fruit and vegetables, as well as children in immaculate uniforms on their way to school. Several of these children, two girls and a boy, sat opposite Otto (pale, scruffy, bleary-eyed and stubbly) and stared at him with round eyes, until one of the girls plucked up the courage to ask him where he came from, what he was doing.

And so the second day began. Otto dozed in the morning, read more, gazed out the window – but by lunchtime he started to feel impatient, wanting an end to his confinement. The final two hours were very long and he found himself counting down the time. He imagined the moment he would see her again, Charlotte, her familiar face in the sea of unknown people at the station, come to collect him, waiting for him on the platform. It was curiously pleasurable, creating this scene. He played out the meeting several times in his mind.

At last, it was over. As they drew into Salem he took down his backpack, said goodbye to the latest instalment of fellow passengers and waited by the carriage door for the train to stop.

Having imagined this reunion with Charlotte, Otto now felt slightly nervous about the prospect of the real thing. He jumped down from the carriage to the platform, the backpack bumping against him, and scanned the crowd for his friend. He didn't see her right away – too many people milling about and the distracting noise of the arrival announcement. He moved uneasily through the crowd, occasionally walking into other passengers, wondering which way to go and worried he might miss her. He'd texted his arrival time the previous morning, and she'd offered to collect him from the station. Now he took his mobile out again with the intention of sending another message – I'm here, where are you? – but just as he began to type, he heard her voice:

'Otto? Otto! Over here!'

He looked up. There she was, on the platform the other side of the rails, waving her arm. She looked a little thinner and more tanned, but charged with energy as usual.

'Hey, Charlie!' How familiar and, at the same time, how different she looked in this new environment. The meeting was not as he'd imagined, being both less, and more.

'Otto?' It was a little difficult to hear her above the hubbub. 'Meet me outside the station!' He lost sight of her then, but followed the exit signs and then they were side by side, and she reached out to hug him with a big smile on her face.

'It's great to see you!' Charlotte had a faint dappling of bruises on one side of her face and forehead and she walked a little awkwardly.

He reached out his hand but didn't quite touch her cheek.

'From the accident?'

'Yes. Knee's a bit better today, fortunately.'

'My god. It must have been terrible. You could have been killed.'

'It was terrible, yes. It's odd: at the time, when it happens, you don't realise fully how terrible it is. You just deal with it, get on with it. It's only in the days after when you have the time to go over it in your mind and deal with it, that you feel the full impact of how awful it was.' She lowered her face, frowned and gave her head a little shake, resisting the lure of thinking about it again.

Otto put his hand on her upper arm.

'Well, tell me about it if you want to. Or not. Or when you're ready.'

She lifted her head again, looking up into his face. 'Thanks,' she said. Then with a smile: 'It really is wonderful to see you. Thanks for coming all this way. How was the journey?'

They walked across the road to a pick-up parked on the other side. Otto dropped his luggage in the back and climbed into the passenger seat.

On the drive to the Golden Tiger Reserve, Charlotte asked him about Mumbai and his travels, and she told him about her work and the problems they were facing with the funding application. She mentioned the illegal quarrying, obliquely referring to the train crash, but didn't go into any detail. The conversation was easy and pleasurable, seeming to slake a thirst for Otto. It felt like coming home.

He was impressed by the way she drove on the chaotic Indian roads, so relaxed and competent, negotiating the darting scooters, trucks that hogged the space, men on bicycles, the occasional oblivious mid-carriage cow, cars that undertook and queue-jumped, drivers jabbing noisily at their horns. Gradually the roads grew smaller, the traffic less intense. They moved into a wilder land-scape of forest interrupted by spaces of untended grassland.

The conversation died back. Otto noticed how hungry he was, and tired too, despite all the sedentary hours. Charlotte wrinkled her brow and cleared her throat.

'Otto, I want to ask you something,' she said. 'It's a bit weird, and I hope you don't mind.'

'Of course not. What is it?'

'Well, I was wondering if you might pretend to be my boyfriend when we get to the reserve.'

'What?' The word came out a little sharper than he had intended.

'I'm sorry, I know it's ridiculous, but it would be a real help.'

'Sure, I mean of course.' Ridiculous? He felt a tumbling of emotions: first at the idea of pretending to be Charlie's boyfriend, and then that she'd described the possibility as ridiculous. What was the matter with him? 'Why?' he added.

'There's a guy I met on the train. We were together after the crash and he's kind of latched onto me in a rather creepy way. He's even got himself a job volunteering on the reserve and I'm sure it's because he wants to be close to me. If he thought you were my boyfriend, well, that might warn him off.' She took her eyes from the road for a moment and glanced at Otto.

'Yeah, sure. Of course. What's the creep's name?'

'Jack,' she said. Then, in a rush: 'I feel a bit mean talking about him like this, I'm sure he's okay deep down, probably just a bit freaked out by the crash. But it would be simpler all round if he thought I was already taken.'

'Well I'm happy to play along,' Otto said. 'Darling.'

Charlotte seemed to relax then. She tipped her head back and laughed.

'Honestly, Otto. I've never heard you call any of your girlfriends *darling*. Try and be a little bit convincing.'

'Okay. Shall we snog in front of him?' The comment was glib, without forethought, and Charlotte blushed in response. Otto swallowed and felt his own face burn.

'No it's okay.' Charlotte shook her head, regaining control of the situation, keeping things light. 'The occasional peck on the cheek will suffice.'

'So what's he like, Jack the creep? What's he said and done?'

Charlotte told him then, about the accident and the moment in the carriage with the dead woman, and the various interactions

61

that had followed. He was shocked to hear what she'd gone through, the horror of the crash and its aftermath.

'I think you're being kind. This guy sounds seriously weird,' he said. 'I'm even more glad I came down to see you. You should have told him to eff off.' Except that Charlie, to his knowledge, had never told anyone to eff off, even when they'd deserved it. She was brisk and efficient, yes, but she was also too kind-hearted for her own good.

At last they drew up outside a pretty white house.

'We're here,' Charlotte said. 'Welcome to my new home. You won't be staying here – Jaideep said there was space in one of the lodges. Jack's staying with one of the other wardens.'

'No worries. I'm sure I can handle Jack.'

No-one was home. Charlotte showed him around. It was an attractive, comfortable place, simply furnished, very tidy. Then she prepared cups of tea in the kitchen. It was odd seeing her in this new place, out of the usual context. It made Charlotte herself seem different, as though he were meeting her for the first time – except that she was also so known and familiar.

'What are you thinking?' She was smiling at him.

'Oh, I don't know. How strange it is, us both being here. Everything that's happened.'

'Well yes, a lot's happened, certainly.' Sunlight from the window fell on her face, illuminating the bruises. She held out a cup of tea.

'So have you seen a tiger yet?'

'No,' she grinned. 'Well, not in real life. I've seen bits of tigers, in pictures from the camera traps. They think about forty live on the reserve but nobody knows for sure. It's a big place and wild tigers are hard to count. I'd love to see one though, a real one, in the wild. I've seen some pugmarks though – that was very exciting.'

'Pugmarks?'

'Paw prints. They're huge! We have to record the sightings, measure them, take pictures. You can learn a lot about a tiger from its pugmark and the length of its stride. Gender, size. You can even take a stab at its age and health.'

'Wow,' Otto said. 'You're learning a lot. So what work are you doing?'

'All sorts of stuff. Anything they need. From cleaning the lodges to answering emails and data entry,' she shrugged. 'A lot of it's pretty mundane, but I don't mind. Sometimes I go out with the reserve wardens. They look out for the tigers, keep an eye out for illegal activity and they're very involved with the people who live around the reserve. They need to be onside, to help watch out for poachers. I'll take you down to the office and introduce you to Jaideep, and then I'll show you the lodge. It's not exactly salubrious, I'm afraid. And there's no mobile signal on a lot of the reserve so you might feel a bit cut off. The best lodges are full of tourists.'

Otto finished his tea, availed himself of the shower to wash away the accumulated grime of the long train journey, shaved and changed his clothes. Then back into the pick-up.

'Are you okay driving, with your bad knee?' he said.

'Actually driving is less of a problem than walking,' she said. 'Anyway, it's less painful than it was yesterday. But thanks for asking.'

They drove along dusty tracks through forest and openings of tall, yellowish grass, to a low, wooden building, the reserve head-quarters. Despite the thatch, it was smart and contemporary in style, with photovoltaic solar panels and a satellite dish. Inside, in the reception area, were white-painted walls with framed posters of tigers and a large map of the reserve. Photographs depicted the reserve's other residents – leopards, hyenas, Indian bison and a species of wild dog, apparently called a dhole.

'Nice place,' he said.

'Yes. Funded by World Wildlife. Money comes in from tourists, but international charities contribute too. They pay for various special projects.'

Otto peered at the map. 'Where is everybody? It's a bit quiet.'

Charlotte was evidently asking herself the same question. She opened a door and looked into a deserted office. She looked puzzled.

'I've no idea. There should be someone here.' Two computers were running. A cup of tea waited on a desk.

'D'you think something's happened?' Otto shifted uneasily from one foot to another. Before Charlotte could answer, a jeep screeched to a halt outside the office and a middle-aged man jumped out.

'That's Jaideep,' Charlotte said. And he didn't look happy. A second man climbed out of the cab. Another three men, not wearing the reserve uniform and looking like local farmers, jumped out of the back, all shouting and gesticulating, angry and animated about something. Jaideep's expression was thunderous. He stormed into the office, barely registering the presence of Otto and Charlotte, picked up the phone, tapped in a number and began a barked conversation with whoever was at the other end. The other men followed him into the reception area and continued to shout and argue. Otto glanced at Charlotte.

'Have you any idea what's going on?' he whispered.

She shook her head. 'Something bad,' she said. 'Whatever it is, we don't need it. Not after the train crash.'

She went up to the other man in the reserve uniform, tried to drag him away from the dispute with the farmers.

'What's happened?' she demanded. 'What's going on?' Although she was speaking, the farmers continued to gesticulate and quarrel, speaking over each other in loud, agitated voices.

Jaideep scowled and waved his hand, as though trying to turn down the noise. He turned to Charlotte.

'We've lost another tiger,' he said, his hand over the receiver. 'Poachers. They've killed one.'

Charlotte's face froze for a moment. Then she said, 'What? How do you know?'

'Someone reported finding a trap and blood,' he said. 'On one of the paths we know a tiger uses. Tyre tracks, broken ground. We had reports of disturbances last night – vehicles driving into the reserve. It's taken us most of the afternoon to find out what happened.' He wiped his forehead with the palm of his hand, and returned to his telephone conversation. Then he ended the call, dialled again and began talking to someone else.

Otto felt uncomfortable and useless, standing around like an idiot while the storm proceeded all around him. What could he do to help?

Jaideep put the phone down and sucked in a deep breath. For a moment, everyone else stopped talking.

'The police are coming,' he said. 'The press will soon be here too. We've lost another tiger.' He seemed to dwindle physically as he spoke. 'I'm going back to the place. You stay here,' he said to his assistant. 'When the police arrive, you show them where to go.'

'Can I come too? How can I help?' Charlotte demanded.

Jaideep shook his head, Charlotte just a useless nuisance at this time of crisis. A teenage volunteer, not an expert or an authority.

'Okay, come along if you like,' Jaideep relented. 'But keep out of the way.' It was no time for introductions; he barely registered Otto's presence. Jaideep went back out to his jeep; his mobile rang and he began to speak to someone else. The local men followed him, still voluble, and jumped into the back.

'Can I come?' Otto followed Jaideep. 'I'll take my camera.'

Jaideep finished his call but he didn't seem to register the question, so Otto decided this was permission. Despite the loss of the tiger, Otto was feeling a buzz of excitement, the adrenalin rush of the great story. It was an opportunity for him – something he could use. They hurried out to Charlotte's pick-up. She started up the engine and set off after Jaideep. It was a longer drive than Otto had expected. The reserve covered about two hundred and fifty square miles, and once they turned off the track it was hard going, driving along stony lanes, through the trees and bumping over the grass. Once in the distance he saw deer, like shadows. Huge trees towered over them, and then a valley opened up in which a dark river passed over smooth, round boulders. A primeval place, not like England, where every square yard was parcelled off, owned, cultivated or developed. He took his camera from his backpack but missed a chance to take a photograph of the deer. Beside him, Charlotte perspired and cursed, concentrating on driving the temperamental pick-up over the challenging terrain. She struggled to keep up with Jaideep. Otto realised her knees must be hurting more than she let on.

'Would you like me to drive?' he said. 'I'd be happy to give it a go.'

'No I'm fine,' she said. 'If we stop for a moment we'll lose Jaideep.'

At last, after they'd been travelling about an hour, the men in the back of the jeep stood up and started gesticulating.

'I think this is the place,' Charlotte said grimly.

The jeep slowed and two of the three men jumped out as it trundled to a halt. They ran ahead into the woodland as Jaideep parked up and climbed out of the cab. Charlotte stopped the pick-up. She and Otto followed at a cautious distance, wanting to see but not wishing to get in the way. They plunged into shadow underneath the trees, walking over the dry, reddish soil. Otto found it hard to keep up: the other men were nimble and accustomed to the terrain and he was tired from his long journey. But he felt for Charlotte more. He could see her knees still hurt, and she was struggling.

'Why don't you go back to the pick-up and wait for us?' he said. 'I'll take some pictures. I'll tell you everything.'

But she shook her head and bit her lip, although her face was pale and strained, determined not to give up.

At last they reached the place.

The scene of carnage.

The body of the tiger still lay there, skinned, monstrous in size

66

and glistening pink. Hard to identify it as a tiger, stripped of its regal black and white and gold. Now, like a carcass in a slaughterhouse – bereft of head, paws, hide. It was a repulsive, lifeless weight of meat, all honour and dignity gone.

Otto looked away. Beside him Charlotte put her hand over her mouth, forcing herself to see what had happened.

'Oh my god,' Otto whispered. He couldn't get over how huge the animal was. He took up his camera and scanned the scene, looking for shots. The carcass sprawled over the ground. Several large, smooth steel traps were still visible in the clearing and high up, in the trees, he could see makeshift platforms, made of fallen branches, where the poachers would have hidden out while waiting for their prey.

'It's awful,' Charlotte said. 'Awful! That was a tiger. How could anyone do that?'

Jaideep and the other men were checking out the scene. Jaideep was silent, furrowing his brow, but the other men were still talking and talking. What were they saying? All around them the forest was silent, breathless, as though stunned by the brutal, unnatural slaughter.

'Why didn't they take the entire body?' Otto wondered. 'Aren't the bones supposed to be valuable for medicine?'

'No time.' Jaideep overheard the question. 'We think they were interrupted, so they took the hide, head, paws, and left the rest.'

A fly buzzed beside Otto's head and landed on the shining carcass. He stepped over to the traps, gingerly pushed one with his booted foot. He tried to imagine the scene, the great beast thrashing about with its leg caught.

'The traps don't have teeth because that would damage the hide,' Charlotte said, her voice subdued. 'A perfect tiger skin sells for twenty thousand dollars in China.'

Otto took some photographs of the tiger's remains and the traps. He felt a twinge of unease doing so, recording this desecration, but it was an opportunity he couldn't resist. He wondered if Jaideep might stop him, but the reserve warden seemed at a loss. How long till the police arrived?

'Otto, I want to go back now. I've seen enough,' Charlotte said.

'You don't want to hang on till the police get here?'

She shook her head. 'There's nothing we can do to help. I don't like to be standing here gawping, it seems wrong. Disrespectful.'

Otto hesitated. A part of him wanted to be part of the process, to see what would happen when the police arrived. A photo opportunity surely? Another part felt uneasy about the prospect of encountering the Indian police again. During the investigation of Maria's murder he'd been treated fairly enough: nonetheless these weren't memories he wanted to bring back.

'Otto, please? I don't feel good.' Charlotte reached out for his hand. She didn't look well. Despite the heat her skin was chilly and she faced a fair walk back to the pick-up, and then the drive.

'Sure,' he said. 'Let's go.'

Charlotte told Jaideep they were leaving, but he was too distracted to do anything other than nod.

It was a tough journey home and Otto could see Charlotte was suffering, though she didn't complain. Instead she went very quiet, conserving her energy. He knew she'd been through a considerable ordeal these last few days.

She did accept his offer to drive back, and directed him to his lodge, about a mile from the reserve office. It was a single-storey building, made of rough wood and raised above the ground, with a terrace offering views over grassland and forest.

The door was fastened with a simple padlock and opened onto a single, spacious room, rather gloomy, with a table in the middle and beds in alcoves to left and right. It didn't smell entirely clean.

'There are toilets of a sort outside, and a shower – cold, I'm afraid.'

'No kitchen?' Otto poked about, seeing spiders run into the crevices in the timber wall.

'I said it was basic.' She smiled. 'If you want food, you can order it at the reserve office. There're some local people who'll bring you meals. Otherwise, you can come to Jaideep's. He told me you'd be welcome. They're a very hospitable family: I'd like you to meet them, especially Amrita. She's lovely. It was her idea I should pretend you're my boyfriend.'

'Won't Weird Jack think it's a bit odd I'm not staying with you, if we're an item?' He tried to keep his voice light, but it was diffi-cult to conceive of this idea, that he and Charlotte were romantically involved, without feeling awkward. He distracted himself by think-ing about Amrita instead, wondering if she were pretty.

'I share a room with Amrita, and don't forget, they're quite conservative as far as that kind of thing goes,' Charlotte said. 'No boyfriends staying over. Amrita told me she'd have an arranged marriage one day.'

'An arranged marriage? Ugh!' Otto shook his head.

'Oh it's not as bad as all that. When you decide it's time to marry, your family gets on the case to find appropriate candidates, that's all. Arranged isn't forced. Is it better to hope to run into the love of your life in a bar or a club?'

'What about all that dowry stuff? Wouldn't suit me,' Otto said. 'What kind of woman would my mother approve of, for her one and only son?'

He glanced across the room at Charlotte. She was standing beside the open door; sunlight brushed her face and picked out copper strands in her hair. She gave him a grave smile and shrugged. 'I really don't know.'

Otto followed her out of the lodge and they sat on two rustic chairs on the terrace, staring out across the reserve. The sun was declining, making the tall, dry grass golden. In the distance, only just visible, a herd of deer passed through a gap in the grass, like a mirage. The air cooled by a degree or two. Charlotte took a bottle of water from her bag, took a swig and passed it to Otto. The water was warm but Otto drank it gratefully. A light breeze lifted, touched his sweaty face with delicious, cool fingers.

'I like this,' he said. 'Sitting here watching the sun go down, enjoying the view. It's a beautiful place.'

Then he remembered the murdered tiger, the butchered body and settling flies.

'So what will happen now? About the tiger?'

'It's not the first poaching incident. Things aren't looking good for the reserve management. If they don't get this funding, we'll lose conservation projects.'

'But what more can they do? The reserve's huge – how can you patrol such a large area all the time? They're up against it, aren't they?'

Charlotte shifted in her chair and rubbed her knees.

'Still hurting?' he asked.

'Yes,' she nodded. 'Overdid it this afternoon. I should be more patient with myself.'

'So will there be some kind of investigation into this crash? What's happening with that?'

'Mark said an inquiry was underway. They shored up the embankment pretty quickly so the trains could run again but the investigation will take a lot longer.'

'Mark?' he said sharply.

'The journalist guy from Goa, remember? The one you liked so much.'

'Yes, I know who he is,' Otto jumped in. 'But how come you've been talking to him? Has he been down here?'

'Oh no. He saw me on the news, after the accident, like you did, and of course he phoned me up to get a story. I haven't seen it yet, but I phoned my parents so they wouldn't get too worried if they saw the story in the newspapers. They did get pretty upset when I told them what'd happened, even though I toned it down a lot.'

'I'm not surprised. You could've been killed, Charlie.' Even now, two days after seeing the news report, the realisation of how close he'd come to losing her was a jolt.

'They asked me if I'd go home,' Charlotte said. 'But I'm certainly not leaving now. I want to see this through.'

The conversation died away and the two friends sat side by side, as the sun plummeted below the horizon. Moments after it disappeared, light leaked from the sky and a chorus of animal and insect noise filled the air. Charlotte stood up.

'Will you come to the house and eat with us tonight?' she said. 'Meet the rest of the family. Maybe I can introduce you properly to Jaideep too.'

'Sure. I'm starving,' Otto said, remembering that he'd eaten nothing since lunch on the train, and that seemed a very long time ago.

Jen

Jen and Kumar were sitting at a round, wrought-iron table, on the flat roof of a whitewashed house, enjoying a view of the Minakshi Sundareshvara Temple in Madurai. In front of them rose huge pyramidal towers covered in a forest of brilliantly painted statues, marking the gateways into the temple, north, south, east and west. Pilgrims moved unceasingly, creating a din in the street below. The perfumes of burned incense, sweet blossoms, charcoal and cow dung mingled in the air. So much noise and activity – it was a relief to be out of it, in the relative space of the rooftop, with this spectacular view: the walled temple complex – so outlandish and unexpected, almost unbelievable, like something from an exotic fairy tale or film. The towers, more than fifty metres high, bustled with hundreds of stucco figures – heroes, gods, monsters and mythical beasts. The statues were many-armed, jewelled and adorned, in a great swarm and a host of vivid colours, entirely covering the surface of the towers, the *gopuras*.

It was late afternoon, a pale powder-red on the horizon above the town. The air carried the faintest coolness, a promised relief from the day's intense heat. A man emerged onto the rooftop with a tray bearing teacups and sticky sweets. After serving the tea he hovered for a minute or two, wanting to entice Jen and Kumar inside, into his brother's shop.

Jen had yearned to visit India for as long as she could remember. It had always fascinated her: the people, the landscapes, the buildings, the colours – the sheer beauty and strangeness of it. She'd watched films, read books, collected art and photographs, even transformed her bedroom at home in London into a kind of fantasy Indian temple. And then she'd met Otto and Charlotte, drawn them into her dream, and together they'd embarked on a gap-year adventure to this most fascinating of places.

Only things hadn't turned out as they'd expected. In Goa Otto had found himself involved in a murder investigation and a racket selling a drug called Kharisma. And Jen had followed her destiny, so she thought, letting Charlotte and Otto depart without her so she could spend time on a holy island, by a holy spring, unlocking the secrets of existence with Kumar and her other new friends.

These last weeks had been extraordinary. She'd sunk into a slow, satisfying rhythm of sleeping, rising, walking, meditating, talking. She'd drawn dozens of sketches and countless little studies of the sea, the Goan coast, the island itself and the visions she'd experienced after drinking water from the spring. They lived very simply, under makeshift shelters. Sometimes she'd spent days at a time on the island, until it seemed to her the rest of the world had faded and disappeared, and there existed only this beautiful place, with its temple ruins, flowers, birds and the all-encompassing sea.

Jen felt cleansed and purged, enjoying each long day, thinking, losing herself in long reveries of sea and sky, watching the long arc of the bronze, burning sun from east to west, the loops of the silver moon and the wheel of the stars in the night sky. When she slept, brilliant, complex dreams had filled her mind and lingered on into the morning after she'd woken, seeming to colour reality. They dined on fresh fish, rice, vegetables and fruit. From time to time she left the island on a boat, usually with Kumar, to buy supplies and the outside world came as a shock, the noise and bustle of it, the complex crowds, fishermen, tourists on the beach, the scooters and cars and music blaring from beach bars. It was always a relief to return to their little Eden, the island.

Then, a little over a week ago, she'd begun to emerge from this peculiar Goan dreamtime. Something was changing. The long days began to seem empty. This contemplation of eternity and the absolute was all well and good, but now she wanted something else. Could it be she was getting bored?

'Why don't we go on a pilgrimage?' Kumar had said, sensing her restlessness. Kumar, the young Indian tattooist with a Birmingham accent and floods of luscious black hair.

'A pilgrimage? Oh yes! Where to?'

And so, here they were, in the great temple town of Madurai in Tamil Nadu, sitting on a rooftop overlooking the complex, two among the thousands of tourists and pilgrims.

They'd arrived just that afternoon on the train, and the following day they planned to pass beneath the decorated tower, through a gateway, into the temple compound. It was dedicated to the Hindu god, Shiva – though here he was called Sundareshvara, the Handsome God – and to his consort, Meenakshi. This information Jen had gleaned from the man who had enticed them to the rooftop for tea and sweets, and a visit to his brother's shop. Now she jotted these facts in her notebook, alongside a quick biro sketch of the pyramidal tower and its cargo of bizarre, multicoloured statues.

'Shall we go?' Kumar said. He reached for her hand, squeezed it. 'We need to find somewhere to stay tonight.'

It was hard for Jen to quantify their relationship. These last weeks she and Kumar had grown very close. They'd spent a lot of time together and talked for hours. They were physically affectionate and, without a doubt, she thought him very beautiful. Still, against the odds, they hadn't quite crossed the line from being friends to something more serious. After the brief romantic episode with Otto – well, she was all too aware how quickly her emotions could get out of hand, how difficult it could be. That wasn't the sort of situation she wanted to have to handle, out here in India.

Kumar had been given an address by one of his Goan friends, which led them to a small, stone house overlooking a sandy court-yard, and a cheap room for a few nights. The owner was very friendly and his wife cooked them a good meal for a modest price. Jen, who'd always suffered with delicate health and a host of allergies back in England, didn't seem to have the same problems here in India. Which was a little perverse considering all the travellers' tales about the stomach infections and exotic illnesses tourists were prey to. The food she'd eaten in Goa had been fresh and wholesome, the sun and sea and air had reinvigorated her body. In fact, Jen couldn't remember having felt so healthy and energetic before. She wondered if the holy spring on the island possessed healing properties, or if perhaps this sense of well-being was simply the result of independence and the new adventure.

The two-storey house they were staying in had seen better days. Paint peeled from its exterior walls, although frescos of gods and what appeared to be a wedding indicated it had once been a prosper-ous household. Several skinny hens and a small but lordly golden cockerel scratched about in the courtyard. A white goat tethered to a post munched a pile of coarse green vegetation. Beyond the high wall Jen could hear traffic passing and the voices of pedestrians. They were eating beneath a thatched lean-to outside the house as the last light seeped from the sky and a string of pink electric light bulbs snapped on. As the daytime heat ebbed away, the perfume of the air altered as innumerable cooking stoves lit up filling the night with a haze of smoke. They dined on coconut rice, lentil curry, curd and pancakes, followed by cups of strong, searing coffee.

Jen was sleepy after the long day, the journey, and the assault of the new town with its thronging crowds. When the owner of the house came out for a friendly chat with Kumar, she seized the opportunity to excuse herself and retire to bed.

The interior of the house was cool and peaceful. She took her shoes off when she stepped inside, walking barefoot across smooth stone slabs. The shutters were open still, the house full of shadows. In a niche stood a small, elegant effigy of Shiva, with offerings of flowers, a cone of incense and oil burning in a copper dish. The wife was sitting quietly on a stool, embroidering a piece of saffron-coloured cloth. She nodded and smiled shyly at Jen as she walked past, through a thick wooden door to the room Jen and Kumar had rented.

Lying in bed, Jen could hear Kumar's voice from the courtyard outside and further away, the sound of discordant recorded music. It was odd being in the thick of a town after so long on the island but the house itself possessed an atmosphere of calm and the sheets on the simple single bed were clean and sweet. Jen, pleasantly tired, took a deep breath and closed her eyes.

She didn't fall asleep right away. Instead she drifted between dreaming and thinking, deliciously relaxed. Distantly she heard Kumar talking and laughing and the soft sound of the woman's bare feet on the stone floor in the next room. Mind soft and receptive, she became aware, as she so often did, of presences in and around the house, the resident spirits. She sensed them, although her eyes were closed – a little girl who stood on a bench to peer out of the window at the night, standing on tiptoes, exposing the pale soles of her bare feet; and a coil of energy, rolling itself upright to stand, like a cloak, by the door. Jen had felt these strange presences around her since childhood. Sometimes she spoke to her close friends about what she experienced, and they variously did or didn't believe her, which didn't bother Jen. Why should it? She knew what she knew. In any case, Kumar and the others on the island had faith in her – they'd all shared their own tales of strange visitations and extrasensory perception. It was part of the tie that bound them together.

The coil of energy curled up, slipped under the door and into the next room. The little girl by the window faded away, like steam on the air. Other presences drifted in and out, unhampered by the material boundaries of walls. None were threatening: on the contrary, Jen found them comforting, a constant wherever she went, making her feel at home.

Her thoughts drifted, as beyond the window and the garden a boy started to sing in a high, fragile voice. Jen sank into sleep.

The forests of night. The black stripes of trees broke the burning moonlight. A dense, monochrome landscape, strangely two-dimensional, as though created from layers of cut-out paper in a pop-up book.

Jen ran through the trees. The undergrowth seemed to draw back from her path, left and right, showing her the way to go. Swords of cold light pierced the dark. Animal noises – the raucous cries of monkeys, the shrieks of invisible birds – filled the air. On she ran.

Ahead something flashed red and gold, like a fire in all the black and white. Jen ran after it, the creature brightly burning. She saw it again, for a moment, and then it was gone. The tail, orange ringed with black, flicked through the grass and disappeared. She pursued the animal for a long time, never seeming to catch up as she followed the path through the unchanging, cut-out jungle.

Suddenly the path opened up, to reveal a clearing in the forest, an oval framed by the silhouettes of trees, illuminated by a brilliant moon. The creature stood in the middle, in a glorious blaze of orange and gold. It turned to face Jen, the great striped mask with yellow eyes aflame. The tiger, like a god, with its fierce, painted face.

In what distant deeps or skies burned the fire of thine eyes? And what shoulder, and what art could twist the sinews of thy heart?

The words chimed like bells in Jen's mind as the tiger raised its head and gazed at her, its legs like columns, the huge, majestic body.

Then a second splash of extraordinary colour in the black-and-white forest: a movement of blue, as a naked man stepped from the trees and stood beside the tiger. The most beautiful man Jen had ever seen or imagined, slender and graceful, with long, slim legs and a narrow waist, almost feminine except for the widening of the shoulders and the lightly muscled arms. A dancer's body, imbued with energy; long black hair framed a perfect symmetrical face, with large, expressive eyes; a small mouth, lips shaped like a Cupid's bow. The man rested his elegant hand on the tiger's head and the tiger closed its eyes in a moment of bliss.

In her dream, Jen was both thrilled and afraid to be witnessing this moment between the perfect beings but the pale-blue man raised his other hand in a gesture of reassurance. Do not be afraid! And in that instant Jen knew he was the god Shiva, patron of the temple at Madurai, the Handsome God, the dancer who made and unmade the universe.

Shiva beckoned her forwards. Trembling, she bent down to take off her shoes and stepped into the clearing, onto holy ground. As she advanced, the god retreated, backing away from the tiger and into the trees, and a horde of men rushed in from left and right, carrying spears and guns. Two-dimensional, like shadow puppets, they descended on the tiger and stabbed their weapons into its hot, living body. Jen watched helpless as the tiger collapsed and the flame retreated from its eyes. The shadow men lifted the empty tiger skin. Soundless, they ran back into the trees carrying the golden hide like a banner over their heads. And Jen was left alone, in the white pool of moonlight. The trees bowed over, bent with grief.

The stars threw down their spears, and watered heaven with their tears . . .

Jen woke up. She felt a weight on her chest, making it hard to breathe. The room was dark and silent, the shutters drawn closed. Her eyes adjusted. Dimly she made out the shape of Kumar, sleeping on the bed against the opposite wall. What time was it? She fished under her pillow for her mobile phone. Four in the morning. The dream burned in her mind, potent and laden with meaning.

She wouldn't fall asleep again now so she sat up, swung her legs over the side of the bed and pulled on her clothes. She rummaged in her backpack for notebook and pens and quietly left the room.

The oil still burned before the little effigy of Shiva in the niche, though the house was silent and dark. Glimmers of light played over his slim, golden body. Grains of rice and petals lay at his feet. Jen stood before the niche for a moment or two, staring at the calm, lovely face – then she crossed the room, unbolted the front door and headed out of the house.

At this hour, the town was as quiet as it ever would be. The streets were almost still. A sleeping dog beside a flaking yellow wall woke and raised its head as she walked by. Street lights at random intervals, here and there a small fire of dried dung. Beneath a wooden shelter half a dozen pilgrims slept on makeshift beds. Passing an open window she heard a baby crying.

Jen had no goal in mind, only a need to be walking. The dream played over in her mind. Shiva, the Handsome God, the great tiger slaughtered for its skin. She'd been called to witness the killing – but what could she do about it?

She walked, and looked, and walked, taking random turnings. Impossible to lose herself for long – the temple towers, the *gopuras*, always orientated her sooner or later. Houses, hostels, shops, and then the poorer part of town where people slept under makeshift shelters made of crates, sticks and sheets of plastic, whole families sometimes. Here one or two people were still awake, sitting beside fires, talking and singing. Someone called out to her but Jen didn't stop.

In the hour before sunrise, in the day's first pale light, the town began to wake. Scooters puttered along the roads and men pushed barrows of vegetables. A woman brushed the ground outside her front door and began drawing an elegant pattern in rice dust, a *kolam*, a circular pattern with loops and coils, to bring prosperity to her home and ward away evil spirits. In the temple itself, the day would begin with the wakening of Shiva and Meenakshi in their bedroom and the offering of breakfast to the deities, later to be shared with the town's poor.

The sun rose over the buildings, pouring down heat. Jen stopped to buy coffee, sat at a table overlooking the road and opened her notebook. In quick, clever lines she tried to capture the essence of her dream – the black, cut-out trees, the shadow puppet hunters, the tiger and the god. Hard to draw Shiva. He eluded her. His beauty was absolute, not to be captured by a humanly flawed heart and hand. Still. She tried her best.

When the drawing was done, Jen thought of Charlotte, because her friend was working at the Golden Tiger Reserve. She hadn't thought of Otto or Charlie very much over these last weeks; they were part of another world. Her decision to stay with Kumar on the island had been a severance – a distancing from her British best friends. Since then her personal experience of India had filled her mind so that now it was odd to think they were also in India, having their own adventures. Charlotte – how was she getting on? Was this dream a sign Jen should contact her? She felt a strange reluctance to do so. She didn't want to be reminded of home and life in England, which reconnecting with Charlotte would inevitably do. And Charlotte could be, well, a little domineering at times, even if that bossiness was intended as caring for Jen, who was frail and unworldly. Only now Jen didn't feel so frail. She was evidently quite capable of looking after herself and here in India her otherworldliness felt less like a handicap. If she returned to Charlotte's side, wasn't there a danger she'd become the old Jen again?

Madurai – Temple City, Festival City, Lotus City.

Pilgrims filled the streets again, men dressed in orange or black *lungis*, wearing strings of beads with coloured chalk marks on their foreheads. Would Kumar be awake by now, and wondering where she was? He wouldn't worry, at least, not for some time, respecting her need for time alone. They'd planned to visit the temple in the early afternoon, when it would be quieter, so she still had a few hours. Jen ordered bananas, chapattis and orange juice for her breakfast and then set off walking again.

Noise, heat, crowds. From time to time she was pestered by people wanting money or trying to sell something. A young man tried to strike up a conversation and entice her to his shop. On stone steps around a tank of murky water, a group of women in bright saris squatted between supple thighs and pounded soapy washing, brown arms shining in the water.

What should she do? Jen didn't want to return to Goa. She'd spent all the time she needed on the island. Now it was time to move on and learn something new. Kumar had suggested they visit other holy sites in the south of India but the dream flagged up another possibility, that she was called to do something. She stopped by the tank and watched the women chat and laugh as they washed their clothes. One of them noticed her, called out and waved. Jen smiled in return. She took out her mobile phone and started typing a text to Charlotte – asking how she was, what she was doing. But she hesitated before pressing the send button, unwilling to commit herself. Instead she saved it to the drafts folder. Maybe she'd send it later.

As she'd thought, Kumar hadn't worried at her absence. He was sitting in the courtyard outside their lodgings, drinking a bottle of Indian beer, chatting and laughing with a couple of local men Jen hadn't seen before. Kumar could evidently get quite blokey on time-out from his spiritual quest. He raised his bottle in greeting when he saw her.

'Hey, Jen! You okay?'

'Yes, yes thanks.' She nodded, unaccountably annoyed. Had she, after all, wanted him to ask where she'd been, why she'd gone off on her own for so long? The men barely acknowledged her presence. It took a little getting used to, her seeming to belong to

Kumar. When they ate out together waiters would only address him, asking him: 'What does she want?' They were being respectful and polite, but it grated on her nerves as an emancipated Western woman.

She went into the house, where the shy wife was sitting on a rug preparing vegetables, slicing green bananas and peeling cassava roots. The wife glanced up at Jen when she came in, gave her usual quick nod. Jen walked to the door of her room, but hesitated on the threshold. She took a deep breath, plucked up her courage, and went over to the woman, who gave a timid smile but indicated Jen should sit opposite. She didn't speak English, which would make communication difficult. For a couple of minutes the two women didn't speak but friendliness and goodwill were evident between them. Hard to say how old the woman was. Early thirties perhaps, very dark-skinned, with a flawless, chiselled face, her thick hair tied in a perfect bun and adorned with blossom. She had long, slender fingers and was deft with the knife, paring the reddish roots, piling the scraps of skin in one dish, the peeled cassava in another.

Jen was happy to watch. When the task was complete the woman put the dishes to one side – bananas, cassava roots, peelings. Jen lifted her notebook and turned to the page where she'd drawn the sketches from her dream. She held out the open book. The woman looked at the book and back to Jen.

'Please, have a look,' Jen said. The woman took it with great reverence and considered the drawing.

'It's Shiva,' Jen said, gesturing to the god in the niche. The woman stared. She touched the drawing very lightly with her fingertips and nodded.

'This is what I dreamed, last night.' Jen mimed sleeping, pointed at the picture and then to the side of her forehead. What was she expecting? Some sign, an interpretation? The woman looked up at Jen again, very intently. She closed the book and handed it back with a smile. Even if she knew what it signified, how would she communicate it to Jen?

They headed for the temple gates at two, Kumar and Jen. The throng in the streets had calmed a little. This was the time of day when, apparently, the god and goddess were resting.

Any annoyance Jen felt with Kumar melted away as they wandered, agog, like children, through the astonishing temple complex. They strolled to the Golden Lotus tank, down the steps to the pool of water, and then along pillared corridors decorated with a multitude of statues and paintings. They passed countless shrines, some containing the smooth black cylinder of the Shiva *lingam*, the symbol of the god as the absolute source of the universe, honoured with garlands of flowers. They were not allowed into the central sanctuary, but just beyond it was a shrine to Nandi, Shiva's bull, and then a statue of the goddess Kali, many-armed, slaying a demon, full of ferocious energy and grace.

They spent a couple of hours drifting around the temple, hardly speaking except to point something out, or share an impression. Outside, afterwards, the peace of the complex melted away and they were swallowed instead by the familiar noise of the town. They stopped at a cafe next to a stall selling all sorts of religious paraphernalia, beads and statues, garish pictures and posters of the Hindu gods and goddesses. Kumar ordered coffees and when they arrived, leaned back in his chair, considering Jen.

'So what is it, Jen?' he said. 'What's up?'

'What? What do you mean? Nothing's up.'

He smiled, folding his arms. 'Ah Jen, you think I don't know when something's going round inside your head?' He was wearing a loose blue vest top. The dark skin on his shapely shoulders and arms glistened with a faint sheen of perspiration.

Jen sighed. She reached for her bag and took out the notebook.

'I had a dream last night,' she said. 'About Shiva and a tiger.'

She opened the book, showed him the sketch as she had done earlier, with the wife in the house. Kumar took the book.

'This was your dream? Wow. A visitation.'

'Charlotte's working at a tiger sanctuary.'

'Your friend.'

Jen nodded. 'I should visit her. It seems obvious.'

A look of shock and appalled surprise tumbled over Kumar's face.

'You're going to leave me?'

Jen blinked, taken aback at the strength of his reaction. 'Well, I – you could come with me.' Curiously she felt some reluctance about his coming along too. She had imagined herself setting off alone. It hadn't occurred to her Kumar would be so upset.

'Just for a visit,' she said. 'I have to go, don't you see? That's what the dream was telling me.'

Kumar looked away, frowning. 'That's a very literal interpretation. Mightn't your dream mean something else?' He looked very tense and awkward, trying to contain his emotions.

'Why don't you come too?' Jen repeated, wanting to stop the hurt he was feeling and that she, unintentionally, had caused.

He shook his head. 'With you and your old friends from home? Don't you see, you'll be different when you're with them. You'll change and I'll be the outsider.'

'No, don't be silly, of course it won't be like that.' Except, of course, she had been afraid of the same thing, that she would become the old Jen when she reunited with Charlotte.

'When are you going?' Kumar said.

'I'll call Charlotte this evening. If I can get a train tomorrow, then I'll go.' She hadn't formulated any concrete plan till she spoke the words out loud. Then it seemed obvious that was what she should do.

Kumar shook his head again.

'I won't be long,' she said hurriedly. 'I'll come back. We'll meet up again. Continue our tour, yes?'

'You won't come back,' he said. 'I know it. You'll be different. You'll think differently. It'll all be over between us.' He sounded almost comically crestfallen and Jen couldn't help but laugh.

'Oh Kumar, don't be ridiculous! How little you think of me, that I'm so easily swayed. Don't you think I have a mind of my own? Don't you see how much I've learned over these last weeks in India? How much more myself I've become?'

'Jen, your friends are so worldly. And you – well, you're extraordinary.'

'Thank you, I think. Then can't you trust me to preserve myself? I need to see Charlotte. Don't you see that?'

'Sure,' he shrugged. 'If that's what you think. I can't stop you.'

They went back to the house by the courtyard. In the evening Jen phoned Charlotte. They hadn't spoken for several weeks, though Charlotte had sent several brief texts, mostly checking Jen was okay. So Jen felt oddly nervous when the phone rang and she waited for Charlotte to answer.

'Hey, Jen! How are you?'

'Yes, I'm fine thanks. Not so far from you actually – I'm in Tamil Nadu too, visiting Madurai. How are you?'

A pause before Charlotte replied, as though she were waiting for something. Then she said: 'I'm fine now. Did you call because . . . well – did you see the news?'

'News? What news?'

'Ah – you didn't see it. I thought maybe that was why you'd phoned. There was a train crash, close to here.' So Charlotte explained, briefly, what had happened.

'I want to come and see you,' Jen blurted. 'Would that be okay?'

'Of course. Yes, of course. I don't think there's any more accommodation free on the reserve but we could find you something close by, I'm sure. Otto's here too.'

They made arrangements. Jen said she'd call when she'd finalised her travel plans and the call ended affectionately.

Kumar defiantly spent the evening outside with the guys, talking and drinking beer. Jen passed the time helping the wife in the house; even though they had no common language they enjoyed each other's company. Later Jen washed and repacked ready for the morning. She was still awake but lying in bed when Kumar came into the room. He wasn't quite steady on his feet and smelled of beer. He hesitated by her bed, dropped to his knees and touched her face. She could feel his warm breath on her cheek.

'Can I lie beside you for a minute?' he whispered.

'Sure.' She wriggled across to make some room on the narrow bed. Kumar clambered on, awkwardly put his arms around her. She rested her head on his shoulder and placed her hand on his warm, T-shirted chest.

'I don't like letting you go,' Kumar said. 'But I can't go with you either. I just can't.'

' 'S okay,' Jen said. 'It'll be fine. I'll call you. Send you some texts.'

'No. Don't do that. Don't contact me at all. Not until you want to come back to me.'

Kumar, tipsy, lying on his back, was soon snoring very gently. Jen stayed awake a little longer, thinking about her journey the next day and the dream that had prompted her to contact Charlotte. What would it be like to be together again?

She woke up early the next morning, just before dawn. The wife took Jen outside the front door in the pale, early light, so Jen could watch how she swept the dirt away and created a large, complex *kolam*, expertly spilling rice dust from her hand to draw the lines and curls. They embraced as they parted. Kumar lay in bed, heavily asleep. Jen decided not to wake him. She didn't want to say goodbye.

Charlotte

Amrita drove the pick-up, Charlotte sitting in the passenger seat. Jack was perched in the back, bumping about as the pick-up bounced over potholes or swerved around the occasional scooter or bike, or young girls carrying unfeasibly large bundles of sticks from the forest.

Jaideep had organised a meeting at a village bordering the sanctuary, for residents from the locality. At the sanctuary office first thing that morning he'd briefed the wardens on the tiger poaching incident and he'd asked Charlotte and Amrita to join him. Jack had attended the meeting too, lurking uneasily at the back of the room. At the end, as Jaideep was about to leave, Jack had expressed an interest in coming along – and Jaideep had agreed.

Charlotte tried not to worry about Jack. She felt safer now Otto was close at hand – easier in her mind. Besides, they all had plenty to think about with the poaching, the aftermath of the train accident and the upcoming funding application. She needed to focus her energies – couldn't let Jack distract her.

The presence of Otto hadn't entirely deterred Jack. The previous night, just as she was going to sleep, her phone had bleeped beside her bed announcing the arrival of a text from Jack, saying simply that he was thinking about her, and goodnight. She didn't reply and deleted the text. Amrita, lying in the other bed, had asked her who the text was from and giggled when Charlotte told her.

'He's very keen,' Amrita said. 'But don't worry. If you don't respond and he sees you hanging out with Otto, he'll soon lose interest.'

'Yes, I expect you're right,' Charlotte said. In truth she wasn't so sure. The more she got to know Jack, the more she was coming to believe something wasn't quite right about him. Like this latest text. He didn't seem to know when he was crossing the line and behaving inappropriately.

Sitting in the passenger seat of the pick-up, Charlotte shifted and frowned, wondering if Jack's eyes, even now, were boring into the back of her head through the window at the back of the cab. She wanted to turn round and check, but didn't dare. If he saw her looking, wouldn't that seem like encouragement? She was afraid that he was so infatuated that everything she said or did seemed to be taken as a confirmation of what he believed and wanted to be true.

However, she reminded herself, she didn't want to spend any more time or energy worrying about it. Too much else was going on.

Charlotte stared out of the window at a stand of teak trees. A crowd of brilliant green parakeets circled in the air. The pick-up lurched into and out of a rut in the road.

They drew up at the village an hour later. It was a remote place, accessible only by the rough track they'd taken in the pick-up. Around twenty simple wood and thatch homes crowded together in an undulating grassy plain at the edge of the forest. People were already gathering under a veranda made of rustic wood and bamboo, talking. The noise increased as Jaideep walked towards them. Men and women, children of all ages, including a couple of infants cradled in their mothers' arms and some gawky young teenage boys loitering, as Charlotte guessed, in the manner of teenage boys in any part of the world.

Amrita and Charlotte got out of the pick-up and Jack jumped down from the back. A gang of children ran up to them, chattering and pointing, the little girls grinning and shyly covering their hands with their mouths.

Jack came up close to Charlotte and Amrita.

'What a place,' he said. 'Talk about off the beaten track. It's hardly somewhere you're going to chance upon, is it? What time's the meeting?'

'Another half an hour,' Amrita said. 'Anyway, they'll be serving tea and something to eat before the talking starts. Come and have a look round the village first.' She said something in Tamil to the one of the children, a girl of about eleven, who nodded and gestured them to follow.

A water pump and a red stone trough stood in the dusty square at the centre of the village, the houses massed around. Chickens wandered. A goat and two kids lay beneath a tree in the shade. Amrita asked the children questions, which she then translated for the others. The youngsters had to walk three miles every day to get to the primary school in the next village, she said. In the fields beyond the houses, farmers grew rice, pulses and sunflowers. Some of the villagers had work connected with the reserve but many young men and women had moved away from the place to find work in the towns.

Jack hung around uneasily as they stood talking in the shade of a mango tree. One of the village women came over and ushered them to the veranda where people were gathered around Jaideep. The villagers offered tea to their guests and the conversation grew more heated. Everyone, it seemed, had something to say. At last, one of the local men stood up, called everyone to order, and introduced Jaideep. At least, that is how Amrita translated it. Jaideep explained to the people what had happened to the tiger – creating outrage and consternation. Jaideep urged them to keep a watch out for poachers, to observe what was happening in the forest. The villagers were both a pressure on and an asset to the reserve, Amrita said. They encroached on the reserve because they needed more agricultural land and collected firewood from the forest for fuel. On the other hand, they had a right to live, just as the tiger did. And they were guardians of the place.

The meeting went on for a long time. Various complaints were raised, about deer damaging crops and one man claimed a tiger had killed his livestock, though this was disputed by others in the village. Nothing was straightforward and the discussions were long and complex. Charlotte began to get bored and hot, and Amrita soon tired of trying to translate the conversation, so they quietly left the meeting and returned to the shade of the mango tree.

They started to talk about England. Amrita, bubbly and enthusiastic, always wanted to know more about Charlotte's life and how it differed from hers. Charlotte, who was similarly interested in Amrita, always enjoyed these conversations and the chance it gave her to ask Amrita about growing up in India.

'So tell us about your family, Jack,' Amrita said. 'Do you have any brothers or sisters?'

'I have a sister,' Jack said. 'Well, a half-sister. She's ten years older than me.'

'Like you, Charlie,' Amrita said. 'You have older half-brothers, yes?'

'My father was married before,' Charlie said, filling in the gaps for Jack. 'I have two brothers. They seemed more like uncles, really.'

'My sister and I spent a lot of time together when I was little. So we were pretty close – at least, until she went to college. Things changed, obviously. Didn't see so much of her,' Jack said.

'Tell me about your parents,' Amrita said. 'What do they do?'

'My parents are both doctors. General practitioners.'

Amrita raised her eyebrows, obviously impressed. 'And where did you grow up?'

'Shropshire. Out in the countryside. We had a fabulous place, an old farmhouse, with a big garden and an orchard and all sorts of tumble-down outbuildings. I loved it. With my parents working long hours, well, they had a housekeeper who kept an eye on me, but I had a lot of freedom when I think about it. Used to camp out in the summer under the apple trees, make dens, that kind of thing.'

'It sounds idyllic,' Charlotte said, with a question in her voice. It did sound lovely – a kind of storybook childhood – but something about his tone of voice, the flatness of it, suggested his life hadn't been quite that.

'In some ways, yes,' Jack said. 'Well, in lots of ways really.'

'But?' she pressed.

He'd been looking at the ground but now he raised his face and looked at her. Jack's eyes were brown, rather small, but his expression was intense, as though something inside him was always being restrained and reined in, creating at the same time a kind of frightening pressure.

'But?' he repeated. 'But nothing.' He shrugged and looked away again. 'Nobody has a storybook childhood, do they? Except for children in stories.'

Charlotte smiled.

'What's so funny?' Jack asked.

'I was thinking about the idea of the storybook childhood. Most of the childhoods I read about in stories when I was growing up were pretty grim. You know, broken families, care homes and stuff. And don't even get me started on all those misery memoirs. Even the idea of a storybook childhood in stories seems a bit of a myth these days.'

Jack didn't answer. Something in the shape of his body, the set of his rather bony shoulders and neck, added to the impression he was repressing something. Was that why she found him so

91

physically unattractive? Or was it simply a response to his unwanted imposition of this deep connection between them? He was a nice-looking man, on the surface of it, with the red-brown hair falling to his shoulders, a narrow face with lightly freckled skin, a slim but well-proportioned body. Still, something about him made Charlotte very uneasy. She couldn't forget how he'd behaved in the aftermath of the accident and she wished he had just moved on and left her at the sanctuary, in peace, because now she was stuck with him. Maybe this Otto-as-boyfriend plan would hammer home the message. Thinking of Otto made her smile, filled her with warmth that dispelled the discomfort she felt, being in Jack's presence. Where was Otto now? Probably still asleep in the lodge, flat on his back, arms and legs outstretched. He could sleep for England. They'd arranged to meet in the evening, when she'd finished work, and just now, despite the novelty of the village and the meeting, that seemed a long time in the future.

'So how long are you staying in India?' Amrita said.

Jack shook his head. 'I don't know. I've been here ten months so far. I love it. Haven't got any particular plans though. I'll go where the fancy takes me.'

'What about your future?' Amrita persisted. She was ferociously ambitious, with her place at university lined up, plans for a career as an engineer both in India and abroad.

'Oh, I don't know,' Jack said. 'I don't think much about it, to be honest. I didn't do as well as expected in my A levels, and competition for university places was very tough, so I thought I'd take some time out to decide what I really wanted to do.'

'So how do you fund all these months of travelling?' Charlotte said.

He looked at her. 'My grandmother died and left me some money. Enough for me to travel for a couple of years, as long as I live simply, and I am quite happy to do that. It's all I want, just now, to be free.'

'Free?' Amrita sniffed. 'And what are you going to do with this freedom? If you don't choose to do something, then your freedom means, in essence, you do nothing.'

A faintly patronising smile crossed Jack's face. 'I don't think the same way as you. I don't need worldly success. I just want to experience each day as it comes. What about you, Charlie, what do you want to do?'

Again that intense scrutiny. Charlotte shifted uneasily.

'I want to do development studies and economics,' she said. 'I've got a place, and I'm starting in September.'

'And then?'

'And then, well, I'm not exactly sure. I'd like to work for a development agency or a charity, something like that.'

With Amrita, Charlotte had enthused about her plans and ideas. With Jack she was naturally more guarded, not wanting to give herself away. She wished he weren't with them, so she and Amrita could chat and gossip as usual. Charlotte glanced at her watch. They'd been at the village for three hours now. She was sweating, despite the shade, and hungry. Fortunately the meeting was adjourned for lunch. Jaideep called them over and the three young people sat with the others. The women arrived with pots full of rice, tomatoes, chutneys and spicy lentils which they served on shiny banana leaves.

'The women here have set up a group, along with others from the villages nearby, to help us protect the tigers,' Jaideep explained, gesturing with a chapatti in his hand. 'They're all volunteers, and every day they take it in turns to walk in the forest looking for signs that poachers are in the area. They also alert us if anyone cuts down and steals our teak or sandalwood trees, or if someone starts any illegal quarrying.'

'That's pretty impressive,' Jack said. And he was right. However, it was also a little daunting to think of these dozens of women, on foot, trying to guard the enormous sanctuary. What chance did they have, in truth, of protecting the few, precious tigers from determined gangs of men, many of whom might be armed?

Another of the villagers came to talk with Jaideep. Charlotte finished her lunch, scooping up rice and lentils with her fingers, then folded her banana leaf plate. She felt restless, despite the heat, unsure of herself, mind full of worries. Perhaps it was a consequence of the accident, the physical, mental and emotional shake-up. At the time she'd dealt with it, but now, she found herself replaying scenes in her mind. Memories of the impact and being thrown around in the cabin, and the haunting screams of the wounded . . . Perhaps that was the reason she disliked Jack so much. While he seemed attached to her because of what they'd shared, she felt exactly the opposite. His presence reminded her of the accident and she wanted to put it behind her, to get on with her life.

Jack was talking to Amrita, so Charlotte rose quietly to her feet and walked away from the meeting, and the village, towards the forest. Several small, brown monkeys, little families with mothers and children and tiny, clinging babies, scampered out of the long grass and into the trees as Charlotte approached. She stepped into the emerald shade, playing over her worries in her mind. Was Jack a problem, or was she just blowing the situation out of proportion? Surely something wasn't quite right about him, so shouldn't she be compassionate? Then all the problems facing the sanctuary – the train crash, the death of the tiger, the imminent funding application. And last night – unexpectedly – the phone call from Jen declaring her intention to come to the reserve. Charlotte had heard next to nothing from Jen these last weeks, only brief, intermittent texts. This call had been a complete surprise. Charlotte hadn't been happy to leave Jen with Kumar and the other people from the island, but in the end she'd had to respect Jen's decision: she was an adult after all. She couldn't force her to leave Goa. So Jen's plan to visit should have been unadulterated good news – but it wasn't. Charlotte felt a strange and unwanted twinge of resentment towards her. Why was that? Because of Otto?

Otto. They'd been the best of friends for years. They could talk for hours. She'd encouraged his photography, influenced his tastes and interests in ways he probably hadn't even noticed. Over the last two years she'd seen countless brief girlfriends come and go, while she waited for him to realise the girl he really wanted had been right in front of him all the time. But when he'd come down from Mumbai to see her, she sensed something, finally, had changed. Hard to quantify what, exactly. He hadn't behaved any differently, not overtly, but nonetheless a shift had taken place. She detected a new sensitivity between them, almost a shyness. Why was that? Perhaps she was just imagining it, because of Amrita's plan to present Otto as Charlotte's boyfriend for Jack's benefit. She hardly dare believe it might be true, that Otto was seeing her in a new light. How dangerous to hope that, when she might so well be wrong. But Jen and Otto had history. They'd gone out with each other for a few weeks the previous year. Was that the reason Charlotte felt an unwelcome, irrational spike of jealousy at the prospect of Jen coming to see her? She didn't want anything – or anyone – to damage the fragile possibility of a new kind of relationship developing with Otto.

A narrow stream flowed through the trees, widening into the skim of a pool where some of the monkeys stooped to drink, scooping the water with fastidious little hands. They edged away as Charlotte approached, but when she sat down on the bank they began to creep closer again, peering at her with wide eyes.

She thought it was a beautiful place. Nowhere in England seemed truly wild; pretty much every square mile had been developed, built on, farmed – even the remaining woods. But the pressure was building on India's wild places too. A growing population, the ever-growing need for resources and agricultural land: it was hard to see how all these demands could be accommodated.

'Charlie?'

'What?' The monkeys scattered. Charlotte looked over her shoulder. 'Oh, Jack.'

'Needed to get away, huh? Of course you did.'

Obviously she hadn't gone far enough. The moment of solitary peace was over. Why couldn't he give her any space? She felt the weight of it, his dogged pursuit.

'Jack, I could really do with some time out. Would you mind leaving me to myself for a bit?' Even now she tried to be polite. She just couldn't bring herself to say what she really felt – that she wanted Jack to clear off.

'Certainly,' he said, still drawing closer. 'I won't be a moment. I know how important it is to have time on your own. I'm the same as you, I need it sometimes – solitude, a moment to think properly.' He sat down beside her.

'What do you want?' she said, with a sigh. Then, with a note of hope: 'I was hoping you might like to meet Otto tonight – my boyfriend. We thought we'd all eat out together, Amrita too, and my friend Jen if she gets here in time. She's travelling up from Madurai. Would you like to join us?'

Jack sat with his knees apart, leaning forward, elbows resting on his thighs. 'Sure, I'd love to,' he said.

'Otto's great. I'm so glad he's here, with me. He's a wonderful man,' she persisted, knowing she was larding it on.

Jack didn't even seem to notice.

'We have to talk, you and I,' he said.

'What is there to talk about?'

'What else? You. I need to talk about you.'

'What about me?' Her voice was a little shrill.

'What we're going to do. How we're going to handle this.'

'Handle what?'

Jack shook his head with a wry smile and clasped his square, bony hands together.

'Why do you resist it, Charlie? Why? You can't fight yourself.'

'What are you talking about?'

He shook his head again, seemingly confident and amused, an adult humouring a child.

'You know very well. Okay, I'm talking about you and me. I'm asking how we should handle it. Obviously you need some time to finish things with this boyfriend of yours.'

Charlotte stood up. 'For crying out loud, there is no you and me! Why won't you get it into your thick head? Nothing connects us. We just happened to be in a train accident at the same time, that's all. I'm sorry to hurt your feelings, I don't want to make you feel stupid, but that's the truth of it. There is absolutely no you and me – not now, not tomorrow, not ever!

'I've tried to be sympathetic and polite but you just keep on and on. Please drop it, okay? I'm not happy you're staying here and I don't want to get involved in any more pointless discussions.'

She glared at him, Jack still sitting as he was, looking neither upset nor offended, with a good-humoured smile on his face. Nothing she'd said seemed to have made any impression. He knew what he knew, his expression seemed to say. It was no use her fretting and fighting about it. This self-possession and certainty exasperated Charlotte. What more could she say to the man? So she spun on her heels, stomped away from the stream and out of the forest. Even so, she sensed him watching her as she left, his gaze pinned to her retreating back, smug despite the no-uncertain-terms rejection.

When Charlotte got back to the village, Jaideep and Amrita were talking to the group of volunteer women. Amrita waved, left her father with the volunteers, and ran over to Charlotte.

'Are you okay? Where did you go? When Jack disappeared, well, I was a bit worried. Did you see him?'

'Yes I did,' Charlotte said. 'I just went for a walk and he followed me – wanted to talk. Wouldn't take no for an answer.'

Amrita's eyes widened and her mouth opened: 'You mean he—?'

'No. No! He didn't try anything, not physically. He just – well, in his own little world he and I have something going, and whatever I say, he doesn't seem to hear it. Nothing can dissuade him from believing we're connected. It is infuriating – and it freaks me out.'

'Well, perhaps tonight will help, if Jack sees you with Otto.' Amrita grinned. Charlotte realised this little unrequited romance was providing some entertainment for Amrita, who evidently didn't realise just how odd and intense Jack could be. She felt a pang of isolation. Otto would understand, wouldn't he? She didn't want to be alone in this strange mental duel with Jack.

He didn't return from the forest for a long time. The meeting ended as the afternoon died; Jaideep, who had business to attend to at the office, headed off in his jeep, leaving Charlotte and Amrita to wait for Jack. It was hard to read Jaideep's mood. Had the meeting been a success? He didn't give much away. When he'd gone, Amrita shook her head and worried he had too much on his plate and not enough help. She said the tiger's slaughter had upset him deeply.

'He was talking about it late, with my mother. He's worried other tigers will be killed, that we'll fail to get the funding, and that he'll lose his job,' she said. 'And what would we do then? It would break his heart. This place is his passion.'

The two young women were sitting in silence in the cab of the pick-up, waiting for Jack, as the sun descended over the forest. They watched the goings-on in the village, stoves and fires starting up as the women began to prepare food for the evening, and a boy returning with a herd of goats which he shut into a makeshift paddock for the night.

98

'Why don't we just go without him?' Charlotte said. 'We're supposed to be going out. I have to meet Otto and Jen.' A cold thought drifted through her mind, of Jen and Otto reuniting at the reserve before she returned, and again she felt the stab of jealousy. She clenched her fists. How awful to be thinking this, about her best friends. What was wrong with her? She'd always kept a lid on these feelings before, but now, having allowed herself the faintest of hopes that the relationship with Otto might be progressing onto new ground, she had also opened the door to these far less welcome and less worthy feelings.

She couldn't phone or text. Signal was very patchy over much of the reserve. Otto's lodge was out of reach.

'Leave him behind? Don't think I'm not tempted,' Amrita said.

They stared through the windscreen.

'There he is.' Amrita raised her hand, pointed into the gathering dusk. He loped through the grass and along the track to the village. He waved to the girls in the pick-up, banged on the window in greeting, and jumped up into the back.

'No apology for keeping us waiting? No explanation?' Amrita started the engine.

'Leave it,' Charlotte said. 'Please. I don't want to talk to him. Let's just go home.'

Charlotte

The evening didn't get any easier. They were late back, hurried to get washed and changed, and consequently late to pick up Otto from his lodge, though he didn't seem to notice. He jumped into the back of the pick-up with Jack, after the briefest of introductions, and Amrita drove them all into town. From time to time Charlotte glanced back, trying to work out what Otto and Jack made of each other, what they might be saying. Each had expectations of the other, because of her, and because of what she'd said.

They seemed to be talking and looked superficially friendly with one another, though Charlotte knew Otto well enough to see he wasn't entirely relaxed. She sighed, turned her eyes to the road.

At the house, a text from Jen had arrived, announcing the time of her train – and did Charlie know of anywhere she could stay? The obvious place, of course, was at the lodge with Otto. Charlotte railed at herself for not liking this idea – what was the matter with her?

Amrita, in the passenger seat, was very talkative, excited by the prospect of having four exotic guests to entertain. They were going to a quiet place her father had recommended; he'd phoned the owner to make the booking and request that they prepare something special for them. Also, Charlotte suspected, to ask him to keep an eye on Amrita. He was very protective about his daughter.

It was a beautiful restaurant. They were welcomed warmly then guided through a corridor to the rear of the old, stone building, where a long table waited in a paved courtyard surrounded by high walls, over which ropes of creepers grew, and blossoms with a sweet, sherbet perfume. A quarter moon lay on its back just above the wall in a dark-blue and mauve sky. Candles burned in coloured glass jars, red and blue and acid yellow. Peeling pictures painted on the walls depicted pale-skinned women dancing one behind the other. What a perfect romantic place, Charlotte thought, taking it all in. Moonlight, candles, blossoms, dancing maidens: all the required ingredients for a seduction in the heat of an Indian evening. Something about this incongruity amused her, she wasn't sure why: perhaps that the simple clichés of the setting contrasted with the complexities of the relationships between the guests. Jack was obsessing about Charlotte; Charlotte and Otto were pretending to be in love, while Charlotte, in truth, did love Otto, and meanwhile Otto's ex was on her way to join them. It sounded like the plot of an elaborate Shakespearian comedy, though if that were the case, all would be satisfactorily resolved by the morning – and that was unlikely to happen.

The owner, looking meticulously clean and pressed in a long cream tunic embroidered with gold thread, bustled out to welcome them with drinks of fruit juice. Jack had dug out a pale-yellow collarless shirt to wear, and had showered and shaved before they left. He looked remarkably cool and contained. Otto, in comparison, seemed unwashed and scruffy, in his cut-offs, which probably hadn't been laundered for some time. Still, sitting beside Otto and taking surreptitious glances at him, Charlotte couldn't help thinking how attractive he was, with his long dark-blond hair, his fine skin still pale after all these weeks in the hot sun, the angular face, the sheer masculinity of him. Then he caught her looking at him, and for an instant she was shot through with embarrassment – until he smiled, winked and reached for her hand. The shock of the contact, his smooth, square hand engulfing hers, sent a disconcerting flood of warmth through her body. Of course – he thought she was gazing at him because she was playing a role for Jack's benefit. She was free to moon over him, to sit close, to hold his hand, all as part of the play. This realisation was both pleasing and painful: the contact was real enough, but the knowledge that Otto was acting a part seemed a horrible torture.

Charlotte glanced across the table to see what Jack made of this little performance. He was talking to Amrita, and still looked cool, hands clasped, elbows propped on the table. He'd noticed the affectionate display, but seemed entirely unperturbed. How annoying.

The owner reappeared with two young assistants and a feast of food. Dishes of fried fish, coconut rice, spicy chicken, fried vegetables, pancakes, steamed rice dumplings, bowls of curd and variously sweet and piquant chutneys, were spread over the table. The warm night air in the courtyard swam with the scent of garlic. Otto's eyes widened to see the dinner.

Charlotte looked at her watch. Someone would have to meet Jen at the station and bring her to the restaurant. She didn't want to leave Amrita alone with Jack and Otto, feeling that wouldn't be quite right, but the alternative – to send Otto to fetch her – wasn't what she wanted either. Why not? Why was she thinking like this? She pressed her toes into the ground and gave her head a tense little shake. Stop it. So Otto and Jen had history – well, things hadn't worked out and now they were friends again. Nothing had happened to suggest any romantic rapprochement between them.

'What's up?' Otto said.

'Nothing – well, I was wondering, would you meet Jen at the station, and bring her along? I'd go myself, but I don't want to leave Amrita.'

Otto's face lit up.

'Meet Jen? Yes of course! Where's the station?'

'Ten minutes' walk. Turn right, then just along the road.'

Otto surveyed the table. 'Save some for me,' he said, now reluctant to leave the feast.

As the night had deepened, the light from the candles in their coloured glass intensified. Steam rose from the hot dishes, carrying the spiced perfume of the food. Tonight no traditional banana leaf plates – they were dining off antique Victorian china plates. Where had the restaurateur come by those? Amrita reached out for a poppadam and snapped it into pieces.

'Okay, I'm off to the station. Back soon.' Otto stood up, clearly reluctant to leave the tantalising food. He leaned over, kissed Charlotte on the cheek, and said: 'See you later,' the barest hesitation and then: 'Babe.'

Charlotte snorted, amused and contemptuous. Babe. No-one had called her babe before. And she wasn't sure she ever wanted to be called babe, even by Otto. As he walked away, she caught Jack's eye and read that he was thinking the same thing – that she couldn't possibly be going out with Otto; she could see he was thinking that Otto, for all his boyish charm and geniality, was an intellectual lightweight; that she needed something more, something else. This was all communicated in a moment. Charlotte shifted in her seat, uncomfortable because Jack had somehow tempted her to think this about Otto, except that he hadn't, she'd created the thought herself. She shook her head again, wanting to rid herself of this unnerving spell, the moment of communion with Jack.

They began to eat, not wanting the food to get cold. The restaurant owner came out to check they were happy and chatted with Amrita for a few minutes before turning to Jack and Charlotte to find out who they were and what they were doing in India.

Otto arrived with Jen, carrying her rucksack, to a warm greeting and introductions. Charlotte held back, wanting to savour this moment, reuniting with her friend. She waited till the others had said hello and then held out her arms to give Jen a long, warm hug. Then she drew away and looked into Jen's face. 'You look so different,' she said. Jen's hair, usually dyed a dark crimson, had faded and been recoloured with henna. A medley of bracelets circled her wrists, silver bangles, chains with charms, coloured beads; more beads around her neck, like those the *sadhus* wore, along with silver pendants and curious talismans of wood, shell and stone. This was not the most marked difference, though. Charlotte thought her face had changed. Jen looked older. Some of the fragile naivety seemed to have worn away. It didn't make her look less pretty – on the contrary, it added something, gave her strength.

'I *am* different,' Jen said. 'How could I not be?' This alteration was also evident in her speech. 'You look different too.'

They stood looking at each other for a moment or two longer, till Amrita summoned them back to the table because they needed to eat and further dishes were arriving.

It was quite dark now – the sky a dome of stars above the courtyard wall. Candlelight flickered on the painted dancing maidens, creating an illusion of movement. Charlotte, Otto and Jen – all together again. Charlotte felt a rush of gratitude and happiness to be with them, her friends, after this time of separation, but made sure to include Amrita in the conversation too. As for Jack, well, he could take care of himself.

They ate and talked for hours. Otto quizzed Jack about his Indian travels. Amrita and Charlotte told the newcomers about the Golden Tiger Reserve and the challenges it faced. The plates were cleared away and the waiters returned with dishes of ice cream, then cups of thick, potent coffee.

For a moment they were all silent. Charlotte heard the heavy chorus of night-time insects. Jack picked up his coffee cup, raised it to his lips, then looked directly at Otto.

'So how long have you two been an item?' he said.

Otto blinked. Everyone's attention was focused on him. Charlotte wondered if he'd remembered to brief Jen on the game when he'd collected her from the station.

'Six months,' Charlotte jumped in. 'But we've been friends a very long time. Since primary school.' How hard it was to lie, even under extenuating circumstances. She was starting to regret the whole plan. It was too hard, too complicated. Everyone at the table knew it was a lie, except for Jack – and she had the distinct impression Jack didn't believe it either.

'You're a lucky man, Otto,' Jack said, his voice level.

'Yeah, yeah you're right,' Otto said, dumping a clumsy arm over Charlotte's shoulder. Was he a little drunk? He'd been drinking Kingfisher beer all evening and he sounded gauche, as he always did after too much alcohol.

Jack looked at Charlotte, who was sitting uneasily under the weight of Otto's arm. He didn't say anything and his face was very still, but his eyes held hers with a particular intensity, as though he were drilling into her mind. He was the outsider, the person for whom the rest of them had agreed to create the charade of a romance. To protect her, ostensibly; yet strangely, the fact that they were all prepared to play along with the deception made Jack the strongest person. They were all going along with a falsehood, telling a lie, because of him.

Charlotte looked away from Jack and wriggled out from Otto's arm. She would love to have his arms around her, had imagined it so many times and for so long, but not like this.

Otto looked at her oddly. Jack leaned back slightly in his chair, the faintest of smiles on his face, still looking at Charlotte and then at Otto. Nobody spoke. The sense of tension in the air increased, everyone nonplussed, not knowing what to say. All, except for Jack that was. He seemed entirely master of the situation. Charlotte felt a rising desperation. Why was that? What could he do? Nothing. He had no hold on her at all. Why then did she feel this sense of dread? An image rose into her mind, of a hunter pursuing its prey. Not a tiger, no. Nothing so beautiful or noble. Something like a hyena perhaps: something doggish that would pick out its quarry then lope after it for miles and days, patient, relentless, until its prey collapsed from exhaustion.

She stood up abruptly, knocking against her chair. 'Going to the loo,' she said, looking away from the table, and knowing that by this retreat in disarray she had awarded a victory to Jack. He had succeeded in discomfiting her, in breaking the connection between Charlotte and her friends.

She stumbled across the courtyard and into the toilet, in a lean-to at the back of the building. The electric light was blinding, after the subtle illumination of the courtyard. Cobwebs clung to the wire and around the root of the bulb, massed in the wooden ceiling. Charlotte peed and washed her hands. A tiny mirror hung above the sink. She didn't look great in the harsh overhead light. Her forehead was greasy and bumpy, the pores on her nose congested. What was it that Jack saw? What was it about her, that he wanted so much? She washed her hands again, delaying the moment of returning to the table and the awkward situation. But it was no good. She couldn't stay locked in this spidery place all night, hiding from Jack. She ran her fingers through her hair, took a deep breath, unlocked the door and stepped out.

Charlotte heard a bubble of laughter. In her absence it seemed the atmosphere of the party had lightened. The four were leaning into the table and Otto was recounting a tale that had held their attention and prompted various gales of amusement. With a sense of relief, she returned to her place and maintained a low profile as they finished their coffees and finally wound up the meal.

It took a long time to leave. They paid the bill and enthused about the meal, while the restaurateur shook their hands and entreated them to return again soon. Charlotte drove everyone home, first dropping off Jack, then Jen and Otto at the lodge, before making the final stretch of the journey back to Amrita's house. She felt a pang of envy again, leaving Jen and Otto. They'd have the rest of the evening, the night, and all of the following day to reconnect and share their respective travellers' tales.

She drove the last stretch of the journey in silence. The moon was large and low now, lingering above the horizon, visible only in moments through gaps in the trees.

'Are you okay, Charlie?' Amrita said, placing her hand lightly on Charlotte's arm.

'Sure, yes. A bit tired.' She was grateful for her friend's concern. 'The whole Otto and Jack thing is very weird. I'm beginning to think it wasn't a good idea, this pretending with Otto. I don't think Jack's fooled and I feel very uncomfortable lying – and involving everyone else in a lie. It seems pretty childish.'

'Oh, I'm sorry.' Amrita withdrew her hand.

Remembering this deception was Amrita's idea, Charlotte quickly backtracked.

'It's not your fault, you don't need to apologise. It was a great idea and I'm sure it would have worked on anyone else. But Jack though – Jack is weird.'

After a few quiet moments Amrita said: 'Would you like me to tell my father what's been going on, that Jack's stalking you? If we explain to him, I'm sure he'd dismiss Jack and make him leave. My dad's very fond of you. He wouldn't allow anyone to harass you. He takes his responsibility for you very seriously.'

Charlotte sighed, feeling guilty again: for harbouring such bad thoughts about Jack (was she inventing it, making far too much of the situation?) and for embroiling Otto, Amrita and potentially Amrita's father, when he had so many more important things to be dealing with.

'No,' she said. 'No, don't worry about it. I can handle Jack and I don't want to worry your dad. Let's see what happens. Maybe Jack'll back off now Otto's here.'

It was gone midnight when they parked up outside the house. Jaideep was still awake, at his desk, working late. He looked up and smiled at the girls, glad to see them safely home, but worry and fatigue were evident in his face. He asked them if they'd enjoyed themselves, and Amrita passed on the greeting from the restaurant owner. She and Charlotte retired to bed, but Jaideep remained where he was, head bowed over his papers, gently illuminated by the glow from the screen of his laptop.

Charlotte

The alarm clock bleeped. Charlotte's head was sleep-heavy; she was unable to work out where she was. Had she been dreaming about home? She felt a weight of anxiety, a physical pressure in her chest: the train accident, the dead tiger, the situation with Jack. Worries turned over in her mind. She lay on her back and stared at the ceiling, where a fan had whirred all night long, to keep them cool and ward away mosquitoes.

In the other bed, Amrita sighed and stretched. She looked over at Charlotte and smiled, her face soft and sleepy.

'Are you okay? Did you sleep well?' Amrita said.

'Yes, I did. I couldn't think where I was when I woke up.' Charlotte sat up in bed and rubbed her eyes. The bruising on her face hadn't entirely gone and the most damaged knee was still a little stiff first thing.

They got up, showered and dressed, then she and Amrita sat at the table to eat breakfast. Prina was preparing them all packed lunches of rice, dahl, chapattis and fresh fruit, stored in natty little foil containers.

Jaideep had already left for work. Perhaps he hadn't slept at all. Prina was outwardly serene but Charlotte wondered how worried she must be about the situation at the tiger sanctuary. It was business as usual for Charlotte today, and Amrita had volunteered to help too. Amrita would be starting at university in August, at the beginning of the new academic year. In the meantime she helped her mother at home, made preparations for her undergraduate studies, helped out at a local school and, from time to time, stepped in for some of the routine work at the sanctuary. Charlotte's presence had made this a much more attractive proposition and the two young women had often worked together over these last weeks.

Charlotte and Amrita set off for the reserve office in the pick-up in the early morning cool. A gaggle of tourists stood outside the office, waiting to be collected in one of the sanctuary jeeps and taken on a tour: middle-aged Americans mostly, and a few young European backpackers who maintained a studied distance from the older Americans. When the lodges were fully occupied – as they were now – the sanctuary operated safari tours in the early morning and again at evening, when the light began to fade. It wasn't often the tourists spotted a tiger, but most returned with photographs of wild elephants, deer, peacocks and parakeets. Had they heard about the poaching incident, Charlotte wondered? The sanctuary relied on tourists for income, as did the local people employed in running the lodges, taxi drivers, restaurateurs, and all those who sold tea, refreshments, regional crafts and all the rest to the foreign visitors. If the sanctuary didn't receive its funding, if the poaching continued, if Jaideep lost his job – what would that do for its reputation? And if the tigers all disappeared, and they couldn't offer tourists even the possibility of a glimpse of one – how many would still come? Quite apart, of course, from the greatest loss of all, the slow vanishing of tigers from India's diminished wilds . . .

'Charlotte . . . Charlotte?' Amrita tapped her upper arm. 'What are you thinking about?'

Charlotte shook her head. 'Nothing.' She climbed out of the pick-up and the two women headed into the reserve office to find out their duties for the day.

Charlotte's heart sank when she saw Jack, all ready and waiting.

Jaideep was ensconced in his office, talking loudly down the phone, but he gesticulated to one of his wardens to deal with his young volunteers.

'Hey, Jack,' Charlotte said in a flat voice, forcing herself to make eye contact.

Jack looked remarkably fresh and chipper, his clothes clean, his hair tied back in a ponytail. He grinned, looking open and boyish, the sinister intensity from the evening before seemingly vanished.

'Hey, Charlie, Amrita.' He nodded. 'We're going to be working together today.' He sounded very pleased about the idea and the tone of his voice suggested they should be too.

The warden came over. 'I'd like you to check the camera traps,' he said. 'Take one of the jeeps. Here's the map.'

That was it. He walked off again, leaving Jack with a map in his hand.

Charlotte raised her eyebrows. 'This is a big job,' she said.

Amrita peered into her father's office. 'They're all so busy – too much to deal with on top of the tourist safaris.'

Jack peered at the map. 'You know what we have to do?'

Charlotte nodded. 'In theory, yes. I accompanied Jaideep on the same job a week ago. There are only five cameras, but they're scattered all over the sanctuary and hard to find if you don't know the spot exactly.'

Jack turned the map around. It was old, badly creased, stained with dirt and fingerprints – as well as various pencil scribbles and crossings out – making it hard to work out where the current camera sites were.

They took one of the reserve jeeps, Charlotte in the driving seat, and set off for the site of the first camera trap. This, along with the recording of the tiger pugmarks, was a key tool in keeping track of the number of tigers living on the reserve. After half an hour's driving, Charlotte parked up just off the dirt track and the three set off on foot into the trees. The camera wasn't too hard to

111

find, secured to a tree by a barely discernible animal path leading to a watering hole – a low puddle cradled in the roots of three vast trees, choked with fallen leaves. The water was black in the shade but smelled oddly sweet: insects in a cloud over the tiny pool, a small monkey loping away as they drew near, tail curling like a question mark. Charlotte remembered the barrel of red plastic monkeys she played with as a child, when you looped tails and arms together to make a monkey chain.

'There it is,' she said, drawing back a spray of leaves to reveal the photographic contraption fastened to the tree. It wasn't hard to find; she remembered it from the visit the previous week.

'How does it work?' Jack squatted to look at the camera more closely.

'An infrared beam across the path – that triggers the shutter. The batteries are pretty good – they last about four weeks,' Charlotte said.

She took the camera down and examined it. A picture had been taken but no animal was visible in the shot. She replaced it, checked the batteries were still functioning and recorded the results in a notebook.

'We only check them once a week because, obviously, you don't want to disturb the area too much or the animals will be scared away.'

'Did you get any tiger pictures last time?' Jack asked.

'No. One picture of a monkey's rear end, that was it.' Charlotte was careful to keep her dialogue with Jack neutral, and avoided making eye contact too much. She stood up, brushed off the dry dirt from her jeans, ensured the camera was hidden again and began the walk back to the jeep.

'We need more cameras,' Amrita said. 'They're very expensive. We had funding from a conservation charity for these, but if World Wildlife respond to this new application there'll be money for more.'

It took several hours to locate and check the next three cameras.

112

They stopped after the third to eat lunch, sitting beneath a solitary tree in a sea of long, yellow grass. Jack didn't have any food so Charlotte and Amrita shared what they had, which was plenty. They swigged water from plastic bottles. None of them had been particularly talkative in the morning. They drove and walked in silence much of the time, occasionally pointing out some interesting feature in the landscape. The place seemed to soak into them, the great trees, the silence, the heat pouring from the deep-blue sky. Few people around – a couple of vehicles on one of the roads passing through the reserve, three young girls in saris of amber and red carrying huge, neat bundles of sticks for firewood.

Jack neither said nor did anything out of the ordinary and, preoccupied by the drive and the work in hand, Charlotte managed to stop feeling so uncomfortable in his presence. Perhaps he'd got the message now. He was relaxed, interested and helpful and although they didn't find any tiger pictures in the camera traps, he actually proved to be useful to have around, navigating from the tatty map and finding paths that eluded Charlotte and Amrita.

The final camera was set up beside another, larger, watering hole, where a stream opened into a deep pool surrounded by rough grey boulders. Lemon and pale-green parakeets were sipping water from the stream as the threesome arrived, but they flew up and away, into the trees. Charlotte sighed with pleasure. It was a beautiful place.

Amrita located the camera, on a tree close to the pool's edge. She made some exclamation and said something in Tamil, excitement in her voice. Then, in English: 'Charlie – we have something!'

'What – a tiger? There's a picture?'

'I think! Come and see.'

Charlotte ran over. Amrita frowned, clicked buttons on the back of the camera and peered at the little screen.

'There – yes! It's a little hard to see. Look!' She passed it to Charlotte. It was difficult to make out because, in the partial shade, the viewing screen wasn't bright – but nonetheless, they had a photograph of a tiger. Crouching over the water, massive, limber, with its gorgeous stripped hide, painted face and long, white whiskers the animal was unmistakable.

'My god,' Charlotte breathed, peering at the picture. It was, so far, the closest she'd come to seeing a tiger at the sanctuary. This creature had lapped the water, in the clearing where she now stood, some time in the last seven days. The time and date of the picture would be recorded in the camera.

Jack leaned over her shoulder to take a look. Charlotte passed him the camera.

'Fantastic,' he said. 'How about that? We've got one.'

They shared a moment of excitement and celebration, grinning like fools all three, thrilled by the discovery.

'We have to take the camera back and download the picture,' Amrita said. But none of them moved right away, too enchanted by the moment to want to leave. The clearing was a cool chapel, under vaults of leaves and branches, outside of which the afternoon sun was blazing. Here in the forest it was perfectly peaceful, the air sweet, the grass a vivid green at the fringes of the pool. A handful of golden leaves swirled slowly on the surface of the water, carried by an unseen current. Amrita sat on the ground, leaning her back against the tree, staring at the picture of the tiger. Charlotte sat beside her. Jack stood up and mooched away, hands in his pockets.

'Fabulous, isn't it?' Charlotte said. 'How could anyone kill one?'

'Terrifying too,' Amrita said. 'Look at the size of it. Can you imagine what it would be like if one attacked you? Its paws are bigger than my face. I wouldn't stand a chance.'

They gazed at the photograph again.

'Nothing like that in England,' Charlotte said.

'No, the English felled their forests and killed off all the remarkable animals – the wolves and bears and wild boar,' Amrita said.

Charlotte didn't answer. Amrita was correct of course. Amrita was intrigued by the idea of England but usually she idealised it in the same way Jen had idealised India. Jen's India had always been an exotic fairy tale, a land of deserts and jungles, of peacocks and marble palaces, of gods and pilgrims . . . which of course it was. Those things were still present; but India was so much more modern, gritty, complex, dynamic, more *real*. Amrita's fairy tale England was the land of Beatrix Potter and Jane Austen, authors of books Amrita had devoured as a child and teenager: an elegant, rural England with rose-covered cottages and grand country houses. Oh yes she knew twenty-first-century England wasn't really like that, but still, Charlotte sensed, it was the vision that lingered in Amrita's heart and mind.

'We did, you're right,' Charlotte said, feeling guilty, as though her Englishness meant that she was personally responsible for the extermination of those historic wolves, bears and boars.

She and Amrita had much in common. They were both hard-working and ambitious. She'd seen Amrita studying, her meticulous notes, the ordered files and books. Beneath Amrita's bubbly good nature was a steely determination to succeed, and although they'd become great friends and enjoyed each other's company immensely, there remained an edge of competition between them. Like now, Amrita reminding Charlotte that India was not a backward country because poachers were killing its tigers – after all, the British had exterminated all their major predators too.

'We don't really have any proper wilderness in Britain any more. Well, I suppose the highlands of Scotland are pretty wild, but really, everywhere in England is owned, parcelled up, culti-vated or managed in some way,' Charlotte said.

'Is that what you were looking for, coming to India?' Amrita said.

'I've told you, it was Jen who inspired me to come. Once I started checking it out, what India was like, then I wanted to travel here for a whole variety of reasons; I wanted to know what it would be like living in an entirely different culture; I thought my volunteer work would mean I was making a difference, even a small one; and, of course, I thought the experience would be good for my career. Jobs in development and conservation are hard to come by. I'll need a great CV.'

Amrita didn't answer. Instead she gazed at her feet in their sandals, with ten perfectly painted golden toenails. She wriggled her toes.

'Still, CVs to one side, this tiger photo is something else,' she said.

Charlotte looked over her shoulder at the little picture displayed on the back of the camera.

'Yes. Yes it is. I know it sounds stupid, but till now, it was almost as though the tigers didn't really exist, except in our imaginations. I mean, the carcass I saw didn't look like a tiger. It was just horrible and monstrous. But now – well. The photo – look how real it is.'

A faint splash: Charlotte and Amrita looked up. Ripples on the dark surface of the pool radiated from a point on the far side. Two seconds later Jack's head burst from the water. He gasped, struggling with the cold, flailed his arms about, treading water. Amrita laughed. She scrambled to her feet to see him better.

'Is it cold?' she called out.

'A little,' Jack admitted. 'Fresh, I'd say. Very fresh.' He swam away, on his back, pulling himself through the water with long strokes of his arms.

Charlotte stood up more slowly, holding back. She didn't want to indicate any kind of interest in Jack. He didn't look at her either, keeping his attention fixed on Amrita.

'Why don't you come in?' he teased.

'Oh no.' Amrita shook her head, laughing with embarrassment. 'Oh I couldn't do that, no.' She took a couple of steps back, as though to emphasise how far she was from peeling off her clothes and jumping into the river. Jack looked very natural and happy in the water. His body, what you could see of it in the shadowed

116

water, was narrow and white. Was he entirely naked? Perish the thought. His face was relaxed, smiling, wet hair plastered back on his head.

Amrita giggled again, eyes shining, covering her mouth with her hand. She seemed rather impressed. Had she forgotten how Jack had been hounding Charlotte? Probably she had no idea just how uncomfortable Jack had made Charlotte. She had only seen the situation from the outside, thought Jack was indulging in some unwanted flirting and didn't have any real understanding of just how intent and manipulative he could be. Was this manly diving into the wild waters another way to impress Charlotte? To tempt her into admiring him? Or perhaps Charlotte was being far too paranoid; Jack had behaved impeccably all day. He been rather useful, helping check the cameras.

Jack surface-dived, flicking his feet in the air so drops of water sparkled in a ray of sunlight. He disappeared for several long seconds before emerging again. For a fleeting moment his gaze locked with Charlotte's and she realised, to her chagrin, that he knew she had been thinking about him. With a scowl of annoyance she turned away from Jack and the river, not wanting to honour him with another moment's attention.

'We'd better head back,' she said to Amrita. 'It's getting late and we've a long drive. I want to see what this picture looks like on a big screen.'

She headed back to the jeep, Amrita a few paces behind her. Jack appeared five minutes later, still dripping. He jumped nimbly into the back, water soaking through his clothes. Amrita looked at him again and grinned. 'You'll get cold,' she said.

Jack shook his head. 'I'll dry off soon enough.' He looked cheeky and boyish, river water sliding from his hair onto his T-shirt.

The delivery of the camera and its precious photograph created some much-needed excitement at the reserve office. Charlotte hooked the camera to a laptop and Jaideep broke off from a phone conversation to come and see the picture, so much more spectacular on the bigger screen. The tiger, a striped, gilded orange, stooped over the water. Its heavy body, the very posture it adopted, revealed its weight and strength, the power contained within the animal. No wonder people coveted its hide, Charlotte thought. Was there anything like it? Bold and majestic, the regal colours and slashes of black declared ferocity and grandeur.

One of the other wardens arrived, then a couple of the tourists, readying themselves for an evening safari. They all stared at the picture on the screen. Jaideep and the warden began talking urgently in Tamil. They were trying to assess the age and gender of the tiger, wondering if they'd seen this individual before or if this was a first sighting. Jaideep asked the three young volunteers questions about the site. Had they seen any pugmarks?

The tourists were thrilled, naturally. They were all desperate to see a tiger – it would be the highlight of their holidays. Could Jaideep take them to the area where the photograph had been taken? Jaideep explained that the situation of the cameras was only revealed to people working for the reserve, for the protection of the tigers. They couldn't afford to let the information leak out to poachers.

That evening, Charlotte drove the old pick-up to the lodge where Otto and Jen were staying. What had they been up to all day? she wondered. Amrita stayed at home – to study, she said, though Charlotte suspected Amrita was diplomatically giving her a little private time with her friends.

All day Charlotte had avoided thinking of Otto too much. It hadn't been easy. She recalled how different Jen had looked the previous evening, as though some of her softness and naivety had worn away, and how mature and attractive she was as a result. Of course Jen was beautiful – much more so than Charlotte. Jen's quirky, pretty face and outlandish, arty outfits had always attracted attention. Would Otto like this new Jen? Would the increase in her self-assurance rekindle his romantic interest?

As she drove to the lodge, Charlotte shook her head to dislodge the thought. She wished she could have spent the day with Otto – but then, she'd not have harvested the photograph of the tiger, and she would remember that for the rest of her life. And in any case, if Jen and Otto did get back together, what could she do about it? They were both friends, both people she loved. Her emotions warred with one another, the selfish wish for the long-awaited love of Otto, a painful spasm of jealousy, and perhaps most hurtful of all, the gleam of hope that the young man she'd loved for so long might finally have noticed his feelings for her weren't limited to friendship.

The sun was sinking over the trees as Charlotte halted the pick-up outside the lodge. A single banner of cloud was flung up high, a soft, grainy pink. She hopped down and made her way to the front veranda.

'Jen? Otto? Anyone home?' The place seemed deserted at first and Charlotte wondered, with a pang, if they'd forgotten she was coming, if they'd gone out without her.

'Charlie?' Otto stepped out, rubbing his blond hair with a towel. 'Sorry, I was having a wash. Didn't hear you.'

He looked a little uneasy.

'Where's Jen?'

Otto shrugged. 'Not sure. Haven't seen her all day. She went out this morning. Said she was catching a bus into town for something or other. Should be back soon.'

They both stood looking at one another, neither knowing what to say. It had never been like this before. They'd been friends for more than ten years, since primary school. The atmosphere between them had always been so easy and natural.

'So. What have you been up to today?' Charlie said brightly.

'Oh, nothing much. Went for a walk. Slept a lot. Read. You know. What about you?'

'Oh!' For a moment she'd forgotten about the tiger. 'We caught a tiger in a camera trap! We've got a picture – the first I've seen.'

Otto gestured to one of the rough wooden chairs on the veranda and as he finished rubbing his hair with his towel, Charlotte recounted the tale of the day's events. In the excitement, she forgot the unsettling nervousness, and the conversation between them became natural again, as it always had been.

'So this guy, Jack, did he give you any more hassle? Has he swallowed this story, about you and me being together?'

Charlotte shook her head. Jack hadn't hassled her at all that day. She'd felt manipulated by the river-pool, but quite possibly she'd dreamed that up herself. On the face of it, Jack had neither said nor done anything wrong. Even Amrita had started to think he was fun.

'He was fine,' she said. 'Maybe he's got the message.'

'Great,' Otto said. 'So we can forget about him, hmmm? What would you like to do this evening? Do you know somewhere we can eat? I'm starving.'

Charlotte smiled. 'As it happens, I've asked the lodge caterers to bring us something. I've ordered a meal, only they won't bring it for another hour. Enough for three. D'you fancy taking a walk first, before it gets too dark?'

A cool, sweet breeze freshened the air as they wandered, single-file, through the tall, golden grass away from the lodge. Otto walked in front, unwittingly giving Charlotte an opportunity to admire him, his height, the strong bones of his shapely shoulders and arms, even the slight ungainliness, as though Otto still wasn't entirely accustomed to living in this new man's body. He was pale despite these weeks in India, too fair to tan. He was so known, so familiar, but the sight of him still gave her a jolt of pleasure, just the shape of him, the way he moved through the tall grass, even the fact that he was oblivious to the fact that she was gazing at him so longingly. Or was he? Could he feel her attention, because he stopped, half turned and looked back at her. He didn't say anything, just smiled, waiting for her to catch up.

'Charlie, you okay?'

'Sure. Of course. Why shouldn't I be?' She spoke clumsily and blushed, feeling the heat rise in her face.

Otto didn't answer, only turned his face to one side as though he didn't know what to say. Then he smiled, shrugged and continued to walk, Charlotte close behind him.

They reached a fringe of trees, passed briefly into the shade and then out again into a wider clearing. Here the land dropped away into a wide, gentle bowl. Otto halted, touching Charlotte's arm.

'Look – over there,' he said softly.

Charlotte scanned the landscape. There, amid the golden grass – six deer, a darker gold than the grass and spotted with white. One raised its delicate head and looked towards them.

'D'you think it's seen us?' Otto whispered.

'Scented us perhaps.'

The deer didn't seem overly alarmed. It stared a moment or two then continued to browse. Charlotte sat down on the hard, dry ground, still watching the deer. Otto dropped down beside her. The declining sun infused the scene with a deeper, older gold, gilding the grass, the deer, the edges of the distant trees. Charlotte took a deep, slow breath, wanting to absorb the scene, to take it inside herself so she would never forget it. The sun's warmth played on her skin. The faintest of breezes touched her face. Beyond them, the deer grazing as they might have grazed ten thousand years ago, a million years ago – a scene from time immemorial. A wave of happiness washed through Charlotte, overwhelming, to be here, and now: a sense of physical and emotional well-being. She could think of nowhere else she would rather be, nothing she would prefer to be doing. She turned to Otto, smiling, wanting to connect with him, to know if he too was in this place.

121

His face was gilded too, in the light from the low sun. He sensed her attention and looked away from the deer towards Charlotte.

'Isn't it great?' he said. The words seemed clumsy. He grinned and shook his head.

'I know what you mean,' Charlotte said, reaching out her hand to touch him gently on the arm. 'Isn't it strange where life takes you? This moment – how could we ever have imagined it, before it happened? And yet it's so perfect, as though everything has come together, all the parts of who I am, and they're focused, into this one place.'

She paused, then said: 'You know, most of the time I feel like I'm living in a kind of chaos, and I'm making everything up as I go along, trying to make a shape of it. Like my life is a piece of string that is constantly fraying and coming apart, and that all my energy is spent trying to keep it intact.'

Otto looked at her wonderingly. 'Your life is chaos? But you're the most organised and together person I know. You always seem so calm.'

Charlotte laughed and shook her head. 'Only from the outside.'

Otto was quiet for a few seconds, then said, in a little boy's voice: 'Do you think it is only when you're young, that you have these wonderful moments? Do you think the intensity fades?'

Charlotte considered. How could she know the answer? She suspected – feared – that he was right: that age and time and the routines of life wore away your capacity for these occasional moments of bliss and brilliance. What a cold thought; well, she was never going to let that happen. Never.

'I won't let it fade,' she said. 'I won't forget it, what it's like.' She thought about her parents, how hard they worked, the occasional meals with friends, her father having a few glasses of wine each evening and her worries he drank too much. Did he have times like this, when the sheer beauty of a moment filled his heart and mind?

It was hard to imagine. Perhaps that was why you aged and died; it was a fading away as you lost, or forgot, your ability to be awake, to receive and be amazed, even in these isolated moments.

The deer had moved away. The sun plunged beneath the horizon. Charlotte stood up, the golden time had passed and worries crowded back into her mind. They'd better get back to the lodge in time for their dinner, and Jen. Behind that the bigger concerns, the tiger poachers and the threat to the sanctuary's vital funding application. Otto stood up too, and they set off home in the fading light. Charlotte walked close beside Otto, finding herself gravitating towards him, into contact with him, wishing she could take his hand or feel his arm over her shoulders and knowing that without the excuse of the pretend-relationship for Jack's benefit she couldn't, in a million years, make the move. She and Otto had been friends for too long. One false move, one unwanted declaration of more than friendly affection, and she could alter and damage that long-cherished friendship forever.

The journey back seemed shorter. Jen was sitting on the veranda, a bottle of water in her hand. She stood up and waved when she saw them approach.

'Hurry up! Food's arrived,' she said. 'A man dropped by with a feast for us. He said you'd ordered it.'

The meal was carefully packed in a box, containers of steaming rice, lentils and spicy sauces, chapattis carefully folded, pots of yoghurt, sticky sweets wrapped in paper. Otto, Jen and Charlotte laid out the meal on a table, on the veranda, and they dined outside as the last light died and the stars unrolled across the sky.

Otto

Otto lay in bed, belly pleasantly full, listening to the thrum of insects beyond the wall of the lodge. A mosquito net hung around the bed, ghostly in the darkness. Just as well he had it – Otto could hear the irritating whine of numerous mosquitoes in the room beyond the net, making his flesh quiver. He'd been so badly bitten in Goa.

The room was tremendously hot, even at night. The wooden lodge seemed to trap the heat, like an oven, and the rough walls provided perfect accommodation for all sorts of insects. No wonder this place was rarely occupied. He found it hard to imagine many of the paying tourists would tolerate it for long. And no phone signal. He couldn't even while away the time texting people.

Jen was in the bed on the other side of the room. How strange it had been to see her again. She looked so different – and not just the hair colour. It was as though some of her native softness had been baked away in the Indian heat, creating a more honed, concentrated Jen, someone a little less diffuse, someone tougher: as though she'd finally come into focus. Away from home, fending for herself, she'd had to adapt. Did he like this new version? Yes and no. At the moment, in this foreign land, he relied on his friends to be constant. They were all he had to hold on to.

He turned over onto his back, body sweating. They'd left the door open in the vain hope of encouraging air circulation and he could see the oblique oblong of the doorway, containing a view of the blue-black sky and its smattering of stars. It had been a strange day: he'd slept in, after the meal and beer at the restaurant. He and Jen had walked the fifteen minutes to the reserve office, and bought a breakfast of fruit and yoghurt from a hut, as well as cups of very sweet, spiced, milky tea from a hut next to the road. They talked about their recent adventures, but all didn't seem as it was. He sensed a slight distance between them. Was that because of this Kumar? he wondered. Jen mentioned that she'd travelled to Madurai with him. Were they an item then? For some reason he was reluctant to ask. Jen had always seemed vulnerable – someone he might take care of. Perhaps that had been part of her appeal.

After breakfast Jen announced she was taking a bus into town. She didn't tell him what she wanted to do, but something about the tone of her voice suggested she intended to go alone. Otto waved her off, bought another tea and ended up enjoying a long conversation with the three men working in the food hut. It possessed something of the air of an alchemist's laboratory, with huge silver kettles, bundles of cinnamon and a roaring stove. And the men, short of customers, seemed glad of a distraction. When he bored of the chat, Otto wandered back to the lodge and picked up his novel. He'd finished the Irvine Welsh and was back on *War and Peace*, all these weeks later. Two thirds of the way through: he enjoyed the battle scenes but found all the genteel chit-chat a bit slow.

The afternoon stretched out. He found himself at a bit of a loss – bored even. Neither the odd conversation with Jen nor the bantering with the locals had fed a little hunger he felt inside. He was restless, wanting something. What was it exactly? He tried to identify the source of this nagging need. These last weeks, staying in Mumbai and then moving down to Tamil Nadu, he'd met dozens of new people, both Indians and fellow foreign travellers, had all sorts of variously interesting conversations, seen the highs and lows of the city, the glory of the Indian landscape . . . and now?

He wanted to be with someone who knew him, with whom he shared a more intimate connection, who would listen seriously, giving him attention; someone with whom he could be, simply, himself. He was waiting, of course, to see Charlotte.

It had been strange, at the restaurant, pretending to be her boyfriend. He'd had plenty of girlfriends over the last two years so of course he knew what to do, all the expected behaviour. But with Charlotte this had seemed so clumsy. He'd felt her cringe. Still, this had scared off the creepy Jack guy, so the effort had been worth it. Had Charlotte ever had a boyfriend? Why had this never even crossed his mind before? That was absurd! How self-absorbed he must have been, not to have considered it. But surely yes, she could hardly have got to eighteen without any romance. But she'd never mentioned anyone, and surely she would have done. He'd bored her often enough with tales of his latest crushes. She was so focused on work, though, perhaps she'd sworn off boyfriends in order to get the grades she wanted. Charlie was so organised, so determined and competent. It could be intimidating. Sometimes he'd felt like a bumbling boy in her company.

At the same time . . . no-one knew him better. They could talk for hours, and he enjoyed how she stretched and challenged him, the laughs they had and the knowledge that she gave him her complete and serious attention, that she valued him. He could be himself, say what he felt, and know he would be accepted.

War and Peace lay, face down, on the rough floor of the veranda. He couldn't concentrate on reading. The afternoon drifted past. He went to the cubicle at the back of the lodge to wash, tired of the heat, and tipped cups full of cold water over his head. He was towelling his hair dry when he heard the pick-up arrive, so he stepped outside to meet Charlotte.

She looked different too, with a beautiful golden tan and a sensuousness he hadn't noticed before – or perhaps only noticed once, that night he'd seen Mark the reporter flirting with her. And then, sitting at the edge of the clearing, watching the spotted deer in a shared moment of happiness, she'd looked beautiful – and Otto had wondered: was it possible? Was he falling for her, after all this time?

Now, lying in bed beneath the mosquito nets, listening to the insects whine, aware of Jen similarly stifled by the heat on the other side of the room, Otto found it impossible to sleep. His thoughts revolved around Charlotte. What was going on with him? He'd never thought of her in this way before. He'd always fallen for girls he didn't know very well: it had always been the unknown that had attracted him, the mystery a pretty girl presented, wanting to find out what she was like, to unwrap her, mentally as well, of course, as physically.

Was it just this exotic new setting, casting Charlotte into a new light? Was her attraction just a peculiar form of homesickness? Oh how dangerous it was, to fall for a friend. He couldn't imagine that she'd feel the same way about him. Charlie had such a touch-me-not air about her. She didn't flirt (except, of course, that time with Mark the reporter . . . he felt, belatedly, the sting of jealousy to think of it) and how could he possible make any kind of move without potentially damaging their friendship? She was so important to him, how could he take that risk?

Except that, in the late sun, looking over the lake of grass at the burnished deer, he'd felt such a longing to take her into his arms.

He sighed and turned over again, onto his stomach, put his chin on his arms and stared at the stars through the open door.

'Otto?' Jen's voice, low in the quiet room. 'Are you awake?'

'Yes. I can't sleep. It's too hot.'

'Neither can I.' She hesitated for a moment then said: 'Can I come over?'

'Sure. Bring a drink.' He heard Jen get up and pad barefoot to the tiny, antique fridge in the corner of the room. She ducked under the mosquito net and sat on the bed beside him, the two of them like campers in a tent, and held out a bottle of beer. It was hard to see her clearly in the faint light. Her hennaed hair fell over her shoulders in rough, uncombed clumps. She wore a pair of pale pyjamas, and from time to time her bangles and necklaces gleamed in the dark.

Otto sat up and tucked a pillow behind his back so he could lean against the rough wall. He took the bottle and pressed it against his cheek, enjoying the shock of the cold against his skin.

'So, Jen,' he said. 'Here we are.'

When he and Jen got together last summer, things hadn't worked out and she'd ended it – fortunately before things got too serious. They had retrieved their friendship instead.

'You seem very different,' Otto said.

Jen raised her face. 'I'm not different really. I've just, well . . .'

'Evolved?'

'Yes, evolved. I stepped out by myself, and once you realise you can do it, it's like you own yourself. D'you know what I mean?'

'I guess.' He smiled. 'Actually it's great to see you like this. You always looked like you were scared of everything. Even food – all your allergies. But you were eating like a horse this evening.'

'I still have to be careful, but yes. It's much better than it was at home.' She hesitated for a moment, then said: 'What brought you here? I thought you headed back to Mumbai.'

'I did. Then I saw Charlie on the telly, and the news about the train accident, and then this business with Jack freaking her out. I wanted to come and see her, make sure she was okay.'

Did she smile, in the dark? Hard to say.

'What about you?' he said. 'What brought you back to us?'

That evening, over the meal, they'd shared their adventures of the last few weeks and Jen had told them she'd finally tired of the island. Its time, for her, was over. She had to get out into the world again.

'I had a dream,' she said.

'Ah, a dream. Of course!' Otto teased. Jen lived in a world of dreams and visions. She saw spirits, apparently. While Otto didn't believe in the literal truth of spirits and visions, he was happy to go along with the idea. It was a part of Jen, her strangeness, her appeal. He listened, treated her gently, believed in her faith in this unseen world. 'What did you dream?'

'About a tiger. It was hunted and killed. The dream was a message for me, to come here and help Charlie.'

'So we are both here to help her,' Otto mused. 'All together again.'

'Yes. And it's good. Very good.' She reached out her arms for a hug and Otto responded. Jen was right. After this time apart, he appreciated his friends all the more. For one mad moment he considered telling her about his new feelings for Charlotte – and asking her advice. The urge was strong, to confide in someone about this peculiar inner tumult. But he reined it in. Too dangerous. Too much to lose, when the three of them were all together again.

Charlotte

The meeting began at eleven. The room was sweltering, despite the best efforts of the air conditioning in the sanctuary's conference room. Three officials from World Wildlife were sitting on one side of the table, three trustees of the Golden Tiger Reserve on the other. Jaideep had the seat at the end of the table. Several other people were sitting in the room, on the periphery: World Wildlife support staff, other wardens from the sanctuary, Amrita and Charlotte herself.

The World Wildlife people had arrived by taxi that morning, having spent the night in town. Discussions were scheduled for two days – to include a tour of the reserve and a public meeting with local people. A decision on the grant application would follow within a week.

The officials and their staff had been welcomed with garlands of flowers. The offices had been tided and cleaned the night before to make the best impression. A gala breakfast was served, of rice porridge, *idlis*, chapattis and *sambar*, a kind of vegetable stew. In honour of the American World Wildlife official, the cooks had prepared waffles, fresh orange juice and fried eggs. A huge silver pot dispensed coffee as thick and black as oil. Jack helped to serve.

Charlotte was hungry; she and Amrita tucked into the breakfast with enthusiasm, though the coffee set her brain buzzing. She noticed that Jaideep, whose reserve uniform was evidently clean and pressed, didn't eat anything but constantly checked up on everybody else, making sure the officials had what they wanted, that papers were in order. She could see how nervous he was, and Amrita, consequently, nervous on his behalf.

The meeting began with a PowerPoint presentation about the reserve, its history and the current status of its wildlife. Unusually, it wasn't a national park but a once privately-owned estate, now run by trustees. Smaller than India's national parks, it faced different challenges – such as attracting funding. Jaideep addressed the meeting in English; one of the other World Wildlife officials was French, the other Indian but not a speaker of Tamil so English was the common language.

A host of photographs – of the forest, its ancient hardwood trees, the teak, rosewood and sandalwood, the stands of bamboo, and pictures of the resident wildlife, elephants, deer, leopards and, of course, the tiger. The photograph they had just retrieved from the camera trap was the last to be shown. How spectacular it looked, blown up on the screen, the black and marmalade tiger crouching over the water in all its massive splendour.

Charlotte heard the collective intake of breath when the picture bloomed on the screen. 'Beautiful,' someone whispered. A momentary restlessness passed through the meeting, people shifting in their seats, moving to take a better look.

Jaideep left the picture on the screen, as a kind of presiding deity, as he moved on to talk about the 'challenges' facing the sanctuary. No avoiding this one: both the train accident and the latest poaching incident had been covered in the press. Neither put Jaideep and the sanctuary management in a great light.

'Illegal logging of hardwood trees, unauthorised stone quarrying and the poaching of tigers and other wildlife pose the most significant threats to our sanctuary,' he said, in a low, sober voice. He paused for a moment, as they considered again the photograph of the tiger, shining bright against the black water and the dusky forest. Then the picture snapped off – and was replaced by an aerial photograph of the train, sprawled over the embankment. From this vantage point, the collapse of the embankment at the front of the train, and the oval scar created by the quarrying, were clearly visible. So too were people, passengers and rescuers, gathered about the wreckage of the train.

Charlotte shuddered. The crash had only been a few days before but in her memory it had the quality of a bad dream – something terrible but unreal. Now the bald spectacle of the accident was a shock. The experience was still within her, but the emotional memories had been packed away. The picture conjured up a succession of painful feelings. A hundred miles away, Jaideep was talking about stone quarrying and operations proceeding without the necessary licences, the difficulty of halting a quarrying operation once it was underway – but Charlotte couldn't focus on the words. The crash replayed itself in her mind, the moment of the impact, the bodies thrown around in the carriage, the minutes she spent trapped beneath the body of the injured businessman. She broke out in a sweat, closed her eyes and took a deep breath.

'Charlie, what's the matter?' Amrita whispered.

Charlotte shook her head, but her heartbeat pounded in her ears and she felt sick.

'Sorry – have to get some fresh air,' she said, rising from her seat. She tried to be quiet but everyone – including the World Wildlife people – turned to look as she shuffled out of the room. Jaideep looked annoyed, pausing in the delivery of his speech. Charlotte pulled the door open and escaped into the cooler corridor beyond. She half ran to the reception area and out of the door into the sunshine. Although it was still hot, the air seemed easier to breathe outside of the stifling conference room.

Charlotte sat on a patch of dry grass outside the offices, head pounding, and thought she might be sick. She pressed the palms of her hands against her face, pushing the memories of the crash to one side, willing herself to be strong. How embarrassing, this admission of weakness, and at Jaideep's most important meeting! Guilt needled, and embarrassment, for having bolted out of the room.

'Charlie, you okay?'

Jack, sitting beside her. The last thing she needed right now. She didn't want his sympathy or his help. She didn't want him to know anything about her thoughts or feelings.

'Sure, I'm fine,' she said. 'Too hot in there.'

Jack scrutinised her. 'You don't look great.'

'Thanks.'

'Not well, I mean.' He jumped to his feet, disappeared for a minute, then returned with a plastic bottle of water.

'Thanks,' she said, grateful despite herself. She took several mouthfuls. The nausea receded.

'What happened?'

'I told you, the heat.'

Jack looked at her sideways, a quizzical expression on his face. He knew she was lying.

'Okay,' she said reluctantly. 'They showed a picture of the train crash. It brought everything back. I just felt – well, I had to get out.'

Jack didn't speak for a moment. In fact, he moved slightly away from her and twiddled with a piece of grass. Then he said: 'You can always talk to me about this. No-one else will truly understand. No-one. They weren't there – and I was. Do you hear what I'm saying? I'm the only one who knows what you saw, what you felt. It can never be undone. You will never forget it nor be the same again. That's what I meant, when I said the crash bound us together.'

Charlotte gave him quick glance. Jack wasn't looking at her, focusing instead on the stem of grass between his fingers. He didn't sound so creepy now, only very serious and intense. And in a way, she could see that what he said was true. No-one else would understand.

Still without looking at her, Jack rose to his feet. 'You know where to find me.' And he walked away, back into the offices, and his duties.

Charlotte remained where she was, sipping the water. She wondered how the meeting was proceeding. The World Wildlife officials had been polite and enthusiastic but reports of events at the sanctuary could hardly have painted the management in a good light. And what worthwhile charity would invest money in what seemed to be a badly managed enterprise?

And Jack had been surprisingly considerate. Perhaps his stalker behaviour had been a reaction to the shock of the accident. These last couple of days he'd been rather sweet and much less full-on. Hopefully Otto's arrival had knocked away any thoughts of a closer alliance.

Now Charlotte was feeling better, she longed to get back into the meeting. She'd have to wait though – she couldn't risk disturbing everyone again – so to pass the time she answered some emails. It was hard to concentrate. She wanted to know what was happening, what questions Jaideep had to answer, how well he was responding.

An hour passed, then another. The caterers arrived with lunch, then grumbled about the delay and having to keep the food hot.

Eventually the conference room doors opened and everyone flooded out. They all looked hot and drained, in need of fresh air and cold drinks. Charlotte waited eagerly for Amrita, grabbed her, and demanded to know how the meeting had gone.

'What happened to you?' Amrita said. 'You looked awful! Everyone looked at you when you left the room. Are you okay? It was the picture of the accident, wasn't it?'

Charlotte nodded. 'I'm so sorry. I didn't want to disturb the meeting. I was afraid I would faint.'

'Don't worry.' Amrita put a solicitous arm around Charlotte. 'My father told them you were on the train when the accident happened. And how brave you were, helping people afterwards. Then everyone was so admiring and sympathetic.'

'So what were they talking about all this time?'

'A lot of discussion about the train crash. They wanted to know why the reserve management hadn't stopped the stone quarrying sooner. My father was explaining to them about the disputed ownership of parts of land at the edges of the sanctuary, and how the quarry operators were refusing to stop work while their licensing application was still under consideration. Now though, the quarrying company is carrying the blame for undermining the railway embankment and causing the accident so they won't be troubling us any more.'

'So that lets the sanctuary management off the hook?'

'Only in part. The World Wildlife people didn't seem convinced my father had done a good job, taking so long to sort out the problem,' Amrita said. 'Perhaps if this were the only difficulty they would let it pass, but the ongoing problem with poachers is worrying them a lot. They talked about it, on and on, trying to find out how my father would tackle it, what could be done, who the poachers were, how they were managing to track down the tigers.' She stopped talking and wrinkled her brow, evidently upset and worried by the grilling her father had endured.

'Surely they must see that the lack of resources makes it harder for the sanctuary staff to take care of the place? If they had more money, they could have more staff, more vehicles, better surveillance and all the rest,' Charlotte said.

'That's what we said, but it's a difficult one. They won't invest unless they're happy with the effectiveness of the management, and the management isn't very effective at the moment because we don't have the money to put our plans into action. How do you win that one?'

Now Charlotte put her arm around her friend. Charlotte would be going home in a few months; she was just a visitor at the sanctuary. But this was Jaideep's life's work and if the funding application was declined, if he lost his job, what would happen to his family? Even their home was tied to the post. And the wildlife sanctuary, the remaining tigers – what would happen to them?

Jen, Otto and Charlotte ate together at the lodge again, that evening. It was like a scene from *Out of Africa*, dining on the veranda in the dying day, the wild land spreading all around them.

Charlotte updated them on the meeting and goings-on at the sanctuary. Jen talked about her dream of the tiger hunt. She revealed she'd bought art supplies on her trip into town; she even ordered a large canvas, to be collected the following day.

'I have to paint it,' she said. 'The dream – it was so vivid. I need to paint it. And if it's any good then the sanctuary can sell it. That will be my contribution.'

Otto sniffed and half smiled. Charlotte glanced at him. She knew he was thinking: typical Jen, thinking a painting could save the tigers.

When they'd eaten, Charlotte proposed another sunset walk. Jen declined – she'd walked enough already, she said. And she wanted to start some sketches before it got too dark. What about Otto? He agreed readily.

Charlotte felt a strange tremor of shyness to be alone with him. When they were three it was easy, as it had always been. As soon as they left the lodge behind the dynamic altered. Otto was uneasy too, she sensed it. The conversation became a little strained.

'Shall we try a different direction this time?' Otto said.

'Yes, why not? The river's that way, shall we go there?'

'Sure.'

When Otto wasn't looking, Charlotte shook her head and scowled, telling herself to behave normally. One of the pleasures of her friendship with Otto was the ease of their relationship – why had that changed? It was her own stupid fault for allowing her long-restrained love for him to leak out, to have fed it with a little hope. Is that why he wasn't behaving as usual? Had he, finally, picked up on the fact that she liked him? Heaven forbid. Walking behind him, unseen, she felt herself blush. How terrible that would be, how mortifying.

The river was beautiful, deep and clear before breaking up into bright white ribbons as it fell over boulders to a low waterfall, and then into a basin edged with huge, flat, reddish stones. Sometimes local village women came here to wash their clothes. Charlotte had seen them one morning, squatting at the water's edge in bright-coloured saris, talking and laughing as they scrubbed and mercilessly pounded their washing on the soapy stone. It was quiet now, the women probably at home preparing meals for their families.

Otto climbed up over the rocks of the little cataract, hopping from stone to stone till he stood in the middle of the river on a precarious stone platform. Charlotte followed him, odd splashes of water touching her bare arms, her face. Then they stood on separate rocks with tons of white water rushing past them, down and down, before plummeting into the basin at the bottom. A view of the valley opened, the river weaving through grassland, the dark-green smoke of the forest rising to either side. The vista grew hazy in the distance, blurring into the sky. Charlotte breathed the fresh, water-laden air. All she could hear was the tumult of the water. High up, circling in a thermal, a huge dark bird soared in circles. A tribe of small monkeys wandered out of the trees and played on a patch of sandy soil close to the river's edge, just downstream of the tumbling water.

Charlotte turned to Otto, conscious he was observing her.

'What are you thinking?' he said.

Charlotte blushed, again. 'Nothing. I mean, I was just looking at the monkeys. What a view – even better than yesterday.' Oh how stupid and awkward she sounded.

Otto didn't answer, but neither did he look away. The moment stretched.

'Do you want to swim?' he said suddenly.

'What, here?'

'Where else?'

'There might be snakes.'

'You reckon?' He was already stepping from stone to stone back to the river bank. Then he jogged down the bank to stand on the slabs of stone by the river basin where the women did their washing. He kicked off his sandals then peeled off his T-shirt and cut-offs, and then, entirely naked, leaped into the water. He hollered when he resurfaced, shocked by the cold. Charlotte, still perched on the rocks above the pool, was taken aback by the spectacle of Otto's briefly glimpsed body, the curve of his strong, white back, as he dived into the water. He splashed noisily, whacking his arms on the surface of the river.

'It's bloody freezing!' he shouted. 'What are you waiting for?'

Charlotte, keen runner, swimmer and all-round athlete, who prided herself on her physical courage, couldn't resist such a challenge – particularly from Otto. She followed his path to the flat slabs, took off her jeans, checked the depth then dived neatly into the water in – modestly – her T-shirt and underwear.

The water was even colder than she'd expected. It took her breath away, made her hands and feet hurt for a few seconds, until she started swimming vigorously, building heat in her muscles and restoring the blood circulation. She couldn't even think about Otto at first but once her body had acclimatised she pushed the wet hair from her face and swam in a circle to see where he'd gone.

'I told you it was cold.' He was sitting on the stone slab, grinning, his cut-offs on again, his legs in the river, water glistening on his shoulders.

'It's not cold,' she said. 'It's lovely. Refreshing.' The awkwardness had passed. They were smiling at each other, invigorated by the cold water. Charlotte ducked her arm into the river and sent a spray of water over Otto. He yelled and recoiled, then retaliated by kicking water over Charlotte's head, again and again, till her view of the world was entirely obliterated by a constantly descending curtain of white water.

'Okay, stop, stop!' she called out, laughing. 'Enough!'

Otto desisted – then splashed one more time, catching her out. She surface-dived, flicking her feet in the air as she plunged down into the river. Underwater she opened her eyes, to see the grey screen of rock around the river basin, the darker depths where ash-grey weeds trailed, the silver flash of tiny fish, and then, looking up, the pale white and mirror-grey water at the surface of the river. Charlotte released bubbles of air from her mouth, and watched them rise, like globules of mercury, to the river's surface. Then, running out of breath, she kicked her legs and propelled herself upwards, towards the light.

She burst from the water into the fading sunshine, powered to the river's edge and pulled herself out of the water. Otto was still sitting in the same place. She was bitterly cold for a few seconds, as the water poured from her body, off her hair onto her shoulders. She felt his eyes linger on her, the long, lean, legs, the athletic, exercised body of which she was so proud, now a delicious honey-brown after all these weeks in the Indian sun. The wide stone ledge, sun-heated all day, was blissfully warm beneath her bare feet. She lay down on her front, wanting to soak up the heat and drive away the river's cold. Water from her hair pooled on the surface just beside her face. She turned her head to one side, rested it on her forearms, and looked up at Otto. He smiled, a little uneasily.

What was he thinking?

How absurd it was. She had no idea. She knew what she hoped he was thinking. They had always been such easy friends, so relaxed with each other. How stupid was it that the prospect of moving closer had in fact driven them further apart? Why couldn't she just ask him? Because she couldn't, not in a million years. If she did so, their friendship would be impossible. She'd kept her feelings so guarded these last years. Wrapped it up, tucked it away and kept it hidden. No-one knew about it. These feelings, this longing, was private; it belonged to her.

'Are you cold?' Otto's voice didn't sound quite right.

'I'm warming up,' she said, shifting her arms and legs to absorb more of the stone's heat.

'Charlie?' He sounded a little choked. She heard the nervousness in his voice.

'Yes?'

'We've been friends a long time, haven't we?'

She squinted up at him. 'A very long time.'

He didn't speak for a few minutes, instead adjusting his position so his legs no longer dangled in the river.

'Have you ever been in love with anyone?' he said. 'I mean, you've never talked about it – about anyone. Not like me, I mean, I'm going on about girls all the time to you.'

'Why do you ask?' Now her voice sounded strangled. She wanted to sit up but didn't dare. Lying like this, her cheek against her forearm, she felt slightly hidden.

'Well, you know. I saw Mark flirting with you back in Goa. And now this Jack guy coming onto you. It just made me think.'

Charlotte didn't know how to answer.

'I went out with a boy a few times last year,' she said. 'But it didn't amount to anything. It wasn't right. I wasn't really interested.'

'You never told me about that.' Otto sounded almost wounded by this admission. Charlotte shrugged.

'As I said – it wasn't anything. I was curious, that was all. He was a kid from school. And I wasn't even curious for long. I certainly didn't feel anything for him, it was all a bit of a charade.'

She watched Otto blink. His pale, elegant feet were crossed, water evaporating from his skin. They were silent for a while, then Otto took a deep breath and said:

'You know, you're my best friend, Charlie.'

Ah, the best friend. A friend.

'Have you ever wondered,' he hurried, 'why we've only been friends? I mean, we get on so well.'

Charlotte's heart began to beat very hard. She could feel the strength of it, pounding through her ribs and against the stone beneath her. What was he saying? What did he want her to say? She didn't answer, too afraid to speak, and at the same time, afraid her silence might be taken the wrong way.

Slowly, focusing on controlling her body in case it should give her away, Charlotte pushed herself up so she was sitting, cross-legged, side by side with Otto. Best be honest.

'I don't know what to say.' She could hardly look at him, and at the same time, she was aware of him, his physical presence, the heat of him, his arm just a hair's breadth from hers. She tipped her head forwards, unable to look at him.

'Charlie?'

She was trembling – hardly dared speak again because her mouth was dry.

'Charlie?' Otto stood up. He held out his hand. Charlotte put her own hand into his and he pulled her to her feet. And then his arms were around her, and the length of her damp body was pressed against his. She felt his sun-heated skin through her T-shirt, the hard, masculine front of him, his heart beating as hard as her own. All this in a moment, and then his face came down to hers, and he kissed her very softly. She didn't move, except to melt against him, and he kissed her again, this time with a greater intensity, a dizzying, voluptuous kiss, as his arms and hands pressed against her back. The world seemed to blur away; she lost all sense of anything except the pressure of his mouth on hers, the heat of him, the way her body cleaved to his, the river-water scent of his skin and hair, the imprint of his hands on her back . . . How long? Hard to say; he broke away and then kissed her once, twice, very lightly.

'Charlie,' he said, breathless. 'Charlie.'

He tightened his arms and she pressed the side of her face against his chest, breathing the smell of him, savoured the texture of his skin against her cheek. He lifted his hand to stroke the back of her hair and for a moment Charlie felt her mind soar, high above them, so she could see Otto and herself as though from a height, embraced, standing on the sill of rock by the lush river, beneath the waterfall, the wilderness all around them, the darkening sky in a great arch overhead.

Never forget, a little voice said in her mind. Never forget this, not a single detail, never let it go.

'Charlie,' Otto said again, one hand pressed against the small of her back, the deft fingers of his other hand lightly caressing her head.

Something plopped into the water. The noise didn't greatly impinge on Charlie's consciousness, until she heard it again – closer this time. Then something scudded against the rock. Otto loosened his grip.

'What?' he said.

'Someone's throwing stones at us!' Charlotte said, breaking away. She scanned the vicinity, looking for the culprit. Another stone skimmed the rock and bounced against Otto's bare calf, slicing into the skin.

'Ow!' he cried, hopping on one foot. There – at the top of the cascade – a figure was silhouetted against the evening sky.

'Up there!' she said. 'Who is it?'

Another stone, which hit the water. The figure shouted something they couldn't properly hear.

'It's Jack,' Charlotte said. 'Oh my god, it's Jack.'

Otto shaded his eyes. 'Hey! You!' he yelled. 'What the hell are you doing?'

Jack did a curious angry dance on the rock where he was standing. Then he jumped away and disappeared from view.

Otto

Otto ran after Jack. He leaped over stones at the river's edge then up the slope and through the long grass to a rough path. He was fired up, infuriated by the attack, the pain in his calf, the brutal interruption of this astonishing, passionate moment with Charlotte. Jack was a long way ahead, disappearing into the trees, but Otto kept up his pursuit, feeling the strength of his body as he ran, the energy in his muscles, the heat in his blood.

He'd been so intensely aware of Charlotte's physical proximity all evening – and when they'd walked he found himself unthinkingly drifting towards her, as though her body possessed a gravity his couldn't resist, but his mind had been shouting out warnings. This was Charlotte – his friend. Charlotte the untouchable. Then she'd disappeared under the water, swallowed up by the river, and for several long seconds he was alone. He knew she was okay – Charlotte was a strong swimmer – but even so, this was an unknown river, they were in the wilderness. What would he do if something happened to her? He felt a flood of relief when she emerged again, a smile lighting her face. And then she pulled herself out of the river, water streaming over her face and from her skin, and Otto was suddenly weak, helpless with desire. And then his bumbling conversation, while she lay, glittering, on the rock by the river's edge. Could it be possible she felt as he did? So hard to tell. She gave nothing away, always calm and in control.

Except, when she'd sat up and crossed her legs, he saw something: how her lip trembled. And then when he'd reached out for her without any conscious decision, and he felt how fiercely her heart was beating, and his feelings took over, knowing she'd let the mask slip, he felt an intense, surprising, protective tenderness.

And the kiss. And how it had felt to be in each other's arms, to have heart and mind and body engaged at once, how consuming and compelling it was . . .

'Jack!' he yelled. Otto was running fast but Jack had too great a start and now he'd disappeared into the trees. How long had the creep been watching them? Otto slowed to a walk. He felt sick to think of it. Jack must have followed them out to the river – it was unlikely he'd been there by chance. He'd stalked them and spied on their intimate moment. He'd spoiled it – by the very act of watching them, and then breaking up their connection with his childish and dangerous slinging of stones.

'Jack!' he bawled again, mostly for effect and to release some of his pent-up anger. No chance of Jack replying, nor of catching him up. Otto stopped. It would be better to go back to Charlotte. She was alone and soon it would be very dark. They needed to get back to the lodge. He broke into a jog, suddenly overcome by an irrational fear that Jack might have doubled back in order to catch Charlotte on her own.

'Otto? Did you find Jack? How's your leg?' Charlotte was standing on the narrow dirt path at the top of the cascade. 'I didn't know what to do – whether I should start walking back. Then I thought you'd probably come looking for me so I waited.'

Her voice sounded young and vulnerable. Otto reached out his hand. Hers was very cold.

'He ran off,' Otto said. 'He was too far ahead.'

'How's your leg?' she repeated.

'Oh it's fine.' He hadn't felt the injury while he was running, but now, reminded of it, the cut started to sting. They walked along the side of the river. A half-moon swung into the sky, reflecting on the surface of the water. Otto felt tense and defenceless in the dark, afraid that Jack might return to ambush them with another hail of stones. It would be easy for him to creep up on them now. Otto's body tingled, in anticipation.

'Are you okay?' Charlotte asked. Her tone was tentative.

'Yeah. Worried, that's all. In case Jack is lurking. We're a bit vulnerable. I don't want him to hurt you.' Although their hands were clasped, Otto didn't know what else to say. Where to start? Charlotte didn't speak again either. He wondered what she was thinking. Had they made a mistake? What had he done? But her hand held his tightly.

The lodge hove into view. The light was on, bright yellow in the doorway, spilling onto the veranda. The lodge looked tiny in the darkness, crouched against the earth among similarly tiny shrubs and small trees, while the great sky and its mass of stars reared over. Otto thought the lodge looked very cosy and welcoming, forgetting for a moment the insects and mosquitoes. Just now he wanted to be somewhere safe and enclosed, protected from unseen enemies and flying stones. He walked faster. Charlotte half jogged to keep up.

Jen was sitting on the veranda. She stood up as they approached and Otto felt Charlotte slip her hand from his. What did that mean? Obviously she didn't want Jen to see. Was Charlotte embarrassed about it? It was odd how empty his hand felt now – the sense of severance. He pushed it into his pocket and shook his hair back, over his shoulders.

'Hey, Jen!' Charlotte's voice sounded overly bright and it occurred to Otto, belatedly, that she'd extricated her hand from his for Jen's benefit. Although it had ended amicably enough when he and Jen had split up the previous summer – at least, as far as he was concerned – perhaps Charlotte was worried Jen would be upset by this new development? Perhaps she was simply shy and had no idea how to handle the situation.

'You've been a long time. It's so dark now, I was starting to get worried,' Jen said. 'I felt quite alone here, out in the middle of nowhere in the night.'

'Sorry, you're right, we should've come back sooner,' Charlotte said. She sat on one of the wooden chairs.

'What have you done to your leg?' A trail of blood, blackish in the low light, had dried on Otto's calf.

'Oh, that,' Otto said. His thoughts raced. If he told her about Jack and his stones, she'd want to know why he'd attacked them. 'I was by the river,' he said. 'I cut it.'

Charlotte raised her head and gave him a direct look. He couldn't read her expression. But he'd implicated her in a lie, and she wouldn't like that. He didn't like it himself. What was the best thing to do?

Charlotte opened her mouth, and closed it again. Then she took a deep breath and said: 'Jack did it. He was throwing stones at us. One of them cut Otto's leg. Otto tried to catch him but Jack ran off.' Charlotte kept her voice level, but her face was flushed.

'Jack? The weirdo who's been hassling you? Is that because he saw you with Otto?'

'Yes,' Charlotte said. Another half-truth. Jen was in on the plan in which Otto pretended to be Charlie's boyfriend in order to scare off Jack. Now the pretence had evolved into something else.

'Jack saw us kissing,' Charlotte said. Otto could see how much it cost her to say the words out loud and he was angry with Jack all over again for placing them in this position. He wished they could have kept this tentative, fragile connection between themselves for a little while, to try it out, to nurture it, before the exposure to scrutiny.

Now Jen's mouth dropped open.

146

'You kissed? I mean, you're – you and Otto? I thought it was just a pretence?'

What was Jen feeling about this? Hard to tell. Otto had never been much good at reading people's emotions – at least, according to several of his earlier girlfriends. But how were you supposed to know what someone was feeling if they didn't tell you? What kind of magic enabled you to work this out? He looked over to Charlotte for assistance, then waited for Jen to offer a clue.

Charlotte, agonisingly honest, said: 'It was the first time we've ever kissed.'

Jen blinked. She took a quick little breath and put her hands out to the rail at the front of the veranda.

'Oh, I see.' Her voice was very soft. 'So does this – that is, are you two an item now? Is this the beginning of something?'

Otto looked at Charlotte and she glanced at him. He'd never seen her looking so fragile. He didn't want to hurt her. What did she want him to say? Every thought in his head sounded clumsy and inappropriate. How could he express the emotions he'd felt as they embraced by the side of the river, at the foot of the water-fall? It was all too new, too precious.

'I don't know,' Charlotte said. 'This is all so – unexpected.' She leaned forward, resting her forearms on her thighs, head lowered.

For several moments they were all silent. Otto knew he should speak but didn't know what to say. The things he wanted to tell Charlotte – well, those would be just for her. But now – was she waiting for a declaration, in front of Jen? Jen – who now looked at Otto.

'I don't know either,' he blurted. 'I hadn't . . . well, it wasn't planned. It just happened, and then Jack was throwing stones.' He didn't like how he sounded – like a schoolboy caught in the act of some stupidity. Charlotte didn't deserve that.

'Just happened? How can it just happen? I can't imagine Char-lotte would ever let something like that *just happen*,' Jen said. Her voice was gentle. She didn't sound angry or upset. In fact, he realised, she was amused. How odd that Jen should seem like the adult, the person in control.

Charlotte stood up. 'I need to go home. It's late. They'll be wondering where I am.' She sounded tired. Jen stood up, embraced her, then backed away, giving Otto a quick nod. He followed Charlotte to the pick-up, hovering for a moment, not knowing what to say or do. It didn't seem right to kiss her again.

'I'll see you tomorrow,' she said.

'Watch out for Jack. Any trouble, tell Jaideep. Or get me.'

'Sure, yes.' They hugged then, Charlotte breaking away first. She climbed into the cab and started the engine. Otto watched as she drove into the night. The pick-up bounced and jerked over the rough road. Only one of its headlights was working.

Charlotte

Charlotte couldn't think straight. She tried to focus on driving, keeping on the narrow track from the lodge to the road. The pick-up's lights didn't seem to be working well as she dodged the holes pocking the surface of the track. The vehicle lurched into a rut and she jerked the steering wheel to the left.

Her mind was a storm. And not just her mind – her heart, her body. She and Otto had kissed. The scene by the river replayed itself over and over in her imagination, and each time she felt an echo of the overwhelming rush, the feeling of pressing against him, of his hands on her back, the dizzying longing for him. After all this time, these years . . . And then Jack throwing stones, and the awkward scene with Jen. These following incidents popped up like shadows but still they couldn't obscure the grand scene, the technicolour spectacle of the kiss. She remembered it again, summoning up every detail, unable to resist the heady sensations even the memory conjured up.

He'd kissed her. He'd wanted her. She recalled the way he'd said her name, how he'd reached for her hand. All the tinder of her long-hoarded love for him had ignited in that moment. It was dizzying, and frightening, how overwhelmed she felt, entirely out of control. Now, in this moment, all she wanted was to be in his arms again, to kiss him again, to hear him say her name in the same way he'd said it by the river. Nothing else mattered, really. Not Jack, not even Jen. Only this, here and now, this plummeting desire to be with Otto.

'Otto, Otto, Otto.' She was saying his name aloud, like an idiot. The pick-up plopped into another hole and bounced out again, so she was momentarily thrown out of her seat. Concentrate, she admonished herself. Concentrate. But it was impossible, like throwing a bucket of water on a forest fire.

Then something careered onto the road ahead, a thin, greyish figure in the headlights. Charlotte slammed on the brakes and the pick-up slewed across the road, throwing her against the door. Was it a deer? Had she hit it? The engine stalled. Charlotte unclipped her seatbelt and jumped out of the passenger door. One of the headlights was out, she saw. No deer to be seen, at least not in the puddle of light in front of the pick-up. It was hard to see much beyond that. She peered into the darkness. What if she'd hit it, whatever it was, and the creature had wandered off, hurting and injured, into the night?

Charlotte went back to the pick-up.

Someone was sitting in the passenger seat.

Jack. It was Jack.

She made a slight sound, startled, and stood for a moment, still holding the door handle, too shocked to move or speak.

'Hello, Charlie,' Jack said. 'Get in. We need to talk.'

Charlotte opened her mouth but couldn't get a word out. She gripped the door.

'Come on – what are you waiting for? Hop in.' His voice was calm and level. He sounded like a dad encouraging a daughter. Charlotte didn't want to get into the cab with him but what else could she do, out in the dark, in the middle of nowhere?

'You'll have to get out first. The driver's door doesn't open. And I'm not climbing over you.'

Jack edged out. Charlotte got in, thinking quickly. No time to drive off, the engine wasn't running and Jack jumped in right behind her. The lodge was too far behind, the house too far ahead. Should she have made a run for it? Even if she could find her way in the dark, Jack would be able to run faster and the wilderness was a dangerous place. This wasn't modest English woodland.

Charlotte swallowed. 'What do you want? Why are you out here in the dark? It isn't safe.' She didn't fasten her seatbelt, every muscle in her body tense, ready to bolt.

'You know what I'm doing,' Jack said. 'I was looking for you.'

'Out in the wilds? In the middle of nowhere? Why not just wait till the morning, you'd have seen me in the office. Saved yourself a lot of trouble. I could've run you over.' She tried to keep her tone light, but her voice was shaking.

'I was looking for you,' Jack repeated stubbornly. 'I wanted to see you with him. I couldn't believe it was true – that you and he were together.' He pressed his lips together, face tense and pale. His hands gripped his thighs.

'How could you get back with him, after what we had?' Jack said. 'I knew you had to talk with him – tell him it was over. I knew you'd have to do that gently and kindly. But I saw you, kissing by the river. I saw how you held him. How could you? How could you?' His voice rose in volume, self-control evaporating. 'He's a clumsy idiot. Why are you squandering yourself on a man like that?'

Charlotte took a deep breath. She clasped her hands around the steering wheel and stared straight ahead. She had to keep a clear head.

'I love him,' she said. 'I've loved him for a long time. I've told you, Jack – told you loud and clear – that I feel nothing for you. Why won't you listen? Why won't you hear what I'm saying? This – this pursuit. It's foolish. Can't you see that? All this dramatic stalking and creeping up in the dark!' She tried to laugh, wanting to lighten the atmosphere and turn it into something else.

Jack didn't laugh. 'Start the car,' he said.

'You want me to take you home?'

'Start the car,' he repeated.

Charlotte turned the key in the ignition and the engine grumbled to life. She put the pick-up into first gear. 'Where shall we go?'

Jack gestured forwards. Charlotte started to drive. What should she do? How dangerous was Jack? After ten silent minutes they reached the end of the track. Charlotte turned onto the surfaced road and headed in the direction of Amrita's house but Jack told her to stop.

'Look, Jack, this is stupid. I want to go home – they're expecting me,' she said in a practical and no-nonsense manner. 'Why don't you come too and have some tea? I'm sure they'd love to see you.' She was trying again to lighten the situation, to take the seriousness from it.

'Shut up,' he said. 'Turn around. I want you to go the other way.'

'Look, Jack, I'm sorry. I don't have time for this. I have to get back or they'll be sending out a search party.'

But Jack interrupted. 'Turn around.'

'No I won't. This is stupid!'

Jack moved quickly, leaning over the handbrake so his face was close to hers. Something sharp jabbed her neck and Charlotte realised he'd put a knife to her throat. 'Turn around and drive,' he whispered. She could feel his breath on her skin.

Her heart seemed to stop for a moment, as heavy as a stone, then it started to thunder. Charlotte's thoughts whirled in her head and she struggled to think straight.

'What are you doing?' she said. 'Have you gone mad? Are you really going to kill me?'

Jack didn't answer. He kept very close to her. She could sense him staring at her face, seeming to feed on her. She drove slowly. The further they went, the worse it would be, the harder to get back. What did Jack have in mind?

'Where are we going?'

'Charlie, be quiet,' he said. 'Just keep going. I'll tell you when to turn off.'

'Ah, you have a destination in mind?'

He jabbed her neck with the blade and Charlotte shut up.

They drove for about twenty minutes, then Jack instructed her to turn left down a dirt track into the trees. Now the pick-up jerked and bounced over the rough surface. Once or twice the blade inadvertently pressed into her neck and she instinctively recoiled. They drove for another ten minutes then Jack said: 'Okay, stop here.'

Jack took the keys and got out of the car, then instructed her to climb out too. He kept a hold of her arm so she had no chance to run off. Now they were standing in the trees; the foliage blocked off moon and stars and it was very dark.

'This way,' Jack said.

'It's dangerous at night,' Charlotte said. 'You don't know what's out there.'

'Snakes, wild elephants, leopards – even tigers,' Jack said. 'I know it's dangerous. Why d'you think I brought you here? Come on.' He tugged her arm and drew her away from the pick-up and through the trees, seeming to know where he was going. Charlotte stumbled along in front of him.

The dry, heated air carried the scent of grass and resin. Now and then the canopy thinned to reveal the needle points of stars. In the distance a monkey howled, then another. Charlotte nearly trod on a large bird, which screeched and flew up from her feet, startling them both. She tried to remember the way they'd come, making mental snap shots of dimly seen tree trunks and fallen branches. If she managed to get away from Jack she'd have to run back to the pick-up somehow – but it would be difficult, no doubt about it. The journey was a confusing welter of darkness and trees.

Then the trees ended. Dimly Charlotte could hear moving

153

water and yes, she could smell it too, its freshness. Moonlight flooded over the landscape. Her eyes adjusted, taking in the sweep of stars, a line of silhouetted trees in the distance. They were back at the river, though an unspecified distance downstream. Now, however, the river was flowing through a deep chasm: Charlotte and Jack were standing together at the top of the cliff. It was hard to see the river, except for occasional sparks of moonlight on the turbulent surface.

Charlotte tried to remember the map of the sanctuary, pinned to the wall in the reception area – where this chasm was in relation to Amrita's house and the reserve offices.

'Why are we here?' She exaggerated how out of breath she was, hoping Jack might underestimate her, and let her voice sound a little teary. That wasn't so difficult. 'How do you know about this place?'

'The reserve office has plenty of maps,' he said. Then: 'How are you feeling?' On this promontory, high above the river, Jack's face was black and grey – pale in the moonlight, dark in the shadows.

'How do you think I'm feeling?' she said, unable to suppress the anger in her voice. 'Pissed off, upset and afraid. Why have you dragged me out here? What stupid little game is this?' She regretted the outburst as soon as it was over. She hadn't managed to keep up the weak-and-feeble-woman act very long.

Jack still had a tight grip of her upper arm. She could feel his fingers pressing into the flesh. His face wore the intense expression she'd seen before.

'Do you know why I've brought you here?' he said. 'I wanted you to be afraid. I wanted you to remember what it felt like to be on the edge of life, as we were on the train during and after the accident. When we were together, all the everyday shit of human life swept away, no masks any more. I saw you, Charlie. I saw who you really were – your courage, your strength. You're not an ordinary person. I *know* you. I've seen your soul. That's why we have to be together.'

Charlotte trembled. 'You're wrong,' she said. 'You're wrong about the accident, about fear, about me. You don't know anything about me. It's just shock affecting your brain. Post-traumatic stress disorder, something like that.'

He took a step closer to the edge of the chasm, pulling Charlotte with him. A chilly wind whipped up from the depths, brushing against their faces.

'Be careful,' she said. 'It's dark, I can't see very well. I don't want to fall off.'

'Of course you don't. Neither do I. But the possibility's there. Can't you feel it? How strong is your desire to live? You are most alive when you know how fragile your life is. We spend most of our time in a fuzzy, comfy dream, filling our minds with rubbish. We're inside our lives, thinking it's everything. Hardly anyone ever realises, or not for long, how precious it is to be alive. But you do now, don't you? I could push you over the edge and in just seconds it would all be over forever. All this!'

With his free hand (the blade, a penknife of some kind, was held in his palm) he gestured to the sky, the forest.

'Can you feel me?' he whispered, sliding his hand from her arm and around her waist. 'Can you feel how warm I am? My heartbeat?'

Charlotte was shaking, though whether from fear or because of the cold wind from the chasm she wasn't sure. One part of her was listening to Jack; another part was busy calculating how she might free herself. What did she need to say? How could she persuade him to let her go?

'Stop resisting,' he said. 'I know it's hard to let go of old, comfortable patterns of thinking. But you can do it. You just need to face the truth. If we were together, Charlie – truly together – our lives would never be the same again.'

155

That's for sure, said a wry voice in Charlotte's mind. Jack sounded feverish. Did she have the space to feel sorry for him? Think quickly, she told herself. If she could empathise, perhaps it would be safer for both of them. Antagonise him and they could both end up at the bottom of the chasm.

'I do know what you mean,' she said. 'You're right. Most of the time we drift about in a dream, obsessing about stupid stuff.'

She took a deep breath and tried to relax. Jack loosened his grip, just a little.

'That's one of the reasons I came to India,' she continued. 'To stretch myself. To get out of the rut. Is that what brought you here too? I know so little about you, I mean, your life at home.'

'None of that's important,' he said. 'Only now. Who you are now. Who I am. Our life starts here, in this moment.'

Charlotte took another deep breath and tried, again, to relax. 'Could we sit down? It'd be much easier to talk.'

Jack considered for a moment. 'Sure,' he said. They stepped back from the edge, out of the cold wind, and both sat on the ground. Jack remained close beside Charlotte, one hand on her arm, the penknife cupped in the other.

'Home,' he mused. 'Life at home. What does home mean? This is my home.' He gestured to his body. 'The rest of it – a house, a familiar place – they don't mean anything.' Jack smiled then, a smile made eerie by the moonlight. 'You're my home now. I told you we were bound together. Where you go, I go.'

'But Jack, how can that be true? I don't feel the same way. Can't you see this is something created in your own mind? A fantasy you've projected on me?' She spoke gently, kindly, appealing to his rational mind.

Jack, equally gentle, shook his head. 'Can't you see that your denial exists only in your mind? I am asking you to accept it – to believe it. That's why I brought you here. I promise you, I need you to know the truth. I need you to understand.'

'D'you think you love me?'

'Love? I don't think love is an adequate word. You think you love Otto. What exists between us is final – absolute. It's not about romance.'

That's for sure, said Charlotte's wry observer. Jack let her go and started talking again, the familiar trail about the train accident, the connection between them. Charlotte's mind wandered into calculations of how fast Jack could run, if she could hide from him in the forest, how she might get the pick-up keys from his pocket. None of these seemed very hopeful. Would Jack actually hurt her? Probably yes. His messianic certainty about their mutual destiny seemed so strong and, to him, so incontrovertible, she was afraid he would resort to violence if she said or did the wrong thing. If push came to shove (how apt!) he seemed to prefer the idea of them dying together – tumbling into the chasm.

On and on he talked, trying to persuade her to accept his truth. Charlotte nodded and feigned interest while trying to work out how to get away. If she agreed with him, might he take them back to the pick-up? Or would he demand some horrible proof of her change of heart? That didn't bear thinking about.

'Jack, please,' she interrupted him. 'Please, listen to me. I'm cold and tired; I don't like being here. My family will be worried about me. If you care about me, please let us go home.'

Jack stopped talking. He blinked and gazed at her.

'Listen to you? You're not listening to me. What do I have to do? Is this a test? What is it you want from me?'

'I just want to go home.'

'No, no!' He shook his head. 'You're *still* not listening!' Something inside him seemed to boil over. He jumped to his feet, grabbed Charlotte, and tried to pull her towards the chasm edge. But something snapped in Charlotte too. She jerked away from him and thrust one hand into his face, jabbing his eyes. Instinctively he tried to protect himself, dropping the penknife, which

Charlotte kicked away into the darkness. Now he was tottering on the cliff edge and Charlotte was facing him, knees bent, alive with adrenalin and fury.

'Give me the keys,' she said.

Finally, a look of alarm in Jack's face.

'Give me the keys or I'll push you over.'

'You couldn't do it,' Jack said. But he couldn't keep the note of doubt from his voice and in that moment Charlotte herself wasn't certain that she wouldn't either. Anger overwhelmed her – she was capable of anything.

'Now,' she demanded, stepping closer.

'If you push me, I'll take you down too,' Jack said.

'No you won't.' Strength charged her body, a ferocity she didn't know she possessed.

She moved forward again. Jack teetered above the chasm. Finally he was afraid.

'Okay,' he said, fishing in his pocket. He dangled the keys in front of her. 'Here they are. You can have them. But I've proved my point.' A gleam of triumph in his eyes, as well as fear. 'Have you ever felt what you're feeling now, Charlie? What I've made you feel? Do you know how magnificent you are? Did you know before you would be capable of killing someone? I've made you feel that way. I did! I'm the one who took you to here. I'm the only one who's pushed you to the limit. Has Otto ever made you feel like this? You want to be Otto's mother figure? You want him so you can feel safe? Don't do it. Don't sell yourself short. Come to me. I know how to make you the most you can be.'

Charlotte quivered. The urge to shut him up, to push him off, was compelling. At the same time, his words carried an awful, tempting appeal.

'Give me the keys,' she said. 'You don't know me. You don't know anything about me.'

Jack smiled, an awful, insane grin. He dropped the keys. Keeping her gaze fixed on his face, she grabbed the keys from the ground and backed away. Still Jack smiled. A horrible joy glazed his eyes and for one horrible moment Charlotte was afraid he would fall, willingly, a sacrifice to his obsession. She stepped back again, still watching him. Then she turned and ran, back into the trees and the darkness, her long, trained legs taking powerful strides.

'This isn't finished!' she heard Jack yell after her. 'This is just the beginning! We both know the game. We both know what you are. I'll take you further!' His voice died away as the distance grew between them.

It was hard running. Too dark, the ground uneven. Charlotte ran into branches, tripped over unseen obstacles. She tried to recall the route to the pick-up but it was impossible to distinguish; she was running blind. The night was dangerous, the time many predators hunted. She wasn't on a road, which the animals avoided, but deep in the forest. She might blunder into something, or be attacked. Soon she was sweating. Which way to go? She couldn't even tell if she was travelling in a straight line. What if Jack caught her again? What if he'd found a quicker way to the pick-up and was lying in wait?

Charlotte tried to maintain a rhythm with her running and breathing, but the rough terrain and non-existent visibility made it near impossible. Surely she should have reached the track by now? Sweat dripped into her eyes, making them sting. Her right foot caught on a humped root and she crashed to the ground, knocking all the breath from her body. She clambered back to her feet and set off again, train-injured knee throbbing, along with some new, fresh injuries sustained in the fall.

Where was the pick-up? Where? How long could she keep running? Where was Jack and what would he do next?

She ran under a tree, and above her head a troop of monkeys began to hoot and howl, an eerie, echoing sound that doubtless would alert Jack to her whereabouts. She veered to the left, fighting through undergrowth. Her hands stung, scratched and bleeding. A twig had lashed an eye. An insidious fear of snakes crept into her mind. What if she trod on one? Who (apart from Jack) would find her if she were bitten and poisoned? She had her mobile in her pocket, but signal was patchy all over the reserve and even if she got through, how would she describe where she was? How would they find her fast enough if venom were pumping through her body?

Where was the pick-up? Desperation crept over her. The first flush of energy was seeping away. Her muscles started to ache. She slowed to a walk. There – ahead! Her heart lifted. A pale light appeared through the trees. Charlotte crept forward, cautious now, in case Jack was ahead of her. She peered out, towards the light – but it wasn't the track.

An oval clearing lay ahead, a perfect pool at its heart, reed-fringed, white flowers blossoming from the black mud at its edges. The moon hung overhead, like a lantern, throwing its light on the surface of the water. Despite her situation, Charlotte was enchanted. The clearing was perfect – a scene from a fairy tale. She halted at the tree-line, an unworthy being peering through the bars at an unattainable world. The pool was utterly still. A faint honey perfume drifted on the air. Then – astonishing, miraculous, silent – a tiger stepped from the trees on the far side of the pool. For a moment she forgot about Jack, forgot about everything. Only the tiger existed, godlike, padding on huge paws to the water's edge. Slowly it lowered its head and lapped at the water. She heard the sound of its tongue catching the pool's surface, saw the multitude of tiny ripples expanding across the water. Burning orange, forest-black, moon-white, the tiger seemed to contain and manifest the Indian jungle. The tiger raised the terrible, splendid mask of a face. It twitched its ears. Glittering water clung to the enormous white whiskers. A single drop fell back into the pool, like a pearl. Charlotte heard it strike the water's surface, watched it disappear.

Did she make a sound? Did a breath of scent reach the tiger's sensitive nose? The solemn face turned towards her. The large amber eyes seemed to regard her, clear and enquiring.

Charlotte was too afraid to move. She held her breath, willed her shaking, sweating body to be still. The tiger held its unflinching gaze. One, two, three. The moments stretched.

Then something else caught its attention. The great head turned away. The tiger moved from the pool, its powerful muscles evident beneath the heavy hide, and the forest swallowed it up.

Still Charlotte didn't leave. She was caught in a spell, unable to move or speak. The spectacle burned in her mind, never to be forgotten. Hard to say how long she remained so. Just a few minutes perhaps. Something else moved in the clearing, a monkey perhaps. Charlotte shook her head, remembering she was lost and alone. She had no idea which way to go. All sense of direction had gone.

She set off at a walk, randomly, weary to the bone and dry with thirst, and emerged on a dirt track. Off to her right, about two hundred yards away, stood the pick-up. She felt a moment's jubilation – followed by worry. Was Jack already lying in wait? Charlotte kept close to the trees, hiding in the shadows. She couldn't see him, but in the darkness it would be just as easy for him to hide. The keys were still in her hand, held ready. She crept closer, poised to run, then darted behind the pick-up on the passenger's side. No sign of Jack.

Then something surprising. In the distance she heard an engine revving. Who else could be out here, at this time? Did Jack have another vehicle nearby? How had he organised that? Someone shouted, far away. A male voice.

Charlotte opened the door, hopped inside, clambered to the driver's seat and pressed the lock. Where was Jack? Had he met up with someone? Presumably he was still in the forest, hunting her. If he had a vehicle she needed to hurry. Luck, only, had taken her back to the track and the pick-up.

She turned the key in the ignition, praying the engine would start. Despite her fears, it leaped to life first time. The lane was too narrow for an easy three-point turn so she slammed it into reverse gear and drove away as fast as she could, desperate not to run off the lane. When the lane opened out she turned round, drove to the road and headed for home.

Jen

Jen heard the pick-up drive away. Otto returned to the lodge veranda a moment later and they sat in awkward silence. Charlotte and Otto, eh? What did she feel about that? Of course she'd known a long time about Charlie's feelings for him. She'd seen the way Charlotte looked at him, how she talked about him. Since Charlie had never raised the matter, Jen had kept the secret and pretended not to know. Otto had always seemed oblivious.

And now? She knew from experience what Otto was like with girls. He wasn't hard or intentionally unkind. He loved girls, all girls. They were tantalising, delightful, appealing and he fell in love – or something like it – at the drop of a hat. Like Maria, the beautiful young woman he'd become so infatuated with after a few days in Goa; whom he'd later found murdered at the sea's edge.

He'd fallen for Jen too, for a while, but even then his eyes had wandered. It had proved too much for her. Jen's own feelings were so consuming, so intense, that she had called an end to their fledgling relationship. Let Otto play. It was safer to be his friend. He was a very good friend.

So what about Charlotte? Was Otto serious about her? If he wasn't – if he hurt her – Jen would never forgive him. She knew too well how much Charlotte cared about him. On the other hand, if Otto were serious, how did Jen feel about that? Jealous? Yes,

yes she would feel a bit jealous. But why? She certainly didn't want to go out with Otto. She pushed these thoughts around in her mind, noticing how contradictory they were and unable to find any satisfactory resolution. She wondered about Kumar, waiting for her in Madurai, wanting some kind of commitment. What did she feel about him? How complicated.

'Are you okay, Jen?' Otto sounded worried.

She smiled. 'Yes, I'm fine.'

'I was worried, well, I was wondering what you were thinking. You know – me and Charlie.'

'So what's the deal?' Despite herself, she couldn't stop the icy edge to the question.

'I don't know,' he said.

'But you care about her? This is Charlie we're talking about. Not any old girl.'

He squirmed. 'Of course I care about her. How can you ask that?'

Jen sighed. 'I don't want her to get hurt. She's not like you.'

'What d'you mean by that, not like me?' He looked wounded. Then: 'Is this about you and me?' It cost him to say this, she could see. They'd not talked about it since the day Jen had ended the brief relationship. 'You're the one who finished with me, remember?' he said.

'But . . .' Jen began.

She was unable to finish the sentence. How could she explain? He hadn't truly understood then. He wouldn't understand now.

'Not long ago you were madly in love with Maria,' she said. 'Now it's Charlie?'

'You think I'm superficial, don't you?'

'No.' She shook her head. 'I just wonder if you're ready for a serious relationship – and with Charlie, well, how could it be otherwise?' Jen looked into his face, seeing emotions playing over his face. Doubt, worry.

164

'I love her, Jen,' he said, looking at his hands. 'I've never felt like this about anyone before. It's different, you know? There's the infatuation stuff, sure. But this time – there's knowing her so well too. It's hard to put into words. When I wanted girls before it was always the not-knowing I liked – the mystery. This time it's because I do know her. And being here – in this strange place, seeing how she's handled herself – it's like I've seen her properly for the first time.'

Jen was surprised – and hurt – perhaps just by the memory of her feelings for him, and knowing he hadn't felt the same way. The depth of his feelings for Charlie surprised her. Unexpected tears sprang to her eyes.

'Jen?' Otto said. 'Are you okay?'

'Sure.' It was hard to get the word out. Her vision blurred. What exactly was going on with her? Neither of them spoke for several moments. Jen struggled to control her feelings.

'You've changed too,' Otto said. He sounded almost nervous. 'What happened to you? I've never known you to be so – forthright. You were always so . . . delicate.'

'I told you: I've learned to take care of myself.' This answer sounded more cutting than she'd intended and Otto flinched. Jen stood up, guilty and upset at once. 'I'm going to bed,' she said.

Jen washed behind the bamboo screen at the back of the house, beneath a light bulb swarming with insects. She tipped cups of cool water over her body, washed and dried, brushed her teeth and slipped beneath the mosquito net into bed. Throughout these activities, her thoughts were far away. Later, half asleep, she heard Otto go to bed but he was restless too. The lodge was hot and confining, the whine of insects a continual irritation. Her feelings, too, were confused and hurt. She didn't want to be in a relationship with Otto, and she was happy to be his friend: why then did she feel jealous of the seeming depth of his attachment to Charlie? After all, she'd known for a long time how painful it was for Charlotte,

165

seeing Otto move from girlfriend to girlfriend, his succession of colourful infatuations.

Oh, but emotions aren't logical, she reminded herself. They can be felt and observed, and perhaps you can choose how you respond to them, however hard it might seem. She was worried Otto would hurt Charlie, certainly, but there was nothing she could do about it. And the jealousy? Better not to nurse it. She would try and let it go.

Nonetheless Jen couldn't sleep. In the end she climbed out of bed, pulled on her jeans and T-shirt and slipped out of the lodge. The sky was dark-blue velvet beneath a veil of stars. Poised above the forest behind the lodge, the moon cast long, grey shadows. The night seemed charged and potent. Jen, always open to signs and atmospheres, sensed something ominous. Was she simply projecting her own bad feelings outwards? Something wasn't right: she felt it tickling the surface of her skin and in her bones. Hidden within the forest, in its depths, she sensed disturbance, a destructive intent. Goosebumps rose on her arms, though the air was warm and still. Jen shivered suddenly. An urge came over her, to run into the lodge and wake Otto. She needed company and reassurance. She didn't want to be alone.

Jen shook her head, moving on from the moment of weakness. She should rely on herself – and what could Otto do? His presence might distract her or block out this feeling. But her time on the island, away from her friends, had taught her to embrace her intuitions and that she was strong enough to face them alone.

She had changed, yes. Her body was stronger. She was eating and exercising more, and in a virtuous circle, the stronger she became, the more she enjoyed food, walking, running, swimming. And the loss for the gain? Her spirit world had receded. As she became more rooted in the physical world, the otherworldly presences had faded a little. She could still see them, but only if she chose to. They no longer intruded. She had to look. Jen felt some regret about this, but also a large measure of relief.

She focused now. Sitting cross-legged she drew a circle in the dry dirt, a moon above, the cardinal points. She took a string of tiny white shells from her neck and spread it in an O inside the circle. From a locket Jen extracted three crumbs of spicy resin which she placed at intervals on the circumference. Dried rose petals from her pockets, the faint pink turned grey in the moonlight, were scattered in the centre. Finally, Jen drew out a piece of crimson chalk. She drew an eye, the petals colouring the pupil. This eye regarded her.

Jen took several deep, slow breaths and cleared her mind. The night-painted land spread all around, with its rivers and grasses, forests, its cargo of animals and birds. She tuned in to the strange atmosphere, the premonition of disturbance. Her body seemed to resonate, like a wind harp. Heart and mind open, she sensed dissonance.

The Madurai dream, the tiger in the paper forest, loomed into her mind. And Charlotte too, Charlotte standing on the brink. On the brink of what? Charlie's aura was churning with extreme colours. In danger – coming to pieces.

A surge of emotion washed through Jen, fear that took her breath away, then murderous rage and a lust for revenge so violent it seemed to turn her inside out. Then gone – a storm blown over. Jen stood up, her mind perfectly clear. She picked up the shell necklace and put it back around her neck, stowed the chalk in her pocket and walked back to the lodge.

Otto was lying flat on his back, arms outstretched, snoring very gently. He looked so childlike asleep. Not a trouble in the world.

'Otto? Otto!' She reached under the mosquito net to squeeze his arm. 'Otto, wake up!'

He was difficult to rouse. She shook his shoulder, and finally his eyes flicked open.

'Wake up,' she repeated. 'I need you.'

'What? What is it?' He didn't move, except to rub his eyes. 'You had a bad dream?'

'Something terrible's happening. I think Charlie's in trouble.'

'Trouble?' Otto repeated. He blinked, barely awake.

'Please, please wake up.'

Otto rubbed his eyes and sat up, still in a daze of sleep. 'What's going on?'

'We have to help Charlie.' Finally Jen's words seemed to sink in. Otto's eyes focused but still he wasn't alert.

'Has she called you?'

'No signal.'

'No, no, of course not. So why is she in trouble?'

Jen took a deep breath and told him what had happened. Otto was something of an agnostic when it came to Jen's encounters with the spirit world. He was entirely respectful of her visions and beliefs but at the same time she knew he wasn't convinced they existed except in her own, personal reality. This time, however, he needed to accept what she was telling him. Otto did indeed listen attentively.

'What are we going to do?' he said, fully awake now. 'Where d'you think she is?'

'I don't know. We need to find Amrita and her dad.'

'It's a long walk in the dark. A couple of miles to the house.'

'I don't think we have any choice.' Jen studied Otto's face. Evidently he was wondering how seriously to take her worries.

'Okay,' he said, swinging his legs out of bed, pushing the net to one side. 'Then let's not waste any time. You're good to walk?'

'I am.' Jen ran to her rucksack and took out her pocket torch as Otto pulled on his jeans. He picked up his camera and locked the padlock on the lodge door. Two minutes later they were walking along the track.

Otto

It took well over an hour to reach Jaideep's house. Otto wasn't sure of the way. In the dark everything looked different so they took a wrong turning and had to backtrack. The forest was still, but Otto didn't find it hard to believe Jen's premonition. The night seemed ominous indeed.

Charlotte. Was she truly in trouble? His first thought was Jack. If Jack was capable of hurling stones, what else might he do when thwarted? But Charlotte had left in the pick-up. Surely she would have been safe? Otto should have gone with her, to make sure. Now he was kicking himself.

No sign of the pick-up. At least she hadn't gone off the road. A mixture of emotions jostled: worry and guilt, and a consequent desire to protect and take care of Charlie. They'd kissed. They'd kissed by the river. They'd put their arms around each other. (How had he dared?) She'd kissed him back, and instead of feeling strange or wrong, it had felt entirely, blissfully right and he couldn't imagine why they'd never done it before.

All those girls he'd kissed and more, all the others he'd flirted with and lusted after; girls like Maria. He'd spent several days obsessing about Maria, but he hadn't actually known her at all. Now he was in love (was he? was he actually in love with

Charlotte, finally?) with the girl who'd shared his thoughts, hopes and dreams for years. But where was she?

Hopefully fast asleep in bed. Hopefully Jen's premonition was unfounded. He wasn't entirely convinced by these paranormal glimpses. On the other hand, he felt worried too. Something was up.

'Is that it?' Jen pointed along the road, indicating the house with torchlight.

'I think so.' Then they were standing on the doorstep. All the lights were out. Otto felt uneasy to be waking them up. Was this a fool's errand? He and Jen glanced at one another.

'Shall I knock?' he said, all nervous. Jen nodded.

The sound echoed through the house and the empty street. After a couple of minutes Jaideep answered the door, a dressing gown wrapped around him and his hair standing in tufts. He only opened the door a little way, squinting out at the callers.

'Look, Jaideep, I'm so sorry to wake you at this time, it's just that – well – we wanted to check Charlie was okay.'

Jaideep blinked. 'I thought she was staying with you two at the lodge tonight. She's not here.' He seemed to wake up then. 'So she's not with you. Then where is she?'

'There was an incident this evening – Jack, you know? I'm worried he might have something to do with it.'

'Jack? What incident?' Jaideep stepped back from the door and ushered them inside. What was he thinking? With all the problems he was dealing with at the sanctuary, the idiot adventures of his young European visitors were the last thing he needed. Jaideep knocked on Amrita's bedroom door and asked her to join them. Then he sat down and indicated his visitors do the same. His expression was intent and serious. 'Tell me what's been happening,' he said.

Amrita emerged while Otto was describing the situation with Jack, as Charlotte had described it to him – from their first encounter on the train to the incident by the river, when Jack had assaulted them with stones. He showed Jaideep the resulting wound on his leg. Neither did Otto shirk from sharing the reason Jack had attacked them. Once again Otto thought how, from Jaideep's perspective, they must seem very stupid. If that was what he was thinking, however, Jaideep kept it well hidden. Instead he invited Amrita to sit down and asked her what she knew about Jack and his behaviour towards Charlotte.

Amrita, blushing, shared what she knew.

Jaideep was angry then, with Amrita and Otto, but mostly with himself. He ranted at them. Why hadn't anyone told him about Jack's behaviour? Jaideep had thought Jack was a friend to the others – why, he'd offered him a volunteer job and some accommodation on the sanctuary! Why hadn't anyone explained Jack's motivations? Charlotte was his guest, a young woman who had travelled alone, and he'd failed to protect her!

Amrita hung her head.

'I don't think any of us realised the situation was so serious,' Otto said.

'I just thought he had a crush on her,' Amrita followed. 'But – why are you so sure this is something to do with Jack? How do you know that? Anything might have happened. She might have gone somewhere.'

'At this time of night? Where?' Jaideep demanded. 'She told Otto she was coming home – to us! If Jack hasn't got her, then someone else has.'

'So what shall we do?' Jen had been quiet until now. 'We shouldn't waste any more time. We need to find her.'

'She could be anywhere,' Otto said. His heart lurched to think of it, Charlotte somewhere out in the night, on her own. What if Jack had taken her? Might he hurt her? Rape her? He felt queasy with helpless rage. Jaideep was looking at him, perhaps reading his thoughts, because he stood up and patted Otto on the shoulder.

'We'll find her,' he said. 'I know this area as well as anyone – certainly better than Jack.'

'But where do we start?' Otto was beginning to panic. 'They've got the pick-up – they could be anywhere!'

Jaideep couldn't disguise the fact that he was also at a loss – despite his brave words.

'Should we call the police?' Amrita said.

'And what would they do, right now?' Jaideep shook his head. 'I don't think we can do anything till it gets light. We'd be wasting our time trying to search for her in the dark.'

Prina joined them in the living room. Jaideep laid out a map of the sanctuary, examined the tracks and roads. Prina made tea and food but no-one had any appetite. Another slow hour passed. Otto, agitated, tried not to torture himself with speculations about Charlie's fate. Maybe this was all an insane mistake . . . perhaps she wasn't with Jack at all? But in that case, where was she?

Jen was quiet, sitting in the corner of the room with her knees drawn up to her chest, lost in thought. Otto went to sit beside her, lightly touched her shoulder.

'Something's happening, something else bad,' she said, her expression troubled. 'It's not just Charlie. I think people are out there, in the forest. Men are hunting the tigers.'

'How do you know that?' Otto said. 'I mean, really, how do you know?' He found it hard to think about tigers now. Only Charlotte mattered – Charlotte, who might, even now, be hurting, or frightened, or travelling further and further from him.

Jen closed her eyes. She gave one strange, violent shiver. Then she raised her head, blinked and looked directly at Otto.

'Don't worry about Charlie any more. Charlie's here,' she said.

Otto rolled his eyes. This was too much. He needed Jen to be serious.

At that moment they heard a vehicle pull up outside the house. Otto glanced at Jaideep. 'Sounds like the pick-up,' he said. Jaideep nodded. They both jumped to their feet and hurried to the front door. Forgetting his manners, Otto pushed past Jaideep and ran out.

'Charlie? Are you okay?' His heart raced.

Charlotte clambered out of the pick-up's passenger door and ran into his arms. It was only a fleeting hug because she broke away and shouted out to Jaideep.

'You have to follow me! Quickly! There are people driving about in the forest and I think they might be hunting a tiger. I can take you there, please, we need to go now!'

Charlotte was loud and fired up, trembling, though she didn't seem afraid. She didn't look like a victim; quite the contrary, she was larger than life, charged by whatever it was that had happened. So where was Jack?

'Get the wardens, and the police,' Charlotte ordered.

Jaideep, taken aback, didn't ask what had happened or how she knew about the poachers. Presumably he knew by now that Charlie could be trusted. He did as he was told.

'Amrita, you drive the jeep so I can make some calls,' Jaideep said, getting into gear now, evidently thinking fast.

'Charlie, I'm coming with you,' Otto said, picking up his camera.

Charlotte

A scene of carnage.

They found the tiger's body as the sun rose, crimson light spilling over the rim of trees. The body, hastily skinned, lay sprawled over the dry ground in a clearing. Blood stained the yellow grass. Within minutes Jaideep received a radio message telling him a second tiger had been found butchered.

Two tigers dead – and the World Wildlife officials still visiting the sanctuary. What hope for funding? What hope of protecting the remaining animals? Jaideep shook his head, shoulders bowed, walking in slow circles around the corpse.

Charlotte watched him. She'd started to shiver, though with the sun rising, it would soon be hot. Already flies were buzzing around the tiger's remains, the flayed, shining body.

Jen had absolutely refused to come. Had she already known what they would find? Two tigers. Charlotte was certain one was the tiger she'd seen by the moonlit pool, because the body was so close to the place. And she'd heard those vehicles, the warning to her that something terrible was about to happen. For a few minutes, as she raced to warn Jaideep, the incident with Jack on the cliff above the river seemed unimportant. Now, as shock and adrenalin receded, moments from the unreal drama played and replayed in her mind.

Would Jack have killed her? Perhaps he would. Jack's obsession had run away with him, consumed him. He'd kidnapped her and held a knife to her throat. They had teetered over the edge of the precipice.

Charlotte had told Otto a condensed version of events as she drove through the night, to the place Jack had taken her. It hadn't been difficult to find – the route imprinted on her memory. Now they stood around the carcass, shocked and helpless. Tyre tracks had beaten a path through the dry grass but the trail disappeared at the surfaced road. Who knew where the perpetrators were now? Hours away.

Two dead animals. Charlotte remembered the tiger drinking from the pool – how beautiful it was, how vital. Now it was one of these inanimate piles of sticky meat and bone, empty of life and spirit.

Jen, Otto, Charlotte and Amrita ate together outside the lodge that evening. Jaideep was reluctant to let them go, but Otto assured him he would take care of them and escort them home. Charlotte had told Jaideep, and later the police, about the abduction. The police weren't overly concerned: a 'domestic' between a couple of young foreigners. Charlotte got the impression they thought she had exaggerated the seriousness of Jack's intentions. After all, she'd come to no harm and Jack was probably far away by now. What could they do about this spat between two young foreigners? And the way some young Westerners behaved – well, what could you expect? And the police had their hands full working with Jaideep and the other sanctuary officials on the poaching incident.

Jaideep, however, took the Jack problem very seriously. Although he had so much else to worry about, he listened attentively to her account, asked her dozens of questions and expressed his sorrow that he hadn't taken better care of her.

'He could have killed you,' he said, shaking his head. And of course he didn't want either Charlotte or Amrita to go anywhere unaccompanied.

Jaideep had no time to eat, heading instead for a briefing with the World Wildlife people about the poaching incident. He had several calls from the press to field. Even so, he escorted Amrita and Charlotte to the lodge, following them in his jeep, before exhorting a promise from Otto to accompany them back home at the end of the evening.

They ate together, on the veranda. Charlotte recounted to Jen the tale of mad Jack, the kidnapping and threats, the spectacle of the tiger and the vehicles she'd heard in the forest.

Jen's eyes widened. She went to Charlotte and gave her a fierce, protective hug. 'I'm so sorry,' she said. 'You don't deserve this. It sounds terrifying.'

'Except for seeing the tiger. I'll never forget that as long as I live. I can't bear to think they killed it.'

'Jen knew something was happening,' Otto said. 'She woke me up and told me you were in trouble.'

'So where's Jack now?' Amrita wondered. 'Where did he go, if you took the pick-up?'

Charlotte dipped a chapatti into a dish of lentil sauce and savoured the rich, spicy taste. Where indeed was Jack? Even in the company of her friends she felt an irrational fear of him, that he might at any point spring out and threaten her again. She was jumpy, nerves primed.

At the same time . . . she glanced over at Otto, aware he was looking at her. Despite everything, all the turbulent events, her feverish feelings for Otto hadn't abated. Nor his for her, she sensed. Even as they ate with the others and discussed these terrible events, even though they didn't touch or speak of the new connection between them, Charlotte was conscious of the atmosphere between and around them. She recalled the school physics experiments with magnets and iron filings, the magnetic force creating patterns in the filings. Now it seemed to her that the air between them was electrically charged by the desire of their hearts and bodies to be close again. Even as she thought of the kiss by the river, replayed it in her mind, her feelings intensified. Selfish yes, when tigers were dead, when the future of the sanctuary hung in the balance, but this love for Otto overwhelmed even those.

She'd guarded her feelings for so long, and now the floodgates were open. She had not a hope of putting this cat back in the bag. All the contained, pent-up passion she'd felt for Otto had emerged, overwhelming her. If this didn't work out – if he'd changed his mind, been acting on a whim – what then? Charlotte had no way back now. She was far, far from the shore. Charlotte felt a moment's plummeting panic.

She glanced at Otto again, unable to resist the temptation. He was looking at her too, and when their eyes met, a warm, golden smile illuminated his face. The panic melted. He was thinking of her. Jen and Amrita were talking but Charlotte didn't hear what they were saying. The kiss by the river . . . it rose up again in her memory, just the recollection of it making her skin tingle. Her emotions had slipped the reins. She wanted him again. Want, want, want. She had never imagined it was possible to want something so much.

And then, dread thought, is that what Jack felt?

Is that why he'd gone to such an extreme to get it?

Was it possible for this wanting to trample rational behaviour to such a degree that you'd turn into a stalker and abductor? Clearly, yes. People did just that. People like Jack.

In a strange way she felt sorry for him. On the other hand he was a terrifying warning. Wanting someone, as she wanted Otto, was no guarantee they felt the same way. It was possible to want something this much and to be terribly, utterly deluded.

'Charlie, are you okay?' Otto was still looking at her, the smile on his face. 'Are you thinking about Jack? You've nothing to worry about. I'm not letting you out of my sight.'

Charlotte nodded. 'I was thinking about Jack, yes.' She longed for an opportunity to be alone with Otto, but now wasn't the time, not with Jen and Amrita gathered for a meal. And she was conscious of Jen's eyes on her, watching every move, every word that passed between Otto and herself. What did Jen make of it? Was she upset? They needed to talk. Charlotte didn't want to hurt Jen – and getting together with your friend's ex was hardly honourable behaviour.

Just after ten, Amrita and Charlotte said they had to go home. Otto and Jen locked up, Otto grabbed his camera and they all climbed into the pick-up. Charlotte drove them to Jaideep and Prina's house; Otto would then drive Jen back to the lodge, so none of the women would have to be alone.

Prina invited them all in for tea. Jaideep was still working at the reserve office, she said.

'You had a phone call,' Prina said. 'A reporter. He said he was a friend of yours and asked if you'd call him back as soon as possible.' She'd written a name and number on a slip of paper, which she passed to Charlotte.

'It's Mark.' Charlotte raised her face and looked directly at Otto. 'No doubt he's heard about the poaching.'

'Are you going to call him?' Otto's voice had an edge.

'Yes. Yes I'd better.' The sanctuary would benefit from a positive report, and that's what she wanted to give Mark. Would he actually write fair? Hard to say. She knew that, for all the reporter's affability, getting a good story was the bottom line. He had to make a living.

The phone only rang once.

'Charlie? Thanks for calling back so quickly. How are you?'

'Yes, fine thanks. How are you?' Although every cell in her body seemed to yearn for contact with Otto, Mark's easy, affectionate manner was very engaging. She remembered the evening they'd spent together in the hotel restaurant in Goa, when this same confident, relaxed, good-looking man had enticed her into eating, drinking and talking too much, and they'd kissed, and

Charlotte had been tempted into doing rather more. Except that Mark had drawn back. She was so glad of that now. He'd been surprisingly wise and honourable. And now, of course, she couldn't imagine being with anyone other than Otto.

'I'm phoning about the tiger poaching,' Mark said.

'I rather thought that might be the case.'

'I understand you have the World Wildlife reps at the reserve? What I'd like most is an interview with the reserve manager. You're staying with him, right? Could you set something up?'

'I can certainly ask him,' she said.

'You can tell him we're friends,' he pushed. 'Put in a good word for me, eh? Tell him I'll do a great job – get some international attention.'

'I'm not sure international attention is what he wants just now.'

'I mean, in a good way. Put his side of the story, yes? All the challenges he faces, what extra support he needs, that kind of thing.'

'Sure – look, I said I'd ask him.'

'I'll call you back tomorrow,' Mark cajoled. 'If you get an answer sooner, call me.'

'Sure,' Charlotte repeated. 'Look, I've got to go. It's late.'

'Thanks for your help, Charlie,' Mark said. Then, after a pause: 'It's good to talk with you again. It'd be lovely to see you sometime.'

'You're welcome,' she said, gratified despite herself. 'Bye, Mark.'

Jen and Otto said their farewells and set off for the lodge. A wave of tiredness overwhelmed Charlotte so she said goodnight and went to bed, almost too weary to stand. She thought of Jen and Otto alone in the pick-up, wondered what they were talking about. Her mobile bleeped. She picked it up from the table beside her bed. The little screen flared in the dark. A message from Otto – he must have sent it outside the house, just before losing phone reception. Charlotte opened the text.

I love you I love you I love you. Charlie I love you. Otto xxx

A rush of feeling – as though huge, feathered, ethereal wings had passed through her body. She read the simple words over and over again. She wasn't deluded. He felt as she did. And now she had to wait, wait, wait the long, impossible hours of the night and the following day until she could see him again.

Otto

Otto's finger hovered above the send button for several seconds. Did he dare? Charlotte had seemed a little aloof at times during the evening. Perhaps aloof was too strong a word. Distant would be better. She said she'd been thinking about Jack.

Otto longed to have her to himself, to talk and find out what she was feeling. He was in a tumult of uncertainty. She'd hugged him perfunctorily when they'd parted, and then before that, taken the phone call from Mark the smooth reporter. Mark had taken a shine to Charlotte, back in Goa, hadn't he? At the time, Otto had noted this with some surprise – then forgotten it. Now he was in an agony of doubt and jealousy. Why was she taking calls from Mark? Was he after her? Did she like him?

'Are you going to send it?' Jen's cool, gentle voice broke into his thoughts. He'd been so lost in his musings he'd forgotten she was there, on the seat beside him in the pick-up.

'What?' he said.

'Are you going to send it?' she repeated. Otto pressed the button. There. Too late to recall it now. He was committed.

Perhaps Mark's call had spurred him on to make such a declaration. Jealousy – fear Charlotte might doubt how strongly he felt.

Jen hadn't seen what he had written. He'd told her he wanted to text Charlotte with the time of their meeting at the reserve office the following day. Jen probably wasn't fooled though. She knew him too well and the lie wouldn't be difficult for her to see through. Why not tell the truth? Jen, I've just sent Charlie a message saying 'I love you' four times. Like an idiot.

Had he ever told anyone he'd loved them before? To be honest, yes. He'd even thought he'd meant it at the time, but the feeling had never lasted, and now it seemed he'd had no idea – because what he felt for Charlotte was nothing like his previous short-lived flares of infatuation. Even Jen. Even Maria – Maria who was dead – his crush on her, the fantasies he'd built around her, seemed ridiculous now. Poor Maria. I'm sorry, Jen. I'm sorry, Maria.

He started the pick-up and drove through the night to the lodge. Would Charlotte be reading his text now? What was she thinking? Even if she replied he wouldn't receive it till the morning. Perhaps if Jen hadn't been in the pick-up, he'd have remained parked up outside the house, waiting, poor fool, within range, for an answer.

Jen was talking to him. Otto yanked his attention back to the here and now. She was telling him something about the painting she was planning, a picture of a tiger for the sanctuary. He tried to focus on what she was saying and provide useful responses. They stopped outside the lodge, Otto cut the engine and looked across at her.

'I'm sorry,' he said. 'I'm a bit distracted. Tired.'

Now Jen wasn't paying attention. She was staring straight ahead. She blinked and stretched out her hand to Otto's arm. Then, still not looking at him, she said:

'What's that?'

The temperature in the cab seemed to drop.

'What's what?'

'The light inside the lodge. Did you leave it on? And what's that, on the veranda?' Jen raised her hand to point at an indistinct hump. 'Is it an animal?'

Otto stared into the darkness, trying to make out what it was.

'No. It's too still,' he said, picking up Jen's unease. Something was wrong.

'Wait here.' He climbed out of the cab. Jen ignored his instruction and in a moment they were standing side by side in front of the pick-up. The place was silent, and nothing moved. Still Otto felt wary. Slowly the two of them stepped closer to the lodge, Jen clutching Otto's arm.

'It's my rucksack,' Otto said. 'What's it doing outside? Have we been burgled?' He ran the last few steps, to find out what had happened.

His rucksack, flat on its back, had been emptied. Clothes lay across the floor. The rucksack itself looked as though it had been attacked by an animal, the royal-blue nylon fabric slashed over and over again.

'Oh my god,' Jen said. She was standing in the doorway, looking into the room. 'Someone's taken the place to pieces.'

Shocked and numb, Otto stepped into the lodge and surveyed the scene. The room hadn't just been ransacked – on a first glance it didn't appear that anything had been taken – it had been attacked, defaced and violated. Jen's rucksack lay on the floor, similarly slashed. Their clothes had been ripped and trampled, the beds overturned, toiletries emptied and smashed. Jen's precious art-book had been torn open and pages lay on the floor. She gasped when she saw them and hurried over to scoop them up. Otto stepped forward. His passport lay partially hidden by the over-turned bed. He picked it up. The cover was torn, several pages had been pulled out – and the picture of Otto on the back page had been heavily defaced with an intense scribble of black biro. His face had been obliterated.

Otto shivered. Someone hated him this much? What kind of fury had been unleashed? He put the passport into his back pocket.

'They've destroyed my new canvas and paints,' Jen said mournfully.

'They?'

'We weren't gone that long. I don't think one person could have done all this,' Jen said. Otto moved closer and put his arm around her. She rested her head on his shoulder. They regarded the spectacle with dismay. Nothing had been taken, but all their belongings had been trashed. The violators hadn't even been looking for goods to steal – no, this was a very vindictive, personal attack. A frightening level of anger.

'Jack,' Otto said.

Jen nodded. 'I think you're right. Jack – and friends.'

'Who though? What friends? I thought he was travelling on his own.'

'Do you think he's still here?' Jen turned nervously, looking over her shoulder. 'What if he comes back?'

Otto kept hold of her. 'I won't let him hurt you.'

'But if he's got friends – how could we stop him?'

'We can't stay here.' Otto tried to sound confident but he was frightened too. Jack and these mysterious friends could be outside now: surely they couldn't be far away. If Jack hated him this much, what else might he do?

'We'll go back to Amrita's place,' Otto said. 'They might be able to put us up, when we tell them what's happened. Or they could tell us somewhere else in town we could stay. I don't want to stay here.'

Jen broke away from Otto and picked up various pages from her art-book. She'd started to cry, quietly.

'Leave it,' Otto said, trying to pull her away. 'We need to get away now. This will have to be sorted in the morning, when it's light.'

Jen seemed reluctant to leave her broken possessions but Otto was wondering to what lengths might Jack and these mooted cronies go, to get their revenge? For surely that was his motivation. He'd seen Otto and Charlotte together, and having failed to abduct Charlotte, he'd trashed the lodge to punish Otto, the object of Charlotte's affections.

'Come on,' Otto said. 'Leave it. We have to go.' He raised his voice a notch and tried to pull Jen away. Her tearful face turned to him.

'I know, it's just – I feel so horrible. To think of them going through my things. And especially here – this stuff is all I have. My link with home.' She shivered. 'Why didn't I know? Especially when they trampled on my book. Why didn't I feel it?'

Otto ushered her out, still holding her book and a handful of its scattered pages. He switched off the light and closed the door. The padlock lay broken on the ground but in any case, locking the lodge would be pointless now. He scanned their surroundings. Under cover of the night it would be easy for people to hide. Had their assailants driven out here? If so, where were the vehicles? Perhaps they'd come and gone again. Still, he couldn't be sure. His nerves prickled.

'Get in the pick-up,' he said, looking around for any potential threat. Jen was very quiet. She crept into the cab and sat on the passenger seat, knees hunched to her chest. Otto's camera was still in the cab. Thank god he hadn't left it in the lodge. He was tempted to nip back and take some pictures of the devastation. Jen sensed his hesitation.

'Can we get out of here, please?' she said. He started the engine, turned the pick-up and drove back up the lane, away from the lodge and back towards Amrita's house.

And to Charlotte.

Charlotte.

Jen

She stared through the windscreen. Only one headlight working –
trees loomed from the darkness like ghosts, and disappeared again,
foliage bleached in the electric light. The pick-up jolted through
potholes and dried ruts in the rough lane. Once she saw the eyes of
an animal, reflecting, something small and low – a wild dog perhaps.

Jen hugged her legs closer to her chest, holding on to herself.
She couldn't accept what had happened. She felt violated. The
remains of the art-book rested on the dashboard in front of her,
testimonial to the destruction of her possessions. She'd stuffed
some of the torn pages into her pocket. The act had, presumably,
been carried out against Otto and Charlotte and she, Jen, had been
caught up in the vicious aftermath.

She glanced at Otto. His knuckles were white, gripping the
steering wheel. His face was intent, staring into the night at the
road ahead. He was afraid. Jen squeezed her eyes shut, blocking
out the phantasmal forest.

Otto slammed his foot on the brake. Jen flew forward against her
seatbelt, her head jerking forward and back, as the pick-up ground
to a halt. A large branch lay across the lane, a web of twigs and
leaves picked out by the headlights, white against the blackness.

Otto swore. He ground the gears into reverse and tried to back up
– but too late. Three men ran out into the lane. One grabbed the

driver's door, the other one stood at the passenger door. The third hammered on Otto's window and started shouting something in a language they couldn't understand. Two of the men had spears, the third had a gun tucked into the waistband of his jeans. These things Jen saw in a flash, as the men moved in and out of the pool of light cast by the single headlight. One tugged Otto's door but it wouldn't open. Another tried Jen's door, pulled her out and then reached for Otto. The scene unfolded before her eyes like a series of scenes from a graphic novel, images in black and white that didn't quite flow, but took place, because of the light, in dramatic, isolated moments.

Otto struggled and yelled but the third man took the gun from his waistband and held it to Otto's chin. Jen knew nothing about guns but this one didn't look modern. That did not, however, make it appear any less deadly. Otto stopped fighting. He stood bolt upright, breathing heavily.

The three men appeared to be Indian. No sign of Jack. Had they been wrong about the desecration of the lodge, about Jack? All three were shorter and smaller than Otto, but he seemed awkward and clumsy in comparison; the men all possessed a strength and economy of movement that suggested they were very dangerous.

One man held Jen by her upper arm, his fingers pressing into her flesh.

All this had taken place over a matter of seconds, almost without Jen registering exactly what was going on. Now her emotions caught up, a horrible falling inside, as though her body were hollow.

The men looked at Otto and exchanged words. One pointed at Jen and the pick-up. Apparently they were satisfied because the man with the gun nodded and jabbed the weapon's short muzzle against Otto's skin. Jen was pulled away. Despite the gun, Otto yelped and yanked against his captor.

'Jen!' he called out. 'Jen, Jen! Leave her alone, you bastards! Let her go!'

Within moments she couldn't see him because the man pulled her off the lane and into the trees. Twigs stung her face, her feet stumbled on the rough ground.

'Jen!' she heard him yell again. But the word was cut off. What had they done to him? She listened for a gunshot, but could only hear her own laboured breathing.

Her captor was silent, seemingly able to see in the dark, moving implacably through the trees to a four-wheel drive parked up in a clearing. He yanked Jen's hands behind her back, tied them, and bundled her into the rear of the vehicle. She fell heavily onto her knees and face, bruising herself on the thick, dusty plastic of the interior.

Why were they taking her? What was happening to Otto? At that moment she felt more afraid for him. She was okay – at least, for the moment. But Otto – were they hurting him? Were they going to kill him? What was this all about? Her entire body was shaking and she was breathing too fast. Her body didn't seem to belong to her at all, flailing about in the back of the four by four, joints loose, muscles turned to water. She strained her ears to hear if Otto were shouting again but she could hear nothing but the sounds of her own panicking body.

Time passed. Hard to say how long: perhaps ten minutes, though it seemed endless. The seconds stretched out, terrible imaginings filling her mind. The rest of the world ceased to exist, only the dread she felt, like a huge, cold hand pressed on her head, as she waited for the sound of a gunshot.

The doors of the four by four opened. Jen struggled to her knees. Dimly she could make out the heads of the three men, sitting side by side. The engine started and the vehicle bumped over the rough ground.

'What have you done to Otto?' she shouted. Could they even hear her? No way of knowing. 'Where's Otto? Where are you taking me?'

Otto

One of the men kicked him behind the knees, knocking him to the ground. Then, without speaking, they kicked him again and struck at him with the handles of their spears. Even in this moment of extremity Otto noted some incongruity in the men's contemporary dress – jeans, trainers – and the archaic weaponry. Archaic or not, the spears inflicted pain and damage. Instinctively he curled up against them, trying to protect his face and body. The blows landed mainly on his back and legs. Dimly he noted that his attackers were not trying to kill him – they could have done so easily enough. No, they wanted to hurt, frighten and damage him. They were succeeding.

A curiously cool part of his mind clung on to this belief, even as he flinched and struggled and screamed on the ground, all dignity gone. He found himself numbering the blows, trying to focus away from the pain. If he counted long enough, this undeserved punishment would come to an end. Seven, eight, nine – a trainered foot hit the base of his spine, sending intolerable pain shooting through his back. He screamed, like an animal. Eighteen, nineteen, twenty . . . The beating stopped. A couple of quiet words passed between the men, and then they were gone.

Otto lay perfectly still. It was curiously blissful this moment; the punishment had finished and his body, in shock, had yet to register the countless hurts it had endured. He knew the pain would begin very soon. He was also frightened the men would come back and resume the attack. Most of all, he was afraid for Jen – what were they doing to her?

Through the trees he heard a vehicle starting up and driving away. Otto struggled to move, hardly able to sit upright, catching a glimpse of the vehicle disappearing into the night. Had they taken Jen? Would they hurt her?

He shouted her name.

They'd gone.

The fog of pain came over him, overwhelming. The world faded. He sank back onto the ground and lost consciousness.

He woke just before dawn. The sky was pale, the sun about to rise. Hours had gone by. He pulled himself into a sitting position, his body a cataclysm of hurt.

'Oh my god, oh my god, oh my god.' He was muttering under his breath. What should he do now? Get help. He had to contact Jaideep and the police. He limped back to the pick-up. First he had to move the branch, though this proved easier than he'd expected. The branch wasn't too heavy, only awkward and bristly. He crept into the cab, started the engine and continued the drive to Amrita's house.

With every passing minute his body hurt more and his worries for Jen grew increasingly desperate. What was happening to her? What were those dangerous men doing to her? He couldn't bear to think about it, and he couldn't stop thinking about it either. Fear for her safety and guilt for his failure to protect her beat a twin rhythm. Driving was an immense effort. He had to concentrate on every move, each turn of the wheel, every agonising change of gear. At last he pulled up outside the house, climbed painfully from the cab and knocked on the front door.

Jaideep opened it. 'Who is it?' He squinted through the narrow opening. 'Otto?' Jaideep's mouth dropped open. 'What happened to you?' He backed away from the door, inviting Otto to step inside. 'Prina!' Jaideep called. She stepped into the living room and her eyes widened when she saw Otto.

'I look bad?' Otto said heavily. Prina didn't say a word, but she nodded.

Jaideep ushered Otto to a chair. 'What happened? Where's Jen? Is this Jack's work too?'

'No.' Otto shook his head. 'I don't know who they were. Three men blocked the road and pulled us out of the pick-up. They took Jen! I don't know where they've gone or what they're going to do with her. You've got to help me find her. We've got to get the police.'

He looked at his hands. They were covered in blood, some of it dark and partially dried, some of it moist and fresh. Jaideep went to the telephone and picked up the handset, as a door opened. Charlotte, sleepy, dressed in her pyjamas, stepped into the room. She had her mobile in one hand. She stared at Otto.

'I've just had a message,' she said. 'Jack's got Jen.' She was wide-eyed, like a little girl. 'He says I've got to go to him, or he'll hurt her.' Charlotte glanced at Jaideep. 'Put the phone down,' she said. 'Please, put it down. He said he'll hurt her if we call the police.'

Still Jaideep hesitated.

'Please!' she said. He responded to the note of desperation in her voice, and slowly replaced the receiver.

'What are we going to do?' Otto said.

Charlotte seemed to register for the first time exactly how damaged Otto was. She made an inarticulate sound and came hurrying over to him.

'Did Jack do this to you? Did he hurt you?'

'No, no, it wasn't Jack,' Otto said. 'But Jack says he has Jen now?' He couldn't work out how this had happened. On the other

191

hand, if this were true, then maybe Jen was safe for the time being. He felt a moment's relief.

'So who did this?' Charlotte demanded.

'Three men. Indian men. I don't know who they were,' Otto said. An agonising pounding filled his head. His hands had started stinging, a new note in his body's symphony of pain. 'So that was Jack? Those guys must be helping him. But why would anyone help Jack?'

'He says I've got to go to him, or he'll hurt her,' Charlotte repeated.

'Where? Where does he want you to go?' Jaideep demanded.

'The lodge. I've got to be there at eight – in two hours.'

'You can't go,' Otto said. 'We'll get the police, or I'll go myself. But however we tackle this, you can't go.'

'We can't call the police, not yet!' Charlotte raised her hand. 'He'll hurt her, I know he will. He's capable of anything!'

'Then I'll go.' Otto tried to stand up again, but half fell back onto the sofa.

Charlotte shook her head. 'I'm the one he's asked for – the one he wants,' she said in a low, slow voice. 'You're in no fit state, Otto. I have to go.'

'Wait a minute, how did he text you if he's at the lodge?' Otto said. 'There's no signal.'

'Presumably he wasn't at the lodge when he sent it,' Charlotte said impatiently. 'It wasn't sent from his phone either. I don't know the number.'

'Then how do you know it was even from Jack? You can't go on your own,' Otto repeated. 'Look what they did to me. They're dangerous.'

'He's right,' Jaideep said. He stepped forward, taking control of the situation. 'Otto, you need to take care of yourself. Clean up, attend to your wounds. We can't risk calling the police just yet. I don't want Charlotte putting herself in danger; I want you to send a message back to Jack – tell him you'll be at the lodge. I don't think he'll hurt Jen. It's you he wants, not her.'

Otto was shaking his head. 'I don't get it,' he said. 'Did Jack hire the heavies? Are they friends of his? How come he has those kinds of resources?'

'Otto,' Jaideep said sharply. 'Do as I told you. You're covered in blood and bruises. Do you need a doctor?'

Otto looked up at him. 'I don't think so,' he said. 'They hurt me a lot – but I don't think anything's broken. They knew what they were doing.'

He saw how tired Jaideep looked. Presumably he'd been up all night. He felt again how little Jaideep deserved this to deal with, on top of the other worries – the funding application, the train accident, the poachers, the dead tigers. Hard to imagine he'd ever want to take on another European volunteer considering the trouble they'd brought with them, even inadvertently. Now he had to deal with the press, World Wildlife – and the assault and abduction of overseas visitors staying at the sanctuary.

Otto headed for the bathroom. He closed and locked the door, then stood in front of the mirror. Although he'd prepared himself, his reflection was still a shock. A mask of dried blood covered half his face, from his hairline down to his jaw. His left eye was swollen, and the left side of his mouth. Blood on his neck too, and his shoulder, staining his T-shirt. Purple bruises were blossoming all over his face, and judging from the pain, across his back, shoulders and legs. He made a grotesque spectacle. Lucky he hadn't been seriously hurt. Lucky? Regarding the monster in the mirror, he didn't feel exactly fortunate. Instead he felt a welling rage for the way he'd been beaten and humiliated, for the treatment meted out to Jen and Charlotte. How had Jack – one man – managed to cause so much damage and trouble to so many people?

And Jen. What was happening to Jen? Would Jack hurt her?

Was she afraid? Otto felt profoundly guilty. He'd been useless; he'd failed to protect her.

He unlocked and opened the bathroom door again.

'Charlie? Could you help me please?'

She was sitting on the sofa talking to Jaideep and Amrita but when she looked up at Otto a light seemed to flare in her face. She glanced at her hosts. Jaideep nodded.

'Of course,' Jaideep said. 'Go on. You must help him.'

She came to the bathroom and pushed the door to, so they were close together in the confined space beneath the harsh electric light. Despite his wounds and worries Otto felt acutely conscious of her physical presence, as though he were drawn towards her by a million intangible filaments.

'I can't take the T-shirt off,' he said. 'My shoulder's stiffening up. Could you help? I think you'll have to cut it off.'

Charlotte found some scissors and snipped through the blood-stiffened fabric. When the cold blade touched Otto's skin he flinched. She was slow and painstaking but the process was difficult. Every time he moved a muscle his body screamed in pain. At last the T-shirt dropped to the floor. Charlotte took a breath.

'It looks bad?' Otto said.

'Yes, it looks very bad.' Charlotte filled the sink with warm water and began to wash his back. When she immersed the sponge a second time, clouds of blood drifted away from it into the clean water. She was gentle. Although the washing hurt, it soothed in equal measure.

'Turn round,' she said. 'I'll do your front. Here – would you lift your arm a little?' Now Charlie was standing in front of him, head slightly bowed, focused on the work in hand.

'Sit down,' she said, indicating the edge of the bath. Otto did as he was told and Charlotte washed his face. This hurt most of all. The skin around his mouth was raw, the flesh around his left

194

eye swelling more and more. Charlotte rinsed the sponge one more time and regarded him.

'I think that'll do,' she said. 'But I have to say, you don't look pretty.'

'I don't suppose I do,' he said. 'But you do. You're beautiful.'

'Am I?' she said, wonderingly. 'I've never thought I was beautiful.'

Otto trembled, idiotically shy. He thought about the text he'd sent earlier and realised she was thinking of it too. They were close together, which was unavoidable in the confines of the bathroom, and the tension between them was at once delicious and unbearable.

'Charlie,' he began, the word almost breaking on his tongue.

'Don't say anything,' Charlotte rushed. 'Not now. Just – just wait a little bit.'

Otto sighed, frustration – and relief. He wanted to put his arms around her again but his body hurt too much and he was conscious of how grisly he looked.

'Thank you,' he said. They were silent for a few moments, then Charlotte lifted her right hand and placed it gently on his left cheek, giving him the lightest of caresses.

'We have to find Jen,' she said.

Jen

One of the men pulled Jen out of the four by four. Torchlight shone in her face and a male voice shouted out: 'That's not her! You've got the wrong girl!'

Jen couldn't see him because of the light in her eyes, but she recognised the voice.

'Jack?' Her voice was rough and croaky. 'What's going on?'

'That's the wrong girl!' Jack repeated. He sounded incensed.

Another voice, unmoved by Jack's strop, said: 'She was travelling with the blond English guy. How many girlfriends does he have?'

Someone else laughed. Jen shaded her eyes, trying to make out where she was, and with whom. She was afraid, but Jack's presence allayed her fear considerably. Now she knew why she'd been taken – even if mistakenly – and she knew who was behind it.

'Jack, would you stop shining that light in my face please?' She tried to sound reasonable and ordinary. 'Where are we?'

Jack ignored her, instead beginning to argue with the men who had brought her. These men, much cooler than Jack, didn't sound at all bothered by his outbursts. She could almost hear them shaking their heads and shrugging. They'd brought him the blond man's girlfriend – they'd fulfilled their part of the bargain, whatever that might be.

'Please, Jack,' she said. 'Can we talk? Maybe we can sort something out.'

But Jack wasn't listening to her. He was shouting at the men who'd brought her. She tried to make out what he was saying – something about the risk he was taking, the favour he'd done. But these men were backing away, leaving Jack to it. She heard the doors of the four by four opening and shutting, and the sound of the engine as it drove away.

Her eyes adjusted a little to the darkness. She was standing in the middle of a cluster of wood and thatch homes, beneath a canopy of trees. She could smell smoke and animal manure. A village? How did Jack find it?

The men had driven away. Jack and one other man – from the little village presumably – remained with Jen. Jack continued to rant about the botched abduction, seemingly oblivious to Jen's presence, and to how she might be feeling, having been snatched and carried off to this remote place.

What would he do now? How far would he go to get what he wanted? Jack's tirade eased off and Jen tried again.

'I'm frightened, Jack,' she said. 'What do you want with me? Would you take me home please?'

Who was Jack, that he could command men like that? Had he paid them? Was he secretly wealthy? They didn't seem to respect him very much.

How would he take her home? They'd driven some time to reach this place. Were there other vehicles here? Jack must have been involved in the wrecking of the lodge – the personal vindictiveness of the attack certainly suggested so. Would hired heavies have bothered to scribble out Otto's face in his passport photo? Jack had been at the lodge and returned to the village while his three friends set off to punish Otto and kidnap Charlotte. They'd made a very stupid mistake though, taking Jen. Had Jack not given them a description and clear instructions?

It seemed that they didn't care all that much. They'd carried out their orders lazily.

Still Jack didn't answer. He seemed to be thinking. The other man waited patiently by his side.

'Jen, isn't it? You're Jen – Charlie's best friend,' Jack said at last. His tone was level and calculating.

'Yes,' she said.

'Maybe I can recover something from this stupid mess.' He grabbed her upper arm and pulled her past one of the thatched dwellings.

'Look out there,' he said, gesturing to the dark-swallowed forest. 'We're twenty miles from anywhere. I want you to stay here and I'm going to get word to Charlie that I have you. And I'll invite her to join us.'

Jen shook her head, close to tears, exhaustion suddenly overwhelming her. 'So what are you going to do? Tie me? Lock me up? Threaten me?' She was losing her composure now. This was all too much.

'Weren't you listening?' Jack said. 'I don't need to lock you up. Where would you go?' Still holding her arm, he dragged her to the open door of one of the little houses. He shined the torch inside, revealing a kind of pallet bed and an ancient blanket.

'You can stay here,' he said. 'I'll have to send a message to Charlie. No signal here – we're miles from anywhere.' He said this with a particular emphasis, reminding Jen how isolated she was.

'Don't worry,' he said with relish. 'The people here will take care of you till I get back. I'm sure we'll all be reunited before too long.'

Jack backed away, shining the torch into Jen's face. The other man was still waiting. Jack said something to him and they moved off. A minute later Jen heard a vehicle start up (a motorbike?), the bark of the engine breaking the silence that hung over the village and the forest. The motorbike departed but Jen could hear it for some time, getting further and further away. Then silence again, falling like a curtain.

She was all alone, in this strange little village.

The villagers – all asleep? Did they know she was here? Surely they must have heard everything – the vehicles, the altercation. She imagined them hiding inside their huts, listening, perhaps afraid to come out. What was the relationship between the thugs in the four by four and the people in the village? Perhaps she would find out in the morning.

Jen slipped inside the dwelling and curled up on the bed. Dry dirt on the floor, the scent of wood smoke, spiced food and warm human bodies imbued in the wood and thatch. The blanket smelled, not unpleasantly, of goat and straw. The hard bed offered little in the way of comfort and Jen wondered how she would possibly sleep – though sleep she did, within moments.

A soft, damp nose tickled her. Jen opened her eyes, to see the white face of a young goat looming above hers, its soft lips browsing over her cheeks and nose. Evidently Jen wasn't very interesting – the little goat drifted away, through the doorway, where it joined several others. The adults wore little rusty bells that clanked discordantly. They were followed by a boy of about eight or nine who ushered them along.

Jen turned over on the pallet bed. White light spilled through the doorway onto the dirt floor. Several paper pictures were pinned onto the rough walls – two of Hindu gods, and one, bizarrely, of Elvis Presley. Seeing the pictures, memories fluttered in Jen's head. She'd dreamed of the tiger again, in the black-and-white forest. The hunted tiger, only when the hunters tried to kill it, the tiger broke and became two tigers, then four, eight, sixteen and so on, till the forest was teeming with them. If only, Jen thought, lying on her side, the smell of goat teasing her nose. Another dream too, if she could fish it from the depths of her mind: something flashing in the darkness, winking in and out of the light, a being of bright colours. She thought of the god Shiva, the dancer, the god of making and unmaking. Had he visited her dreams?

Jen sat up and lifted her legs over the side of the bed, planting her sandalled feet on the floor. It was hot, even so early. She felt the stickiness of sweat on her forehead, her back and under her arms. What would happen now? Had Jack contacted Charlotte? What would she do?

A face appeared at the doorway – a young female face, very smooth and beautiful, with huge dark eyes. Gold-coloured earrings, bangles on silk-skinned arms. This lovely face grinned, revealing perfect white teeth. The girl – about twelve or thirteen – said something, but Jen couldn't understand the language she was speaking. Jen shook her head and shrugged. The girl laughed. She crept forward into the doorway, grinning but evidently shy. She squatted so her face was level with Jen's, pointed to herself and said: 'Saanjh.'

Jen smiled. 'I'm Jen,' she said. 'Jen.'

Saanjh's dense black hair fell in a single plait, which hung over her left shoulder and down to her waist. She wore a deep-red sari, the soft, well-worn fabric stitched with tiny flowers. Saanjh said something else Jen was unable to understand – then gesticulated, raising her hand to her mouth. Evidently the question was, did Jen want something to eat? Jen nodded. The girl disappeared.

Jen was bursting with questions. Who were these people? They looked different to the other villagers she'd seen – their clothes, even their faces. She guessed they were Adivasi, tribal people. She'd read a little about them, intrigued, at the reserve office. Apparently many such tribes lived in the state of Tamil Nadu, often in the forests and forest fringes, secretive, living apart. She had not anticipated meeting them.

So what was their relationship with the men who had brought her here – and attacked Otto? Otto. Her heart lurched to think of him. Had they hurt him badly? Had he reached Charlie and Jaideep? They would be worrying about her, looking for her.

Saanjh returned with a cup of milk and a piece of flatbread, still warm from the skillet. Jen took it gratefully. She savoured the peculiar flavour of goat's milk, the freshness of the bread. Saanjh watched her eat.

'Thank you,' Jen said. Was she a prisoner? What would happen if she stepped out of the hut? Would the people try and stop her leaving the village? Then again – where would she go? The language was a barrier in itself.

Saanjh shuffled forwards and sat beside Jen. She touched her hair, marvelling at the colour, then played with Jen's beads and bangles. Jen took one off and handed it to Saanjh, a gift. Saanjh looked thrilled. She slipped it over her own slender hand.

'Can we go out?' Jen indicated at the door and stood up. She had no idea how long it would take Jack to come back from his message-sending and she wanted to learn as much as she could about this place before he returned. Perhaps Jack had underestimated her and she would find a way to escape and get home.

Saanjh, guileless, nodded happily.

The early light of day revealed it was indeed a small settlement: only half a dozen dwellings, some makeshift animal enclosures, the ubiquitous chickens scratching about. Three women were talking together outside one of the little houses, sitting on the dry ground, one with a baby in her arms. They looked up at Jen as she walked past with Saanjh. One covered her face with the end of her sari, overcome by shyness.

'How many people live here?' Jen asked. 'Where are the men?'

But Saanjh just grinned. She couldn't understand. Jen's hundreds of questions would have to go unanswered. Instead she had to observe and work things out for herself. Not much to see in the tiny village though. Beyond it, the forest stretched, with its green shadows and piercings of sunlight. No road to the village, only the tracks beaten through the vegetation by vehicles – presumably the four by four she'd travelled in the previous night.

Jen gazed into the trees. A narrow stream emerged from a stony outcrop and tumbled in a narrow channel past the village, where it opened out into a shallow pool. On the other side of the stream, the trees seemed to huddle together, occluding the light, creating a dark space within the forest.

'What's that?' She pointed. 'Can we go there?'

Saanjh ignored the question. She turned away, beckoning for Jen to follow her, wanting perhaps to introduce her to the women. Jen took a deep breath. She stepped away from the village and walked through the long grass, across the stream and towards the dark trees. Would they stop her? She tried to be confident, striding forward, waiting all the time to be stopped. But nothing happened. She walked further. Finally she looked over her shoulder. Saanjh was standing close to the settlement, gazing after her, perfectly still, except that a breeze plucked at her sari, so the fabric looped over her shoulder fluttered. She was bright like a jewel amid the subdued greens of the forest. One of her golden bangles glittered in a chink of sunlight. Saanjh's young face was solemn. Something symbolic about her, the upright posture, her stillness, as though she were a sentinel, or a warning. Jen looked away and continued to walk.

The trees grew up in a kind of wall, the straight columns of the trunks interwoven with creepers. Jen skirted the place, looking for a way in, or through. She sensed it, a whisper of the supernatural, a prickle running over her skin and in her bones. This whisper had summoned her from the village – was it also the reason Saanjh hadn't followed?

Jen found an opening – a passage through the vegetation, created by an animal probably. She also saw stone – carved stone, a rusty red-brown, and a carved face peeping through ropey creepers and waxy white blossom. Another holy place.

She ducked under the foliage, thinking of Mary Lennox, the girl from *The Secret Garden*. Mary had spent her early years in India.

The path ran under branches and tumblings of red stone. Once or twice Jen had to crawl to pass through. She could smell dirt and the frankincense perfume of the creepers. Insects buzzed on the air, and once she heard the shrill cry of a monkey. Were there snakes? She kept a lookout, taking care where she placed her hands and knees.

The little tunnel opened up. Jen stood up and stretched, grateful to be on her feet again.

A ruined temple. Red-brown stone walls ran to right and left, another in front her. No roof, the place was open to sun and rain. She was standing in a corridor. She felt it again, the note of the uncanny, as though someone were singing: inaudible but registering in the body and soul, disturbing her thoughts.

Silent, and still. Trees had eaten into the stonework, prising it apart with roots and branches. Vines and creepers hung over the walls, creating a cloak of leaves and flowers. Jen moved along the corridor to a courtyard. The place wasn't large. A square tower, ornamented but broken, rose above a black doorway. A smaller courtyard opened to the left. Trees grew all around, high above the walls and the tower, so the temple was contained – perhaps a miniature place in a green bottle. Now she thought of *Alice in Wonderland*. Maybe she had shrunk as she'd entered the temple – and this ruin could be held in the palm of a hand. She felt disorientated. A strange void seemed to open in her chest, just below her heart.

'Curiouser and curiouser,' she said aloud. The words bounced off the walls. Sculptures adorned the stonework, much eroded, though this seemed to add to their beauty: scenes of dancers, hunting, animals, gods – and some of a frankly erotic nature, tender and joyful depictions of love-making that sent a quivering arrow of something through her. Her cheeks burned. She turned away.

Jen walked through the doorway into the body of the temple. The place smelled of cool stone and rotting leaves but it felt empty, unlike the courtyard and passageways, which seemed charged with the lingering presence of whatever spirit it was that haunted the place. She sighed, clearing her mind, inviting a vision or communication – something to tell her why she had been brought here. Jen didn't doubt she'd been brought here, to these ruins, for a reason – she saw signs and omens everywhere. The mistaken abduction, the choice of forest village for her prison – these had all taken her, step by step, to this singular place.

Jen returned to the courtyard and sat, cross-legged, on the warm, dusty stone floor. The presence prowled the temple, like a great cat. She sensed it circling her, sliding through the broken stonework, shadow to shadow. The forest's great trees arched overhead. No noises now, no monkeys or birds, only the singular, intensifying note of the supernatural, heard not by the ears but in the mind and bones.

Jen looked at the ground, drew in the dust with her finger, and waited.

A wave of heat passed through her body, and then a blast of cold that made her shiver. The sun blinked, as though something had passed in front of it. The sculptures on the walls seemed to move, coming to brief, celebratory life – dancing, hunting, lovemaking. A breeze, from nowhere, scooped up a handful of dust, whirled it in the air, let it fall again.

One of the waxy white flowers from the rigging of creepers dropped slowly to the ground. A second blossom fell, and a third, each one step on from the next. The flowers marked a path, dropping one by one, along the side of the courtyard. Something was moving towards her.

Closer, closer. The white flowers lay on the ground, showing the progression of the spirit, visitor – the *something*. Jen quivered, trying not to pay it too much attention – better to acknowledge these visitations indirectly, from the corner of one's eye. She continued to draw in the dust, circles and patterns, like the rice powder designs she'd seen the housewives creating on their door-steps. A flower dropped, seemingly from nowhere, landing on the ground in front of her. Jen raised her head. She kept her attention vague, her eyes unfocused. Something shimmered on the air. The trees moved, seeming to bend over and close in, cradling the temple ruins. The unearthly sound, the powerful, single note, made the walls vibrate. The carved figures swam over the surface of the stone. Fragrance filled the cup of the ruin in waves – attar of roses, then almond and jasmine.

A tremor again, blurring the temple and the trees. Jen took off her sandals and stood up. This was holy ground.

A pillar of white, conceived from air and light. The pillar became a stem, and then a tree with a multitude of branches, blind-ing bright, and the tree became a human form, a woman with ten arms and ten hands. Her glittering hair hung loose to her waist, and her skin, though pale, gave off a fierce golden light. She had jewellery of gold too, earrings, necklaces, a plated belt embedded with huge, round pearls and burning rubies. A quarter-moon shone from her forehead.

Jen bowed her head.

Durga. The divine feminine; consort of the god Shiva.

Durga: creativity and compassion.

She held a lotus flower in one of her ten hands. The others flexed and moved, making ritual gestures. No part of the goddess was still; she seemed to flow, like a waterfall, as though this manifesta-tion was always renewing itself.

Jen couldn't look at the goddess for more than a moment. Durga was too bright, too perfect to gaze upon. She could only be glimpsed, or seen in part.

A low rumble, like thunder. The sound came again, a deep, visceral growl. Nerves prickled along Jen's spine. Now Durga was sitting on the back of a huge tiger. The creature raised its fiery head. Its mouth was open, revealing the rich pink cavern of a mouth with its moist, fleshy tongue and ranks of fierce teeth. Long white whiskers jutted from its muzzle.

The goddess lost definition, her radiance absorbed by the tiger. She faded on the air, as her mount, the tiger, gained in strength. Durga vanished and in that moment the tiger became one, two, four, eight tigers – which leaped over and around the temple. Their great bodies brushed against Jen. She felt the shock of contact – fur, whiskers, hot breath. They ran all around her, heavy bodies impossibly graceful, illuminated by one spirit, the essence that was all tigers, emerging from distant deeps.

And they were gone.

The temple was empty.

Above her head, the trees moved in a breeze. Leaves rustled. Far away a peacock screeched. A monkey, closer, whooped and its companions whooped back. Jen was shaking. She took a long, deep breath. The dust on the ground was undisturbed. Neither goddess nor tigers had left any mark. Of course not.

Jen smeared away the patterns she'd drawn and replaced her sandals. She sat down, her body overcome by weakness, feeling contradictory urges to laugh and cry. She heard a ringing in her ears.

Why had Durga shown herself? What did she want of Jen? Durga, a compassionate creator and a mighty warrior, whose mount was a tiger . . . The confrontation was coming and Jen shouldn't shirk it, this battle with those who would slaughter the few remaining tigers, exterminating the species from the wilds where they belonged.

Jen had never been very brave. She was afraid of so many things in the ordinary, everyday world. She'd learned to rely on herself in Goa, when she'd left the protection of travelling with her friends. Now she'd been asked to take another step. No use hiding away. She had, like Durga, to be a warrior. She needed to act.

The temple seemed smaller and more ruinous now: heaps of stones, weathered carvings, all pulled apart by the forest. Jen found the animal path through the broken wall and the trees. A solitary stone figure, leaning sideways, about two feet high, gripped by stems and leaves, peered out at her. Jen stared into its calm, even face, dropped to her hands and knees, and crawled out into the forest.

Saanjh was standing at the edge of the little village, still staring through the trees. How long had Jen been away? Hard to say. Saanjh had known she would come back. She had waited. Now she welcomed Jen's return with a big smile, grabbed her hand and led her through the village to the women, who were still sitting and talking.

Jen thought fast. She had to find out about the relationship between Jack, the thugs and the villagers if she were going to free herself, get back to the others and join them in the fight against the poachers. If Saanjh and her friends were indeed tribal people, why were they dealing with the gun-toting four-by-four drivers? Were they paid? And how did Jack fit into this – how did he find the heavies?

'Do any of you speak English?' she said. The women looked at her and smiled. The shy one kept a hand over her mouth, hardly daring to make eye contact. The woman with the baby lifted it from her breast and handed it to Jen.

'Oh,' Jen said, awkwardly taking the child. She'd never held a baby before. This one was naked, except for a thong with a pendant around its neck. A little boy, his skin a milky chocolate brown, warm and soft, sweet-smelling with round, brown eyes. He looked up at Jen and grinned, kicking his legs.

'Oh,' Jen repeated stupidly, trying to hold the baby in the same natural, easy way his mother had done. She looked up at the mother, who was perhaps no older than she was. The woman laughed. They were all curious about Jen and, now the ice was broken, touched her skin and clothes and hair, picked at her jewellery, chatted to each other. They seemed so kind and good-natured Jen wondered again how they came to be allied with the four-by-four men, who surely hadn't been Adivasi.

'No English?' Jen repeated again, hopelessly. How could she find out if they couldn't speak together? She had to think of something. With every hour that passed her friends would be worrying more – and what was Jack doing? What was he planning next?

Charlotte

Someone knocked on the door. They jumped at the sound, all of them, sitting anxiously in the living room: Charlotte, Jaideep, Prina, Amrita and Otto.

'Who is it?' Otto said.

Nobody answered. Nobody moved. A second knock broke the spell. Jaideep rose to his feet. Prina said something to him in Tamil, the language doing nothing to hide the worry in her voice. Jaideep took a deep breath, stood up straight and opened the door.

'Who is it?' Amrita repeated Otto's question. She and Charlotte exchanged anxious glances.

The caller, still invisible to the people in the living room, said something in English. A warm, male voice. Charlotte stood up.

'Mark?' She hurried to the door. 'My god, how did you get here so quickly?' Impossibly, he was standing there on the doorstep, looking remarkably bright and handsome for a man who must have spent the night travelling. Even Jaideep looked impressed. He glanced at Charlotte, the question written on his face: you know this man?

'This is the journalist I told you about,' Charlotte said. 'I wasn't expecting him just to turn up.'

In fact, although Charlotte had told Jaideep about Mark and his request for an interview following his call the previous evening,

Jaideep hadn't agreed and with all the tumult of the night, they'd had neither time nor energy to discuss it in any detail. In any case, Jaideep said he'd need the approval of the sanctuary trustees.

They all stood as they were for a moment. Thoughts flashed through Charlotte's head – what was he doing here? This was hardly a good time, with Jen missing, and Jack, and the rendezvous at the lodge in another hour.

'Look, Mark, this is . . .' she began. Mark cut her off with a big smile.

'It's great to see you,' he said, stepping forward and giving her a big hug. 'May I come in? It's been quite a journey.'

He didn't quite push past them, but it wasn't far off. Then he was in the house, taking Jaideep's hand to shake it. Early twenties, suntanned, dressed in obviously expensive blue jeans and T-shirt, sunglasses pushed back on short, newly-barbered spiky blond hair, Mark was just as she'd remembered. He carried a laptop in a case and a small suitcase, as well as what appeared to be a smart camera bag. Clearly he'd come direct from the airport.

'Great to meet you, Jaideep, I've heard a lot about you, been reading up too. You've done some great work here. Terrible bad luck you've been having – anything I can do to help, I'd be only too glad.' This Mark rattled off, smiling goodnaturedly all the while, as though he was thrilled to be there and couldn't imagine that they wouldn't be equally thrilled to welcome him. Even the generally imperturbable Jaideep looked lost for words. He opened his mouth and closed it again.

Mark invited himself into the living room, giving each of the inhabitants a shrewd glance. 'Otto, my god, what happened to you? You looked rough last time I saw you, but this time – bloody hell.' Mark looked at the rest of them. 'What's going on here? What's happened?'

No-one answered for a moment, nonplussed by the pushy, charismatic stranger who'd arrived in their midst. Charlotte glanced at her watch, aware of the minutes ticking by, time counting down to the moment she'd have to meet Jack at the lodge. She thought of Jen. How to handle this situation with Mark?

Jaideep took command. 'I don't think now is the best time. Why don't you go back to your hotel and we'll speak again later today?' He stretched out his arm, to usher him away, but Mark crouched down beside Otto, though he looked at Charlotte.

Prina and Amrita stared at him agog, this stranger who had materialised in their home.

'What's going on?' Mark said. Despite the smile his voice communicated a new steely note.

'Look, you heard Jaideep, it's not a good time,' Charlotte said, uncertainly. But Mark had the bit between his teeth. He persisted.

'What happened to Otto? This is fresh, isn't it? Who attacked you? Have you called the police?'

Charlotte thought fast. Mark had caught scent of the story. If they sent him out of the house, perhaps he'd go to the police. He had contacts. And if the police headed over, asking questions, Jen might be further endangered. She glanced at Jaideep, seeing anger rise in his face. Mark was pushing his luck.

'Jaideep, please, I think we should tell him,' Charlotte said. Otto gave her an incredulous look. Charlie raised her hand. 'I've got to be at the lodge soon. What harm can it do, if he knows? Maybe Mark'll be able to help.'

Otto's look of incredulity deepened. Mark stood up and respectfully introduced himself to Prina and Amrita, who blushed and blinked when he shook her hand.

Jaideep didn't look happy but he said: 'As you like. You know this man better than I do.'

'Charlie? Are you really sure this is a good idea?' Otto reached out a proprietorial hand and touched her arm.

Prina stood up. She addressed Amrita, who was still staring at Mark, her mouth open. She said something in Tamil, and then, in a sharp voice: 'Come and help me get something for our guests to eat.'

Amrita frowned, reluctant to leave the room, but her father nodded in confirmation of Prina's instruction.

As quickly and clearly as she could, Charlotte explained to Mark what had happened, culminating in Jen's disappearance and the instructions to meet at the lodge. The bonhomie faded and he listened attentively, absorbing everything. He asked her several questions to clarify.

'What are we going to do?' he said.

Charlotte

Charlotte drove through the early-morning light along the lane to the lodge. She was alone. She'd dropped Mark and Otto half a mile back, and they were making their way on foot, away from the track, taking a route through long grass and trees that Jaideep had identified on a map of the sanctuary. He'd left at the same time for a final meeting with the World Wildlife people. The situation was grave – the latest double poaching had prompted accusations of incompetence. Jaideep was fighting for his professional life, as well as the future of the sanctuary and its few, precious tigers. Even so, he'd suggested postponing the meeting till he knew Charlotte and Jen were safe. Mark and Otto had persuaded him to go to his meeting – it was far too important to postpone, when the two men could accompany Charlotte.

At first Mark had proposed being Charlotte's sole protector, since Otto had been so badly beaten he could hardly walk. Otto wouldn't countenance this for a moment. Amrita, although she'd pleaded to help Charlotte, was going with her father to provide hospitality for the officials.

Golden light streamed through the trees, flashing into Charlotte's face as she drove. She was so afraid her body felt light and unreal, as though it had turned into air. She had to concentrate on the process of driving, conscious of the dead-snake texture of the steering wheel underneath her hands, the split rubber cover on the accelerator beneath her foot, the flecks of dirt and dead insects on the windscreen. She tried not to think about the lodge and what might happen – better not to let her imagination run away with her. Most of all, she wanted Jen to be safe.

She went slowly, to give Otto and Mark a chance to reach the lodge at a similar time. They would stay under cover and watch the proceedings from the trees. Charlotte was convinced she could talk Jack round. She would lie if she had to, tell him she'd had a change of heart, that she wanted him too, make a promise – anything to get them both away from him.

She was sure she could do it. Of course Jack might have his assistants, the three Indian men – and what if they came along? Charlotte reckoned she could persuade him to send them away but they were hoping that Jack would come alone. Mark and a wounded Otto would hardly be a match for the cold, competent thugs who'd beaten him before. The plan was fraught with difficulties and dangers. At the last moment, Jaideep decided the best option would be to call the police, but Charlotte begged him to give her plan a chance.

The pick-up crawled the last few hundred yards. She scanned the area, looking for a vehicle.

Nothing.

She could see the door of the lodge was open but Otto had told her about the destruction of their belongings and the broken lock so the open door didn't necessarily signify anything. Charlotte cut the engine. She remained sitting in the cab for a few long moments, staring at the lodge, wondering what was inside and how events would unfold. Her body still felt strangely light as she opened the door and slowly stepped to the ground. A breeze picked at the yellow grass, making it hiss. Charlotte scanned the trees surreptitiously, wondering if Otto and Mark had arrived, if they were watching her now.

214

She took a deep breath, willing her pulse to ease up, then began to walk to the lodge.

She climbed the step to the veranda. The place was silent. Nothing moved.

'Jack?' Charlotte stepped towards the open door. A slashed rucksack was lying on the ground, mutilated, a dead thing.

'Jack?' She crept forward and pushed the door. It creaked a little. After the bright morning sunshine, the interior of the lodge seemed impenetrably dark. She peered in.

More scattered, desecrated possessions on the floor. Already these seemed to be covered with a film of dust, as though they'd lain, broken and abandoned, for months, not hours.

Still no sound. Nothing moved. Charlotte stepped inside.

A shadow on the bed, a man-shaped outline. She swallowed, forced herself to breathe again. Jack was sitting close to the wall, legs slightly apart, elbows resting on his knees, hands clasped. Quickly she scanned the rest of the room, looking for Jen.

Jack didn't speak. Instead he stared at Charlotte, apparently perfectly relaxed, a smile on his face.

'Where's Jen?' Charlie cleared her throat and tried again. 'Jack – where's Jen?' Odd how even the sight of him repelled her. She'd never liked him, but after all he'd put her through, that dislike had evolved into something much more visceral. The sight of him, his face, the smile on his face – he repulsed her.

'Jen's okay,' Jack said lightly. 'Good to see you. You're looking great.'

'Please, Jack. I want to see Jen. That was the deal, yes?' She struggled to master her feelings. Charlotte had never been a great actor and dissembling didn't come easily. This time though, she had to overcome her natural inclination and pander to Jack in a convincing manner.

'I am guessing your back-up is hiding in the trees somewhere. Who did you bring? Not the police I hope. Otto?'

Charlotte's face must have given her away because his smile changed.

'Ah yes, Otto,' he said. 'Otto the chump.'

'Those – those people of yours, they hurt him!' Charlotte said, her true feelings getting the better of her. 'How could you? I could kill you, Jack, you little shit! You hurt him – it was you!'

Jack seemed oddly pleased with her outburst. His smile widened. 'You're very beautiful now,' he said. 'I knew you would be. I always knew. I could sense it in you. You have a passionate nature, Charlie, it just needed bringing out. How wonderful that I've been the man to do it.'

Charlotte stared at him, appalled. He had successfully manipulated her emotions, goading her into losing control of herself. That was his victory of course. She mustn't let it happen again. It allowed him power over her. She took a deep breath, trying to master her emotions.

'So – Jen's not here? Where is she?'

'Don't worry, she's safe,' he said. 'I'll take you to see her. But we'll have to leave discreetly, so Otto can't follow. Don't try anything, if you want me to take you to her.'

Charlotte didn't answer. She stared at Jack, waiting to find out what he would suggest.

'I've got a motorbike outside, by the side of the lodge. A trail bike – it's pretty nifty on this kind of terrain. You're going to lead the way, and when I get on the bike you're going to climb on behind me. Do you understand? Any messing around and Jen will be in trouble. You'll never find her without me.'

Charlotte nodded, thinking fast. She had to go with him. Perhaps Otto and Mark would be able to follow. Her first priority was finding Jen and making sure she was safe.

Jack stood up. He reached out a hand to pat her reassuringly on the shoulder. Charlotte tried not to flinch.

'Give me your mobile,' he said.

'Why? There's no signal out here.' Even so, she felt a moment of panic.

Jack shrugged. 'In any case, give it to me.'

Charlotte reached into her pocket and did as he asked.

'Time to go,' he said.

Otto

Otto crouched in the long grass just beyond the trees behind the lodge. His body hurt. The ferocious pain in his head made it hard to think straight. Truly it hadn't been a great idea to accompany Mark on this expedition, but what choice did he have? Otto had to keep Charlotte safe.

Beside him Mark was peering through a pair of binoculars. Where had they come from? For a man who'd travelled all night, he seemed remarkably fresh and fit. Otto sensed the journalist was actually relishing this adventure. He was like an overgrown boy scout, alert, capable – and tremendously annoying.

'She's gone into the lodge,' Mark whispered. 'I'm going to move closer. Stay here if you like.'

Otto knew Mark was aware how much he was suffering, but Mark's sympathy was something he absolutely didn't want.

'No,' Otto snapped. 'I'm coming too.'

He thought of Charlotte. Was she afraid? Not that she would show it. Charlotte always looked calm, even when he knew she wasn't.

'Once we know Jen's okay, we'll move in,' Mark said, taking the lead again. 'You go to the left, I'll go to the right.'

Otto knew it would be pointless to argue and he couldn't let his competitiveness get in the way of a successful rescue, so he shut up and nodded. The sun beat down on his aching head. His mouth tasted of dried blood.

On the journey to the lodge, Mark had explained how he'd reached the sanctuary so quickly. He was a journalist, and it was part of his job to be able to move to the right place as fast as possible. He'd made calls soon after talking to Charlotte the previous evening, secured the first available seat on a plane, taken a taxi. Waiting at the airport, he'd made more calls, received mails, researched online for background to the story. Despite himself, Otto was impressed. He would have to learn this kind of efficiency if he wanted to be a globe-trotting photojournalist.

Charlotte had been inside the lodge for several long minutes and Otto began to feel nervous. What was going on inside?

An engine shrilled.

'Bloody hell, he's got a bike!' Mark shouted, leaping up. 'Quick, they're on a bike!'

Otto rose to his feet, thighs complaining, in time to see Charlotte on the back of a yellow motorbike accelerating away from them through the grass in front of the lodge. Mark yelled and ran after them in hopeless pursuit, but the bike pulled further and further ahead. Within a few seconds it was out of sight. Soon after that, they couldn't hear it either.

'Was that Jack in front?' Mark called.

Otto nodded. Where was he taking Charlotte? Where was Jen? Their plan to protect had utterly failed. Now Jack had both his friends and Otto had no idea where they were.

The two men wandered into the lodge.

'We messed up,' Mark said, shaking his head. 'Any idea where Jack might take her?'

'No, none.' He stared at the wreckage on the floor.

Mark pushed at a torn pair of jeans on the floor, lost in thought. He rubbed his face. 'These guys weren't messing about, were they?' he said. 'I think it's time we called the police.'

'And what will they do?' Otto snapped. 'Will they take it seriously? How will they find them?'

Mark shrugged. 'We'll take the pick-up back to the house,' he said. 'You need to rest. You look awful.'

'Thanks a lot,' Otto said, unable to stop noticing that Mark looked great. The excitement and adrenalin had simply served to give him an appealing masculine glow. He sniffed with disgust, turned away, and sloped out of the lodge to the pick-up. Time to stop feeling sorry for himself. What he had to do now was think how best to help Charlotte and Jen.

Jen

A motorbike bounced over the rough track, sending up clouds of dust. Jen stood at the edge of the tiny village as it approached. Two people on the bike – Jack and his friend were returning? She shaded her eyes, squinting in the bright light. No – somebody else was riding behind Jack.

'Charlotte,' she said out loud. Jack was bringing Charlotte. The bike pulled into the village and Charlotte dismounted, blinking dirt from her eyes.

'Charlie!' Jen ran up and hugged her friend. It seemed to take Charlotte a minute to realise what was going on.

'Jen? Oh my god, Jen! Are you okay? Did he hurt you? I was so worried about you!'

They stared into each other's faces, as though searching for sign of injury, physical or emotional.

Jen shook her head. 'I'm fine, absolutely fine. But what about Otto? Is he okay? What did they do to him? I was so afraid, I thought they were going to kill him!'

'He's okay,' Charlotte said. 'Badly beaten, but nothing permanent. They hurt him though, hurt him badly.'

They both stopped talking, aware that Jack was observing the reunion. The village women formed a second audience, lined up and smiling at the girls, talking amongst themselves.

Charlotte separated herself from Jen and turned to Jack.

'So what now?' she said. 'What exactly do you want? You're going to take Jen home?'

'Was that the deal? You for me? I'm not going anywhere without you,' Jen jumped in. Jack looked from Charlotte to Jen and back to Charlotte again. His confidence seemed to falter, faced with the two of them. Could they overpower him? Take the motorbike, ride away into the wilderness? Jen had no idea how to operate a bike – and didn't think Charlotte did either. In any case, something else was going on and she needed to see the bigger picture.

'I want a night with you, Charlie. One night,' Jack said.

'What?' Charlotte responded, recoiling from him.

'No, no! I don't mean – no not that! Just to talk. Time together. I want you to give me one last chance to find out who I am. And if you don't want me after – well, I'll take you back. I'll leave you alone. I won't bother you ever again.'

Jen and Charlotte both stared at Jack, trying to work him out. He looked vulnerable, making this appeal. Charlotte's face went very still, as though a veil of ice was closing over it. Jen sensed how she was trying to control her reactions, to be cool.

'Of course, Jack. That seems fair,' she said lightly. 'I'll talk to you all night – only talking, mind – and if you fail to convince me we're destined to be together you'll take us safely home.'

Jen blinked. Jack nodded uncertainly. He glanced at his watch. 'I've got something to do first,' he said abruptly. 'The women will give you something to eat. I'll be back in a couple of hours.' Some emotion flickered across his face then: apprehension perhaps. What did he have to do? Was it connected with the men in the four by four? What was he planning?

Jen noticed his hands were shaking. Now the plan had come to fruition, and he had Charlotte, was the situation starting to unravel? Was this not as he'd expected? Jack seemed to be a man operating within a web of delusions. How hard was it for him to maintain his fictions and fantasies?

'You're not going to lock us up? Aren't you worried we'll just run off?' Charlotte said.

'We're miles from anywhere,' Jack said. 'You'd never find your way on foot and you've no way of contacting anyone.' He shrugged. 'I don't think you'd be so stupid. In any case, you know I'm not going to hurt you. I just wanted a chance to talk with you.' Again that look of little-boy-lost appeal.

'You're shivering,' Jen said.

Jack shook his head. 'I'm going now. I'll be back in a couple of hours. Get something to eat.' Jack the solicitous host. He turned away from the girls and half ran to the motorbike. He started up the engine and, with one backward glance, rode away.

Jen and Charlotte didn't move as they watched the motorbike disappear.

'He's cracking up,' Charlotte observed. Now the two girls were together, neither of them felt so afraid.

Saanjh sauntered up to them and Jen introduced her to Charlotte. They smelled wood smoke: one of the women was preparing a meal of stewed lentils and baking some kind of flatbread on a skillet. Jen and Charlotte sat down to eat.

'We could just run – take our chances,' Charlotte said. 'We'll see some tyre tracks, that'll help us find our way back.'

'How far do you think it is?'

'Hard to say. Ten miles? I don't know, that might be way off.'

'I think Jack said twenty miles, but I don't know if that's true. We could probably walk ten miles.'

'With no water, or directions? We could try, Jack's right, it would be dangerous, but I think he's underestimated us. I'm sure we could do it. Do you think the people here would stop us?' Charlotte glanced at the women. Then she tore into her bread, staring out of the village at the trees.

223

'I don't know,' Jen said. 'I found an old ruin in the trees over there, and nobody stopped me going. But I'm not you. You're the one he wants. I don't know what would happen if you tried to escape.'

'We could try.'

'Yes. It'd be dangerous, but so is staying here. Jack's dangerous,' Jen said. 'You're not really going to spend a night with him, are you? He's cracking up. You don't know what he might do.'

'I don't trust him at all. He's very clever. Very – manipulative.'

'So – we've got a couple of hours to come up with something.' Jen thought of telling Charlotte about her vision of Durga but refrained. Instead she said: 'Charlie, I think this has something to do with the tiger poaching.'

'What has?'

'This place. These people. Those men.'

Charlotte considered. 'You think Jack has something to do with it?' Her eyes widened. 'That night, when both the tigers were killed – it was the night Jack drove me into the forest. When I escaped in the pick-up, I heard other vehicles. What if they found him – picked him up? Those guys who beat up Otto – what if they're the poachers and Jack is helping them?' Charlotte shook her head. 'My god, if that's true . . . if he's helping them – he knows so much! He knows where to find the camera traps, the paths the tigers have used.

'We have to get out of here – warn Jaideep! We can't wait! We have to get out of here!'

Charlotte jumped to her feet, but Jen caught her arm.

'Hold on! Think a minute. Even if we did make it back, what would we tell him? We need more information – what their plans are, where they're going to strike. We need to know how to trap them.'

Saanjh was still eating beside them. If Charlotte was right, how had these Adivasi people become entangled with the poachers?

Had they been bought or threatened? Were the men from the village helping the outsiders to hunt tigers?

'What on earth can we do?' Charlotte pondered. 'Just the two of us, with no transport, against Mad Jack wanting a night to woo me, and professional hard men with spears and a gun?'

Despite everything, Jen giggled. How had they found themselves in this astonishing situation?

'It's not funny,' Charlotte admonished. But Jen laughed again, and then Charlotte giggled too. Nervous relief. And despite everything, gladness they were together.

Charlotte

Charlotte and Jen walked through the huddle of huts and followed the vehicle tracks away from the village. A narrow dirt path, one person wide, wound through the long grass. The girls were perfectly open about their intention to leave, holding their heads high, waiting to see what would happen.

At first, nothing. Although she was arm in arm with Jen, Charlotte felt nervous. The skin on her back prickled. She sensed watchers. What would these watchers do?

They walked fifty yards, then a hundred. Nothing. The urge to run was strong but she resisted. Somebody shouted. She almost looked back but Jen gripped her arm more tightly and Charlotte kept her gaze fixed ahead. Another shout – a male voice. She couldn't make out what he said, or even if it was in English; she knew it was an admonishment and a warning. They weren't supposed to leave.

'Keep going,' Charlie said. They took another few steps then heard a gunshot; a bullet whined past them, buried itself in the mud path just ahead of their feet. Both girls stopped. Charlotte took a deep breath. The bullet had come so close she was certain she'd felt it whiz past her leg. It hadn't touched her, but even so, the skin of her calf stung. Jen's arm was tense at first, but a couple of seconds later Charlotte could feel her trembling.

'They shot at us,' Jen whispered.

'Okay. Point proved,' Charlotte answered. 'Turn round, very slowly.' She was afraid the gunman would shoot them again, so they inched round, careful not to make any sudden movement. Then they could see him, standing at the edge of the village, staring after them, a rifle held casually in his arms, its strap over his shoulder.

'Where did he spring from?' Jen breathed. 'Do you recognise him?'

Charlotte shook her head. 'Maybe he was inside one of the huts. One of the women must have seen us leaving and told him.'

The man barked another incomprehensible word and gestured for them to return. The girls started to walk, keeping a wary eye on the rifle. The exercise had proved two things – they were indeed prisoners, and a man (were there more?) was evidently sheltering in the village.

The man didn't move. He watched them. He certainly didn't look like a member of the tribe – someone who herded goats and lived in the forest. He didn't fit in: too modern, dressed in a shirt and tight jeans with a gold chain around his neck, he caressed the rifle. When the girls reached the village he jabbed it at the huts. 'Stay here,' he said.

'You can speak English?' Jen asked. The man didn't respond since the answer was evident. He continued to stare in a way that made Charlotte feel increasingly uncomfortable. They were alone here; very vulnerable. If these men were indeed poachers and criminals, who knew what they were capable of? She dropped her gaze, still clinging to Jen, and they walked past the man back into the tiny village. They dropped down to sit in front of one of the huts. The man was still staring at them, though he'd let the rifle go, so it hung, nose down, from his shoulder. Saanjh emerged from one of the huts, carrying a piece of sewing. She sat down close to the girls, her eyes averted. Had Saanjh informed the guard they

227

were leaving? She was only a little girl, and she seemed so curious and friendly – was Saanjh not to be trusted either?

Charlotte wondered what Jack was doing. If Jack was helping the poachers, was he with them now, telling them about the camera traps and recent sightings of tiger traps? She shuddered to think of it. They couldn't afford the death of another tiger. Surely that would be the end of the sanctuary.

'I wish I could speak your language, Saanjh,' Charlotte said. She'd so many questions she wanted to ask. Saanjh shrugged and smiled, the needle and thread busy in the brightly-coloured cloth in her hands.

'Hold on a minute.' Jen dug in the back pocket of her jeans. She drew out several ripped, haphazardly folded pieces of paper. 'Shreds of my journal,' she said. 'I picked them up in the lodge. The trouble is, I don't think I've got a pen.'

Jen held out the paper to Saanjh and mimed writing something.

'Do you have a pen, Saanjh?' Jen asked. The girl's eyes widened. She looked at the torn paper and back at Jen. Saanjh nodded and shrugged at the same time, stood up, and scampered into one of the huts.

'Be careful,' Charlotte warned. 'We don't know if we can trust her.'

Jen nodded as Saanjh came running towards them. She didn't have a pen, only the aged stub of a pencil. She presented it to Jen.

'Can you read or write, Saanjh?' Jen wrote her name on a scrap of paper and showed it to the girl. Saanjh shook her head. So Jen, in a few canny lines, drew a tiger on the paper. Saanjh's mouth dropped open, clearly impressed with Jen's artistic skills.

'Tiger,' Jen said. 'Do you know what's going on here? Are these men hunting tigers?' She kept her voice low, doubtless remembering the man with the rifle spoke English too.

Saanjh looked at her and back at the drawing of a tiger.

228

'Are the men here hunting tigers? I don't know who they are, but I don't think they're part of your tribe, I think they're outsiders. So why are you helping them?'

'Jen, she's scared,' Charlotte said. Saanjh's eyes were wide, blinking back tears. She gave her head an agitated shake. 'She knows something. Be careful, we don't want to frighten her off.'

Jen waited a moment, then she said, very gently: 'We want to help. These men have to be stopped. Are they threatening you, your family?'

Saanjh glanced at one of the huts, then back at Jen. The other women were wandering off, children in tow, into the trees, perhaps to gather firewood or food. Charlotte was conscious of the rifle man hiding out. He might not be alone. The girl looked anxiously after the disappearing women and then at the hut. She jabbed at Jen's sketch and began chattering in a low voice, looking intensely at Jen all the while. She pointed out at a dense clump of trees in the forest, site of Jen's ruin, touched Jen's hand and then her own forehead.

'Do you have any idea what she's on about?' Charlotte whispered. Jen blinked rapidly.

'I think I do.'

'What? What's this about? What aren't you telling me?'

'Just a minute.' Jen waved her hand at Charlotte, to silence her, keeping her attention focused all the time on Saanjh. The girl looked at the women, retreating into the trees, and back at the hut. She was very evidently afraid, talking all the while, trying to decide something. Decide what?

Jen took Saanjh's hand. She said: 'You know what's going on. You know what you have to do. You saw something, didn't you, at the ruin? When I went there, is that when it happened? You know what I saw. And now you have to be brave. You have to help me.'

Charlotte held her tongue. She desperately wanted to know what Jen was talking about and she was also afraid for Saanjh. It

229

was all well and good for Jen to urge her to be brave (even in a language she wouldn't understand) but they had no idea of the consequences of a betrayal for Saanjh. The poachers were evidently violent criminals and she knew India's tribal peoples led isolated lives, away from the mainstream and often not enjoying the proper protection of the police. And Saanjh was a child, a female to boot. Charlotte didn't want her to be put in any danger.

Saanjh stood up, anxiously peering all around her. She still held Jen's tiger drawing, like a talisman, the paper very white in her slim, brown hand. She touched her forehead again – her mystic third eye?

'Come on,' Jen said, rising to her feet. 'We need to follow her.'

With another glance at the huts and the women, Saanjh, stooped and surreptitious, trotted away into the long grass beyond the makeshift animal paddock, beckoning Jen and Charlotte to follow. They sneaked away. What if the rifle man spotted they were gone? With every step she took, Charlotte felt the terror of discovery, listening for the sound of a second shot, nerves primed, anticipating a bullet.

They pushed their way through thorned, shrubby bushes that scratched her bare arms. A huge, golden-brown bird, startled, flew up in front of them, its wings beating the air like a drum. How far did they go? Probably not so far, as the crow flies. Maybe half a mile. But the journey seemed very long and time stretched out as Charlotte imagined pursuit and they fought their way through undergrowth and tough, razor-edged grasses. Soon sweat coated her skin, dripping into her eyes. Agile Saanjh, accustomed to the terrain, kept urging her to hurry.

'We're here,' Jen whispered.

'Where?' They were squatting in grass amid stands of bamboo. A flock of emerald parakeets squawked noisily in a tree above them. Charlotte could see nothing out of the ordinary; what was Saanjh showing them?

Saanjh raised her finger to her lips. She whispered something and pointed ahead. Another guard? Charlotte peered through the grass, with stinging eyes. She wiped her forehead. Saanjh edged forward.

'What's she showing us?' Charlotte had a terrible feeling of foreboding. She could smell something peculiar. The ubiquitous sound of insects became an intense thrum on the air. Despite the oppressive heat and burning sunlight, she sensed a curious darkness all around them, a warning of something utterly wrong. Something evil: yes evil. It wasn't a word she would normally use or liked, but Charlotte could feel it hanging over the place like a cloud, occluding the senses, so you couldn't hear or see. But they had to see. They had to know. She rubbed her eyes. Charlotte, normally sceptical of Jen's spirits and auras, wondered if Jen was feeling the same thing. Or had Charlotte created it herself, an imagining born of fatigue and shock and fear?

They followed Saanjh, squatting and crawling as she did. Then Saanjh stopped. She dug her fingers into the ground and pulled a piece of rope. The smell grew stronger. What was it? Death, meat, chemicals. Saanjh hauled on the rope. Astonishingly, an invisible door opened – the roof of a pit perfectly camouflaged by a mat of grass. Almost magical, how the secret pit was revealed. A cloud of flies lifted from the dark interior.

Jen and Charlotte looked at one another. Saanjh, her face blanched, beckoned them to hurry and look. They crept forward on hands and knees. Charlotte, reluctant to look, took a deep breath and steeled herself for the spectacle.

Huge boards, on which two fresh tiger skins were stretched and nailed.

Fur against board, the interior skin was exposed to the air. A layer of salt coated the pink surface, though glistening gobbets of flesh and pearls of fat were visible still. The poachers were evidently storing the skins till they departed for wherever it was they would take them, to sell for thousands of pounds. Why hadn't they left at once? Even so cunningly hidden, it was a risk keeping the skins on the very sanctuary they had poached the tigers. The obvious answer – considering the poachers were still around and if they had Jack feeding them information about the tigers – they wanted another strike, another tiger, before making off with their evil harvest. What a gift Jack must have been. They couldn't resist the opportunity to bag another valuable tiger, despite the risks of staying longer in the area. And those risks were growing, now they had assaulted a tourist, kidnapped another. Jack must have promised them a certain catch. One good tiger skin could fetch twenty thousand dollars, remember? For these men, that was a fortune. Jack knew where to find the camera traps. And he knew which one had captured a tiger on film. He'd done a deal: rough up Otto and bring Jack his girlfriend in exchange for the whereabouts of a valuable tiger. If all worked to plan, they'd soon have another skin and be hundreds of miles away, leaving Jack to sort out his own mess.

Jen was pale despite the heat. Her face was greenish and sick-looking. She edged back from the edge of the pit. Would she be sick? Charlotte withdrew too, with one final glance at the tiger skins. Hideous, like something tortured, the tiger hides were spread-eagled, stretched and nailed in place, to be cured. Horribly she couldn't help thinking the skins were still alive, suffering agonies on the drying board, burning and burning with salt.

Then she felt sick too. She nodded to Saanjh, who lowered the lid. The pit disappeared again, expertly hidden. No-one would know it was there, even standing right beside it.

Parakeets launched from the tree, wings clattering. Saanjh froze, putting her fingers to her lips. Then she scurried backwards into the long grass and amid the bamboo. They were scarcely out of sight when Charlotte heard male voices. Evidently a guard had been posted in the vicinity of the pit. She glanced at Saanjh's

232

frightened face. The three of them kept perfectly still, hardly daring to breathe. A short exchange between two men, too distant to be properly heard. Had the girls been seen?

Charlotte glanced at Jen. Her face was still as stone, her hand gripped Saanjh's. The voices disappeared but still they waited an agonising time, for an alarm call or discovery. But nothing happened. Finally Saanjh nodded and they set off back to the village.

Charlotte glanced at her watch. They'd been gone less than an hour. The women had disappeared into the trees. She could see no sign of the rifle man. Was it safe to assume their absence hadn't been noted? Time would tell. Saanjh picked up her embroidery.

Jack should be back soon. What then? What were they going to do? Charlotte turned to Jen.

'I need you to tell me what happened – the ruin, what you were talking about, why you think Saanjh helped you.'

Jen sighed, as though she were reluctant to tell. In the past she had always been frank with Charlotte about her contact with the supernatural. Now, after her time alone on the Goan island, she seemed to feel a little protective of herself, and her visions.

'Please tell me,' Charlotte said. 'I want to know. Whatever it was, however real I believe it to be, it must have been true because both you and Saanjh were affected.'

'I was visited, in the ruin,' Jen said. 'It was astonishing – more than I've ever experienced before.' She spoke slowly. 'I saw the goddess, Durga. She has ten arms. She rides on a tiger.'

'And what did that mean?' Charlotte prompted gently.

'I think it was a request,' Jen said. 'To be involved. To defend her tigers.'

'And Saanjh?'

'Saanjh didn't stop me going to the ruin, and she was watching the whole time. I think she saw something too – or somehow

233

knew what was happening to me. Perhaps Durga asked her for help too. Otherwise, how would she have dared to do it? She's been incredibly brave. You, me, Saanjh – together maybe we can do something.'

Charlotte thought fast. What should they do? Jack was likely to return at any moment so she had to stay in the village to keep him occupied.

'You've got to make a run for it.'

'What?'

'Find Jaideep and the others – tell them what's happening. You've got to warn them about the poachers. Tell them Jack's with them, what he knows, how he's helping them. They're going to try again, aren't they? It's going to be today, or tonight, I'm sure of it.'

Jen quivered. 'What about the man with the gun? How will I find my way?'

'We have to persuade Saanjh to take you. She knows the area. I bet she knows how to get to the reserve office, and she can explain to Jaideep how to get to the village. I'll distract the rifle man, at least till you get a good start. And as you said, it's me Jack wants. I don't think they'll worry too much if you go. They don't know we've worked out who they are, what they're planning.' Charlotte saw the doubt in Jen's face. Saanjh had already put herself at risk by helping them – why should she take this even bigger, more dangerous step? They didn't know anything about the relationship between the tribal people and the poachers, and when Saanjh's role was inevitably found out, how might her own people feel about her actions?

Charlotte remembered the tiger skins in the pit, the flayed bodies left in the forest. She thought about Jaideep trying to raise money for the sanctuary, to protect all its forests and wildlife, and about the few remaining tigers themselves, precious and vulnerable, and her desire to protect them. Did all these factors balance the trouble they could bring upon Saanjh, if she agreed to help them? No easy answer.

'I'll ask her,' Jen said. 'But I'm not going to pressure her.'

Charlotte nodded. She knew they both felt uneasy about enrolling Saanjh but she couldn't see a way round it. Saanjh had been waiting patiently beside them all this while, her beautiful, trusting face rather anxious as though she knew they were talking about her.

Jen took out another scrap of paper from her pocket and drew the reserve office – another canny sketch. Saanjh didn't look surprised. Perhaps she had anticipated this next step.

'What do you think?' Charlotte said. 'Will you take Jen?' She gestured to her friend. 'I won't go. I'll stay here.' Saanjh twiddled with one of her bangles. She took a deep breath and nodded. Charlotte surveyed the little gathering of homes. The other village women were still working in the fringes of the forest. Distantly she could hear the peal of their voices.

Charlotte gave Jen a hug. 'Okay. Go as quickly as you can. You know what to tell them.'

Jen nodded. She stepped back, gave Saanjh's hand a quick squeeze, and said to Charlotte: 'I don't like leaving you here, on your own. I have no idea how long we'll be and we don't know what the poachers will do. Nor Jack.'

'I'll be okay. Just make sure you hurry.' They hugged again, holding tight. Then Charlotte hugged Saanjh too. They looked at each other, all three.

'Go, go now,' Charlotte said. 'Don't take the main path, skirt round the village so nobody sees you.' She turned away, not wanting them to see how anxious she was. A thought of Otto flashed into her mind, and with it, a wave of longing. What was he doing now?

Otto

Mark called the police from his mobile as soon as he had a signal, on the approach to Jaideep's house. He didn't try the local station but a mysterious contact he had, wanting advice on the best way to handle things and an opinion about the local police chief. He drove and chatted at the same time, while Otto slumped against the door, head aching, barely able to keep himself awake. No-one was home – Prina was helping Amrita organise the final day of negotiations with World Wildlife – so Mark drove them to his hotel in town.

'I found it on the internet, made a booking,' he said. 'It's not grand, but it's clean, and there's hot water.'

From the outside the building didn't look promising but Mark was right – the interior was neat and uncluttered. His room, at the back of the hotel, overlooked a lush garden where peppers and melons grew. The furniture might once have furnished a Victorian bedroom, with an aged iron bedstead and great oak chest of drawers – everything old and worn, but scrupulously clean. A man knocked on the door and invited them to order refreshments.

Otto called Jaideep on his mobile and told him the bad news about Charlotte.

Jaideep was mortified to hear she had disappeared with Jack, but Otto reassured him they had called the police and talked Jaideep out of pulling the plug on the World Wildlife meeting.

'You have to carry on,' Otto said. 'Just keep going. Keep your mind on the meeting. There's nothing you can do now. I'll call you again as soon as I have information from the police.'

Otto ended the call and sat on the bed, overwhelmed by exhaustion.

'Have a shower,' Mark said. 'You can borrow some of my clothes.'

'Thanks.' Otto picked up a towel and went into the bathroom. In keeping with the room, a stained claw-footed bath stood on a green-tiled floor, a shower suspended above it. A gold-framed mirror, dark-flecked, hung above a huge white sink. Otto filled the bath, took off his clothes and sank gratefully into the water. Hard to resent Mark when he was so generous, and at the same time, Otto found himself resenting him because he was hard to resent.

Otto's mind was a dark blizzard, full of worry about Charlotte and Jen, but he was so hurt and exhausted he could hardly keep awake. Even lying in the bath, sleep was snatching him away. He forced himself out of the water, patted himself dry very gently with the towel and donned a spare pair of jeans and a white T-shirt from Mark's suitcase. Once, a few weeks ago (a hundred years it seemed) Otto had been mistaken for Mark. They were both tall, blond and English. Otto was evidently the slimmer of the two – the clothes didn't fit him so snugly: more narrow across the shoulders, more boyish, less muscled. This wasn't a comparison Otto enjoyed.

He stepped out of the bathroom. Mark was focused on his laptop.

'My contact is getting back to me as soon as he can. He's making some calls with the local police, checking things out,' Mark said, glancing round at Otto before returning to his laptop.

'We can't hang around!'

Mark swivelled on his chair. 'I'm not hanging around,' he said. 'Don't you think I'm worried too? I'm busy, okay? I'm on the case. Look, you need to sleep. You're hardly able to stand. Now lie down and rest. You're no use to me, Charlotte or anyone like this. As soon as I have some information I'll wake you up.'

Mark began to type furiously on his laptop.

Some time later, Otto woke up, with a gasp, from dreams of jackals. Brown and gold, they pursued him over grasslands as he ran and ran. The light in the room had changed. Mark was still poring over his laptop. Otto sat up.

'How long have I been asleep?'

'About six hours.' Mark didn't look away from the laptop.

'Six hours!' Far too long. What had happened to Charlotte and Jen in that time? Otto stood up.

'Stay calm. I've ordered some food,' Mark said. 'I've found out some interesting stuff. We need to eat, and then we need to move. How are you feeling?'

Otto tested himself, flexing his limbs. 'Headache's gone. Stiff, bruised – but better, yes.' His body ached, but his mind, at least, was clear again. He felt like himself again.

'You were in a terrible state – I don't think you even realised. Fancy hauling yourself to the lodge with me like some stupid bloody hero. Sometimes you have to know when to take care of yourself, or you're of no use to anyone.'

'Thanks for the lecture,' Otto bristled. Mark was only a few years older than he was but those few years made a vast difference. Otto was fresh out of school, Mark had made his way in the world, personally and professionally.

One of the hotel staff knocked on the door and delivered a tray of rice, spiced lentils, chapattis, fruit and yoghurt, along with huge cups of sweet tea. Otto hadn't noticed his hunger but he ate ravenously, tearing into the food his body craved to heal itself. He didn't speak, hardly tasted the meal, focused only on consuming the fuel he needed. Slices of banana and papaya vanished into his mouth, and then a bar of Dairy Milk Mark had produced, miraculously, from his suitcase. A taste of home.

'Thanks,' Otto said at last. 'Really, I mean it. Thanks. I feel almost human again. Now, we have to get moving. What have you found out?'

Mark picked up the laptop and placed it between them.

'I sent some emails, made some calls, checked out a few things based on what you've all told me about Jack.' He opened an email and clicked on an attachment. A photo opened on the screen. 'Is that him?'

'Yes. That's him.'

'I thought so, but I wasn't sure. Didn't get much of a look this morning.'

A colour picture of Jack, several years younger, all smiling and fresh-faced with a long fringe draped over his eyes and a My Chemical Romance T-shirt.

'Where did you get the picture?'

'Internet. Our friend appeared in a newspaper report two years ago, after a court appearance. He was convicted, received a community penalty which included an order for anger management.'

'For what? What did he do?'

'Offences under the 1997 Harassment Act. Stalking, in other words. He got obsessed with another student, a girl at his college – and when she turned him down he started harassing her with nasty letters, phone calls, cyber-stalking and so on. In the end he broke into her house and threatened her – actually brandished a knife. She wasn't hurt, fortunately, or Jack would have received a much stiffer penalty. He was thrown out of the college.'

'Okay, so we know he's done it before. And we know he's dangerous. That certainly fits with Charlotte's experience. What else have you found out? What I'd like to know is, does he have money? How did he manage to recruit the hit men?'

'I haven't found anything to suggest he's rich. The story says his parents had split up and he was living with his mum. His parents are doctors, apparently. The house looks nice, but it's unlikely he's super rich. So how did he find the guys who beat you up and what was he offering them? If they had a big vehicle and a gun, they sound professional.'

Otto sighed. 'So what about the police? What have you found out about them?'

Mark opened another email, clicked on the attachment and opened three grainy photographs. 'Recognise any of these guys?' he said.

Otto blinked. 'That one.' He pointed to the middle picture. 'That's him. That's the man who did this to me, the one with the gun.' Otto hadn't been able to summon their faces into his mind, but he had no doubt, looking at the photograph. Seeing this face, vivid memories of the beating sprang into his mind.

'What about the other two?'

'Not them. Just the middle guy. Who is he?' Otto tore his gaze from the picture and focused on Mark.

'A wanted criminal. A gangster, you could say. Suspected for involvement in poaching and the illegal trade in tiger parts.'

'So Jack's hand in hand with a poacher? My god! And this is the man who's got Jen and Charlotte? How did you find the picture?'

'My police contacts. I told them what had happened – and it turns out they've been watching this man and had some inkling he was in this region. They sent me the photos. I wonder if Jack knows what he's got himself into,' Mark mused.

Otto jumped to his feet, worried and impatient. 'So how are we going to find them? What about Charlie and Jen? We can't wait any longer!'

Mark looked up at him. 'The police are onto it,' he said. 'I told them everything we know and we've got their interest. They might not be too worried about a domestic between foreign kids – but a known criminal involved in poaching and kidnapping, that seems to have galvanised them. They're on their way to the reserve office now. And so are we.'

Jen

They crept away from the village, Jen keeping a watch over her shoulder. Saanjh knew the area intimately, guiding them through the trees, skirting the open places. They disturbed a baby deer, curled in a kind of nest in the tall, dry grass. Monkeys shrieked at them from the lower branches of a tree. Luckily they were, by then, too far away for the noise to alert their guard.

Saanjh was agile and fit. Soon Jen was sweating in the intense heat, and scratched and out of breath. No let-up though. They couldn't afford to stop and rest.

The journey seemed to last forever. Sometimes they walked along dirt tracks, once on a rough piece of road, but more often than not they made their way through wild places. Once Saanjh seemed unsure which way to proceed (presumably the further they got from the village, the less well she knew her way around) but she made a decision and they strode on again.

All the while, Jen worried about Charlotte. What would happen when the guard found out she and Saanjh had gone? How would she handle Jack when he returned? Would they hurt her? Jen ignored her own aches and pains, the heat and knocks and scratches: Charlotte's best hope, and the best hope for the tigers, was to find her way to the reserve office, to call for help and rescue.

Was Saanjh afraid? Probably yes, though, focused on walking

and finding the way, her face revealed little. She didn't sweat as Jen was sweating, and although she was so young and smaller, she didn't seem to tire.

Time stretched out interminably. How far did they walk? Hard to measure. The journey seemed to last for hours. They crossed a stream, and then some indeterminate time later, hopped from one smooth, hot boulder to another in order to pass over a river.

At last, in the distance, Jen saw a familiar huddle of wooden buildings, a road between them, and the dots of people moving around outside.

'We're there!' Jen called out, without thinking. Energy renewed, she broke into a jog. Saanjh, who had previously taken the lead, dropped in behind. As they drew closer Jen slowed down again.

'What's going on?' So many people and vehicles outside the offices. Men in uniforms. Were the police already on the case? Saanjh stopped altogether, clearly afraid. Jen took her hand.

'Don't be scared,' Jen said. 'I'll take care of you. I won't leave you on your own. We have to do this.' She wasn't sure how much of this Saanjh understood. 'Think of Durga,' Jen urged. 'She's a warrior. She'll give you courage.'

Saanjh blinked rapidly, holding back tears, but she allowed Jen to lead her forwards.

Dozens of police officers swarmed around the reserve headquarters. Many carried guns. Their vehicles shone in the sunshine, police cars and four by fours. Keeping a tight grip on Saanjh, Jen approached the office. Her eyes were drawn to the blond man standing outside the main door.

'Otto! Otto!' She started to run, half dragging Saanjh. He looked up, hearing her voice. His left eye was swollen and badly bruised, but nonetheless it was a joy to see him. Her heart jumped in her chest. 'Otto!' she called again.

He hurried towards her, surprise and delight evident in his damaged face. He flung his arms around her, almost knocking her off her feet. Jen hugged him back with one arm, the other still attached to Saanjh.

'What happened? Are you okay? Where's Charlie?' The questions bubbled over.

'She's with Jack,' Jen said. 'We've got to help her! Jack's mixed up with the poachers and we think he's told them where they'll find tigers. We've got to stop them, I think they're out there now, trying to kill more!'

Otto absorbed this new intelligence surprisingly quickly.

'You already knew?' she asked.

'Some of it, yes. We worked it out – that's why the police are here. And Jaideep – he was pulled out of his meeting. You have to talk to them – tell them what you know. Who's this with you?'

'This is Saanjh. She guided me here – and she can take us back to Charlotte, and we can show the police the pit with tiger skins in.'

Saanjh hung her head, too shy to look Jack in the face. She was trembling, clearly overwhelmed by the place, the police, the sheer number of people.

'Come inside,' Otto said. 'Bring Saanjh. Keep a hold of her. You have to talk to Jaideep and the police chief. They're inside, trying to work out how to start a search. You're just about to make things a whole lot easier.'

Otto held out his arm, to welcome them inside. Beyond the door Jen could see the journalist, Mark, listening in to a conversation between Jaideep and a police officer, as they pored over a map. Too many people were talking, all raising their voices to be heard. Nobody, it seemed, could decide what to do.

Otto tried to attract Jaideep's attention but too much else was going on. He took a deep breath and raised his voice: 'Jen's here! She got away from the poachers. She can tell us where to go!'

Everyone stopped talking. Jaideep lifted his head and stared directly at Jen. The police chief gestured: 'Is this her?'

Jaideep escorted her into his office, along with Saanjh, Otto and one of the policemen. They had just sat down when Amrita opened the door and hurried into the room, carrying a jug of cool lemonade and two glasses. She filled the glasses and presented them to Saanjh and Jen. Then she demanded:

'Where's Charlie? Is she okay?'

Charlotte

An hour passed. Charlotte stared at her watch, thinking about Jen and Saanjh, wondering how long it would take them to reach the reserve office. Did Saanjh really know the way? Would they be safe from the poachers, from wild animals?

Charlotte walked among the little homes. The man with the rifle was sitting in the doorway, smoking a cigarette. 'Your friend has gone,' he said.

Charlotte didn't know how to respond. So he was aware Jen had escaped and hadn't tried to stop her?

The man shrugged. 'You're the one I watch,' he said. Evidently guarding Charlotte wasn't a job he relished. He looked fed up.

Charlotte took a proper look at the man. In his twenties, she thought, with a moustache and the gold chain shining at his neck. His accent was strong. 'When's Jack coming back?' she said.

The man shrugged again. He stubbed out the cigarette and stood up, the rifle still dangling from his shoulder.

'Soon I hope. Then I'll get paid and I can go home.' The man wandered away, clearly not interested in being drawn into a conversation. He was watching her closely though, with quick, sidelong glances. It didn't sound as though he were a poacher – just a local lackey they'd taken on for guard duty? Did he know these men were killing tigers? Maybe when it came to easy money, he was prepared to turn a blind eye.

And then, as though in fulfilment of the man's wish, Charlotte saw a cloud of reddish dust, heralding the arrival of a vehicle. A yellow motorbike hove into view. Jack had returned.

Dust covered him, congealed in the sweat on his face. He cut the engine, climbed off the bike and, without a word to Charlotte, walked to the guard. They exchanged a few words that Charlotte didn't hear and then Jack said to him: 'You can go now,' handing over money from a roll of notes he pulled from his pocket. Jack's voice was low and flat. The man took the money and started walking away. Jack called out: 'Leave the gun.' The man shrugged and regretfully dropped the rifle on the ground inside the hut where he'd been sitting. He climbed on the yellow motorbike. With a quick nod to Jack, he started the engine, wheeled the bike around, and drove away from the village.

Charlotte glanced at the rifle, left so casually on the floor. For a moment she considered grabbing it but Jack picked it up first.

'You know how to use that thing?' Charlotte said. Jack shrugged.

'I'm full of surprises,' he said. 'Remember the idyllic childhood I told you about, in the country? I did some shooting.'

'Not a gun like that though,' Charlotte said. 'Be careful.'

Jack shook his head dismissively but she could see he didn't look entirely comfortable with the weapon.

'So, the guy told me Jen ran off. She took her chance,' Jack said. 'That really surprises me. I didn't think she'd have the guts. She didn't seem the brave type to me. Not like you. How will she find her way?'

Charlotte didn't answer. Jack shrugged. He didn't suspect she'd been helped by Saanjh, and plainly wasn't bothered about Jen.

'So, it's just you and me.' Except that he spoke too soon. The women returned with enormous, neat bundles of sticks and branches, carried by straps around their foreheads. One had the baby bound by cloth to her front. The little children trotted after them. The women glanced at Charlotte but lowered their eyes in front of Jack, the male outsider. Were they wondering where Saanjh had gone? Would they say something? Evidently not.

'Let's go,' Jack said.

'Go where? We haven't got any transport.'

'We don't need transport. We're walking.'

'Walking where?'

'Somewhere special. You'll see.'

Charlotte eyed Jack. Something was wrong – something more than the usual mad-stalking-obsessive Jack behaviour: his voice, the strange slackness in his body, the odd opaque quality of his eyes. Something had happened.

'Okay, which way?'

Jack ducked into the hut and picked up a backpack. He took out a plastic bottle of water and handed it to Charlotte. 'Take this. I've got another,' he said.

'So where are we walking to?' She found she didn't want to leave the relative safety of the village, where at least she had other people around. Though would the women step in if Jack tried anything? She wasn't sure. They seemed downtrodden. On the other hand, she thought they'd noticed Saanjh and Jen's disappearance and hadn't said anything, so perhaps some quiet rebellion was taking place?

'Wait and see.' Jack's voice was oddly grim, for a man planning a romantic assignation. Or had he given up on that? Once they were alone in the wild, Jack armed with a gun, who knew what he would do? This new mood of his frightened her. She thought of making a run for it – surely Jack wouldn't actually shoot her? But glancing again at his closed face, she couldn't be sure of that. She would have to rely on her wits.

'Let's go,' she said brightly, as though anticipating that this jaunt might be interesting and fun.

Jack led the way. They left the cluster of huts and walked towards the dark stand of trees where Jen had found the temple ruins. This wasn't his destination, however. As they skirted the trees Charlotte glanced up, trying to see the place, but nothing was visible from the outside. The forest had locked it away. The shade offered relief from the fierce sun, but walking was slow through long grass and increasingly dense vegetation. Jack went confidently, seeming to know where he was going, though no obvious path suggested itself.

Charlotte studied his back as he walked, the thin shoulders and narrow head, the reddish-brown hair sticking sweatily to his neck. He'd lost weight, hadn't he? Was that possible in the few days she'd known him? Perhaps the stress of his obsession and now his involvement with such dangerous men was burning him away. Every few seconds he glanced back, to be sure she was following still.

'Come on,' he urged. 'We've got a way to go.' Clearly he was anxious to get away from the village.

Charlotte tried to memorise their route. She wondered how far Jen and Saanjh had walked and how long it would take them to share their news about the poachers, and to rescue her, and she thought about Mark and Otto. Mostly about Otto. Even now, in this dangerous time, her mind played over the moments they'd shared, the text he'd sent saying he loved her. She wanted him, for this ordeal to be over, so she could take him in her arms and be held, and know she was wanted and loved. Even the imagining, even out here, filled her with warmth: the thought of Otto, her faith in him, gave her a core of strength. She had to get through this, so they could be together again.

Jack stopped walking and swigged water from his bottle. When she caught up, Charlotte said: 'How far is it?'

Jack was sweating profusely but his face was oddly pale.

'Jack, are you sick?'

But he shook his head. 'Let's get going,' he said. 'Make sure you drink. I don't want you to get dehydrated.'

They walked for another hour, passing through stands of emerald bamboo, glades of long, bleached grass and cool forest of teak and rosewood. Once Charlotte saw three pale deer grazing ahead of them, but otherwise the place was eerily silent; no monkeys, no birds. She started to feel tired.

'Might I rest a bit?' she called. Jack certainly looked like he needed a rest.

'No, keep going. It's not far now. You'll love this place. It's worth it.'

Charlotte jogged to catch him up. 'How did you find it, this mystery destination?'

'Someone told me about it.'

'Who?' She tried to keep her tone light, as though they were any two friends on an outing. But Jack shook his head and didn't answer. Unusually, he had no desire for her conversation.

They walked into denser forest and then downhill in the deep shade and comparative cool. Red soil, almost bare of undergrowth, was soft beneath their feet. The decline grew steeper. Tree roots poked above the soil, like long clinging fingers. Stones erupted. Jack jumped into a narrow streambed, dry now.

'I think we're nearly there.'

'But you don't know? You haven't been here before?' He'd seemed so confident of the way. Jack didn't answer but picked up pace. A stone post, about four feet high, adorned with eroded carvings, appeared on their left. Jack touched it, as they passed. Perhaps this indicated to him they were on the right track?

White, cream and ochre stones lined the streambed. Now and then a vein of quartz glittered when a stray sunbeam penetrated the leaf canopy. Ten minutes later they passed a second stone pillar. Was this some ancient route of pilgrimage? So far away now, lost in the middle of nowhere. What was Jack planning?

He could kill her out here. No-one would know. No-one would ever find her.

Charlotte stopped this train of thought. Jack's only advantage was the gun. She was as quick as he was, and probably as strong. It was a contest between them, and her wits were as keen, and her will to survive. She didn't want to die – and why should someone like Jack take this life away from her? She wasn't going to let that happen, no way. Let the battle begin. Bring it on, she told herself. Bring it on.

Ahead, the trees opened, bringing a glare of bright sunlight and the sound of water. Jack slowed, shading his eyes. They had arrived. Charlotte stepped forward, and despite everything, as the view opened before her it took her breath away.

A deep, romantic chasm: a lush hill sloping steeply down. Tall dun-coloured cliffs, crowned with trees, from which a narrow waterfall jetted, sending a plume of white water down and down to a pool with a hem of pale gravel.

'What do you think?' Jack was also impressed.

'It's beautiful, Jack. Astonishing.' She stepped in front of him and down into the narrow valley. The sound of the falling water grew louder. The pool was churned white where the water fell, but otherwise as clear as glass, revealing polished boulders in its depths, some the grey of shark's skin, others white and amber. Creepers twined the trees with red ragged flowers. The air carried the perfume of cold water and something sweet, like marzipan and burned sugar, from the flowers perhaps. Charlotte surveyed the place, like a painting, impossibly perfect. No other obvious way in, or out, short of scaling the cliffs. She would have to leave the same way they'd arrived.

'I knew you'd like it,' Jack said. 'When they described it to me, I knew this was the place.'

They. The poachers?

Charlotte made her way to the pool's edge. A mist hung over

the surface, around the tumbling water. Was that a ledge behind the fall, a cave perhaps? To one side, close to the trees, she saw the remains of a stone hut, the roof caved in. She wandered over. A hermit's home? Some connection with the stone pillars?

'Look!' Jack stood beside her. He gestured to the cliff wall. A picture of the elephant-headed god Ganesh had been carved into the surface of a smooth slab of rock. Charlotte slowly shook her head.

'Amazing. Really. I wish Jen were here. She would love this too.' She turned to Jack. 'Thanks for bringing me here. How would I ever have found it otherwise?'

Something like a smile flickered across his face. Did he think she was sincere? He sat on the gravel at the edge of the pool.

'I wish you'd give me a chance,' he said. 'I want you to know me, Charlie. And I think, deep down, you do know me – know who I am. If only you'd acknowledge it – let yourself believe it.'

Charlotte sat beside him. The rifle, slung over his shoulder, looked like a dangerous black insect perching on his back.

'Go on then. Convince me.'

He seemed uncertain then, as though he hadn't expected she would open the door so easily. Uncertain and then suspicious.

'Are you humouring me?' he said quietly. 'I don't want your pity. I want your respect.'

Respect? Angry thoughts clambered over each other in Charlotte's mind but she didn't say anything. Jack was so unpredictable. If she made the wrong response he might flip again, become aggressive. Better to let him take the lead.

'We spend most of our lives alone,' he said. 'I know, we have families of one kind or another, but we don't choose them and god knows they aren't always much good. And there are friends who come and go. But we all want something more, don't we? We all want to meet someone who'll know who we are – I mean, truly know. Recognise us. Like I recognise you. I've told you this

– when we were on the train, all manners and games and stuff stripped away, I could see you, Charlie, who you really are. I know we're made of the same material, deep down. We're bound together. And I don't understand why you won't accept it. You must know what I say is absolutely true. You *must* know.

'I'll stay by your side always. I'll never let you down. I'll understand you. Isn't that what you want? That boy, Otto – do you really think he knows you? He can't possibly. He hasn't got what it takes to recognise a woman like you.'

Jack's hands were shaking, emotion overcoming him. Had he rehearsed this speech? As he spoke, he looked intently into her face, searching for a reaction.

Charlotte thought of Otto, how long it had taken him to realise he loved her, the long years he'd been oblivious to her feelings, his gauche enthusiasms, his occasional clumsiness, and his ability, from time to time, to hurt her with the things he said and did. Was he the right man for her?

She shook her head. This mustn't happen. She couldn't allow herself to fall for Jack's manipulations.

'But you do. You think you know me,' Charlie said. 'What is it that you know?'

'Stop trying to analyse it. Just put your intellectualising to one side. We're together in this place, you and me. A bond exists between us, something no-one can destroy. You're the part of my life I've been missing, that I've been searching for all this time. You are it, Charlie. Without you, I'm nothing.'

For a moment he looked small and vulnerable, like a little boy.

'I want you to accept this,' he continued. 'I want you to acknowledge the truth. When that happens, when you're prepared to commit yourself, the whole world is waiting for us. We could go anywhere. Do anything.'

Charlotte took a deep breath. 'May I ask you something, Jack, please?' she said gently. 'Is it possible for you to entertain the idea that you might be mistaken? That this is all in your head? The train accident was terrible. I'm not surprised it's had a big impact on you. We saw shocking things, like nothing we've ever experienced before. Do you see that might have skewed the way you perceive things? You know, post-traumatic stress syndrome or something.'

She waited for his response. Jack went very still, and then shuddered.

'Jack, are you okay?'

Still he didn't speak. His body seemed to swell with anger.

'Say something,' she said, with a rising sense of alarm.

Then, without warning, he jumped to his feet and belted her across the face with the back of his hand. Shock and pain. Charlotte was knocked back onto the ground and before she could think, Jack was upon her, squatting over her body, grabbing her wrists, pinning them to the ground above her head. Charlotte cried out and began to struggle but Jack was heavier and had the advantage of his superior position. The weight and heat of him, the strong odour of his body, filled her with revulsion. Her body bucked, desperate to throw him off, but Jack was tenacious, an expression close to hatred on his sweaty face.

'How do I make you listen?' he said. 'Why do you refuse me? What do I have to do?' He held both her wrists in one hand and slapped her face again, hard enough to sting and humiliate. She could see he enjoyed this, the power he had over her. Where words had failed, violence succeeded. Jack slipped the rifle from his shoulder. Still sitting on her hips he said: 'I want you to get up. Walk over to the hut. Don't say anything, don't try anything.'

Charlotte cursed herself. She was hurt and frightened yes, but more than this, she was angry with herself for letting him get the better of her. She hadn't been alert enough – hadn't paid attention. First round to Jack.

They walked to the stone hut, between the cliff and the squat, lush trees growing at the bottom of the chasm. Although the roof had caved in at the front of the little building, a second room at the back seemed to be intact, with a relatively new-looking wooden door. The vegetation had invaded the walls, tough creepers winding their way through the open doorway and over the tops of the walls. Three leathery saplings had sprung up just beyond the threshold, bursting through the dirt floor. Jack indicated with the point of the rifle.

'That door should open,' he said. 'Try it.'

Charlotte drew back the bolt and the door swung inwards, revealing a small, dark interior. No windows, only a dappling of light from various rifts in the roof. Evidence of recent visitors though – several plastic cups on the floor, cigarette ends, empty wooden crates. A hide-out of some sort?

'Go inside,' Jack said. 'Stand by the wall, over there.' He took a piece of blue nylon rope from his backpack. 'Give me your hands.'

Charlotte hesitated. If she was tied, what chance did she have of escaping? It was an advantage she didn't want to give him. She cursed herself again for pushing him too far. She'd said the wrong thing. She should have been more accommodating, more agreeable.

'Now!' Jack said, sensing hesitation. He jabbed her in the ribs with the end of the rifle, hard enough to hurt. Would he actually shoot her? The calculation ran through her mind in a moment. He looked sick and deranged. In this state of mind, so far away from their ordinary, ordered home world, he might be capable of anything.

Charlotte gave him her hands.

Jack wrapped the hard rope around her wrists, scanned the wall and located an iron ring about five feet from the ground. Clearly he'd been briefed on that too. Jack looped the end of the rope through the ring and tied it tight. The rope bit into the soft skin of her wrists and the height of the ring would oblige her to stand. How long would he keep her here? What would he do now?

Once the rope was fastened to his satisfaction, Jack stepped

254

back and gazed through the doorway, evidently thinking about something.

'I'll be back later,' he said. Again Charlotte noticed how pale he was. Sweat beaded on his forehead. One fat drop spilled over and fell on his cheek. Jack wiped his face with the back of his hand, then tensed and clutched his stomach. The spasm of pain lasted several seconds. He straightened up again, taking several deep breaths.

'Jack, you're sick,' she said. 'What is it? Did you eat something bad?'

'Shut up.' He stepped backwards, away from her, out of the door. He pushed it to and drew the bolt on the outside.

It took several seconds for Charlotte's eyes to adjust to the darkness but the holes in the roof provided just enough comforting light to see the form of the room.

How long would Jack be gone? Surely he wouldn't leave the valley, abandoning her in the wilderness with no hope of rescue? Perhaps he'd gone to rest and recover from whatever ailment was troubling him. Dysentery perhaps – not an uncommon traveller's gripe, but a nasty one. Fever, pain, diarrhoea. She hoped he was suffering.

Charlotte tested the rope and the ring, but Jack had tied her securely and the ring was firm. Minutes passed. Very soon she was uncomfortable with her hands held at shoulder height against the wall. She leaned against it, letting the wall take her weight. After all that had happened, culminating in the long walk, she was tired physically and emotionally. All she could hear was the distant rush of the waterfall. In the hut's twilight, and the relative cool, the urge to sleep overwhelmed her. Charlotte closed her eyes, wondering if it was possible to fall asleep like this, propped against the wall. Her eyes closed, her head slumped forward – but as her knees relaxed her hands jerked against the rope and she woke again. Charlotte reached out with her foot for the wooden crates. If she could haul one over, manoeuvre a second on top of it, perhaps she could sit down. The first was easy. The second was further away. She stretched out her leg, extended her foot, angled her whole body as far as she could, straining to catch it. No good. Just out of reach. She tried again. Just an inch or two short. Hopeless, helpless tears sprang to her eyes.

Hard to say how long she waited. Minutes, an hour – Charlotte lost track of time. For a while she drifted in dreams, partly asleep and partly awake. Sometimes cramps would wrack her arms and ribs so every minute (she counted aloud, in an effort to distract herself from the pain) seemed an unending hour. The rope dug into her skin, an itch which became an agonising burn. She longed for escape.

She opened her eyes: less light in the hut now. The sun had moved on. Her fingers were numb, deprived of proper blood circulation. Her entire body ached but her mind was lucid. A moment later someone drew the bolt and the door swung open. Charlotte blinked in the brighter light. Jack stood silhouetted in the doorway.

'Would you like some water?' His voice was gentle. He had a bottle in his outstretched hand. 'We'll talk a little, and then you can have some.' He picked up the crate Charlotte had failed to reach, turned it over and sat down.

'I had a sleep,' he said. 'Feeling a lot better now. It's a beautiful place. I thought we could swim in the pool. Would you like that?'

'Yes, I would.' Charlotte was torn. On the one hand, she wanted to plead with him to untie her. On the other, she didn't want to give him the satisfaction of knowing how much pain and discomfort she was suffering. Why satisfy his need to affect and control her? She would hold out against him.

'So where do we go from here?' Charlotte said. 'Since charm has failed, are you hoping to beat or starve me into submission?'

'We don't go anywhere from here,' Jack said. 'This is it.'

'What do you mean, this is it?'

Jack didn't answer. He took another gulp of water and screwed the top back on the bottle.

'There's no going back for me,' he said. 'And so, no going back for you either. This time we have together, that's it. Enjoy it while it lasts.'

'What are you saying?' A sensation of cold, a knot of ice in her belly. Jack looked at her with empty eyes.

'I can't go back,' he repeated. 'I've gone too far.'

'You'd be in too much trouble, is that what you mean?'

Jack nursed the rifle, pondering. Was he going to kill her, or himself? The worst case scenario. He'd lost all grip on reality.

'I did it all for you,' he said. 'If only you'd understood, if only you'd admitted the truth to yourself, the situation would be so very different. This is all your fault. All you need to do is accept me – to have faith in me, and us.' His tone was mournful, almost pleading.

Charlotte sighed. Her body was shaking. She was desperate to pee and her hands throbbed. What was the correct response? What words did Jack want from her? She'd say whatever he needed if he'd set her free – but use the wrong words or seem insincere and she was afraid he would become violent, or murderous. She drew a deep breath.

'I'm scared, Jack,' she said. 'I want to leave this place. I want us both to leave. You haven't gone too far. You're still here – still alive. So it's not over. There's a way back.'

Jack stood up, making no response, as though he hadn't heard her. He took out a penknife from his pocket and cut the nylon rope binding her hands.

'Go outside,' he said. 'It's very beautiful. I don't want to finish things in here.'

Blood pumped painfully into her hands. Charlotte staggered into the light. The sun had crossed the chasm and settled on the cliff-tops. Soon it would pass out of sight, casting the valley into shadow. Now though, sunlight played on the white water plunging over the cliffs, creating fragments of rainbow on the mist above the pool. Underwater, the coloured rocks nestled like eggs. Sugar-almond scent drifted from the flowers.

They walked to the pool's edge, Jack standing behind her.

'I love you,' he said. 'I love you so much.'

In that moment she remembered the text Otto had sent her the previous evening, and the time they had put their arms around one another by a pool not unlike this one. I love you, Otto, she thought. I'm not dying here. I'm going to be with you again.

She glanced over her shoulder. Jack had raised his rifle, but another spasm of intestinal pain overwhelmed him, sweat erupting on his face, and he doubled over with a gasp of pain. Charlotte didn't hesitate. She bounded towards him, two, three steps, and kicked the rifle out of his hands. Jack was so incapacitated his grip was weak. The rifle leaped away, turning in the air in a steep, spectacular arc – and dived into the pool. Charlotte kicked again, at Jack this time, catching him on the shoulder and then the stomach. He crumpled to the ground with a moan of pain, not even defending himself.

'Damn you, Jack,' she shouted. 'Damn you to hell, for all you've done, you shitty little creep. I hate you! I hate you!'

He didn't move, curled over on the ground in a ball. Charlotte didn't waste any more time. She reached into his pocket for her mobile, then she turned and ran, fired with adrenalin, stretching out her long legs and taking giant strides away from the pool, the stone hut and the chasm. Away from Jack.

Otto

Confusion. Chaos.

At least, this is how it seemed. People milling about, shouting, giving orders, demanding answers to questions. Policemen, many carrying firearms, vehicles arriving, others stationary but engines revving, reserve wardens, the World Wildlife officials and increasing numbers of random people, materialised from he knew not where.

Mark, the journalist, moved among this crowd apparently at ease in the environment of stress and confrontation, asking questions and taking notes. He looked thrilled to be in this challenging situation, witnessing and taking part in a time of crisis – a big adventure.

Jen and Saanjh, both weary and subdued, had been ushered into the reserve office for questioning. Now both were sitting in the shade waiting for the moment of decision and the next step.

Jaideep, engaged in a heated discussion with the police chief, gesticulated, mopped his forehead, and issued orders which were ignored or countermanded. Although the afternoon was in decline, the heat was relentless, adding to the sense they were all in a crucible – a time of testing, breakdown, and remaking. So much depended on the outcome of the next few hours. Reputations and careers; the lives of precious tigers, the future of the reserve. And justice, yes, justice.

And Charlotte – most important of all for him. What was happening to her? Where had Jack taken her? Was she safe?

Otto was impatient, wanting them to get on with the job, but the plan of action evidently had to be thrashed out with loud voices, argument and confrontation.

Then something happened. The situation crystallised, though Otto couldn't work out how or why. The police mobilised. Jaideep jumped into his jeep, giving instructions to his wardens. The police chief ushered Jen and Saanjh into one of the police vehicles and Mark (invited or not, Otto wasn't sure) leaped in behind Jaideep. In danger of being left out, Otto jumped to his feet and hopped in alongside him. At first Jaideep looked as though he might protest (did he want to be taking random tourists on a dangerous mission?) but Otto pre-empted him.

'I have to help you find Charlie,' he shouted, over the noise of the engines.

Perhaps Jaideep didn't have time to argue because without a word he put his vehicle into gear and they accelerated along the track.

'What's the plan?' Otto asked. The jeep threw up clouds of dust and bounded along the track, throwing him against Mark. Otto clutched the side of the vehicle, his bruises complaining.

'As far as I can work out, the police are taking Jen and Saanjh to the village to show them the pit with the tiger hides,' Mark said. 'The rest have divided into teams, each of which will check the area around one of the camera traps, and other places of recent sightings that Jack knew about and might have passed to the poachers.'

'Where is Jaideep heading?' Two police vehicles followed them. Otto had to shout above the noise.

'The camera trap with the most recent capture. Apparently it got a picture just a couple of days ago. He thinks that's the most likely target.'

The jeep swerved onto a dirt track. The police vehicles bumped after it.

'But what about Charlotte?'

Mark raised his hand to his ear. 'What?'

'Charlotte – what about her?'

'If she and Jack are at the girl's village, the other police team should pick her up.'

Otto sat back, accommodating the jolts and swerves of their route through the reserve. In theory, Mark was right. Why did he have a sinking feeling it wasn't going to be so simple? What if Jack had taken her away from the village? Hurt her, or worse? Perhaps he should have gone with Jen and Saanjh instead of leaping, gung-ho, into the jeep with Mark. Time to put this macho contest with Mark aside. Clearly it was one he couldn't win. And Mark – well, no getting away from it, he was proving to be a useful man to know. Otto glanced over at him, Mark with his expensive shades and tight white T-shirt, gripping the bar above the back of the jeep and so displaying his tanned, muscled arms. Who could blame a girl for liking him: what wasn't to like?

What mattered most was Charlotte's safety – to get her away from Jack.

How long till Otto saw her again? And what would that be like?

As the journey proceeded Otto started to feel afraid. He resisted it but the impulse seemed to rise from his body rather than his mind. His bones remembered the beating he'd endured at the poachers' hands. He wondered what would happen if they ran into the criminal gang – surely violence would ensue.

Jaideep slowed the jeep, cut the engine and jumped out. The police cars stopped behind him, blocking the lane. The apparent chaos at the reserve headquarters was far behind now. Jaideep spoke briefly to the highest ranking officer, who issued instructions to the eight police officers. They set off for the forest and started to move, wordless but coordinated, through the trees and undergrowth.

'Stay there,' Jaideep admonished Mark. He hardly seemed to notice Otto. 'I don't want you getting in the way. Keep out of sight. I'll call you when it's safe.'

Jaideep took a rifle from the cab and then he was gone too. His dark-green reserve uniform blended with the leaves and shadows.

'I'm going to follow them,' Mark whispered, a few seconds later. 'I don't want to miss this.'

'But Jaideep said—' Otto began. Mark shook his head.

'I know what he said.' He was already moving towards the trees. Otto hesitated for a few moments, torn between his training to obey instructions and his desire to prove himself, to see the action. Didn't he want to be a courageous photojournalist? But where was his camera? He'd left it at Jaideep's house and now it was time to go.

As soon as Otto reached the tree-line, he heard men shouting. A branch cracked loudly. Silence for a few seconds – and a single gunshot, the sound tearing the quiet, echoing amongst the trees. Ahead of him Mark cursed, presumably because he was missing the confrontation. Mark started to run, snatching a small camera from his bag.

A flash of gold and marmalade among the trees, and a deep, hoarse roar. They had the tiger already? Otto raced after Mark. A tiger was thrashing about, a front paw gripped by a smooth metal trap. A young tiger, Otto thought, slightly gawky and not as large as some he'd seen in the reserve photographs. It roared again, in pain and panic. The police had guns levelled. A dozen other men were standing at a distance from it – frozen in attitudes of surprise and shock, not knowing what to do. Otto recognised the three who had accosted him. The others, some young, some middle-aged, were dressed in more traditional Indian clothes. For a few moments nobody moved – only the tiger, who tugged helplessly at the trap. Jaideep dashed forward, bravely within reach of the injured animal's claws and teeth, and kicked away a second trap before the tiger caught another paw. Mark, cool-headed, took several pictures in quick succession.

Jaideep shouted instructions and the police officers moved in. The chief poacher glowered with rage. The local men cowered, backing away from the guns, raising their hands and apparently pleading for their lives. Slowly the police edged forwards, herding the poachers together, away from the tiger. One of the chief poacher's henchmen tried to make a run for it but one of the officers jumped on him, knocking him to the ground, fastening his wrists with handcuffs.

The chief poacher didn't say a word. He didn't look frightened at all, only angry. He glared at the police, and at his men.

One of the officers barked an instruction – to drop their weapons presumably because, as one, the local men dropped their bamboo spears. The second henchman hesitated before letting his gun fall to the ground. The leader didn't respond until the instruction was issued a second time. Then, with a grimace, he obeyed. Instantly the officers stepped forward and snapped on handcuffs. He offered some slight resistance, perhaps only to indicate he wasn't beaten and afraid, and apparently insulted the police and his men, earning a blow to the back of his head.

'What about the tiger?' Otto murmured. How would they set it free? Hurt and frightened it lashed out at the men, revealing its giant, brilliant white teeth.

Jaideep summed up the situation and ran from the clearing, returning several minutes later with another gun, armed with a syringe, presumably containing some kind of tranquilliser. Taking careful aim he fired the syringe into the tiger's shoulder, eliciting another outraged roar. Then, slowly, the tiger lost strength and spirit. It slumped heavily onto the ground, blinking slowly, taking long, deep breaths. Jaideep picked up one of the bamboo spears, which had been filled with lead to make it heavy and strong. He moved closer. The tiger lifted its head and flicked its tail in warning, as Jaideep edged bit by bit towards the trap. He wedged the spear into the trap, pinned it with one foot and, watching the tiger all the time, levered the metal jaws open. Beside Otto, Mark took more photographs. If only I'd brought my camera, Otto thought. He'd not been clear-headed or professional enough to think about it – too much personal stuff going on. He'd missed the photographic opportunity of a lifetime.

The tiger's paw slipped free and Jaideep jumped back. The tiger, groggy but not unconscious, lay where it was for a while, its huge amber eyes gazing at the congregation of men. Its leg didn't seem to be broken: it jerked its paw back, flexing the joint.

They all watched the tiger, mesmerised. Otto's eyes fed on the spectacle, the great body lying on the soil, its hide white and orange, painted with black, tribal stripes. The long, ringed tail flicked. The tiger struggled to its feet, the weight and strength of it evident in its movements, despite the lingering effects of the tranquilliser. It stood for a few moments, dazed like a drunk, surveying the men. They backed away, opening a path for its departure. The tiger didn't leave at once, its mind perhaps foggy. Then, at last, it staggered away from the clearing with a limp.

The tiger disappeared into the trees.

For a few seconds the enchantment lingered. Nobody moved or spoke. The lead poacher broke the spell first, spitting loudly on the ground and shouting some insult to his men. He received another cuff from one of the police officers, which didn't stop him issuing some other contemptuous comment. One of the officers, clearly riled, was about to punch him again but the police chief (with one eye on Mark's camera?) ordered him to leave the captive alone.

The confrontation was over. Instructions and information were relayed over a radio. Officers herded the local men towards the vehicles. The leader and his two men followed on under close guard. Jaideep attended to the traps, disarming those remaining.

'May I help?' Otto stepped forward.

Jaideep scowled – he shouldn't have been there after all – but accepted the offer and asked him to help clear the scene.

Laden with weighted bamboo spears, Otto walked to the jeep.

Slowly adrenalin drained away and excitement receded. The tiger had been saved and the poachers rounded up.

Now what about Charlotte – and Jack?

Charlotte

She ran along the dry streambed, and passed the first stone post.

Despite the long ordeal she didn't feel tired. Relief to be free and exhilaration at her victory fired her up, filled her body with unnatural energy. She'd always loved running and kept very fit, and now her athleticism paid off. Her legs responded to the demand for action, striding up the hill.

Now and then a flicker of doubt crossed her mind, fear that Jack was chasing her. She glanced over her shoulder just in case he was following, jumped when a bird clattered out of a tree. Should she have tied him up? Locked him in the stone hut? What if the rifle had survived its dunking in the pool? She thought she could outrun Jack – especially when he was so crippled by whatever illness he was suffering. But outrun bullets? No, she couldn't do that.

Don't stop. Keep running. She leaped over boulders and broken ground, powering through the forest, breathing even, muscles strong. A slight sweat broke out on her face and back but in the shade the heat was tolerable.

After half an hour, her strength began to wane. She slowed to a walk and caught her breath. Jack should be far behind now, but she'd left the guidance of the streambed and would have to rely on memory for the way back to the village. Emerging from the denser forest, she reckoned it was another hour's walk – if she could remember the way.

Charlotte set off. As she walked, thoughts of Otto filled her mind. Perhaps he was looking for her. If Jen and Saanjh had been successful, the police would be on to the poachers, the hunters becoming the hunted. What dramas were unfolding without her?

Now tiredness caught her up. The aggressive heat soaked up her strength and thirst became an issue. She was fairly confident about the route but now out of immediate danger, her energy was fading. Just keep walking, she told herself sternly. Keep going. Don't think about how tired and thirsty you are. Don't think about the possible dangers – snakes, elephants, even tigers. Focus your attention elsewhere. And so she did. It wasn't difficult, of course, because Otto, her feelings for him, loomed so large in her mind. She replayed from memory the scenes they'd shared: the evening by the river, the strange moment in the bathroom when she'd bathed his battered body and he'd almost declared what his braver text had shouted over and over. I love you. I love you. Delight and anticipation clouded her mind, an almost painful longing to be physically close to him again.

The silent landscape, golden in the fading afternoon, she barely noticed – nor the creeping exhaustion sapping the strength from her body. Thirst she put to one side. An intense longing for Otto blocked out these lesser sensations, and Otto she couldn't see until this journey was complete.

Once or twice she thought she'd taken a wrong turning, back-tracked and tried again. From time to time she worried she was walking in entirely the wrong direction, and then panic threatened. What if she were lost in the wilderness? How would anyone find her, and night would fall, with its potentially dangerous animals. Again, she pushed the fear aside. She had to reach Otto.

The sun touched the horizon, molten red above the trees. Was that dense grove the place Jen had found her temple ruins? If so, the village was just beyond. Charlotte quickened her pace. There – ahead of her, caught in a warm beam of sunlight, up to her waist in pale-green grass, a girl dressed in red, like a poppy.

'Saanjh! Saanjh!' Charlotte started to run. Saanjh turned and smiled. Then she looked over her shoulder and beckoned.

'Charlie?' Jen's voice. She appeared beside Saanjh, taller but no less slight. 'Charlie?' she repeated, as though she couldn't believe the evidence of her eyes. And then they were together, Jen and Charlotte, hugging each other while Saanjh grinned and grinned beside them, and the women emerged from the huts to see the reunion, smiling and making expressions of delight.

'You made it? You got to the reserve office? What happened? Did they catch the poachers?'

Jen held on to Charlotte. 'It's okay,' she nodded. 'We did it. Everything's okay.' Then: 'Where's Jack? Did he hurt you?'

'I'm fine,' Charlotte reassured. 'I'm not sure where Jack is. I escaped from him, in this little lost valley. He was ill, bad I think. I don't know if he followed me or if he's still there. I suppose someone will have to look for him.'

She looked over Jen's shoulder. 'Where's Otto?'

Jen gave a small, knowing smile.

'Back at the reserve office. They caught them – the poachers. They didn't kill another tiger, we were just in time.'

Police officers and a reserve warden were still hanging around the village, talking among themselves. Jen said they'd guided them to the pit where the tiger skins were curing. The site had been photographed, notes taken in evidence ready for a trial. The skins would also be presented in court. Since the poachers had been caught in the act a conviction seemed almost certain. Jaideep was relieved. The police were jubilant. They'd detained, red-handed, a well-known player in the world of organised crime.

Three tigers were already dead though, Charlotte remembered. No way to bring them back. How long could the species survive in the wild, when growing populations and demands for resources ate into their habitat, when poachers were so hard to foil?

Jen took Charlotte to one of the police officers. They didn't seem quite as excited to see her, caught up in the news of the arrest and the collection of evidence. Doubtless the whole Jack-and-Charlotte drama seemed like a sideshow to the police in comparison to the big arrest. After all, here she was, safe and sound, and it wouldn't be obvious to these officers how dangerous her situation had been.

'Did Saanjh get in trouble?' Charlotte asked. 'Was she okay?'

'Look.' Jen gestured to the women and children, who were patting and hugging Saanjh, talking to her in cheerful, animated voices. 'They're proud of her. You know, I think those women orchestrated a lot of this. I'm not quite sure, how and why, but I think they told her to help us.'

Charlotte was desperate to get home, to eat and rest, and most of all to see Otto, but the police didn't seem to share her sense of urgency. She and Jen rested in the shade while all sorts of apparently useless hanging around ensued, conversations among the officers, amicable arguments and note-taking. The Adivasi women brought Charlotte and Jen huge cups of sweet tea, and then prepared them lavish dishes of rice and stewed lentils. Saanjh joined the feast and they sat in a circle, away from the men and around a little fire, talking to each other. Jen traded her jewellery for some of the bangles worn by the forest women. Charlotte held the baby at the insistence of its mother.

Finally the reserve warden came for the girls, telling them it was time to go. The police departed noisily in their vehicles. Jen and Charlotte hugged Saanjh and waved to the other women before jumping into the back of the Golden Tiger jeep.

'Where are their men? The husbands and fathers and brothers?' Charlotte wondered.

The drive home seemed to last a long time. Charlotte fell asleep for a while, head bouncing on Jen's shoulder, unable to keep her eyes open. When they pulled up outside Jaideep's home, the door opened, spilling warm electric light. Jaideep, Amrita and Prina hurried out. Amrita and Prina folded her in their arms, expressing their delight to see her safe and unharmed. She was ushered into the house, into a comfortable seat, plied with food and fruit juice, and a hundred questions ensued. What had happened, where was Jack, how had she escaped? Charlotte answered as best she could, though weariness slowed her brain. One question hovered in her mind, one she hardly dared ask a second time. Where was Otto? Why wasn't he here to greet her?

In the end Jen put her out of her misery. She asked Jaideep where Otto was.

'He's staying in town, in a hotel with the reporter. We didn't have room for them both here,' Jaideep said. 'I've phoned to tell them you're home and safe, and I said you were too tired for more visitors tonight. They'll see you tomorrow.'

Charlotte's heart plummeted. Not see him till the morning? If Otto loved her, as she loved him, he'd be over here now, banging on the door, desperate to see her. She was so disappointed tears threatened and her voice choked. Why had Jaideep warned them off? How could he!

Don't be stupid, she told herself. He was trying to be helpful. He doesn't know what you're feeling, or how important this is. She swallowed the urge to cry.

'Thanks so much,' she said. 'I am so tired I really have to go to bed. Would you excuse me?'

'Me too,' Jen said. 'I'm sharing your bed with you tonight, Charlie, I hope that's okay.'

Charlotte took a long, delicious shower. She was barely able to stay awake though, and leaned against the wall of the cubicle. Even standing was too much effort. She crept into bed while Jen took her shower, and picked up her mobile. He'd have sent her a text, surely? Light flared from the screen into the dark room.

Nothing.

No message. Not a single word.

Charlotte was alone in the room. Amrita hadn't yet gone to bed, Jen was in the bathroom. An astonishing, stunning feeling of hurt and loss crashed over her. All those hopes and dreams, all the love and desire that had fuelled her escape and the long walk home, all the anticipation of joy and fulfilment – now so many bitter ashes. Otto hadn't even bothered to text her. He'd changed his mind. He didn't even care enough to send her a message after all she'd been through.

Should she text him? No. Why wasn't he wanting to look after her, to find out how she was? Didn't he care?

Exhausted, overcome, sobs overwhelmed her. She pressed her face into the pillow and cried. The pain of it, her thwarted longing to be with him, was unlike anything she'd felt before. Is this what love was? How stupid she'd been to lose control, to let her feelings run away with her. Still sobbing, she picked up the phone and opened the previous text, Otto's declaration of love, trying to gain some hope or nourishment from it. Then she rested the mobile on the table, close to her face, and stared at it in the vain hope that a text might still come – that Otto was thinking of her and would find some way to communicate a love and longing that matched her own.

Otto

Mark put his iPhone down.

'She's home, she's safe,' he said, with a grin. He picked up a glass of whiskey and took a sip. 'Have another drink. All's well. Now you can relax.'

Otto felt a profound sense of relief. He'd spent the last few hours tense and restless, churning with worry for Charlotte and frustration at his own helplessness. They'd had word that Jen and Charlotte were together and safe at the Adivasi village with the police just after sunset, then no further information for several hours.

'Thank god,' he said. 'Thank god. I don't know what I'd have done if anything had happened to her. I'd better give her a call.'

Mark held up his hand. 'Give her a little time,' he said. 'She'll be shattered, needing a rest. Call her later.'

Otto hesitated. He wanted to talk with her, but perhaps that was selfish. Maybe Mark was right.

They were sitting in a little restaurant, close to Mark's hotel. They'd eaten well; even worry couldn't thwart Otto's need for food after all that had happened. Now though, he could afford to savour the meal. He picked up his glass. 'To Charlotte,' Mark said. 'She's quite a woman.'

'Charlotte,' Otto echoed, clinking his glass against Mark's. She's safe, she's safe: the words repeated themselves over and over in his mind. He knocked back the whiskey and ordered another shot. His body still hurt and he was tired, but none of these mattered compared to the happiness he felt, knowing Charlotte was out of danger and that tomorrow he would see her again.

Mark took a deep breath. 'You and Charlotte have been friends a long time, right?'

'Yes, a long time.'

'I've been so impressed by the way she's handled herself. She's clever, and cute too – I hope you don't mind me saying that. And I think she's likes me.'

'Likes you?' Otto couldn't hide the shock in his voice. What exactly was Mark saying?

'Don't sound so surprised! In fact, I know she likes me. I expect she told you, back in Goa, we had, well, a romantic moment.'

Thoughts tumbled over one another in Otto's head, a horrible crashing of emotions. He could hardly believe what he was hearing. It didn't make sense. He'd never felt anything like this, the sheer hurt of it.

'A romantic moment?' His voice sounded strangled.

Mark carried on oblivious, evidently unaware of the storm inside his companion.

'Well, a kiss, nothing more. I didn't push it. But now – well, she is very impressive. Maybe I'll ask her out again before I go.'

Otto couldn't think straight. Every word Mark pronounced so blithely felt like a knife stabbing into his heart.

Mark and Charlotte *kissed*?

She hadn't told him. Suddenly events of the past few days replayed themselves in his mind. He remembered the moment in the bathroom when Charlotte had bathed his wounds, and he'd been about to tell her in person that he loved her. She had stopped him. Because the moment hadn't been right, he'd assumed. What if he'd misunderstood? She'd talked to Mark on the phone. Had she changed her mind about the romance with Otto, with Mark reappearing on the scene?

One cool part of his mind told him this was ridiculous, to stop worrying. Another besotted, jealous, insecure part of him was screaming with hurt and suspicion. The image of her kissing Mark (why hadn't she told him?) was a horrible kind of torture.

What should he do?

He swallowed his feelings. If she wanted Mark – well, that had to be her choice.

He'd taken a room of his own in Mark's hotel, another clean, airy place furnished with elegant, faded furniture. They drank and Mark talked, enjoying a vicarious sense of accomplishment after the capture of the poachers. Otto was too upset to say much, and excused himself, saying he was tired. Lying in bed, he spent a few intense minutes thinking of Charlotte, wondering what he would say to her, how he'd feel when he saw her again. No pressure, he reminded himself. Give her space if it's Mark she wants. Strange how hard it was to conjure her familiar face in his mind: though he could remember her hands so vividly, the golden brown of her skin on her back, just beneath her neck.

Then sleep came, obliterating. No dreams he could recall. He woke up suddenly, at eleven. Sunlight filled the room and he was hungry again. A moment later someone knocked on the door.

'Otto?' Mark's voice. 'Are you up?'

Otto jumped out of bed. 'Yes, almost.'

Mark laughed. 'I'll order you a coffee. See you in the cafe.'

Otto showered, wishing he had some razors. His stiffness had eased, and while the bruises were still painful his body was healing fast. His heart though, that was a different matter. How could he bear to lose Charlotte so soon?

He wondered how he would replace the stuff Jack had destroyed – including his passport. Jack. What had happened to him? Presumably the police had arrested him? He wanted to know Jack was locked away somewhere, out of the picture.

Fifteen minutes later he was sipping thick, sugared coffee on a little terrace overlooking the main street, where vehicles carefully dodged a large, white cow lying peacefully in the middle of the road. Mark was poring over his iPhone, apparently checking emails. He looked, as always, bright and energetic, ready for anything. One angry, insane part of Otto's mind hated him – wanted to push him over, stamp on him. He looked away, tried to think of something else.

'I wrote up some of the story this morning,' Mark explained. 'I need to get some information from the police, and I'd love to get some comments from Jaideep. But it's quite a coup. I'm feeling ridiculously pleased with myself.'

'Who will you sell the story to?' Despite himself, Otto was curious how the process worked.

'Oh, I've had a few offers already.' Mark grinned at the iPhone, his fingers brushing the screen, scrolling through the inbox. 'We'll see who comes up with the goods. The pictures I got – well, they really make it.' He seemed to glow with pleasure.

'It's a bit early, but, well, I think I'll call Charlie in a bit, find out how she is. I 'spect you'll want to talk to her too,' he said.

Otto didn't answer. He didn't know what he'd say to her, didn't know if he'd even be capable of speaking. He needed to see her. He had to find out the truth.

They breakfasted on bananas, scrambled eggs and toast, then a taxi arrived (Mark had organised that as well) to drive them to the reserve office.

Jaideep welcomed them both, shook Otto's hand, and ushered Mark into his office. It looked like Mark had secured the interview he wanted. Then again, this was Jaideep's long-awaited moment of triumph. At last he had an opportunity to celebrate a success and to prove the competence of the reserve management.

Otto sat outside. He felt at a complete loss. Jaideep had told him Charlotte and Jen were still at the house, but should be arriving sometime soon. All he could do was wait.

Half an hour passed. Otto wandered into the office in the hope of chatting to the other reserve employees but they were also preoccupied. He did learn that the World Wildlife officials had left – and a decision on funding was expected within five days. Despite the successful detention of the poachers, Otto sensed no-one was confident of the outcome. Too much had happened. Too many bad things: an ongoing battle with loggers and illegal quarrying, the struggle the few staff had to protect wildlife over the huge area of the tiger reserve, the loss of three tigers over the course of a week. Was it possible yesterday's success could outweigh that?

Neither Jen nor Charlotte appeared. After an hour, Mark emerged from Jaideep's office looking pleased with himself. He set up his laptop among the other reserve staff, making himself quite at home, and used their landline for a long conversation with the local police. Then he started typing. Otto waited all the while, bored and restless, wanting to talk to his friends, aching to see Charlotte. Why hadn't they come?

Otto went and stood beside him, like a pestering kid. 'What happened to Jack?' he said. 'The police got him, right?'

Mark looked surprised. 'Jack? I don't know where he is. They didn't arrest him, no. Jaideep said Charlotte left him in this little valley place, right out of the way. Some old pilgrim path, can't be reached in a vehicle. I don't think the police were that bothered about him once they'd got the poachers. Too much effort to trek all the way out there on foot last night.'

Otto was surprised Mark didn't seem more worried. If Jack was on the loose, didn't that mean Charlie could still be in danger? Mark was so caught up with his big story that didn't seem to have occurred to him. How much did he care about Charlotte? Not so much. Why should he? It was an idle fancy (like all the many idle fancies Otto had indulged in, his conscience reminded him).

When he'd finished writing, edited his photographs and checked final details with Jaideep and the reserve staff, Mark gestured to Otto.

'I'm heading back to the hotel. You coming with?'

'What about Jen and Charlie? I wanted to see them.'

'I'm sorry, I forgot to say. Change of plan. Jaideep's taking us all out for a meal this evening. We'll see them then.' Mark grinned. 'Could be my chance, don't you think? I hope you don't mind me talking to you like this, I know she's your friend. I'm perfectly serious about wanting to know her better. And Jaideep said he knew a great place for us to go – you've been there before?'

'Oh, yes. A great place,' Otto echoed mechanically. But the rest of the afternoon stretched emptily ahead of him.

He passed the time lying on his bed at the hotel, gazing at the ceiling, dreaming about Charlotte, running through conversations in his mind. None of them seemed to work out well. Why hadn't she told him she kissed Mark? He thought about phoning Jen but didn't know what he would say. He didn't trust himself to be sensible. Better to wait till the evening when he'd see them and perhaps could then gauge the situation. He'd handle it better when Charlotte was there in the flesh.

Through the wall he could hear Mark talking loudly, on his phone or Skype maybe, thrashing out the best deal he could get for his cracking news feature.

Otto fell asleep for a while. When he woke the room was silent. He sat on the step outside the hotel willing the next hour to pass.

He and Mark were first at the restaurant. The owner welcomed him warmly, remembering him from the previous visit. He joined them at the table in the courtyard while his guests drank beer.

Daylight faded. For a few minutes, carmine light coloured the dancing girls on the walls. As the restaurateur lit candles on the tables, Otto heard a commotion as new guests arrived. He stood up. Prina stepped through the door first, glittering in a blue-and-silver sari, then Amrita in jeans and a primrose blouse, and Jen, looking unlikely in an outfit similar to Amrita's (she, presumably, had also been obliged to borrow clothes) and finally Charlotte herself.

Charlotte.

His eyes locked on her, hardly registering the other people around them. He wanted to hug her, but held back. Charlotte looked stunning. Slim and golden, her hair loose on her shoulders, dressed in her usual simple style, jeans and a long-sleeved T-shirt; no jewellery except for her wristwatch. No make-up, because she didn't need it.

Jen gave him a fierce hug and a kiss on the cheek. Charlotte caught his eye then quickly looked away. 'Hey, Otto,' she said, maintaining a distance.

The meal began. Charlotte was quiet, though the rest of the party was in celebratory mood. Mark was entertaining, with stories to tell, clearly out to impress. He flirted with Charlotte, but Otto was gratified to see she didn't seem to be responding. Jaideep was expansive too, letting his guard down for a change. Amrita giggled and made eyes at the handsome reporter, while her mother frowned and tapped her daughter's arm in admonishment from time to time.

After the first course, the gathering began to talk about the events of the previous two days. They had all heard parts of the story, but now was an opportunity for each piece to be shared and made into a complete picture. Charlotte described the time she had spent with Jack, how he'd tied her up, threatened her, how afraid she'd been that he would kill her, and himself too.

They all listened attentively. Otto found it hard to bear, hearing what she'd been through and what Jack had done to her. He was also overwhelmed at her courage and quick thinking, the way she'd handled herself. They all were.

'So where's Jack?' Otto said. That question again.

'I don't know,' Jaideep said. 'I wasn't able to send someone to the valley till this afternoon – it's a long way by foot, and as you'll understand, we were preoccupied. And he wasn't there. The rifle was still in the river, but no sign of Jack.'

'Aren't you worried? What if he comes after Charlotte again?' Otto's voice sounded angrier than he had intended.

'We'll take care of Charlotte, don't you worry,' Prina spoke up. 'If anyone sees Jack, he'll be arrested.'

Finally Jaideep spoke. He told them the police had charged the three chief poachers. Their local helpers, it turned out, were the men from the Adivasi village. They had all been released.

'The poachers went to the village and threatened them,' Jaideep explained. 'They set up camp, took over the place, and told the tribespeople they'd destroy the village, assault the men and violate their wives if they didn't cooperate. And they promised to give them a large quantity of money if they did help them kill tigers.'

'Why didn't the Adivasi come to you? Or the police?' Mark said.

'They live in a remote place. They had little contact with us, and to be honest, little faith in the police to protect their interests. And the poachers were there, virtually holding them captive.' Jaideep shook his head. 'If we are successful with this funding application I'd like to help them, and for them to help us. There are several hundred tribal people living all over the reserve and it would be excellent to create some kind of schooling for the children, and to engage the adults in watching and protecting the wildlife in the reserve.'

'The women had a plan, I think,' Jen said. 'They told Saanjh to help us. They didn't want the poachers to succeed, and they didn't want tigers killed. They were clever. Very discreet, and very clever, helping us without seeming to be involved.'

'So what about the funding?' Amrita asked. 'Are we going to get it?'

Jaideep shook his head. 'I don't know. I wouldn't care to guess. Two days ago I had no hope at all, after everything that happened.

Now, who knows. Perhaps Mark's story will help – give us some positive publicity.'

'I mentioned your pending application in the story, and the World Wildlife connection,' Mark said. 'Maybe that will persuade them a little. After all, they wouldn't want to be seen refusing help to such an heroic enterprise.'

'Maybe,' Jaideep shrugged, not seeming convinced.

'Charlie, are you okay? You're very quiet.' Amrita put her hand on Charlie's arm.

'I'm sorry.' Charlotte shook her head, as though dislodging unpleasant thoughts.

Jen, who was sitting beside Otto, reached out and squeezed his hand. 'I think Charlie needs some fresh air,' she said. 'Why don't you take her for a walk? We can meet up with you later.'

Otto glanced at Charlotte, his face burning, his heart beating so loud that surely Jen could hear it.

'I don't know if Charlie wants to walk,' he said.

She looked at him again, a flare of something in her face. Anger? Did she think he was reluctant to be alone with her?

'Charlie?' Jen's voice was bright.

Otto knew they were being manoeuvred, but however generous Jen's intentions, perhaps Charlotte didn't want to be alone with him. Nothing about her behaviour this evening had suggested she did.

'Charlie?' Otto stood up. 'If you'd like.' An excruciating moment. The rest of the party watched the little drama, and Otto thought, they all know what's going on. What if Charlie refused? What if she said yes out of politeness and a desire to save him from humiliation? What if she'd rather Mark had asked?

Questions and no answers.

Except that finally Charlie made a response. She stood up too.

'I could do with a walk,' she said, still not looking directly at Otto. 'Just be ten minutes. Order me some pudding.' Everything about her body seemed to deny him, to block him out. Was she angry with him? What had he done? He'd never seen her like this before. She was usually so open and straightforward.

Charlotte led the way out. Suddenly they were in the street, alone.

'Which way?' Why wouldn't she look at him?

'That way,' Otto indicated. 'There's a cafe, ten minutes' walk. It's got a nice terrace. I had breakfast there this morning – great scrambled eggs. Weird toast though.'

Shut up, he told himself. Shut up. All the rehearsed conversations had vanished from his mind.

Charlotte walked beside him in silence. He sensed her turmoil – emotions tightly contained. Why didn't she tell him what she was thinking?

'It sounds like you went through hell,' he offered.

Charlotte took a deep breath, seeming to have to force herself to speak. 'You know, none of the hell with Jack hurt me as much as your silence last night.'

'Silence?' He felt whipped. 'What do you mean, I didn't even see you last night, what do you mean?' The words raced out.

'You didn't send a message. You didn't phone me, you didn't even text me, after all I'd been through. The only thing that kept me going was thinking about you, wanting to be with you, and you didn't even bother to send me a word!'

She spoke in a rush. They'd both stopped. Otto turned to her.

'Why didn't you tell me you kissed Mark? Have you changed your mind about us, is that it? Because he's come back? Would you rather be with him?' His voice sounded strange, hurt rather than angry, though he realised he might sound angry to her.

He realised she was crying.

'What are you talking about? I love you! And I thought you loved me,' she said, naive like a child. 'I thought you loved me. You said you did! But you don't, and I feel like such a fool. What a mistake it was, screwing up our friendship like that. I was always so worried that would happen. I can't bear it. I can't bear how I feel.

'Yes, I kissed Mark, but that was weeks ago, and I was drunk and all the stuff going on, and you were mad over Maria. I didn't tell you because I felt embarrassed about it. It wasn't any of your business then. Have you told me about every girl you've ever kissed?'

Otto felt a flood of emotions – mostly relief and happiness. She did love him. The business with Mark was truly not important. Why hadn't he trusted her?

And she'd said 'always' so worried? How long did that 'always' mean?

'Oh my god, I'm sorry,' he said.

She was sobbing now, standing in the street. Otto put his arms around her, held her tight, kissed the top of her head as she cried. He glanced around the street, suddenly afraid of passers-by and the scene they were creating.

No-one about. Only a skinny dog, sniffing about in a mound of rubbish in a gutter. Lights in buildings indicated the presence of others, but for the moment they were alone in the relative darkness of the street.

'I do love you,' he whispered.

'What?'

'I do love you. My god, I love you.' He stroked her back, feeling how she clung to him, how her body seemed to melt into his.

'Do you really?' She lifted her head to look into his face. All the Charlotte confidence and competence were gone. She seemed so vulnerable and exposed. He felt a wave of tenderness.

'Really,' he said. 'Really and truly.'

They stood for several moments more, pressed against each other, Otto caressing her all the while.

'We'd better text the others, tell them to continue the meal without us,' Charlotte said, taking out her phone. Then they broke apart and continued to walk along the street, hand in hand. Otto felt a moment's fleeting triumph. When Mark heard Otto and Charlie weren't coming back, he'd know what was going on.

Charlotte

All the grief drained away.

They passed cabin-shops, some of them still open, selling mobile phones, lighters and bottled drinks, takeaway food, shoe repairs, haircuts.

Holding Otto's hand, Charlotte felt an energy running between them, her body's desire for him, the heat of his blood. How ridiculous it seemed now, the storm of emotion stirred up by his failure to contact her. Is this what love would be like for her, this terrible tempest? Don't think about it now, she told herself. Relax. Enjoy this long-awaited moment.

They didn't speak again till they reached the cafe. No other customers – Otto ordered a couple of coffees. He was still bruised but in the dim light, this and his two-day stubble made him look disreputably rakish. She smiled.

'You're beautiful,' she said.

'Me?'

'Yes.' Their hands were still clasped.

The coffees arrived.

'Mark told me he fancied you – told me about the kiss,' Otto said. 'That's why I didn't text you. I know that's a rubbish excuse, I should have done it.'

'Mark? Why would you think that I wanted him – after everything we said by the pool?'

'I don't know,' he said. 'I wasn't thinking straight. I was so jealous.'

Charlotte sighed. He could be so obtuse. That wasn't going to make life easy. She pushed her chair closer to his so she could lay her head against his shoulder. Such a display of affection might not be the done thing here, but the street and the terrace were quiet.

'I wouldn't blame you for liking him,' Otto persisted. 'He's a great guy, got everything going, and if I were a girl, well I'm sure I'd fancy him myself.'

Charlotte laughed. 'You idiot.' Her voice was fond. 'I don't want Mark. I want you.' She thought, he will probably hurt me like this from time to time, but he will never intend to hurt me. Was that good enough?

They talked awhile. Otto asked again about her time with Jack, wanting details. She felt him tense with anger as she recounted the ordeal. It helped though. Each time she told the story its impact lessened.

Otto hesitated. 'Are you going to stay with me tonight?'

Charlotte felt a drumming through her body, like horses galloping. Her face flushed.

'I don't know what Jaideep and Prina would think of that,' she said. 'I'd better not stay all night. I need to behave appropriately, as their guest. But yes, let's go now.' She longed to be somewhere private.

They crept through the hotel, surreptitious, not wanting to be seen or waylaid. Charlotte loved Otto's room, the ancient but fragrant cotton sheets, the old furniture. They sat on the bed side by side, both tense with nerves and anticipation. She had wondered about this moment so many times over the last two years – what it would be like if he loved her, how she would feel if they were lovers.

284

Now the reality was both more and less than she had imagined: less because they were each so familiar with the other, and so comically awkward – and more, because her feelings, physical and emotional, were so intense. Just now nothing mattered, except to be in Otto's arms, to feel him close to her, kissing her.

Otto kissed her again. His warm hands slid beneath her T-shirt, caressing her waist and back. He kissed her forehead and nose, her chin and neck. She was almost faint with longing.

'Shall we get into bed?' he said. Charlotte nodded. In the low light from the lamp by the bedside she pulled off her clothes and jumped neatly under the sheet. Otto embraced her and she pressed herself against the length of him, feeling the smoothness of his skin, the hard, masculine front, the muscles in his arms and legs. She wanted to savour every moment of this, each passing sensation. They kissed again, longer and deeper this time. Her mind seemed to spiral away, overwhelmed by the clamouring sensations in her body.

Otto drew back. 'Have you done this before?' he whispered. 'I mean, have you ever . . . ?'

'Yes,' Charlotte said. 'A year ago. I told you I had a brief relationship – and, well, it didn't really work out. It wasn't what I wanted. I mentioned it before, remember?'

'Yes but – you never told me it got that serious.' Otto sounded pained by this admission.

'No, I didn't.' She was reluctant to admit that this foray into the world of romance had been cut short because she couldn't get Otto out of her mind. Perhaps she'd only embarked on it because she was afraid Otto would never want her, that life would pass her by while she fruitlessly waited. Nonetheless, the relationship hadn't been a success.

Otto kissed her again. Charlotte, braver now, ran her hands over his back, enjoying the firm velvet texture of his skin, the hardness of bone and muscle underneath. She pressed her face against his neck, breathing in the precious smell of him, the clean, masculine fragrance.

'Do you want this now?' he said. 'I mean, we don't have to. We can wait, if you're not ready.'

'I am ready,' she said.

'Are you sure?'

'Yes! For god's sake, I'm sure!' she laughed.

'I love you,' he whispered, kissing her again.

Jen

Prina kept a beautiful little garden at the side of the house. Every morning she rose before dawn and watered the neat vegetable bed, where she grew onions and peppers, various green and yellow gourds, cucumber, fenugreek and various other herbs Jen didn't recognise. A mango tree, with dense, dark leaves, grew in the corner of the garden, cast welcome shade in the afternoon.

It was still early. The soil hadn't dried yet, and smelled sweet. Inside the house Jen could hear Prina working in the kitchen, singing to herself. Amrita was studying in the living room. The family had been very kind, finding room for her in the already-busy house because she was Charlotte's friend, and in trouble, but today she had to sort out her possessions, replace those too damaged to salvage and find out how to replace her ruined passport. What then?

Ah yes, what then?

Charlotte had returned late the previous night. How did Jen feel about that? Although Charlotte had said nothing, Jen had known Charlotte had been hurt and upset the previous day. It hadn't taken any psychic powers to see this, or to guess Otto was the reason. That had been confirmed when Jen had seen how Charlotte and Otto had behaved with each other at the meal – and Jen herself had suggested the walk she'd hoped would break the impasse between them.

Did that mean Jen was okay with the situation? She loved Charlotte, and she loved Otto too. Things hadn't worked out when she'd become romantically involved with Otto all that time ago (it seemed such a long time, now) and she could see he wasn't the right man for her. Still, she felt something. A twinge of regret, the sting of jealousy, and a sense this relationship between her two best friends would exclude her. Wouldn't she lose them both, to some degree, if they were committed to each other? Certainly travelling with them might be uncomfortable. However hard they tried, she would feel like a gooseberry. Couldn't they have waited till the end of the trip before embarking on a romance?

She gave her head an impatient little shake. It was a selfish thought. She wanted them to be happy. And she had behaved selfishly when she'd stayed on in Goa despite Charlotte's protests. At what point did the fulfilment of your own needs shift into selfishness? Perhaps no clear line existed. Jen had insisted on staying in Goa to follow her chosen path, even though it upset Charlotte. Now she would take the pain and accept Charlotte's long-awaited relationship with Otto. Charlotte, one of the least selfish people Jen knew, certainly deserved this.

'Jen? Charlie's up. She's just got out of the shower,' Amrita called from the kitchen. Jen went inside. Prina had just gone out.

'Charlie?' She looked great, glowing with health, a shy smile on her face as though unsure of the welcome she could receive. Jen hurried over and gave her a big hug. The three young women sat down. Amrita was evidently bursting to question Charlotte about her night out and the romance with Otto, but didn't dare ask. Instead, she and Jen looked at Charlotte expectantly, burning with curiosity and wondering what Charlie might reveal.

Charlotte glanced from face to face, and laughed.

288

'I'm not saying anything, okay? Except that, yes, Otto and I are together now and I'm very, very happy.'

'That's all we need to know,' Jen said, hugging Charlotte again.

That afternoon, Jen and Charlotte left Amrita to her studies and went into town, so Jen could buy a few new clothes. She picked up a pair of jeans and three loose cotton tops, before chancing upon a narrow side street, lined with tiny workshops. The women wandered down, past a man mending shoes and another selling a cornucopia of nails, screws, bolts and keys, to a wooden cabin where a very elderly man sat cross-legged with a thick needle in his hand, sewing pages into a notebook.

Jen stopped. The old man glanced up. He was naked to the waist, and despite his age, had a young man's body, with dark walnut skin and without an ounce of superfluous flesh. The book in his lap had a black leather cover and pages of soft ivory paper.

'I need a new book,' Jen said. 'Jack . . . I mean, well, the other one was pulled to pieces.'

A pile of ready-made notebooks of various sizes waited on a shelf inside the cabin. The old man put down his work, rose to his feet and beckoned to Jen. She felt a little shy but the man picked up one of the books and held it out to her. A leather cord bound the mottled cover. She examined them all, before deciding on a notebook with a red leather cover. The man indicated she might like a second book, and then invited Charlotte to buy one too. In the end they agreed a price for the red book and Jen tucked it into her bag. A new book, a new start?

They stopped for drinks of orange juice and talked about practicalities – how Jen might best patch up her rucksack till she found a new one; how Mark had already left town and was flying back to Delhi that afternoon. Then the conversation died away. After a couple of minutes, Charlotte opened her mouth to speak, but hesitated. Jen put her hand on Charlotte's arm.

'It's okay,' she said. 'You and Otto. Really, I don't mind. You deserve it. I only hope he knows how lucky he is.' She was thinking, I hope he behaves himself, though she didn't say this aloud. Otto had a good heart, but he could be, well, a little thoughtless at times. Was he ready to focus his attention on a serious relationship?

Charlotte lifted her head and looked directly at Jen. 'Are you sure? Are you absolutely sure you don't mind?'

'Absolutely. Stop worrying. Enjoy it. And last night – was it lovely?'

Charlotte blushed. 'I didn't want to say anything before, especially as Amrita told me she'd never have sex with anyone till she married. But yes, it was lovely.'

They were quiet again. Charlotte had a faraway look in her eyes, clearly thinking about her beloved. Then she sniffed, sat up straight and said:

'What about you? You haven't told me much about you and Kumar. What are your plans now? Are you going to stay around here for a while?'

Jen drained the last drops of juice from her glass and stared from the cafe terrace to the road, where an ox pulled a wooden cart full of dried palm leaves.

'I don't know exactly what I want to do,' she said. 'Kumar and I – well, we're friends but he'd certainly like it to be more than that. He's a lovely man, and I think he's so beautiful – but, you know,' she hesitated, 'something holds me back.'

'What?'

Jen ruminated. 'I think it's just, well – a relationship takes up so much energy, doesn't it? Emotional energy. Thinking time. I don't think I want to make that kind of investment right now. I want to be free to focus on other things.'

Charlotte arched an eyebrow. 'Your spiritual path? Your art?'

'Yes. Those things. They amount to the same thing.'

'So, you're not going back to Madurai?'

'No. Kumar was right. He said if I left I wouldn't go back. I want to go to Rajasthan.' The word evoked many images for her, gleaned from books and photographs – cities in the desert, palaces, camels and sand-dunes, men in turbans like characters from the *Arabian Nights*, women dressed in rich colours and jewels.

'When are you going to go?'

'Tomorrow. I'll take a train north. I'll phone Kumar tonight and tell him. If he wants to come with me, well he'll be welcome. If he doesn't, I'll go alone.'

Charlotte looked into Jen's eyes. 'You're very brave, to travel so far on your own. You take care of yourself. Don't take any risks.'

'Don't worry. I'll be careful.'

They talked more, about the events of the previous days, and their plans for the forthcoming weeks. Charlotte had a few more weeks working on the reserve – she hoped Otto would stay on too.

In the afternoon, Charlotte drove them out to the Adivasi village so they could see Saanjh. The women welcomed them with open arms, and Saanjh ran out to give both her visitors a hug. The men were evident this time too, but they kept their distance, leaving the women to entertain the guests. Jen wandered to the edge of the settlement and stared out at the stand of trees obscuring the temple ruins. She thought the Adivasi people had a connection with the temple, the goddess and the tigers. Perhaps that was the reason they lingered in the vicinity of the ruin. She closed her eyes and remembered the visitation, when carvings had moved on the walls and the goddess Durga had appeared before her. Jen was tempted to go again but something held her back.

'Saanjh?' The girl had appeared beside her and slipped a small, warm hand into Jen's. Saanjh smiled and drew her back to the fire, where tea was brewing and Charlotte was, once again, uneasily cradling the naked baby.

As the sun descended, Jen and Charlotte decided it was time to leave. Jen communicated her farewells to Saanjh and the women, who made a voluble and heartfelt response, taking her hand and, so it appeared, asking her to return some time.

That evening Prina prepared a meal for her family and invited Charlotte, Jen and Otto to join them. Amrita seemed a little crest-fallen Mark had departed so soon but cheered herself with some discreet teasing of Charlotte and Otto. When the meal was over, Jen retired to the bedroom to make the phone call to Kumar. He hadn't contacted her since she'd left Madurai, true to his word. Jen wasn't looking forward to this call, even though Kumar had accurately anticipated this outcome. Maybe he'd come to Rajasthan too. And if he wouldn't – well, she would find other adventures on her own.

Her gaze fell on a picture hanging from Amrita's bedroom wall – an English landscape, with lush fields and hedgerows. It reminded Jen of home, with a pang, and also of her promise to paint a picture for the Golden Tiger Reserve.

No time now – she had to leave. She'd accepted the relationship between Charlotte and Otto, but she didn't necessarily want to spend a lot of time with the lovebirds just now. Give them some space. And the painting – she would fulfil her promise from Rajasthan, and post it back to Prina and Jaideep, as thanks for all their kindness and hospitality.

The phone still waited in her hand.

Time to call Kumar.

Charlotte

Charlotte and Otto were sitting beside the waterfall, where they'd first kissed. Sunset soon. Along the horizon a few fragile clouds burned copper and orange.

Charlotte recalled how Jack had spied on them here – Jack, who still hadn't been found. She tried to put these thoughts of him out of her mind. She didn't think he would hassle her again. He would be in so much trouble now his association with the gangster poachers was known. He was wanted by the police for his role in helping the criminals kill tigers. Hopefully he struggled out of the valley and headed far away, and she would never have to encounter him again. Still she was careful. Jaideep wouldn't let her out on her own.

'What are you thinking about?' Otto asked. He stroked her upper arm as he asked.

'Nothing,' she said. They'd swum earlier, then reminisced about their fledgling relationship, the events and hitches that had led them to be here, now.

'When did you first think of me as something more than a friend?' Charlotte asked. 'Honestly, tell me. What happened?'

Otto furrowed his brow. 'I hate to admit it, but the first inkling was – well, when Mark flirted with you at the end of our Goa trip. And then when I heard about the train accident, it got me thinking.

I don't know what I'd have done if you'd – if anything had happened to you. So, what about you?'

Charlotte immediately regretted asking the question. She was still loath to admit how long she'd cherished this affection.

'A long time,' she said, playing it down: 'Though not in a keeping me awake at night kind of way.'

'You know, I think it was a long time for me too.'

'But the possibility that someone else might snatch me away crystallised your feelings?' she teased.

'Maybe,' Otto smiled. He kissed her cheek. Charlotte turned and they kissed again, more passionately. As soon as their lips touched the fever burned up again and she felt again the intense rush, her body's clamour to be close to him.

Otto broke away first. 'I need to find a room for a couple of weeks. The hotel's too expensive,' he said. 'I want to stay here with you until you've finished this stint on the reserve.'

They lay back on the slab of smooth, sun-heated rock, side by side.

'We'll have to go soon, it's getting dark,' Charlotte said. Her thoughts drifted away for a moment, thinking about Jaideep and the reserve. In another three days they should hear from World Wildlife with a decision on the funding application.

She and Otto had said goodbye to Jen at the railway station that morning. The rest of the day she'd worked at the reserve office.

Newspapers had arrived, Mark's feature spread over the pages, with his shocking photographs of the tiger caught in a trap, the men with their bamboo spears. Newspapers from Britain and Europe, from America and, of course, India itself. Jaideep, his family and all the reserve staff pored over the coverage, analysed it endlessly, picked out Mark's mistakes, speculated what effect this might have on World Wildlife's decision. For a day or two the phone didn't stop ringing as other journalists called to follow up the story. Then, as quickly as it arrived, the media circus moved on. Other news grabbed the headlines and life returned to normal.

Except that it wasn't normal, at least not for Charlotte. She continued her work – data entry on the computers, writing information for the reserve's website, visiting local villages with Jaideep to talk to residents about the reserve and any problems they were having, any worries that illegal logging or quarrying might take place.

But when the working day was over, she went to see Otto. They spent their evenings together, talking and walking, eating out, taking coffees after dark in the town. She knew Otto was lazing away his days, sleeping late, but he made some progress in the quest to replace his passport and damaged possessions. Some afternoons, while he waited for Charlotte to finish work, he took out his camera and explored the town, taking pictures he would later show her.

All day, even as she worked, Charlotte thought of Otto. The long hours away from him lacked substance. She seemed to be a kind of puppet acting out a role, waiting, waiting for the time they were together again.

Friday morning. Jaideep gave a roar from the interior of his office. Everyone outside – Charlotte, two administrators, a warden and the cleaner – fell silent. What had happened? Hard to say what the roar betokened – triumph or rage?

They didn't have long to wait. Jaideep flung the door open and stood looking at them all, wild-eyed. He didn't speak at once, only looked at them like a showman standing on a stage.

The warden asked something in Tamil.

Jaideep grinned and nodded.

Another question from the warden, and Jaideep nodded again, his grin stretching even wider. The room erupted. Everyone jumped to their feet and cheered.

Charlotte turned to her neighbour and said: 'We've got the grant? That's it, isn't it? We've got the grant!'

And they were all jumping around like children at a party,

clapping each other on the back, embracing and weeping. Jaideep picked up a phone to call Prina and Amrita, and within fifteen minutes they'd arrived too, and the afternoon became a party, as the other wardens dropped in, and the vendors of food and drink who were passing through, and a taxi driver, and various local residents, so by the end of the day people crammed the reserve offices, talking, laughing and celebrating. Charlotte and Amrita hugged and cheered.

Charlotte called Otto and he joined the party. Together they phoned Jen and Mark to tell them the good news.

After dark, Jaideep ordered an impromptu banquet which the food vendors hurriedly assembled from their wares. He even dispatched a man to buy some fireworks, which they set off in the little clearing behind the offices. Plumes of golden and royal blue crackled in the night sky. Everyone cheered again.

Towards the end of the evening, Charlotte grabbed a chance to speak with Jaideep about the grant. They had agreed the full amount he said, but it wasn't without strings. 'I'm sure the press coverage helped,' Jaideep said. 'The world saw the problems we face and how – this time – we overcame the poachers. Everyone loves tigers. No-one wants to see them wiped out.'

'What are the strings?'

'They want us to draw up a detailed, costed strategy on how we'll deal with illegal loggers and poachers. Some of the money they give us has to be set aside for this purpose, which is what we want too. They also want a commitment from the local government for tougher action against companies and individuals who start quarrying without a permit. That might be harder to do – we've been pushing for that over many years. And they'll give us the money bit by bit, so they can see we're fulfilling these commitments. World Wildlife will be keeping a close eye on everything we do.'

'Is that a problem?' Charlotte asked.

'Hopefully not,' Jaideep smiled. 'I can see we'll be having many negotiations with World Wildlife over the next three years, and while their ways might not always be our ways, we have the same end in mind. We want the reserve to flourish. We all want tigers to survive.'

Jaideep moved away to talk with Prina. Amrita, Charlotte and Otto sat on the grass as firework chrysanthemums of acid green and candy pink blossomed in the sky above their heads.

'Another couple of weeks and you'll be gone,' Amrita said mournfully. 'It's been so exciting having you to stay.'

'Perhaps not the kind of excitement you'd want all the time,' Charlotte smiled. 'But you'll come and visit me in England, won't you?'

'Yes, I would love to,' Amrita said. 'I'm longing to visit England. I have to find a way to pay for it, that's the problem.'

Prina called, apparently needing some help. Amrita jumped to her feet, leaving Otto and Charlotte alone.

Charlotte kissed him surreptitiously, shadowed, as they leaned against the wall. How long till this felt ordinary? Hard to imagine that could ever happen. Otto slid his arms around her waist and pulled her towards him. Out on the grass one of the tea-sellers, who must have been about seventy, was cavorting like a goat, skinny arms and legs outstretched.

'They certainly know how to have a good time out here,' Otto observed.

'They deserve to. This was important for all of them.' Charlotte leaned her weight against Otto, resting the side of her face against his chest.

'I love you, Charlie,' he said, kissing the top of her head. Each time he said it, in that wondering naive tone, it seemed to Charlie the feeling had totally surprised him.

'I love you too,' she replied.

They were standing side by side on the busy railway platform, ready to leave Tamil Nadu and begin the long journey to Varanasi, the holy city on the Ganges River.

They'd made their farewells to Jaideep, Prina and Amrita at the house and taken a taxi to the station. The parting was difficult. Amrita and Prina wept a little. Jaideep shook her hand for a long time.

The train arrived. They found seats and helped each other stow their backpacks in the luggage racks. Charlotte took a seat by the window and stared out, hungrily absorbing her last view of the place. She caught her breath. There – on the other platform: a thin, pale man with reddish-brown hair and a backpack, walking away from her.

Was it Jack? Could it be? She couldn't move a muscle. Fear spread through her body in a wave, from the pit of her stomach and out along her limbs. She tried to swallow, but couldn't.

'Charlie, what is it?' Otto had noticed something was wrong.

She didn't answer, keeping her eyes fixed on the person who might or might not be Jack. Hard to tell. Was her imagination playing tricks? Otto put his face beside hers, trying to see what had caught her attention.

'What is it?' he repeated.

Still she didn't answer. No way of knowing if she'd glimpsed Jack – it could easily have been another white backpacker. And in any case, he'd got on a train travelling in the opposite direction. No need to worry.

'Nothing, I'm fine,' Charlotte said, turning away from the window. The train began to move, creeping out of the station then picking up speed as they reached open countryside. Charlotte was nervous at first, remembering the trauma of her last train journey, but as the hours passed she began to relax.

India rushed by, the lush landscapes of the south, the rural villages and busy towns, with their markets, temples, grand houses and hovels. Passengers came and went. Day and night.

Charlotte and Otto changed trains and continued on the long journey north.